BETRAYAL
in TIME

BETRAYAL
in TIME

A Kendra Donovan Mystery

JULIE McELWAIN

PEGASUS CRIME

NEW YORK LONDON

BETRAYAL IN TIME

Pegasus Crime is an imprint of
Pegasus Books Ltd.
148 W 37th Street, 13th Floor
New York, NY 10018

First Pegasus Books edition July 2019

Interior design by Maria Fernandez

Library of Congress Cataloging-in-Publication Data is available.

ISBN: 978-1-64313-074-3

10 9 8 7 6 5 4 3 2 1

Printed in the United States of America
Distributed by W. W. Norton & Company

For Nikki and Shawn
In Memory of Margaret Leake—a true British lady

BETRAYAL
in TIME

1

Edward Price almost caught the bugger, could actually feel the coarse wool of the boy's raggedy coat skim across his fingertips as he reached out to snag a bone-thin arm. But the urchin evaded him with a twist of his narrow shoulders, and in a spurt of youthful energy, he sprinted across the cobblestone street, slick with sleet and snow, leaving Edward clutching only cold air.

"*Oy!*" he shouted. "Halt, thief!"

Even though his watchman duties wouldn't begin for another eight hours, Edward pelted after the young criminal, annoyed that the boy had gained a sizeable lead already. A more seasoned watchman would most likely have let the brat go, he knew. But he was only two nights into his job—tonight would be his third—and Edward was still filled with the bright earnestness of a new recruit called upon to keep the peace in London Town. He could hardly look the other way when the bold little napper snatched an apple—never mind that it was shriveled and wormy—off the costermonger's cart right in front of his very own peepers. And certainly not when the costermonger himself and at least a dozen witnesses had turned to fix their eyes on him, expecting him to do something.

"Stop! Stop, I say!" Edward bellowed, his gaze locked on the small figure running ahead. The thief dodged pedestrians and peddlers' carts with the agility of someone who belonged in the city's criminal class.

Even though he hadn't yet reached his nineteenth year, Edward was less nimble. As he raced after the boy, he crashed into three wooden crates stacked on the pavement, having just been hauled off a wagon. He winced when they toppled and the slats cracked, and he had to dodge the potatoes, onions, and turnips spilling underfoot. The two burly men who'd been unloading the wagon stopped long enough to hurl curses after him. Edward gritted his teeth and ignored them—as well as the stitch that had begun to pulse in his side—and plowed on.

He was pretty sure that he was gaining on his quarry. Elation gave him a burst of speed. Edward smiled grimly when the thief tossed him a quick look over his shoulder, his eyes going wide. *You'd better be afraid, brat.*

As quick as a fox, the boy darted to the right, vanishing from the wider street into a narrow, twisting lane. Edward didn't waste his breath—he didn't have any to spare—on ordering the two men loitering outside a candlestick shop to try to capture the urchin, or on again demanding that the boy halt. Instead, he barreled after him, gasping when his boots hit a patch of ice crusted over the dirt road. Arms flapping, he managed to right himself before he fell on his arse.

Bleeding hell. He heard the two men laughing behind him, but he tightened his jaw and renewed his pursuit. The stitch in his side was beginning to feel like someone was jabbing him with a red-hot fire poker. Despite the temperature hovering near freezing, the exertion made him sweat. He could feel perspiration pool in the pits of his arms and slink uncomfortably down the base of his spine.

Still, he ran on. His gaze was fixed on the thief, a small shadow against the area's crumbling buildings and broken cobblestones. Edward wasn't sure exactly when it began to dawn on him that no one else seemed to be about. He'd chased the boy into one of London's more derelict sections. A narrow, unkempt park of dead trees was in the center of the street, creating a poor man's version of a square. Four- and five-story buildings rose up on either side of the street, the windows either boarded up or the windowpanes broken, the glass like jagged teeth. Snow drifted across steps and stoops, piled in shadowy corners, stained revolting yellows and browns. Even though it was still morning hours, the abandoned buildings cast deep bluish-gray shadows across the square. The back of Edward's neck prickled with unease.

Bugger it. Edward slowed to an unsteady stop as he sucked in great gulps of cold air, ready to abandon the chase. He swallowed hard, his eyes flitting this way and that. You couldn't swing a cat without hitting someone in London, so it was peculiar to be in a section of the city that was as desolate and silent as this. The only sounds came from pigeons cooing from rooftop ledges, and curtains that fluttered and snapped in the breeze against empty window frames. And his own pounding footsteps and ragged breathing.

The thief glanced back at him, flashing a cocky grin before scampering up the steps of a building across the square and ducking through an open doorway.

Anger surged through Edward. The thief's blatant insolence renewed his flagging spirits. His lungs were still burning something fierce and the stitch in his side had yet to subside, but he pushed himself forward into a half-running, half-loping gait. A moment later, he was up the short flight of stairs and clearing the doorway. Only when he was through the door did he register that the building was a Catholic church, long since abandoned. The vestibule was barren, with two water fonts carved into the granite walls left dry and filled with spider webs. Puddles, now iced over, spread across the entrance's flagstone floor.

Chest heaving, Edward slammed through the swinging doors, hinges shrieking, into the nave of the church. Like the vestibule, the nave was empty of its popery trappings. The pews and wall plaques had been removed, the sanctuary stripped bare. A chorus of pigeons cooed from up high, where the birds had made nests in the vaulted ceiling niches. Weak light came through the stained-glass lancet windows, and rainbows fell across the stone tiles of the floor, which was crusted white in places with dried pigeon droppings.

Edward only glanced at the surroundings, as his attention was on the thief. Surprise and triumph flitted through him when he approached his quarry, and saw that the boy had come to a standstill in the middle of the room. The boy looked around, and Edward noticed that the bold smile was gone. Now his small face was pinched, his eyes round with something approaching horror. Still, it never occurred to Edward that the boy's horror wasn't about his imminent capture until his gaze dropped to where the scamp stood.

"Good God . . ." Edward came to a stumbling halt, his breath catching painfully in his throat.

For just a moment, he thought that maybe the wretch lying on the floor was a wax sculpture, like the ones Marie Tussaud used in her traveling exhibits, maybe placed here by schoolboy pranksters. Except who was around to fool?

The man was naked, his flesh nearly blue, his body hair shimmering silver with frost. Edward was no stranger to death. Two nights ago, his first night as a watchman, he'd been the one to discover a poor sod who'd frozen to death huddled outside a coffee shop, across the street from St. Paul's.

But this . . . *this* . . .

Edward's shocked gaze traveled across the dead man's face, which was swollen and appeared to be twisted into a silent scream. The watchman tried and failed to suppress a shudder.

Someone had cut out the old man's tongue.

2

The church had probably been beautiful at one time, with its flowing arches, marble columns, and delicate workmanship. But now it had a hollowed-out feeling, Sam Kelly thought, like someone had scooped out its guts, the pews, altar, religious statues, and candles all gone. The church and its congregation had most likely fled these bleak streets for the more prosperous sections of London. Or, rather, for neighborhoods that were more Irish, and, therefore, more Catholic. Sam understood. As the son of Irish immigrants, he'd spent his childhood in those streets and squares that echoed with cheerful brogue and drunken bellows, the latter of which could either end in violent fisticuffs or laughter and friendly backslaps.

"By God, I think it's colder in here than outside," complained his companion, Dr. Ethan Munroe, as he blew a warm puff of air into his cupped hands. Though they should have been warm enough, encased as they were in brown kid leather gloves.

Sam shot a sideways glance at Munroe as they entered the space. He was a big man, although anyone above five feet, ten inches seemed big to Sam, who barely scraped the five-six mark. At least a decade older than Sam's forty-one years, the doctor was blessed with a thick silvery mane that he wore tied back into a queue, a style more suited to the turn of the century than the more modern age of 1816. Sam had always thought it was an odd, old-fashioned quirk for an enlightened man like Munroe, who'd been trained in the prestigious schools of Edinburgh to become a doctor. Why he'd abandoned that respected profession to work as a lowly sawbones and then an anatomist—a profession not even acknowledged by Polite Society—Sam would never understand. But he was grateful. As a Bow Street Runner, Sam had called upon the doctor's services in more than one murder investigation.

Like now. Sam's gaze skimmed across the dead man lying on the floor to fasten on the four men huddled together about five paces away from the body. Sam recognized three of the men as constables. The fourth man—tall, chubby, and ridiculously young, with a mop of carrot-colored hair—was a stranger. But it was his gaze that swung toward Sam and Munroe, and he was the one who stepped forward, raising his hand with the puffed-up authority of a new recruit. He ordered, "Hold!"

Sam was already yanking out his baton, with its distinctive gold tip, which identified him as a Bow Street man. "Sam Kelly. This is Dr. Munroe," he said, thrusting the baton back into the deep pockets of his greatcoat as they approached the circle of men.

"Kelly," said Dick Carter with a nod. He was as short as Sam, but round, and as dark as a Spaniard. His black eyes glinted with amusement. "Ye're bringin' yer own sawbones ter crime scenes these days?"

"Dr. Munroe and I were at the Pig & Sail breaking our fast when I got word. Who found the body?"

Sam wasn't surprised when the redheaded lad spoke up.

"I did," he said.

Sam eyed him. "And who are you?"

"Edward Price." His chest swelled slightly. "Watchman."

"You're a bit early for your duties, ain't you?"

Edward frowned. "I was chasing a thief. Swiped an apple in front of me, as bold as you please."

"Where is he?" asked Sam. He didn't bother looking around. He knew the church was empty except for the six of them. And the dead man.

"The little guttersnipe got away when I was flaggin' down help. But I've seen him about. Snake's his name—"

Sam couldn't control his start of surprise. "*Snake.*"

"Aye. Not his real name, mind you—"

"I know who Snake is," Sam said, cutting off the watchman. In fact, the Bow Street Runner had come into contact with the young scamp the previous year, when Alec Morgan, the Marquis of Sutcliffe, had been accused of murdering his former mistress, Lady Dover.

"You didn't see nothin'?" asked Sam. He had light brown eyes, so light that they appeared gold, but there was nothing soft about them as he fixed his gaze on Edward Price.

"Nay." Edward swallowed hard enough to cause his Adam's apple to click. As though he couldn't stop himself, he slid his gaze back to the body. "I found him just like that. Why'd anyone want to do that ter his tongue?"

Sam grunted, but ignored the question. He was going on twenty years as a Bow Street Runner, and the profession had given him a decidedly jaundiced view of humanity. Cutting out someone's tongue was odd, but not the strangest thing he'd witnessed.

He shifted his attention back to the corpse, studying the naked body. He wondered if some scavenger had stolen his clothes after the man was dead, or if the fiend who'd killed him had wanted the victim to be found naked as the day he was born. And if the killer had stripped him—or forced the man to strip before death—why? What was the point of his nakedness?

The body looked frozen. Probably *was* frozen, given the cold temperatures inside the church. Sam let his gaze travel from the dead man's chest up to the throat, ghost-pale except for the nasty red abrasion that blazed across it. Obviously strangulation. Sam knew that would account for the man's swollen, distorted face, and the broken capillaries around the eyes.

But it wouldn't account for the mutilated mouth. Cutting out the poor wretch's tongue would require a sharp blade. *Christ. The lad asked the right question,* he decided. Who would do that? What kind of madman were they dealing with?

Maybe it was that savagery that had been done to the dead man, or maybe it was the bloated features, but it took Sam a full minute to realize that he actually recognized the victim.

"God's teeth." Only years of experience kept him from giving a startled jolt. "Do you know who that is?"

"Yes." Munroe was squatting down to examine the corpse more closely. His black brows, a distinctive contrast from his silver hair, collided in a deep frown. Slowly, he raised his gaze to meet Sam's eyes. Sam realized the doctor had pinched his round gold wire spectacles onto the bridge of his hawklike nose. Behind the lenses, Sam could see that Munroe's intelligent gray eyes reflected his own awareness. And wariness.

"Sir Giles Holbrooke," Munroe identified.

"Shit," one of the other men muttered.

Munroe nodded at the man who'd issued the profanity, his expression grim. "Former secretary of state of foreign affairs, one-time undersecretary for the Home Department. I believe he is—*was*—a member of the Privy Council advising the monarchy . . . and by all accounts, a close friend to our future king, the Prince Regent."

Sam couldn't shake his sense of disquiet as he followed Munroe down the stairs to the autopsy chamber. That particular room was in the basement of the doctor's anatomy school, which he'd opened more than two years ago in Covent Garden. Their boots thudded against the stone steps. Even though he'd descended these stairs to the subterranean chamber countless times before, Sam couldn't control the spasm of distaste as cold air wafted up, brushing against his cheeks like spider webs. Around them, wall torches flickered, causing the thick ebony shadows in the passageway to weave and dodge on the walls, like a pugilist match from the underworld.

A grim atmosphere certainly, and yet it had nothing to do with why Sam's gut was churning now. That, he knew, had everything to do with the man lying on the autopsy table, awaiting Munroe's ministrations. Sir

Giles's murder would draw the attention of Polite Society, Whitehall, and possibly even the Prince Regent himself. The idea of presenting himself to the future king of England or one of his palace emissaries to explain that Sir Giles had cocked up his toes with his tongue cut out, naked in what had been a church—a *Catholic* church, for Christ's sake—made Sam's blood run cold.

Of course, it probably wouldn't come to that. Sir Nathaniel Conant, the chief magistrate of Bow Street, would most likely become involved before any of that. Bow Street and the Home Office had a very close connection, often working in tandem on behalf of king and country. Sam would report his findings to Sir Nathaniel, and Sir Nathaniel would be the one to inform the home secretary, Lord Sidmouth, about the investigation. Lord Sidmouth would then be the liaison to the Prince Regent and his court.

Sam bit his lip to stifle the put-upon sigh that threatened to burst forth. The murder of a man like Sir Giles could easily become a political firestorm.

Munroe shot him a shrewd glance as they walked into the autopsy chamber. But he offered no commiserating words in response to Sam's sigh; his attention was immediately claimed by the cadaver on his table. Mr. Barts, Munroe's pallid, weak-chinned apprentice, was already inside the room, lighting lanterns and candles to chase away the gloom.

"'Tis an ignominious end for a man such as Sir Giles," Munroe finally said, removing his gloves and unbuttoning his greatcoat.

"Perhaps that was the point," Sam murmured. "Perhaps."

The doctor tossed his greatcoat on one of the counters that ran the length of a wall, and peeled off his dark gray jacket, leaving him in white shirt, white cravat, and brown tweed waistcoat over black pantaloons and boots. He slipped on the leather apron that he always wore to protect his clothes from the unexpected sprays of bodily fluids. Across the room, Mr. Barts lit two more lanterns, carrying them over to the autopsy table. As Sam watched, he set one down, and lifted the other to attach it to the wheel-like structure centered above the autopsy table. It was a clever contraption that Munroe had designed himself, to infuse the area with light without having wax drip on the corpse below.

"I pray that such barbarism wasn't committed until after the poor sod was dead," Sam muttered, his gaze falling on the dead man's face and mutilated tongue.

Munroe said nothing. Rolling up his sleeves, he walked back to the table. "We shall begin with the visual examination," he informed them.

"One moment, sir." Barts bent to retrieve the last lantern, but paused, frowning. "How very odd . . ."

Munroe asked, "What's the matter, Mr. Barts?"

The apprentice continued to frown, obviously puzzled. "I'm not certain, sir. The cadaver appears to have a tattoo of some kind. . . . Ah, actually several tattoos . . ." Barts squatted down to examine the symbols on the dead man's leg before glancing up at Munroe. "I do not recall the body being marked in such a way when he was brought in, Doctor."

"That's because he did not have any such bodily mutilations," Munroe said sharply. He came around the table, snatching the lantern away from his apprentice to peer closely at the area in question. Sam heard his gasp of surprise. "My God. What *is* this?"

Sam scooted around the autopsy table, nudging aside Barts to stare down at the dead man's leg. "I don't remember seeing them, either," he admitted slowly, and felt his lips part in astonishment as he watched two more intersecting lines begin to appear on Sir Giles's flesh. "Jesus," he whispered, and had to curl his hand into a fist to stop himself from making the sign of the cross. He looked at Munroe. "What witchery is this?"

Munroe said nothing, but behind his spectacles, his gray eyes narrowed. He hesitated, then carefully moved the lantern down the length of the leg, letting the light play over the corpse's flesh.

Sam leaned closer, waiting. He was mildly disappointed when nothing happened.

Munroe pressed his lips together as he contemplated the leg. After a moment, he brought the lantern closer to the body. Nothing happened at first, but then slowly two more symbols appeared like mystical stigmata.

Someone gasped. For a second, Sam was embarrassed to think he might have done it, but then he realized that Barts had made the sound.

Dr. Munroe lifted his hand and pressed two fingers against one of the images. He brought his hand back toward his face, thoughtfully rubbing his index finger and thumb together.

"'Tis no witchery, Mr. Kelly," he finally murmured. "I believe it's some form of secret ink. I've read about such things."

"The light from the lantern is making the symbols visible?" Sam guessed. Intrigued, he leaned forward to watch as Munroe continued to move the lamp closer to the skin. The process teased out more of the markings.

"Not the light, Mr. Kelly. The *heat*. Mr. Barts, please bring another candle."

Sam didn't wait for an invitation. He retrieved a candle from one of the wall sconces as the apprentice had, and joined the men in bringing the flames near enough to heat the dead man's flesh without setting it on fire. Despite having already seen it happen, Sam was still amazed when dark images began to bloom. Twenty minutes later, Sam took a step back and surveyed the corpse with appalled fascination. Sir Giles was no longer pale in death; his skin had become a canvas for about a hundred markings—the same symbol, etched over and over again on the warmed up flesh.

It took him a moment to be able to speak, and even then his voice was hushed. "God's teeth. 'Tis a crucifix . . . ain't it?"

"I'm not certain," Munroe admitted. "Initially, I thought it might be an X, but one of the lines of the symbol is consistently longer . . . . I believe you may be correct, Mr. Kelly." He turned to meet Sam's gaze. "He was found in a church. Do you think this might be some form of religious zealotry? Or a political statement? Sir Giles was not a proponent of Irish emancipation."

Sam frowned, troubled by the implication. "I don't know," he finally said, and his mind instantly conjured up an image of a certain dark-eyed, dark-haired American. "There is someone who might be able ter help answer that question, though."

"Kendra Donovan," said Munroe without hesitation.

"Aye." Sam nodded, and nearly smiled. He knew that a year ago, neither he nor Munroe would have ever considered the idea of a lady involving herself in something so gruesome as murder, much less actually welcome her presence. But a year ago, they'd never known a female quite like Kendra Donovan.

The American was a puzzle. Her guardian, the Duke of Aldridge, had spread the story that Miss Donovan was the daughter of a close friend who'd emigrated to America, and he'd taken her in as his ward when her parents had perished in that rough-hewn country. Of course, Sam knew that story was as false as the one that Kendra had told his Grace—that she'd traveled to England in 1812 and had been stranded when war broke out between the two countries. The Duke must have had his suspicions; he'd asked Sam to investigate. It was during the course of that investigation that Sam had discovered . . . nothing. He'd found no ship carrying a passenger by the name of Kendra Donovan, and no captain who admitted to having transported a woman that answered to her description.

It was odd. But then, so was the American. There was no disrespect in Sam's observation. In fact, he'd developed a deep admiration for the lass. He'd never met a female more courageous or more clever when it came to the criminal element. He'd seen her study a corpse with as detached an eye as Dr. Munroe. She even seemed to know things that the doctor did not. There were times when it was damned unnerving. If Kendra Donovan didn't wear skirts, Sam would have been tempted to persuade her to become a Bow Street Runner.

Well, that, he amended silently, and the fact that she was the ward of the Duke of Aldridge. Members of the Ton did *not* become Bow Street Runners.

Although . . .

He scratched the side of his nose, and glanced at Munroe. "The Duke of Aldridge *is* a man of science. He would probably find this secret ink interesting, wouldn't he?"

Munroe's mouth curved in a knowing smile. "He is indeed a natural philosopher. I can attest that His Grace's laboratory at Aldridge Castle is one of the most impressive I've ever seen. I agree with you that this is something that would intrigue him."

"Aye," Sam said slowly, his mind already churning with the possibilities.

"Mayhap you ought to send a messenger to Aldridge Castle, Mr. Kelly. At least to inquire about his Grace's interest in this matter." The doctor's hand dipped beneath the apron, and he fished out his fob watch from his waistcoat pocket, studying its face. "A fast messenger ought to be there in two hours, maybe sooner. It would depend on the condition of the roads, I suppose. We could receive a response from the Duke by early afternoon. In fact, I wouldn't be at all surprised if His Grace himself ventured to London immediately . . . along with his lovely ward."

Sam exchanged a glance with Munroe and grinned. "I wouldn't turn her away." He hesitated, his gaze becoming thoughtful. "You know, His Grace's participation would be helpful for another reason. Sir Giles belonged ter his circle." He didn't have to remind the doctor that a lowly Bow Street Runner such as himself had limited access to his betters in the Beau Monde, even when investigating a murder.

"Yes," Munroe agreed. "His Grace would be extremely helpful in this matter. I know a fast rider."

The Bow Street Runner's gaze drifted back to the cadaver. Even as he watched, the symbols were beginning to fade. One by one, the marks disappeared as mysteriously as they had appeared across the dead man's cold flesh. Sam had to fight the shudder that suddenly seized him.

"Aye," he whispered. "The faster the better, I think."

3

Kendra Donovan's gaze followed the Boeing 747 as it angled to the side, white wings against a brilliant blue sky, circling around and around in a graceful glide. Lower. Lower still . . . Then it flapped its wings.

Kendra blinked as the plane was transformed into a bird—a seagull or an egret, she couldn't be sure—riding the air current in a descending spiral until it disappeared behind the frost-covered trees.

Kendra slowly released the breath she hadn't realized she'd been holding. She wasn't delusional, but there were moments when her imagination transported her back into the past—*her* past—which was actually two hundred years into the future. *And isn't that a kick in the ass?*

She'd been living in the early 19th century for six months now. She'd watched the leaves of England's trees change from the late summer greens to the rich rubies and flamboyant oranges of autumn before falling to the earth, where they shriveled into rusty browns. She'd watched the snow drift down to blanket those same leaves, and ice etch itself into the corners of windowpanes. A little over a month ago, with varying degrees of emotion, she'd listened to the clock strike midnight, and mentally flipped the calendar to 1816.

New year. New life.

Outwardly, she was adapting. Her dark hair had grown out from its blunt-cut bob, now long enough for her maid, Molly, to easily style into the trendy hairstyles of the era: simple topknots with wispy tendrils or more elaborate braids and bouffant curls. She could use a tinderbox in less than three minutes—which was still two-and-a-half minutes longer than anyone else here. But for someone who'd spent her life pressing buttons to light up rooms, she considered creating fire by striking a piece of flint against a metal container stuffed with scraggly bits of linen fibers and jute to be a hell of an accomplishment.

She'd learned to play whist. What else was there to do here in the evenings without internet or TV? She was even learning to dance—quadrilles, minuets, and reels—and was shocked to discover that it was more enjoyable than she'd ever imagined.

There hadn't been dancing in her childhood. It was too frivolous. Her parents, Dr. Eleanor Jahnke, a quantum physicist, and Dr. Carl Donovan, a biogenetic engineer focusing on genome research, were fervent supporters of positive eugenics. Her very existence could be attributed to their almost evangelical desire to demonstrate to the world that society would be vastly improved if genetically gifted individuals would marry and procreate. Not that they'd left their experiment entirely up to the whims of nature. Her childhood had been a ruthless regime of tutoring and testing. While other preschoolers were scribbling outside the lines with a choice of 120 Crayola hues, she'd been given a No. 2 pencil to carefully fill in the circles on the latest aptitude test.

Kendra shivered, though whether from the memory of her bleak childhood or the fact that she was standing outside in a temperature cold enough to frost the trees in early February, she couldn't be sure. She pulled her fur-lined pelisse closer to her throat, her gaze drifting to Aldridge Castle, spread out below from the sloping hillside upon which she stood. The ancient fortress, with its craggy gray stone, central tower, and castellated chimneys, was her one constant in time, looking exactly the same today as it had when she'd first seen it in the 21st century.

She'd been a special agent for the FBI then. Or, rather, she'd been a special agent who'd gone rogue. At the time, she had known she was making a decision that would change her life. She'd planned on being forever on the run, in hiding. She'd been prepared for that. But not this. How could she ever have envisioned *this*?

Another shiver raced down her arms. Life could change in an instant, forever dividing it into *before* and *after*.

Before she'd gone rogue, she'd been the youngest person accepted into the FBI. The Bureau had put her in cybercrime to take advantage of her computer skills; her own ambition had propelled her into the Behavioral Analysis Unit to work as a profiler. Her career had been on the fast track. Then she'd been loaned out to a terrorist task force.

Before and after.

On that last, disastrous mission, she'd nearly died. And she'd been one of the lucky ones. Beneath her pelisse and dove-gray velvet walking dress, the cotton chemise, petticoat, and stays, her scars seemed to throb at the memory.

If she could go back—*forward*?—in time, would she do anything different? The question haunted her. God help her, she'd made the decision to flout the FBI's edict and go after Sir Jeremy Green, the man responsible for getting half her team killed. He'd died, but not at her hand. Instead, she'd fled the assassin who'd killed Sir Jeremy, running into the hidden stairwell in the study of Aldridge Castle.

Christ, if she lived to be a hundred, she'd never forget what happened next: the plunging temperature, the dizziness, the sensation of being shredded, shattered. A vortex or wormhole. That was the only explanation she could come up with for suddenly finding herself in the early 19th century.

A movement in the distance caught her eye, and she shifted her gaze to the three horseback riders coming out of the dark woods, trotting into the snowy parkland. They were too far away to distinguish their features, but Kendra knew their identities: Albert Rutherford, the seventh Duke of Aldridge; his nephew, Alexander Morgan, the Marquis of Sutcliffe; and his goddaughter, Lady Rebecca Blackburn. The trio urged their horses across the parkland at a brisk canter.

In the 21st century, Kendra had always viewed herself as an outsider, a freak. First, her odd childhood. Later, she'd been a fourteen-year-old at Princeton, out of step with the older college students. At the Bureau, she'd had colleagues, and outside work, she'd formed a few romantic relationships, but they'd never survived the demands of her career. She couldn't say that she'd had any deep friendships. How odd to have that change in this era. There was no denying the deep affection she felt for the Duke of Aldridge or the bond she'd formed with Rebecca. And Alec . . . God, she'd actually fallen in love with him.

It was completely insane, she knew. She might have been adapting in her own way, but that didn't mean she belonged in this century. And yet . . . *Everything old really is new again.* Her parents may have lived in the 21st century, but their views were remarkably similar to those of the 19th-century English aristocracy, who believed in protecting the upper class bloodlines from their social inferiors. Like her parents, the Beau Monde had a sense of superiority in its own genetics. Although here, she realized, marriages were as much about securing legacies and increasing family wealth.

Something else moved in Kendra's peripheral vision. She glanced over, surprised to see a horseback rider coming in fast, snow spitting like bullets from the stallion's hooves as he charged down the long drive. The Duke, Rebecca, and Alec had also spotted the stranger, wheeling their horses around and galloping to intercept him. The rider yanked on his reins, bringing the powerful-looking stallion to a prancing stop.

Curious, Kendra watched the man retrieve a letter out of the pocket of his greatcoat and pass it to the Duke. Before she'd became an involuntary time traveler, Kendra would have sworn that she didn't have a superstitious bone in her body. She'd been trained to think logically, both by her parents and the Bureau. But now her nerves tightened in a strange and entirely illogical sense of urgency. *Something happened.*

She was too far away to hear the words, but they were obviously engaged in some sort of discussion. Then the rider touched his tricorn hat, and kicked his heels against his horse's flanks, sending the beast bolting down the drive, which curved around the castle's courtyard to the stables in the back. Kendra knew the messenger would receive hot food and refreshments in the kitchens, and a coin for delivering the letter, while his horse would be tended to by the stable hands for his return journey home.

The Duke, Alec, and Rebecca remained huddled in their semicircle. From her position on the hill, Kendra could see the Duke breaking open the seal, reading the letter.

She picked up her skirts. Instead of retracing her steps along the path, she cut down the hill. The snow wasn't too deep, the powdery stuff only coming up to her ankles, so she was able easily to churn through it.

She was about a hundred yards away when they noticed her. She raised a gloved hand in acknowledgement. Rebecca was the only one who returned her wave. Then she gathered her reins, bringing her mare around. Kendra was surprised when Rebecca leaned forward in the saddle and, instead of galloping toward her, sent her mare pelting after the messenger.

Something happened.

Kendra shifted her gaze back to the Duke and Alec. They appeared to be arguing. Alec glanced in her direction. She was still too far away to see his expression, but she recognized the angry set of his shoulders, the straight line of his spine. After a moment, Alec broke away, and, like Rebecca, directed his prized stallion, Chance, toward the castle, while the Duke turned his big bay toward her.

"What's going on?" she demanded as soon as the Duke brought his horse to a full stop next to her. Her gaze roamed over his longish face and bold nose before meeting the pale blue eyes that seemed overly bright in the shadow of his beaver hat.

He said, "We must leave for London immediately, my dear. Mr. Kelly has requested our assistance."

Kendra stared at the Duke. "What happened?"

"There has been a murder. Mr. Kelly's letter is scant on details, but he says there is something peculiar in the nature of the crime. He believes our counsel would be helpful." A perceptive gleam came into his eyes. "I believe Mr. Kelly is actually being considerate of my feelings, and is, in truth, seeking your expertise, my dear."

Kendra said nothing. Her gaze drifted beyond the Duke to the white-blanketed countryside and cloudless blue sky. Another bird was being buffeted on the air currents high above the crest of trees. This time she didn't imagine it was an airplane.

Something shifted and settled inside of her. A sense of satisfaction. Or, no. A sense of *purpose*. This might not be her world, but she could still find a purpose here.

She became aware that the Duke was watching her. She nodded. "Okay."

The Duke's saddle creaked as he leaned over and stretched out a gloved hand to her. Kendra's wary gaze moved to the horse, and her stomach knotted. Learning to ride had been one of the lessons she'd avoided. It was the reason she'd been walking this morning while everyone else had been galloping across the fields. She didn't exactly have equinophobia, but horses made her nervous. Jumping on the back of a thousand-pound animal seemed foolhardy to Kendra. And jumping on a sidesaddle was just begging for a broken neck. Ladies riding sidesaddle because it was more feminine and modest was about as asinine to Kendra as five-inch stilettos or rib-breaking corsets.

"If we double up, it shall be faster, my dear." The Duke's blue eyes twinkled down at her as though he'd read her thoughts and was amused. "There's nothing to fear."

"Who says I'm afraid?"

He smiled. "We ought to leave for London immediately."

Kendra blew out a breath. He was right, damn it. She reached up to clasp the hand he was offering. "Okay. Let's go."

4

Y e'll be dealin' with another murder, then?" Molly paused in her task of pulling gowns out of the large mahogany wardrobe to glance over her shoulder at Kendra.

The maid's matter-of-fact expression spoke volumes. It occurred to Kendra that five months ago, Molly would have been wide-eyed and horrified at the thought of a murder having been committed. But being Kendra's lady's maid had obviously hardened the fifteen-year-old to the grisly side of life. *I'm not the only one who's adapting*, Kendra thought suddenly. *We're changing each other.*

"Mr. Kelly has asked for our help. He found a body." Kendra crossed the room to the mirrored vanity. Opening one of the side drawers, she retrieved a cedar chest, and set it on the vanity.

Molly sniffed. "'Tis London Town. Oi'd wager they're always finding bodies."

"Apparently there was something strange about this particular homicide."

"Like w'ot?"

"I haven't the faintest idea."

Kendra lifted the chest's lid and surveyed the muff pistol resting against the velvet lining. Compared to the firepower available in the 21st century, it was a nonentity. But she knew that the dainty weapon with its polished walnut stock and exquisitely engraved gold plate could be deadly. She'd used the weapon to defend herself not more than four months ago.

"'E didn't say?" Molly asked.

"No."

The Duke hadn't been kidding when he'd said that the Bow Street Runner had been scant on detail. She'd read more descriptive messages in fortune cookies.

Your Grace. I most humbly request the presence of you and your ward, Miss Donovan, in London. A man of consequence has been murdered in a most peculiar fashion. The body is at Dr. Munroe's anatomy school in Covent Garden. I eagerly await your response.

The Duke's response had been to have his carriage readied for the journey to London. Because there was no such thing as a quick trip in the early 19th century—it would take four hours to travel by carriage (if the snow didn't hinder them)—Kendra knew that they wouldn't be returning to Aldridge Castle tonight. Or anytime soon. They would stay in town, at the Duke's mansion at No. 29 Grosvenor Square. That meant trunks were now being packed, and Mrs. Danbury, the Duke's frighteningly efficient housekeeper, was divvying up the servants into those who would stay behind at the castle and those who would travel to London. After all, a duke couldn't be expected to get his own cup of tea.

"It'll be excitin' ter return ter London," Molly admitted as she began searching through the mountain of gowns she'd thrown on the bed. With a smile of triumph, she pulled out a small drawstring pouch decorated with roses and ribbons. The accessory was called a reticule because it was considered ridiculous as a fashion accessory, too tiny to be truly serviceable. Yet Kendra had found it the perfect size for a pistol designed to fit into a muff or a pocket.

"Thanks," she said as Molly handed her the reticule.

Kendra was in the process of stuffing the pistol into the purse when the door suddenly opened, and the Duke's formidable sister, Lady Caroline Atwood, sailed into the bedchamber. *Oh, crap.*

"A word, if you please." The Countess's tone was needle-sharp. She didn't spare Molly so much as a glance, but the former tweeny didn't need a verbal command to know that she was being ordered to leave the room. Hurriedly, the maid squeezed around the bed, and vanished out the door like a puff of smoke.

Coward, Kendra wanted to call after her. Yet she knew that the number one rule for household staff in this era was to operate in the background, to blend in with the furniture. Meeting Lady Atwood's hard gaze, Kendra only wished she could join Molly in her escape.

The Countess had the same blue eyes as her brother, eyes that could appear gray in a certain light or certain moods, and their fair hair was slowly turning silver in their fifth decade. But the resemblance ended there, at least as far as Kendra was concerned. Whereas the Duke always regarded her with sharp intelligence, gentle humor, and overall goodwill, Lady Atwood viewed her with deep suspicion bordering on dislike.

Part of Lady Atwood's dislike stemmed from the Duke appointing himself Kendra's guardian, which had always struck Kendra as ironic, since she'd thought that needing a guardian at the age of twenty-six was both ridiculous and insulting in the first place. But it would have been a major scandal if she'd remained at Aldridge Castle without being part of the household staff, so the solution was either to become the Duke's ward or be kicked out on her ass. Kendra knew which one Lady Atwood would have preferred.

They'd reached an uneasy truce during the Christmas holidays, but by the older woman's stiff expression, Kendra suspected those days were over.

"Aldridge has told me that you shall be departing for Town momentarily," the Countess said.

"That's the plan," Kendra agreed carefully.

Lady Atwood arched her neatly plucked eyebrows. "Indeed. And is it also the *plan* to embroil my brother in yet another one of your outrageous investigations, Miss Donovan? Bertie is the Duke of Aldridge, not a costermonger to brush up against criminal society!"

"Mr. Kelly was the one who asked for His Grace's assistance," Kendra said. "This has nothing to do with me."

"Don't be stupid. It has *everything* to do with you. Bertie would never have made this thief-taker's acquaintance if it hadn't been for *you*." The Countess's nostrils flared as she sucked in a furious breath. "Before your appearance in his life, my brother's only interest was investigating the natural world, not this *un*natural world of cutthroats and scapegraces. Bertie informed me of your disgraceful adventure several months ago in Yorkshire, Miss Donovan."

Kendra had to count to ten before she answered. "Someone was murdered, your ladyship, and Mr. Kelly is asking for our help. I think you know that His Grace isn't the kind of man to refuse such a request."

The older woman's eyes flashed a dangerous blue. "Don't you dare take that tone with me, young lady, or tell me what kind of man my brother is! I know his character far better than you."

Ah, and wasn't that the crux of the issue? Among her sisters, Lady Atwood had always been the closest to her brother. Kendra knew that the older woman thought she was brazen and odd, and way too common to associate with their ancient Rutherford bloodlines. But what really irked her was the closeness that had formed between Kendra and the Duke. What Lady Atwood didn't know—and never could—was the secret over which their bond had been forged.

"Bertie has always been intellectually curious," the Countess was saying. Her lips thinned as she appraised Kendra. "But his pursuits have been socially acceptable. He is a member of the Royal Society, for heaven's sakes! But your influence has brought him into contact with the most common, crass element of society."

Kendra didn't know how to respond. This was a world where the upper classes found it embarrassing if one of their members was caught working in trade, where doctors distanced themselves from surgeons because it was considered ill-bred to work with one's hands.

"You have bewitched my brother, Miss Donovan," Lady Atwood went on furiously. "But have care. He shall come to his senses one day. And you . . ." She let her angry gaze roll over Kendra. "You are like one of those automated toys Bertie was intrigued by when he was a child. Personally, I cannot comprehend what it is about you that so entrances him, but like those toys, his interest will undoubtedly wane."

Kendra's gaze fell to the muff pistol inside the reticule. Slowly she pulled the drawstrings shut, concealing the weapon. "I'm sorry. I don't know what you think I can do."

Lady Atwood let out an exasperated hiss. "If you truly cared about my brother, you would refuse the thief-taker's request. You would insist Bertie not involve himself in this folly. You—" Lady Atwood broke off when a knock came at the door, and Rebecca came into the room.

"Kendra, I came to—Oh." Rebecca stared in surprise at the Countess. "Forgive the interruption, my lady. I only wanted to inform Miss Donovan that I shall be accompanying her on the journey to London."

Lady Atwood frowned. "Your father has given you permission?"

"Yes, ma'am," Rebecca said with a polite smile, unoffended by the comment.

At twenty-three, Rebecca was still living at home, subject to her father's authority. Most ladies of the same age and station would have already been establishing their own households as married women. The reason for Rebecca's single status was on her face, which was pockmarked as the result of having suffered from smallpox when she'd been six years old.

Kendra had often wondered if she would have ever met Rebecca if the other woman hadn't been disfigured. The aristocrat's life would have been completely different, managing a household and raising a family. Or if they had met, would Rebecca have shared Lady Atwood's opinion of Kendra?

It was impossible to imagine Rebecca as anything other than the independent woman she was, but if she hadn't suffered from smallpox, and the resulting disfigurement, her parents might not have felt the need to compensate by encouraging their only child in her intellectual and artistic pursuits. They might have pressured her to conform to the rules that governed women of the day.

Before and after, Kendra thought again. She wasn't the only person who had an event change her life completely.

"Papa is speaking with our coachman," Rebecca told the Countess. "As soon as the servants have finished packing the trunks, they will follow, and open up our town house."

"Hmm." Lady Atwood shot Kendra a disapproving look, as though Lord and Lady Blackburn's decision to allow their daughter to go to London was her fault as well. She released a put-upon sigh. "I suppose nothing can be done except prepare for the journey."

Kendra's heart sank at the implication. "You're not staying at Aldridge Castle, my lady?"

The older woman's lips knotted into a sour smile. "You'd like that, wouldn't you?"

With all my heart. But Kendra said nothing.

Lady Atwood narrowed her eyes. "Someone must manage the house-hold and ensure that Bertie doesn't forget his place in society. Besides, London is not without its amusements. The Season began several weeks ago. Our family has obligations, Miss Donovan."

The Countess retraced her footsteps to the door. She paused there, and Kendra's stomach tightened when she looked back at her and smiled slowly. "You can no longer claim you don't know how to dance, Miss Donovan. As the Duke of Aldridge's ward, you have responsibilities as well. I shall be on hand to make certain you fulfill them."

Kendra kept her lips pressed together until Lady Atwood left. Then she sagged against the bedpost. "Oh, my God. Did you see that smile? It was evil."

Rebecca laughed.

"I think she's looking forward to torturing me," Kendra said. "It almost sounded like a threat."

"Oh, my dear," Rebecca said, and grinned. "There is no *almost* about it. It was most definitely a threat."

5

Fifteen minutes later, Kendra was tugging on her kid gloves as she left her bedchamber. The heavy, blue-velvet carriage dress that Molly had insisted she wear for the journey made a swishing sound against the floor as she moved down the hallway. That was joined a moment later by the light but firm tread of a man's boot. Kendra wasn't surprised when Alec emerged from a shadowy alcove and fell into step beside her.

"It's about bloody time," he muttered, his straight dark brows pulling together in a scowl. "I've been waiting to have a word with you."

Kendra shot him a sideways look. In this era, 'bloody' was considered a profanity, never to be spoken in the presence of a lady. Even though Alec often relaxed his own code of etiquette when they were alone, especially given her own propensity toward colorful language, she suspected that it was irritation behind his lapse this time. She didn't resist when he grasped her elbow and steered her to a stop against the wall.

He fixed his eyes on her. "I don't suppose I could convince you to send Mr. Kelly a polite refusal?"

He was six feet tall, tall enough that she had to tilt her head up to gaze at him. Sunshine streamed in from a nearby window, delineating the hard planes of Alec's face: the square jaw, sculpted cheekbones, and straight, narrow nose. Kendra had a ridiculous urge to brush back the silky dark lock that fell over his brow. They'd been together for more than four months, and she'd thought the crazy physical attraction would have faded a little by now. But it was just as strong as ever. As she met his green eyes, her stomach gave a delicious flutter.

She huffed out a sigh. "Why does everyone think I'm in the position to refuse? Mr. Kelly sent the note to His Grace. Why don't you talk to your uncle?"

"Don't play coy, Kendra. We both know Mr. Kelly's true purpose in sending the letter. Just as we both know you want to go."

He knew her too well. "Alec . . ." She was close enough to see the gold flecks around the pupils. "This is what I do."

By the way his lips pressed together, Kendra could see that her answer didn't please him. She nearly sighed again, but managed to stifle the sound.

It was odd, but despite the centuries that separated them, they'd actually had similar childhoods. After his mother, Alexandria, an Italian countess, had died when Alec was still an infant, his father, Edward, had remarried. When he'd died, Alec's stepmother, a cold, controlling woman, had shipped him off to boarding school as soon as she was able. The Duke had invited his nephew to spend the holidays at Aldridge Castle, but still, Kendra knew that Alec's childhood had been as lonely as hers.

And like her, he'd been born with a destiny in mind. His was to fill his father's shoes as the Marquis of Sutcliffe and run the estate he'd inherited in Northamptonshire. The weight of responsibility on Alec's shoulders had increased when the Duke lost his wife and daughter twenty years before. The Duke's refusal to remarry meant Alec was in line for the dukedom, a duty that included the stewardship of Aldridge Castle and surrounding lands, and the livelihoods of all the people who lived there. It also meant ensuring that the estate and his lineage survived into the future by marrying and producing children—*male* children. Wives, mothers, and daughters had no right to inherit their family's entailed estates. If they were lucky, they'd receive a stipend that would allow them some sort of independence. If they were unlucky, they'd be forced to find work as a companion to the more affluent ladies in their family tree.

Kendra drew in an unsteady breath and lifted her gloved hands to press against Alec's chest. The reticule that had been dangling from her wrist slid down, weighted with the pistol inside. She kept her gaze on his. "Alec, this is who I *am*."

And that was the root of their problem, wasn't it? In spite of the strange parallels in their upbringing, Alec was very much a man of the early 19th century. He wanted to marry her, to protect and provide for her. He didn't understand her determination to be self-reliant, her desire to keep her independence. She'd had a purpose in the 21st century. Maybe it wasn't the one that her parents had envisioned, but she'd felt *useful*. She still wanted that feeling here.

"I know." He put his hands over hers. He leaned down and rested his forehead against hers. "I know this is important to you, but I dislike the thought of you becoming involved in another murder. Of placing yourself in danger."

"There might not be any danger."

He straightened, then raised a skeptical brow. "Do you take me for a flat?"

"I don't even know what that means."

"A gullible fool."

"Oh. No. But I can ask the same of you. I'm not a child, Alec." She lifted her reticule and pressed it against him so he could feel the weight of the gun. "I know how to take care of myself. You should know that better than anyone."

He was silent for a long moment, then he released a sigh. She heard frustration and capitulation in the sound.

"Promise me you will be careful," he said. "Promise me that whatever happens, you shall not take any unnecessary risks."

Kendra smiled. "Of course."

She started to step away, but he grabbed her elbow, his gaze locked on hers. "Promise me."

Kendra nearly gave a flippant response, was opening her mouth to do just that. But something in his face stopped her. This time she was the one who capitulated. *Is this love?* she wondered. *This give and take?*

She leaned into him, her hands settling on his shoulders as she kissed him softly. "I promise," she whispered.

She meant it. But no one was more aware than she that life could change in a second. *Before and after.* And promises, no matter how sincere, could be too easily broken.

London might not have grown to the size it would become in the 21st century, its urban sprawl gobbling up towns that in this day stood on their own, surrounded by vast swathes of countryside, but the city was still massive. Kendra had forgotten the noise, the people, the pollution, the poverty.

The colder temperature and snow seemed to mute the noise somewhat, muffling the clip-clop of horses' hooves that carried riders and pulled carriages, hackneys, and wagons loaded down with supplies and coal. The streams of pedestrians were thinner, and there didn't seem to be as many costermongers about, pushing their carts and trying to cajole the public into buying their wares. As the Duke's carriage joined the city traffic, Kendra gazed at figures huddled in doorways and alleys—chapped, red hands worrying the edges of raggedy blankets, or standing around barrels in which wood and coal burned, to keep warm. The smoke pumping out of the city's million chimneys for those lucky enough to have a home and a hearth darkened the afternoon sky into an early twilight. The air was heavy with the acrid stench, as well as other odors, ranging from the god-awful—something that smelled like rotten eggs, dung, and decaying vegetation—to the more pleasant smells of roasting chestnuts, meats, and pies.

"Where is Dr. Munroe's anatomy school located?" Rebecca asked. She gathered her heavy pelisse closer to her throat and scooted forward on the seat to peer out the window. Her cornflower-blue eyes filled with pity as the carriage passed two hollow-cheeked women standing in a doorway with babies clutched to their breasts.

The Duke carefully placed the ribbon inside the book he'd been reading and set it aside. "Covent Garden. Dr. Munroe's rider ought to have informed him of our impending arrival by now. I expect Mr. Kelly shall meet us there as well." He hesitated, a frown pulling his brows together. "We shall most likely be going down into Dr. Munroe's autopsy chamber."

Kendra looked at him curiously, wondering at his cautious manner.

He cleared his throat, his gaze on Rebecca. "I must insist that while we go below stairs, you stay in the doctor's office, my dear."

Rebecca's head whipped around. "But, Your Grace!"

He said firmly, "I must protect you from whatever gruesome sight might await us on Dr. Munroe's table."

Rebecca turned in the seat to face her godfather fully. Her eyes had taken on a militant gleam. "If you recall, sir, I have seen such gruesome sights before, when your very own ice house was used as a makeshift autopsy chamber. I did not swoon then, and I will not do so now, if that is what you fear."

The Duke heaved a sigh, clearly not happy to be engaging in this particular argument. "That is not my fear, my dear," he said gently. "I think you know very well that your father would never have given you permission to travel with us if he thought it would lead you into an autopsy chamber to view a cadaver. He would expect me to protect you from that."

"Sir, I implore you to reconsider. 'Tis most unfair to restrict me because of my sex." She glanced at Kendra, and her jaw tightened. "I'm certain you will not be barring Miss Donovan from the room, will you?"

"No, but Miss Donovan has a certain expertise that is needed," the Duke said.

"For heaven's sake!" Rebecca threw up her hands in a testy gesture. "My sensibilities are not so delicate. Ladies are not restricted from viewing hangings, you know. Some ladies have even rented rooms across from Newgate and brought their opera glasses to view the hanging more closely!"

"Where in blazes did you hear that?" demanded Alec, appalled.

Rebecca gave a temperamental shrug. "I read it in the *Morning Chron-icle*, if you must know. My point is that the rules that ladies are forced to adhere to are arbitrary. I may watch some poor wretch being choked by a hempen quinsy, but not view a body laid out for dissection?"

Alec winced. "Becca, really."

Kendra had always thought Rebecca would have made a kick-ass lawyer if she'd been born in a different era. "She's making a good point," Kendra offered, and earned a grateful smile from Rebecca.

"This is not *your* America, Miss Donovan," the Duke said sharply, frowning at her.

It was a rare reprimand, which made Kendra bite her lip. He meant 21st-century America, not the country of this time period.

The Duke turned back to Rebecca. "Mr. Kelly said that the victim is a man. He will most likely be on the autopsy table . . . *unclothed*. Now do you understand why I cannot allow you to accompany us, my dear? I cannot put you in a position that may harm your reputation. Your father would never forgive me."

Kendra had to suppress laughter at the way the Duke lowered his voice to say *unclothed*, but then she saw Rebecca's eyes widen and her mouth part slightly. Rebecca was an excellent artist, and had undoubtedly viewed sculptures and paintings depicting *unclothed* men, but she was also a sheltered, unmarried maid in the 19th century, and the idea of seeing a naked man—albeit a dead one—was obviously shocking to her.

Rebecca closed her mouth and shot Kendra a quizzical look that Kendra had no trouble interpreting. She'd seen it countless times throughout her life. *Who are you really? Why are you so different?*

Kendra dropped her own gaze to her gloved hands, her stomach churning suddenly. She didn't blame Rebecca for her suspicion and resentment. Hell, she'd have felt the same. That pinch of guilt made her weigh the pros and cons of telling Rebecca her secret. She'd need to think about it carefully, though. *Impetuous decisions aren't my strong suit.*

She was relieved when the carriage began to slow, finally jerking to a stop. Coachman Benjamin jumped off his perch and came around to open the door, oblivious to the awkward silence within the cab as he unfolded the steps.

As she descended onto the pavement, Kendra's gaze traveled to the nondescript, three-story brick building that housed Dr. Munroe's anatomy school. The doctor deliberately kept a low profile. A wise choice, in Kendra's opinion, given the superstitious public's tendency to view his profession somewhere between that of a witchdoctor and an occultist.

They climbed the steps in silence. The door opened easily, and Kendra was assailed with memories from the last time she'd walked through this darkly paneled foyer lit by wall sconces. Straight ahead was a set of closed double doors, but Kendra knew that beyond them was an auditorium with old-fashioned wooden seats raised above the floor, so students could observe Dr. Munroe's lessons on anatomy and watch him conduct autopsies.

The corridor branched to the left and right. They went right. Kendra caught the murmur of voices through the half-open door before the Duke rapped his knuckles against the panel, and then nudged it open.

"Your Grace!" Dr. Munroe had been sitting behind his desk, holding a glass of whiskey. But upon their entrance, he hastily set the whiskey aside, and thrust himself to his feet. "Lord Sutcliffe, ladies—good afternoon. The messenger returned with word to expect you around four. Thank you for being so prompt."

Aldridge said, "We were fortunate; the roads were in excellent condition, despite the snow. One never knows what hazards one will encounter. 'Tis good to see you again, Dr. Munroe."

"Likewise, sir," Munroe said, and gave an abbreviated bow.

The Duke was already pivoting to the fireplug of a man in the room, who'd also put down his whiskey and risen to greet them. "And you, Mr. Kelly," the Duke said. "You are well since we last met?"

"Aye, sir, quite well, thank you, Your Grace." Sam grinned, shifted his attention to Alec, and gave the marquis a nod of acknowledgement. His golden gaze traveled to Rebecca. "Milady, I confess that I didn't expect ter see you here."

"My parents and I have been staying at Aldridge Castle since Christmastide, so I was in residence when you sent word."

"Ah, I see." If he was concerned about Rebecca descending with them into the bowels of the building, he didn't let on. Instead, he turned toward Kendra, and his grin widened. "Miss Donovan, you appear well. Recovered from your adventure in Yorkshire?"

Kendra returned his smile. "Yes, thank you, Mr. Kelly. You look well too." He actually looked like an elf, with curly, reddish-brown hair and gray sideburns. His gold eyes could dance with good humor, like they were now, but Kendra had also seen them go as flat and hard as any cop she'd met on the job in the 21st century.

Munroe said, "Please, would everyone like a drink? I have Madeira and brandy, as well as whiskey. Or tea? I can call Mr. Barts to brew a cup for the ladies."

"Why don't you tell us what's going on?" Kendra said, tugging off her gloves.

"Please be seated," Munroe said, and pulled out his chair for the Duke.

Sam waited for Rebecca and Kendra to settle into the remaining chairs in the room before he cleared his throat. "Well . . . this mornin', a watchman was chasing a thief." He paused. "Actually, the thief was Snake."

"*Snake,*" Kendra and Rebecca said in unison.

Sam nodded. "The watchman chased him into a church. It was abandoned, and empty, save the dead man on the floor."

"Good heavens," Rebecca murmured, shaking her head in amazement. "That must have been traumatizing for him. How is he?"

"I don't know," Sam admitted with a shake of his head. "I didn't see him. He slipped away from the watchman—Edward Price—when he was gettin' help. Price says he didn't see nothin', just the dead man." He hesitated. "Sir Giles Holbrooke."

"Sir Giles?" Alec said, startled.

"Good God," the Duke added. "You mentioned in your letter that he was a man of consequence . . . Sir Giles is—*was*—one of the Prince Regent's advisors."

"Aye." Sam looked at the Duke. "You knew him?"

Aldridge shook his head. "Only by reputation. How did he die?"

"He was strangled—garroted, actually," Munroe answered. "It might be best if we continue this discussion in the autopsy chamber. I have something to show you."

"Certainly," the Duke said, and pushed himself to his feet. "Lady Rebecca shall wait for us here, if you don't mind."

"Oh. Of course." Munroe nodded, his gaze moving to Rebecca. "Shall I pour you a glass of wine, or have Mr. Barts make you a cup of tea while you wait?"

For a moment, Rebecca's eyes flashed with resentment, and her mouth took on a mulish pout. Kendra wondered if she was going to rebel and insist on accompanying them to the autopsy chamber. But then her shoulders sank a notch as the tension went out of them. "A glass of wine would be lovely," she said softly. "Thank you, Dr. Munroe."

When Munroe went to the counter that held several bottles and tumblers, Kendra followed. "Do you mind if I borrow this, Doctor?" she asked, hefting up a bottle of whiskey.

"Do you want a glass, Miss Donovan?" he inquired, puzzled. He finished pouring burgundy wine into a glass and brought it to Rebecca.

"No, that won't be necessary."

Before Munroe could inquire further, Alec cleared his throat in such a way that commanded their attention. He said, "I was acquainted with Sir Giles. For two years during the war, I worked as an intelligence agent on the Continent."

The Bow Street Runner's eyebrows shot up. "*You* were a spy, milord? But you are His Grace's heir. What were you doing in service?"

As a firstborn son, Alec was in line to inherit. Only second-born sons in the aristocracy were allowed to risk their lives and shed their blood in war.

"'Tis what I had wanted to know at the time, Mr. Kelly," the Duke agreed.

Alec ignored his uncle, keeping his eyes on Sam. "My mother's family lives in Venice. Sir Giles approached me because he thought my connections in Italy could be useful. I am fluent in the language and can blend in easily enough."

Aldridge looked at his nephew. "I did not realize that Sir Giles was the man who recruited you. Or that you worked for him."

"I shall state for the record that I did not murder Sir Giles." Alec's mouth curved into a smile, but it didn't reach his eyes. Having once been accused of murder was still a sore spot for him, Kendra knew.

"No one will accuse you of this atrocity, my boy," said Aldridge.

Alec shook his head. "Forgive me, sir. It was a joke—a poor one."

Sam rubbed the side of his nose as he considered the latest information. "Obviously I'm aware of Sir Giles's current position in government, and his importance in the War Department. But I didn't realize he was actually a spymaster." He hesitated, his gaze on Alec. "It would be helpful, milord, if you shared any information that you know about him."

"I'm not certain I have anything relevant to tell you," he admitted with a frown. "I didn't maintain my connection to Sir Giles after I returned home. In truth, the association to the man was tenuous even when I was in the field gathering intelligence for him. I dealt primarily with another man, who acted as a courier. I have maintained an acquaintance with him, and know he continues to work in government. I shall send him a note and request a meeting."

"Aye. That would be helpful. Thank you, milord."

Kendra said, "Sooner would be better than later."

Alec smiled at her. "I shall send the note tonight."

"Do you think Sir Giles's murder has anything to do with his work as a spymaster?" asked the Duke, looking troubled.

Kendra noticed the glance that the Bow Street Runner exchanged with Munroe.

"I think it may be possible," Sam said slowly.

Munroe moved to the door. "Let us go downstairs. There is something you need to see."

6

Kendra remembered Dr. Munroe's subterranean autopsy chamber very well. In contrast to the sterile M.E. rooms of the 21st century, this was the stuff of nightmares. Workbenches, cupboards, and shelves held an assortment of large glass jars that had God-knows-what floating inside the murky greenish liquid. Ancient microscopes were lined up next to scalpels, saws, and pruning shears, the last of which were used to snap off a cadaver's ribs. Two wooden buckets filled with bloody water had been set next to dirty sponges. The sight reminded Kendra of the whiskey that she held. She crossed the room, and carefully set the bottle down on one of the cupboards.

She turned, letting her gaze drift across the three tables, finally settling on the one that was occupied. Amusement flickered through her when she saw that someone—most likely Dr. Munroe—had apparently considered her feminine sensibilities and draped a linen blanket across the victim's pelvis. Rebecca could have come down, after all.

"Do you have an idea of the time of death?" she asked as she removed her bonnet and pelisse. Even though it made her shudder, she put them down on the counter. To the naked eye, it appeared clean. She didn't want to think about what was happening on a microscopic level.

Munroe said, "The body was in full rigor mortis when Mr. Kelly and I arrived at the church. I would say Sir Giles was dead at least eight hours before. But in my experience, external temperatures can skew the results. The church was quite cold when we found the body this morning. Still, I don't think Sir Giles was there long."

The Duke's eyes were curious as he regarded the doctor. "Why do you say that, Dr. Munroe?"

"I have only conducted a visual examination of the body at this point, but if you look closely at the earlobes, fingers, and toes, you will see that the flesh has been torn. Wild animals, I believe, caused the lacerations. Most likely rats. God knows London is besieged by the vermin."

"Do you have a magnifying glass?" Kendra didn't really need the instrument to see the shredded flesh, but there were other things she wanted to examine more closely. "And paper and pencil?"

"Certainly. Mr. Barts?" Munroe shot his apprentice a look that sent the other man scurrying to the cupboards. He turned back to the cadaver and pointed. "If you note, very little damage was done, which leads to my supposition that Sir Giles was not in the church for long."

Sam nodded. "Aye. He'd have been nibbled clean ter the bone if he'd been there longer than a couple of hours, I'd say."

"Dear God," murmured Aldridge.

Kendra silently agreed with the Bow Street Runner. Forensics in this era was primitive at best, but she was always surprised by the deductive reasoning of her 19th-century counterparts. It was her own bias, she knew. Every generation felt intellectually superior to the previous one, as technology and general knowledge of the world advanced. But human nature seemed pretty set.

She asked, "Was he killed in the church?"

"Nay." Sam shook his head, his tone certain. "He wasn't killed there. There wasn't any blood."

"There wouldn't necessarily be a lot of blood," Kendra murmured, bringing up the magnifying glass to study the red ligature mark around the victim's throat. It was about half an inch wide. The indentation wasn't deep; it hadn't even cut the skin. "If he'd been garroted with something thin, like a wire, there would have been more blood." Hell, she'd seen victims nearly decapitated with a simple wire. "This injury looks like it was made from a rope."

Munroe appeared pleased by her conclusion, like she was one of his star pupils. "Exactly right, Miss Donovan. It was a rope. Hemp, to be precise. I extracted fibers embedded in the wound."

Kendra brought the magnifying glass down to study the victim's hands.

The doctor realized what she was looking for, and said, "'Tis difficult to tell because of the animal activity, but I believe his fingers were also abraded by the rope."

Kendra nodded, and returned to study the throat. "The victim's fingers may have been compromised, but see there? Those scratches?" She twitched the magnifying glass upward to show the ugly marks, for the Duke's and Alec's benefits. "He tried to claw at the rope when his windpipe was being crushed. A primordial reaction to being strangled."

No one said anything; it was obvious they were imagining the horror of Sir Giles's last moments on earth.

"The laceration from the rope is about two inches below the jawline," she noted, inspecting the wound. "The killer came at our victim from behind. They were both standing."

The Duke stepped closer to examine the wound himself, intrigued. "How do you surmise that?"

"Well, they both could've been sitting," Kendra qualified. "But that's an awkward position. Why would our vic sit in a seat in front of the killer? Where would that happen? The only place I can think of would be an auditorium, but they'd presumably have other people around them. No." She shook her head "The simplest explanation makes the most sense. The killer would have better leverage standing. And if he stood behind the victim while he was sitting, the ligature mark would have been positioned differently, higher up and at an angle, snug under the victim's chin. See how it's lower on the throat and straight across? That indicates they had to be roughly the same height."

"So the killer is as tall as Sir Giles?" Sam speculated.

"Yes. Or, if the killer was a woman or a shorter man, he or she could have been standing on something to boost their height."

Alec looked at her. "Surely you can't think that the fiend was a woman?"

"I don't think we can rule out a woman at this stage." Kendra straightened, and examined the body again. "Sir Giles is, what? Five ten? Five eleven? A tall woman would be able to cause the same injury."

"A woman would have to be very strong," said the Duke, sounding skeptical.

"Strong, yes. But not abnormally so," Kendra said. "Like I said, it's a question of leverage. And taking your victim by surprise. All he—or *she*—would have to do is come up behind Sir Giles, loop the rope around his neck, and twist it with enough force to cut off his oxygen."

"Sir Giles would hardly have just stood there." Aldridge glanced at the cadaver. "He's not a feeble old man. He would have fought back."

"He did fight back," Kendra said. "He clawed the rope around his neck, his fingernails gouging his own flesh. But once the carotid artery and jugular veins in his neck were cut off, he would have become disoriented pretty fast and lost consciousness. Ten seconds. That's how long it would've taken to knock him out."

Alec frowned. "Ten seconds can be a long time if a man is thrashing and fighting for his life."

"I agree. But a little strength and a lot of determination can overcome the victim's resistance."

"Jesus," Sam whispered.

"After the victim is unconscious, the unsub only needs to keep up the pressure," she continued. "Starved of oxygen, the brain would cease to function in four to five minutes."

The Duke said, "So . . . five minutes and ten seconds to kill?"

"Yes. We're dealing with a murder that happened relatively quickly."

"Why'd the fiend cut out the poor wretch's tongue?" Sam asked.

Kendra shifted her gaze to the victim's bloated visage. The mouth was agape, and what was left of the pulpy tongue was clearly visible. "I'm not sure. Maybe the unsub is trying to send a message."

Sam swung his golden gaze around to lock on her. "A message? Ter who?"

There was something in his tone that made her narrow her eyes. "I don't know. It might not be anyone specific. It might have been something that the unsub felt compelled to do only for himself."

Sam raised his eyebrows. "Why'd he want ter send a message ter himself?"

"Not a message, per se." She struggled to explain. "It might be a ritual. Something that he felt was important to do, that had meaning only to himself. If he thought Sir Giles had talked about him, insulted him, he might have felt compelled to cut out his tongue. A final act of vengeance, or closure." She shook her head. "We don't have enough information to go on at this point."

Kendra saw Sam exchange a glance with Munroe before the Bow Street Runner said, "The madman is fond of messages."

Alec frowned. "What do you mean?"

"It means . . . this." The doctor retrieved a stout candle from his work-bench. Kendra watched as he returned to the autopsy table and moved the flame down the length of Sir Giles's leg.

"What the devil are you doi—*Hell and damnation*." Stunned, Alec jerked forward to take a closer look. "What *is* that?"

Kendra found herself equally stunned. Sam and Barts joined the doctor, grabbing candles and bringing the flames close to the dead flesh. By the time all three men had set their tapers down, more than a dozen symbols covered the marble-white flesh of Sir Giles.

Slowly, Kendra raised her gaze to look at Munroe, who was standing on the other side of the autopsy table. The candlelight bounced off the lenses of his spectacles, but Kendra could still see his gray eyes, and the solemn expression in them.

"I think you had the right of it, Miss Donovan. The killer *is* sending a message. But what message? And why?"

7

It's some sort of secret ink, isn't it?" the Duke said, his voice infused with wonderment. Reverently, he traced his fingertip up one line and then across one of the symbols that had become visible after the heat from the candles had warmed the flesh, apparently oblivious to the fact that he was also touching a dead man's bicep. "*Fascinating.*"

It *was* fascinating, in an eerie way. Kendra let her gaze travel over the victim. Twenty minutes ago, Sir Giles's flesh had been pale gray. Now he looked like a hardcore gang member who'd gone wild with his tats. Except these were no spider webs or teardrops or tribal tattoos. It was one symbol, repeated over and over. Two intersecting lines, one a little shorter, one a little longer. The shorter line tilted upward on the left and angled downward slightly. Depending how you looked at it, it could have been a slightly skewed *X*. Or maybe a lowercase *t*. Or a—

"Crucifix," Aldridge said. "It's a crucifix."

"That works with dumping the body in a church," Kendra said, and frowned. There was another parallel that she couldn't ignore. She said slowly, "Steganography is common in the intelligence world."

Sam glanced at her. "Steganography?"

41

"Hiding a message inside another source. Like writing a message with invisible ink inside the pages of a letter or a book."

The trick had been around for centuries in every culture, but its covert nature would keep it within the intelligence community until the latter half of the 19th century. Then the public would become aware and interest in the topic would explode. The phrase "reading between the lines" was a direct reference to the practice of writing invisible coded messages between the visible sentences of a piece of writing.

The Duke rubbed his thumb and index finger together, sniffing experimentally. "I cannot detect any odor or adhesive quality. What can it be made of?"

"I'm not entirely sure," Munroe admitted. "I would say it's a chemical mixture of some kind, except that usually requires a reagent to activate the ink so it can be seen. Applying heat to activate the secret ink would mean the ink is organic in nature, perhaps lemon, vinegar, or onion, or the juices of certain plants. I've read Pliny the Elder's *Natural History*, where he describes concocting secret ink with the milk extracted from a tithymalus plant."

Aldridge smiled, his blue eyes brightening. "I have been fortunate enough to read the ancient Roman's writings myself. 'Tis fascinating."

Kendra nearly smiled. The Duke was getting his geek on. She knew that he'd forgotten they were standing in a morgue, with a dead body laid out in the middle of the room and the stench of decay surrounding them. She'd seen him become enthralled like this when he gazed into the stars on the rooftop of Aldridge Castle, or found a unique fossil. Or when he managed to pry some tidbit of the future out of her, like the invention of the iPhone. He was still coming to terms with having so much information available in the palm of one's hand.

Aldridge went on, "I know Scotland's Queen Mary used to send and receive letters with hidden messages in them while she was imprisoned. If I recollect properly, she created her secret ink by using both nutgall and alum. It was really quite ingenious, but this . . ." His gaze traveled across the symbols, and he shook his head. "I do not know of any organic liquid that would adhere to the skin like this."

"Neither do I," admitted Munroe, as puzzled as the Duke. "'Tis why I believe we're dealing with a chemical compound of some type. But as I explained, that would require a reagent to activate the ink. Heat would not have been able to do such a thing."

"And yet here we are," Kendra said drily.

"It is quite clever." The Duke's voice was infused with admiration, his eyes still trained on the symbols. "Is there any way to determine the formula that was used to create this ink, Dr. Munroe?"

"No. And we'll most likely never know it."

It took Kendra a moment to realize that Munroe's apprentice had been the one to speak. She swung around to look at Barts. If Sir Giles had sat up and begun speaking, Kendra didn't think she would have been more surprised. Normally, Barts stood in a corner, as silent as a shadow, only emerging when Munroe asked for his assistance.

Barts's eyes widened when he realized he'd become the center of attention. He clutched the parchment paper and pencil she'd requested earlier to his chest. His pale, chinless face flooded with color. "I-I was only thinking of the stains . . . the stains used by General Washington," he stammered. "W-white ink. That's what h-he called the formula."

In the small silence that followed, Barts looked like he was going to faint. Since she didn't have any smelling salts on hand, Kendra nodded. "Yes, I remember reading about that." *In textbooks that won't be printed for another two hundred years.*

Most Americans knew George Washington had been America's first president, and before that, a general in the Revolutionary War. They might even have visions of him crossing the Delaware. But what few people realized was that he'd been America's top spymaster, and the invisible ink created to pass messages within the infamous Culper spy ring was a large part of America's winning the Revolutionary War.

Barts cleared his throat self-consciously. "No one ever figured out how General Washington created his stain."

"Washington actually didn't create the ink himself," Kendra said absently. But Barts was right about the secrecy of the formula. Even in her era, the formula remained shrouded in mystery. Some scientists believed they knew the ingredients; others disputed their findings. "It was created by Sir James Jay."

"Sir James?" Munroe gave a surprised jolt. "Good God. I am—or, rather, *was*—acquainted with the man. He died last year. We attended the same functions and belonged to the same clubs. He was a doctor, you know. I had forgotten that he was one of your countrymen, Miss Donovan."

Kendra blinked. Would she ever get used to the fact that people she'd read about in history books were now alive? Or, in the matter of Sir James Jay, recently alive? She licked her suddenly dry lips. *Get a grip, Donovan.* "Most people in America are more familiar with his younger brother, John Jay."

Though she had a feeling that if she polled the average citizen in her time, they'd think John Jay was a rap singer or reality TV star—not one of America's Founding Fathers, first secretary of state, and first chief justice of the Supreme Court. In *this* America, John Jay was actually still alive. It took her a moment to absorb that. Then she let it go. They were getting off track.

She forced herself to turn back and scan the body again, studying the bizarre tattoos. "If the killer didn't actually create the formula himself, he purchased it from someone. Where would you go for invisible ink?"

"A chemist or alchemist," suggested the Duke. "Or another physician like Sir James."

Kendra noticed that the symbols farthest from the heat source were already beginning to fade. "Mr. Barts, if I could have those." She stretched out a hand for the paper and pencil he held.

For a moment, he looked at her blankly. "Oh, yes . . ." Flustered, he handed her the papers and pencil.

"Thank you." She moved forward, positioning herself next to Alec, who was staring down at the body. His face was expressionless, but Kendra was reminded that he'd known Sir Giles. She touched him lightly on the arm. "Are you all right?"

He glanced at her. "I told you. We were not close."

In all their late-night talks, Alec rarely spoke about his two years as an intelligence operative. He'd mentioned it, but she'd never thought to press him about it.

She hesitated. "Did you ever use a certain kind of invisible ink?"

"There were a variety of ways that we communicated." He stepped back, his face somber as he thrust his hands into his greatcoat pockets. "But I was given a vial to use. It was a chemical formula, not organic. Messages sent and received would need an agent to activate the ink. I never thought to inquire about the formula."

"I can have me men make inquiries, but it'll be difficult ter find the chemist, physician, or alchemist who sold it, I think," Sam said.

"We need more information before you do that," Kendra said. She settled down to make her sketches. She wasn't much of an artist, but the symbol was easy enough to draw—just two lines. One long. Then a quick, shorter slash bisecting the longer line. Off center, near the top.

She set aside the sheet of foolscap and pulled out another. Here she sketched the crude outline of a man's body, back and front. She drew a line across the throat to indicate the ligature mark. "Are there any other wounds?" she asked Munroe.

Sam reminded her, "There's his tongue."

Kendra nodded, and made a corresponding line where the mouth would be. Her gaze returned to the victim, studying the mutilation. "It looks like a sharp knife was used. The tongue appears to have been excised cleanly."

"The blade was sharp," Munroe agreed. "Probably a boning knife, or carving knife. The tongue is a muscular organ, so you wouldn't be able to use something dull to cut through. Or if the killer did, the edges would have been much more jagged."

Sam frowned. "If the fiend had a knife on him, why didn't he just gut Sir Giles? Seems queer for him ter be using two different murder weapons for the same bloke."

"He didn't use two separate murder weapons," Kendra murmured, and looked at the Bow Street Runner. "The rope was the murder weapon, Mr. Kelly." She looked at her rudimentary drawing of the body. She scanned it, making sure she'd included all the relevant details. "The knife was used for one purpose only—to cut out our victim's tongue."

Munroe said, "Strangulation was a good choice for the killer then, if he planned to cut out the tongue. The tongue has a tendency to swell and protrude while being choked. I think it took very little effort for the killer to slice it off postmortem."

"Did you examine the victim's esophagus, Doctor?" Kendra asked, as she carefully rolled up the foolscap.

"Not yet, no."

Kendra set aside the drawing materials. She moved back to the victim, hating what she needed to do next. When the hell were latex gloves invented? she wondered. Obviously not now. She clenched her jaw tight as she slide two fingers into the cadaver's mouth, nudging it open. Even though the orifice wasn't wet anymore—the saliva had dried, the blood congealed, the teeth smooth, the lips rubbery—a shudder rippled through her.

Sam asked, bewildered, "What are you doin', lass?"

"Checking to see if the killer shoved the victim's tongue down his throat."

"God's teeth," whispered the Bow Street Runner, looking like he wished he hadn't asked. He swallowed. "Another message?"

"It's been known to happen. But I don't see anything." Kendra withdrew her fingers, and stepped back. "Was the tongue found near the body?"

"Nay. Unless . . ." Sam's eyes fell to the dead man's gnawed fingers. "It could've been eaten by the vermin that did that."

"It's soft tissue," Kendra said. Rats loved soft tissue. Another quick tremor ran down her arms as she imagined the rodents carrying off Sir Giles's tongue. "It's possible," she forced herself to say, and was pleased that her voice was steady and revealed none of the revulsion she was feeling. "It's just as possible that the killer took it with him as a trophy."

The Duke's blue eyes flashed with a terrible comprehension. "A trophy. Are you saying this monster will kill again?"

Kendra was silent for a long moment. "It's too soon to say," she finally answered. "I don't know."

Her gaze traveled back to the victim. Most of the symbols had vanished, but in her mind's eyes, she saw them as they were—stark images inked onto the dead man's flesh.

What type of killer *were* they dealing with here? Intelligent, definitely. Ruthless, absolutely. Calculating . . .

The unsub was all those things, she thought. And maybe something else. Maybe just a little insane.

8

Rebecca prowled Dr. Munroe's office with an impatient swish of her skirts. Her own company had begun to pall about five minutes after everyone left the room, and she was now feeling quite ill-tempered. She paused in front of one of Dr. Munroe's bookshelves, scanning the book titles. *Travels in the Ionian Isles, Albania, Thessaly, Macedonia, Mimibukuro*; *The Anatomy of Melancholy*. She wasn't interested in reading such weighty fare, and pushed herself forward, her attention switching to the large glass jars filled with bilious green liquid, and what seemed to be strange amoebic creatures. She frowned into one murky jar. A chill raced down her spine when she had the unsettling notion that whatever was inside the jar was frowning back at her.

Good heavens. Uneasily, she turned her back on the specimen containers. She took a sip of the burgundy wine and continued pacing. Almost against her will, she shot another look at the plain wooden clock on the shelf. She could hear the tick of the minute hand. If she was a more fanciful woman, she'd think the clock was a conscious being, mocking her.

Twenty minutes had passed since everyone—*everyone*, including Kendra—had marched off to the autopsy chamber below stairs. It wasn't fair that she'd been left behind to pace the room.

Rebecca sighed. Her godfather was sincere in his desire to protect her. She *knew* that. He was absolutely correct that her father would never have given permission allowing her to go into the autopsy room, especially not when the dead gentleman was lying there au naturel. She could only imagine the gossip if that ever got out.

But why should I care? she wondered with a peevishness that was not normal to her nature. It wasn't as though she wanted to court society's approval. In truth, she'd always preferred country life to the restrictions of town.

Of course, it wasn't only the restrictions of town that scraped at her nerves. If she were being entirely honest with herself, Rebecca knew there was more. She was well aware that behind every fluttering fan, the cats of society whispered about her flawed face. Sometimes they didn't bother to hide behind their fans. Rebecca thought back to a well-meaning matron, who'd advised her to paint her face with the white lead used by the ladies of two generations ago, having apparently forgotten that many of those ladies had succumbed to mystery illnesses where they'd doubled over in agony, or shrieked at any slight, imagined or otherwise.

Rebecca didn't care. As far as she was concerned, Polite Society could go to Jericho. But being separated and isolated from her friends was another matter entirely.

She took another sip of her wine, but it seemed bitter on her tongue. For heaven's sakes, she was three and twenty—no longer a young girl to be taunted and tormented by unkind playmates. She was a woman. Nearly a spinster. And wasn't that the problem? It was her unmarried state that restricted her from entering Dr. Munroe's autopsy chamber.

So why was Kendra Donovan in that forbidden room? Why was she allowed to break those rules imposed on unmarried ladies? This wasn't the first time that Rebecca had cause to ponder the mystery surrounding the American.

Just who was Kendra Donovan?

They were friends—Kendra had even saved her life last year when she'd nearly drowned. One moment she'd been in the Thames, icy water rushing over her, and then the next, she had cast up her accounts on the riverbank. She'd been told Kendra had used some trick to bring her back to life. Impossible, of course. What could bring someone back from the dead?

The whole thing reminded her of the newspaper accounts she'd read long ago about Italian physicist Giovanni Aldini's experiments with electricity. She'd only been ten at the time, but she still remembered the way her skin had tingled with horror as she'd read about his visit to Newgate. Aldini had placed metal rods into the mouth and ears of a recently hanged murderer, causing the corpse's jaw to contort, and one of his eyes to pop open. The newspaper account had even reported that the dead man had raised his right hand in a fist.

Rebecca shuddered, and she had to remind herself that once the metal rods were removed, the corpse had gone back to being dead. Aldini's exhibition had simply been a bizarre hoax. Whatever had happened, she most certainly had *not* cocked up her toes.

Impatiently, she pushed thoughts of dying or nearly dying away, and resumed pacing. Kendra Donovan was remarkably reticent about speaking of her past, her family. Whenever Rebecca quizzed the American about her life before England, she always gave vague answers.

It was frustrating, especially when she saw the looks so often exchanged between Kendra and the Duke, and Kendra and Alec. She was well aware of the amusement in their eyes when nothing had been said that warranted the reaction. Then, like now, she was on the outside, isolated. Her throat tightened unexpectedly. She knew what it was like to stand on the sidelines, to not be included, but not with Alec, the Duke, and Kendra.

Her skirt swished again as she pivoted, retracing her footsteps. My God, they were treating her like some feeble-minded female. It was galling.

Rebecca came to a halt at one of the windows and peered down at the street. Daylight was slowly receding, leaving thickening shadows in its wake. Despite the cold, the area was congested with carriages and people, many of whom were drawn to the entertainment provided by the nearby Royal Opera House.

And other entertainments. She was aware of Covent Garden's more lurid reputation. Even as she watched, a man and woman disappeared into one of the dark alleys. The man's dress indicated that he was a gentleman, or at least a wealthier merchant. However, Rebecca could see by the woman's more garish clothing that she was *not* a lady.

Rebecca spun away from the window, her thoughts returning to Kendra. Why wasn't the Duke concerned with Kendra's reputation? Why did he always let her do as she pleased?

She hesitated mid-stride, recognizing the fallacy of that argument immediately. The Duke *was* concerned with his ward's reputation. She'd seen it in his eyes. She'd heard him argue with Kendra on points of etiquette. She knew that he feared that Kendra would someday cross a line and be ostracized from Polite Society, where even his title and position couldn't protect her. If the Duke—or Alec—had their wish, Kendra would be in this room, pacing right alongside Rebecca.

But the Duke didn't *allow* the American to do anything. Kendra made her own decisions, despite His Grace's arguments. She never appeared to be intimidated by the possible consequences of those decisions. Or if she was, she never let on.

Rebecca's gaze fell on the wineglass as her mind raced. As difficult as it was to admit, she had only herself to blame for prowling Dr. Munroe's office instead of being downstairs with everyone in the autopsy chamber. She wasn't a child. And yet she continued to allow herself to be treated like one.

So what am I going to do?

She drew in a long breath. Despite reading—and advocating for—Mary Wollstonecraft's *A Vindication of the Rights of Woman*, as well as French playwright Olympe de Gouges's *Declaration of the Rights of Woman and of the Female Citizen*, the argument had always been a philosophical one for Rebecca. Until Kendra had appeared in their lives, she'd never actually had a reason to defy the rules. Or to stand up to her father—and the Duke.

Her stomach churned. The harsh reality was that she didn't want to be an outcast in society. She might not venture to London often, but she couldn't imagine being cut dead by the town's matrons. Still, she could probably face that more than she could face disappointing her father or mother.

On the other hand, she didn't want to disappoint herself. Maybe the time had come to put into practice what had been so easy for her to preach.

She let out a shaky breath, squared her shoulders, and moved toward the door. Her heart seemed to bounce around in her chest, and she paused in an attempt to steady her nerves. Good heavens, she'd never been one of those silly chits to have vapors, and she wouldn't begin now. Tightening her jaw, she hurriedly moved into the hall. Her fingers convulsed around the wineglass. She frowned. She'd forgotten that she was holding it until that moment. Briefly, she considered returning the glass to Dr. Munroe's office, but was too afraid that her nerves would fail her, and she'd never leave the room.

Keep going. She marched down the corridor, and was forced to open doors, peering into shadowy rooms until she found the door on the opposite end of the building that opened to a stone staircase leading down into the subterranean chambers. A shiver darted down her spine as cold, dank air rose up to greet her. The rough stone walls reminded her of the caverns she'd explored as a child. At the bottom, the corridor was wide, though; the flickering light from the torches revealed three doors cut into the stone.

And something else. Rebecca stifled a gasp as her gaze traveled to the far end of the hallway, locking on the man standing outside a slightly ajar door. He was wearing a rumpled brown greatcoat and a battered tricorn hat. His hessians were scuffed white around the toe and heel. His head was cocked to the side, revealing his profile. Straight nose, prominent chin. From what she could see of it, his hair appeared to be a bright reddish gold. Given the fact that he had his ear nearly pressed to the door, it was quite obvious that the stranger was eavesdropping on whatever conversation was going on inside.

Outrage swelled Rebecca's bosom. She didn't even realize that she'd begun moving again until she was halfway down the corridor. "Here there, you scoundrel!" she yelled, and her arm came up in an instinctive swing as the stranger pivoted around to face her. She'd forgotten about the glass that she had been holding until it went sailing through the air. Rebecca caught a flash of cerulean blue as the man's eyes widened, then they squeezed shut as the wineglass and the droplets of remaining wine hit him above his left brow with a loud *thunk*, before bouncing off and shattering on the stone floor.

"*Ow!* Bloody *hell!*" the man cried out, slapping his hand over the injury. He took a step back—probably because Rebecca was still striding toward him—but he'd forgotten about the partially open door. His sudden weight sent it flying inward with a loud bang, and the man lost his balance. He yelped as he went down in an ignominious heap on the floor.

"What the devil? Who the blazes are you?"

Though her heart was pounding in her ears, Rebecca recognized Alec's voice.

"He was spying!" she announced breathlessly, her gaze fixed on the man sprawled on the ground.

"I was not!" The man had a faint Irish lilt.

Rebecca glared down at him. He was younger than she'd realized, no more than thirty. "I *saw* you. You had your ear pressed to the door!"

He gave her a crooked grin, pushing himself to his elbows but making no other attempt to get up. "I didn't want to interrupt, and was merely judging the best time to make my entrance. How would I know that these gates would be protected by a Cerberus?"

Rebecca gasped, indignation rising up and nearly strangling her. It took her a moment to find her voice. "How dare you, sir!"

"'Tis not meant to be literal, but rather in spirit—a guardian." Wincing, the man finally thrust himself to his feet, and dusted off his hands. "My manners may be rough, but I am not so ill-bred as to make such a comparison, Princess. Although my wits may have fled after you brained me with your glass." He rubbed his forehead. "A simple shout would have sufficed, you know."

Rebecca's pulse throbbed. She couldn't remember the last time she'd been this furious. The man was obviously an insufferable lout. It took every ounce of her control to stop herself from screaming at him. "*Lady*

Rebecca. My father is *Lord* Blackburn. And I did call out. I suspect your wits had fled *before* I brained you—most likely years ago."

She was confounded when he laughed.

"Who the devil are you?" Alec repeated, his green eyes darkening with temper. "What were you doing eavesdropping?"

"Which is *quite* ill-bred," Rebecca put in testily, sweeping past him into the room. The smell hit her then, and she nearly reeled back, her eyes watering. "Dear heaven," she muttered, and quickly opened the embroidered reticule dangling from her wrist to retrieve a blue silk and lace handkerchief to press to her nose.

"Phineas Muldoon," Sam said before the stranger could reply. He scowled darkly at the young man. "He works for the *Morning Chronicle*."

The man whipped off his tricorn hat and bowed deeply. For some reason, that annoyed Rebecca all the more.

He said, "I prefer Finn, if you should call me by my Christian name. Good afternoon, one and all."

Sam kept his flat gaze on the younger man. "What are you doing here, Muldoon? Listening at doors?"

Muldoon's eyebrows wriggled mischievously. "Some interesting information comes from listening at doors," he quipped, unrepentant. "I heard Sir Giles had stuck his spoon in the wall—with a little help from an assailant—and was transported here." His gaze shifted to the body on the table.

Handkerchief still pressed to her nose, Rebecca followed his gaze with some trepidation. Never, not even under threat of torture, would she confess to being relieved that a sheet covered the cadaver's nether region. It didn't even occur to her that she was more concerned about the dead man's state of undress than the injuries he'd sustained. Now, as her eyes traveled to the poor wretch's swollen face, it took all her will power not to react with horror.

The reporter continued, "As you are undoubtedly aware, Sir Giles is—*was*—an important figure in Whitehall. His murder is being remarked upon. Was he really found as naked as the day he was born in a church in Trevelyan Square?"

"Who's saying that?" Sam demanded.

Muldoon put a finger to the side of his nose and winked. "I picked it up on the wind." His gaze drifted back to the body, and he let out a low whistle. "It looks like the other whispers are true, and the fiend did cut out Sir Giles's tongue. Apparently, the killer has a sense of humor."

"Humor?" The sharp word came from Kendra. She stepped toward him, studying the reporter with interest. "What's humorous about that, Mr. Muldoon?"

Rebecca was baffled as to how Kendra could bear being in this chamber without a handkerchief to protect her from the stench. How could any of them ignore the ghastly smell in the room? Even with her handkerchief, she had to struggle not to gag.

Muldoon was giving Kendra equal measure. "You must be Miss Donovan. There's been whispers about you as well—*ow!*" He yelped when Sam grabbed his collar and wrist, twisting the younger man's arm behind his back and using it as leverage to propel the reporter to the door.

"Never you mind who she is," the Bow Street Runner growled. "Go on. Off with you!"

"You helped with the investigation into the murder of Lady Dover last year, didn't you?" Muldoon called over his shoulder at Kendra. "We haven't been properly introduced!"

"Wait a minute, Mr. Kelly," Kendra said. The Bow Street Runner paused, but didn't let go of the journalist. She asked again, "What do you mean the killer had a sense of humor?"

"Now, see, I'm having a difficult time thinking, what with my arm being twisted about behind my back like it is."

"Speak or I'll be twisting more than your arm," Sam warned.

Kendra waved her hand. "You can let him go, Mr. Kelly. I've dealt with the press before."

"Have you now?" Muldoon lifted a brow, his eyes curious. He gave Kendra a roguish grin as Sam released him.

Rebecca could feel her lips thinning as she regarded the reporter. She still held the handkerchief pinched to her nose as she said, "Try not to be any more of a simpleton than you already are, Mr. Muldoon. A man is dead." Rebecca was surprised when that reminder appeared to sober him.

"Right you are, milady," he agreed, glancing at her. Then he turned his attention back to Kendra. "I often write about Parliament and politics for the newspaper. Sir Giles has a certain reputation."

Kendra looked at him. "And what was that?"

"He was willing to do anything for king and country."

The Duke frowned. "I would expect nothing less, given his position."

"Ah, well." The reporter tugged on his ear. "Given the king's state of mind . . ."

"You would do well to be careful in that regard, Mr. Muldoon," Rebecca snapped. "What you say may be perilously close to treason."

Muldoon shot her a lopsided grin. "I didn't say the king was mad," he pointed out, eyes twinkling.

"Muldoon," Sam growled, and made a move toward him.

The reporter threw up his hands to ward off the Bow Street Runner. "All right! It has been whispered that Sir Giles orchestrated campaigns against anyone he deemed a threat to the kingdom."

Kendra frowned. "What do you mean?"

"Politics at its most base, Miss Donovan." Muldoon's humor vanished. He looked grim. "There is plenty of dissatisfaction in this country, but men like Sir Giles have deliberately sowed lies about people and causes that they disagree with in order to keep them under their thumb. They're terrified that England will have a revolution to throw off the yoke of monarchy, like France or America. Making rebels into monsters is a relatively simple way to rally the masses. And it very cleverly deafens the masses to what the rebels might be saying."

Some of his humor returned as he added, "How do you think the milk-maid in Devonshire or the farmer in Kent comes to believe that Americans have forked tails and cloven hooves, Miss Donovan? Or that the Irish, if given their independence, will murder the English in their beds?"

"You're saying Sir Giles was responsible for churning out government propaganda," Kendra said slowly. "And someone cut out his tongue because he spread lies."

Muldoon rolled his shoulders in a loose shrug. "It sends a message, doesn't it?"

Sam's eyes narrowed. "You heard that, did you?"

The reporter wisely kept his mouth shut.

"Do you know who would want to kill Sir Giles?" Kendra asked bluntly.

"I've heard stories."

"I want more than stories."

Muldoon went quiet for a long moment. "Someone comes to mind," he finally said. "But I can't imagine him doing what was done to Sir Giles."

Kendra regarded him closely. "Why not?"

"Because I speak of Mr. Gerard Holbrooke—Sir Giles's son." Muldoon's gaze traveled to the body on the table again, and Rebecca was surprised to see a shadow pass across his countenance. He shook his head. "What son could ever cut out his father's tongue? 'Tis unimaginable."

9

Kendra wasn't sure what it said about her that she could too easily imagine a son cutting out his father's tongue. Her work in the 21st century had been filled with such atrocities. Now she eyed the reporter. "Why do you think Mr. Holbrooke killed his father?"

"Ah—I told you that I actually do *not* think he killed his father," he reminded her. "However, about two weeks ago, the two were involved in a rather public argument at Tattersalls."

"So what? People argue all the time. It doesn't necessarily lead to murder."

"Yes, but more than sharp words were exchanged. I wasn't there, but I was told that Mr. Holbrooke became violent against his father."

Kendra perked up. "In what way?"

"He tried to plant a facer on Sir Giles, but apparently Mr. Holbrooke was deep in his cups at the time, so one could say his aim was off." Muldoon grinned. "The two scuffled a bit before Mr. Holbrooke's friends dragged the young buck away. The way I heard it, Sir Giles stalked off, embarrassed and livid."

"I should imagine," the Duke said, shaking his head. "To have one's own son behave in such a manner, to strike one's own father, is shocking."

"Well, now, in all fairness, he *attempted* to strike his father," Muldoon said, lifting his finger. For the first time, Kendra noticed that his fingers were stained with ink. A trademark of this era's journalists, she supposed. He added, "He actually didn't manage to do so."

Rebecca lowered the hankie she'd been holding to her nose. She was taking shallow breaths. "Only because he was foxed," she retorted.

Kendra looked at the reporter. "What were they arguing about?"

"What many fathers and sons have been known to argue about. Mr. Holbrooke has a reputation for spending much of his time in gaming hells."

"Losing?" Kendra guessed.

"If he'd been winning, I don't think Sir Giles would have blinked an eye. As it was, Mr. Holbrooke has plunged himself into the River Tick. And something was mentioned about his wenching . . . ah." He coughed, looking suddenly sheepish. "Pardon me, ladies."

"We're standing in the middle of an autopsy chamber, Mr. Muldoon," Kendra pointed out drily. "I think we can dispense with the formalities."

The reporter appeared startled for a moment, then his grin returned. "I'm beginning to believe the rumors that I heard about you are true, Miss Donovan."

"Watch yourself, Mr. Muldoon," Alec warned in a low voice.

"I didn't mean any disrespect, my lord. Quite the opposite, in fact."

"It doesn't matter," Kendra said, shooting Alec an irritated look before she turned back to Muldoon. "You—"

"One moment, Miss Donovan," the Duke interrupted, lifting his hand. "You make a good point about the autopsy chamber. If this discussion continues, I suggest it be in a more appropriate setting." The Duke retrieved his fob watch. "I'm certain Caro and the servants are still en route. Dr. Munroe, is there a dining establishment with a private parlor in the area that you would recommend?"

"Covent Garden might not be an area that you wish to linger, sir," said Munroe. "The crowds can become quite boisterous, and not at all suitable for young ladies. If you venture to Regent Street, the Lantern Tavern is a respectable establishment, Your Grace."

"Aye," Sam put in. "They make an excellent leek soup, and roast beef."

"Very well. The Lantern Tavern it is." Aldridge calmly tucked his watch back into his pocket. "Mr. Kelly, Dr. Munroe, will you be joining us?"

The Bow Street Runner grinned. "Aye, thank you, sir."

Munroe shook his head. "Thank you, sir, but no." His gaze fell to the body. "I'd like to finish my work with Sir Giles. I've found that it's best not to let the dead stay too long. Being below ground helps slow the natural decomposition process, but one cannot stop it."

Kendra hesitated. "If you discover anything else of relevance, you'll let us know?"

"Certainly." Munroe caught her eye. "I believe you have already observed the most important thing, Miss Donovan."

Kendra nodded, understanding that he was referring to the symbols in invisible ink. The doctor wisely decided to err on the side of caution, and not mention it in front of Muldoon.

"I don't imagine there will be any more surprises," he added. "The manner of Sir Giles's murder seems to be self-evident."

"Strangulation?" Muldoon said, and ambled over to study the laceration on the neck.

"Yes." Kendra looked at the reporter, and came to a quick decision. "Mr. Muldoon, you'll join us for dinner. I have a few more questions for you."

Kendra didn't realize how high-handed she sounded until Muldoon gave a theatrical bow. "I would be honored, my lady."

Smart ass. Kendra's lips twitched. She didn't know what to make of the man, but she was finding his flippancy refreshing in an era of tightly controlled social etiquette.

Apparently, Rebecca didn't feel the same way. She was scowling at Muldoon, her mouth tight with disapproval that reminded Kendra oddly of Lady Atwood.

Kendra moved to the counter, grabbed the bottle of whiskey, and indicated one of the buckets. "Do you mind if I use this, Doctor?"

"Of course."

"Could I borrow a towel?" This was another decision she'd made, to bring a bit of the modern world into the 19th-century autopsy chamber.

"Certainly. Mr. Barts." Although he was clearly puzzled by her request, Munroe nodded at his apprentice, who hurried to one of the cupboards and retrieved a thin strip of rough linen for her.

"Thank you." Aware that everyone was now watching her with perplexed expressions, Kendra uncorked the whiskey, and tipped the bottle over the dirty water, pouring the alcohol onto one hand, and then, switching hands, splashing the whiskey onto the other. The fumes were strong enough to briefly obliterate the stench of death in the room.

"God's teeth, lass, what are you doin'?" Sam's voice rose up behind her in a distressed howl. "You're wasting good whiskey!"

Munroe cocked his head as he regarded Kendra. "I am not distressed over the loss of my whiskey, but I am curious as to know why you are washing your hands with it instead of drinking it, Miss Donovan."

Kendra put down the whiskey bottle and picked up the rag to pat her hands dry. What to say? What *not* to say? Microbes and germs had been studied as far back as ancient Rome, she knew, but it would be another fifty years before the British doctor Joseph Lister would make the leap that disinfectants and antiseptics could be used to stop the spread of infections. And even then, it would take several more years before doctors would accept his research.

The Duke came to her rescue. "Miss Donovan is a proponent of Mr. Richard Bradley's philosophy that infectious diseases are spread by poisonous insects, which can only be detected under the lens of a microscope."

"Ah." Munroe's features relaxed, and he nodded. "I have read Mr. Bradley's work, and found his hypothesis intriguing. However, his theories have been rejected by the medical community."

"That doesn't mean he's wrong," Kendra said. She tossed the rag aside. Whiskey wasn't the same as the medical-grade antiseptics in her own era, but she felt marginally better as she pulled on her coat and gloves.

You can take the girl out of the 21st century, but you can't take the 21st century out of the girl . . .

"Do you recommend that I begin washing my hands with whiskey from now on?" Munroe asked Kendra. "To kill any poisonous insects that may exist upon my person?"

Sam muttered something beneath his breath that she didn't catch, but she understood the sentiment very well.

Kendra kept her eyes on the doctor. "I think that is an excellent idea for you to do after you conduct autopsies."

He seemed a little surprised at her answer, and his gaze turned speculative as he looked at the whiskey bottle she'd left on the counter. Kendra swung around, heading for the door. She'd done her good deed, she thought. Imparted a small slice of knowledge from the future that would one day save millions of lives. Maybe it would save Dr. Munroe or Barts from becoming seriously ill. Or from infecting others.

Was she saving someone who should have perished? And would that change the future? As with most other things in this time, she had no way of knowing.

10

Forty minutes later, they were comfortably seated in the private parlor of the Lantern Tavern, a rambling Tudor that looked like it should have been in the middle of a forest, not on a crowded London street. A blazing fire crackled in the hearth, a nice contrast to the light snow that had begun to fall outside. A young maid moved around the shadowy room, filling their goblets with homemade blackcurrant wine, while the proprietor himself, Mr. Flock, sliced off thick slabs of roast beef with a large boning knife.

In the candlelight, the blade glimmered. Kendra couldn't help but think about how Sir Giles's tongue had been cut out by his killer.

Yet even that gruesome mental imagery couldn't stop Kendra's stomach from growling as the savory scents from the roast beef and side dishes—boiled turnip greens and potatoes—filled the room. She was only mildly disappointed that the meal didn't include the freshly baked brown bread that had become her greatest culinary weakness.

Kendra waited until their plates were loaded and Mr. Flock and the serving maid had left the room before turning her eyes on the reporter.

"Okay, Mr. Muldoon. Tell me what you know about Mr. Holbrooke. The son."

"What do you want to know?"

"Let's start with the basics. How old is he?"

Muldoon pursed his lips as he picked up his knife and fork. "Four and twenty, I think."

"What does he do?"

"Do?"

"Yeah. For a living." Kendra cut into her roast beef. "How did he get the money to gamble?"

The reporter frowned. "I assume he has an allowance, but most likely moved on to credit. 'Tis a common enough practice."

"How did his father find out about his debt?"

Muldoon shrugged. "I'm certain Sir Giles was well aware that his son was a wastrel. The man knew how to ferret out secrets. He'd hardly be ignorant to what was happening in his own household."

"You might be surprised by how many people are oblivious to what goes on under their own roof." Kendra leaned forward and stabbed a buttered turnip with her fork. "By the way, whatever we discuss here at this table stays off the record."

A sly smile curved the reporter's lips. "Well, now—"

"We won't be able to talk freely if we know we'll be reading our words in tomorrow's newspaper." Not that she was going to be talking too freely around the man anyway, but Kendra wanted to set the parameters. "It either stays private, or we can ask Mr. Flock to pack up your meal and you can take it home with you."

Muldoon leaned back in his chair to study her. "You are a hard woman, Miss Donovan. I'm just a poor scribbler, and you're interfering with my livelihood. Would you have me starve?"

Sam snorted. "You're doin' it up too brown, me lad."

Kendra said, "That's the deal. Take it or leave it." When he said nothing, she put down her knife and fork and began to rise. "I'll get Mr. Flock."

"All right! All right! 'Tis a deal you have, Miss Donovan. But whatever I find out elsewhere, I shall do as I please," he warned.

"Fair enough. But if you find out something that's relevant to the investigation, I want you to bring it to us first. I don't want any surprises waiting for us in your newspaper. Deal?"

Muldoon grinned. "And you'll keep me informed?"

"Yes." *Maybe.*

"Then, deal."

Kendra switched her attention to Sam. *First things first.* "I assume you notified Sir Giles's family about his death?"

"Aye."

"Did you have a chance to interview Mr. Holbrooke?"

Sam swallowed the food he'd been chewing. "Nay. Mr. Holbrooke was not in residence at the time I called upon Lady Holbrooke."

"How did Lady Holbrooke react to her husband's death?" she asked.

"Shocked, of course. But she appears a sturdy woman. She didn't swoon or go off into a cryin' jag." The Bow Street Runner shrugged. "In my experience, folks react differently ter bad news."

"When was the last time Lady Holbrooke saw her husband?"

"Yesterday morning. They had breakfast together before he left for his office in Whitehall."

"She didn't think it was odd that her husband never returned home last night?" Kendra wondered, but then waved the question away. She'd been in this century long enough to become familiar with the patterns of husbands and wives in society's upper circles. It was the norm to keep separate bedrooms and, often, separate lives—or at least distant lives. "Was there any other family member in residence?"

"Aye." A small smile tugged at the Bow Street Runner's mouth. "There's a daughter. I spotted her hidin' behind a great hulking urn."

Kendra frowned. "Why was she hiding? That's a little strange."

"Well, the lass is only nine, if I had ter guess. Her name's Ruth, and she was hidin' from her nanny."

"Oh." Kendra lifted her glass of wine as she thought about that. "Are there other children?"

"Not living ones," Muldoon supplied.

The statement was blunt and brutal, but Kendra understood. It was a fact of life in this century that many children simply didn't make it to adulthood. Her gaze drifted to Rebecca. The light from the candles was not kind, casting too many shadows across her pitted scars. It was a miracle that she had survived.

Sam said, "I spoke ter Sir Giles's coachman. He said that he brought Sir Giles ter his offices in Westminster yesterday mornin', and picked up his master later, about half past six, which was his custom. He left him off at his club, which was also his custom on several nights, including last evening."

Kendra lifted her glass of wine. "The coachman didn't pick Sir Giles up to return him home?"

"Sir Giles told him that he would hail a hackney."

"Is that usual?" Kendra wondered, taking a slow sip of the blackcurrant wine. Like many of the homemade wines, Kendra found it to be surprisingly good. And potent. She set down the glass as the Bow Street Runner lifted his shoulders in a shrug.

"It seems ter be. The coachman said that his master never knew how late he'd be at his club. It was quicker for Sir Giles ter hail a hackney and send the coachman home for Lady Holbrooke's use."

"He's a member of Whites, I believe," put in Muldoon. He glanced at Sam. "Have you questioned the club's butler?"

Sam's eyebrows lowered, clearly not liking the reporter's participation in their discussion. "Aye," he finally answered, spearing a potato, and cutting it in half. He added a large pat of churned butter, smashing it into the potato with his fork. "But I only spoke ter the day porter. He saw Sir Giles briefly when he first arrived at the club. The night porter doesn't begin his duties til half past six. I'll go back this evening."

Kendra looked across the table at Muldoon. Something had been niggling at the back of her mind. "You said Sir Giles already knew about his son's debt—and his wenching. So what set off the argument?"

The reporter pursed his lips, looking thoughtful. "'Tis a detail that I have yet to ferret out."

"Is Sir Giles a wealthy man?" she asked.

"Compared to most of the poor wretches of London, yes," Muldoon replied, his jaw tightening. "Compared to Prinny, no. Then again, Prinny isn't all that wealthy, if you tally it against the debt he's incurred."

"Careful, Mr. Muldoon. Your Whig politics are showing through," Rebecca said, eyeing him over her wineglass.

He grinned at her. "It's right up front for all to see, Princess."

Rebecca's eyes narrowed.

"Mr. Muldoon, I would advise you to tread lightly," the Duke cautioned.

"Forgive my sense of humor, Your Grace," the reporter offered quickly, and shifted his gaze back to Kendra. "Sir Giles can afford a nice residence in Berkeley Square. I believe his pockets are quite plump."

"And yet his son is in debt?" Kendra said. "Is he in line to inherit?"

Alec said, "The firstborn, and only son? I would imagine so. Although Sir Giles's title is a matter of courtesy, and has no estates or wealth that is entailed."

"So you're saying Sir Giles could disinherit his son?"

"Yes."

"Money is always a motive for murder," Kendra murmured, but frowned.

Alec was regarding her, and he knew her too well. "However?"

She twirled her wineglass, watching the firelight strike ruby sparks off the spinning liquid. "However . . . killing for greed tends to be more straightforward. Strangulation makes sense." Stabbing, shooting, bludgeoning, drowning, burning—she'd seen it all when it came to crimes motivated by avarice. "But cutting out the tongue? Why do that when your purpose is financial gain?"

She didn't mention the invisible ink symbols. She wasn't ready to share that information with Muldoon. Still, the same question remained. If the motive for murder was greed, why spend the time to draw crosses on the dead man's flesh that were invisible to the naked eye?

No one answered her. There really was no answer. Not yet, anyway.

Kendra looked at Sam. "Did Lady Holbrooke mention if her husband had received any threats recently? Or did he have any enemies that she knew of?"

"She couldn't recall any, but she might've been in shock."

It was probably too late to call upon the new widow, Kendra supposed, glancing at the dainty ormolu clock on the fireplace mantel. It was approaching nine o'clock. In her era, that wouldn't matter. But here, propriety overruled a murder investigation. Lady Holbrooke would be entering her year-and-a-day mourning period. Tomorrow morning, though, Kendra had every intention of visiting her, the rules be damned.

She turned to Muldoon. "Can you think of anyone else besides his son who might have wanted Sir Giles dead? He was in government." As far as Kendra was concerned, that could be a motive right there. Politics, perfidy, and murder swam in the same dirty pool.

The Irishman sipped his wine. "Plenty of people wished him to Jericho in the opposition party. I don't recall anyone issuing specific threats, though. And to do the deed? In such a peculiar way?" He shook his head. "No."

Kendra frowned. She knew enough about the politics of this era to know that Tories leaned conservative and Whigs leaned liberal. "Do you know what he might have been working on that would have caused someone to murder him? Like that?"

"Again, it may have upset the Whigs, while it pleased the Tories. But that's typical. I'll look into it."

She asked, "What can you tell us about Sir Giles's background?"

"I only know the bare bones," Muldoon admitted. "He comes from humble stock. I believe his father was a bookseller in Hammersmith. Or was he a butcher?" He paused, then shrugged. "Well, no matter. Sir Giles joined the military when he was a lad and went to fight the colonists when America revolted against English rule. By all accounts, he was a brilliant strategist, and steadily moved up the ranks. King George gave him the title of baronet sometime during the French Revolution. Sir Giles left the battlefield to join the War Department. He managed to train as a barrister, and then transferred to the Home Office, where he plays—*played*"—he frowned slightly—"his spymaster games."

Kendra pushed her empty plate away, her mind returning to the mutilated tongue, the strange symbols in invisible ink. A game was still being played, she thought. Whether it was professional or turned out to be personal, they would have to see.

11

Grosvenor Square, where the Duke's enormous buff-colored mansion was located, was darker than the other sections of the city. The fashionable residents who lived there had declined the new technology of gas lighting, preferring to keep to the tradition of lighting their doorsteps with oil lamps. It was a sore spot for the Duke, who continued to rail against his neighbors' lack of progressive leanings.

Still, Number 29 was lit up like a Christmas tree, with warm amber light spilling from every window. Lady Atwood had arrived.

Kendra wished that didn't give her a tight knot in her stomach.

The Duke looked at Rebecca. "You shall stay here until we send a footman to see if your parents have arrived at your residence, my dear. I'm not turning you out to await them in a cold, empty house."

Benjamin came around to unfold the steps and open the door. Snow was falling steadily, dusting the coachman's hat and shoulders.

"I shall have Harding retrieve the slate board that we used last year," Aldridge continued as he stepped down, then turned to assist first Rebecca, then Kendra. "I know it's around somewhere."

"Thanks." Kendra paused, lifting her face up to the black sky spinning with white crystals. For a moment, she stood there, absorbing the cold air scented with fireplace smoke. Alec stopped beside her, his gloved hand capturing hers.

"What are you thinking?" he asked.

She shook her head. "I suppose I'm thinking about how nothing changes, not really. People will always kill each other. For the damnedest reasons." She sighed, and tugged Alec's hand. "C'mon, my lord. Let's go in before we turn into popsicles."

"What the devil is a popsicle?"

Kendra laughed, and pulled him down the path. Harding was eyeing them from the door he held open. Hurrying up the steps, they joined Rebecca and the Duke, who were divesting themselves of their outerwear. Servants were bustling around the mansion, opening up rooms, taking linen covers off the furniture, dusting and sweeping. The scent of lemon, linseed oil, and beeswax drifted on the air. Even though kindling and coal had been brought in, and fires started in many of the hearths, it was still cold enough for Kendra to lament the lack of central heating as she handed her cloak, gloves, and bonnet over to one of the waiting footmen. Kendra kept her reticule, which contained the muff pistol, and her notes.

"Lady Atwood is with Mrs. Danbury in the morning room, sir," Harding informed the Duke in his characteristically grave manner. "Shall I let her ladyship know that you have arrived?"

"Thank you, but I shall go to her myself. Send someone to Lady Rebecca's residence to find out if her parents have arrived. Has my study been made ready?"

"Yes, sir. A fire has been lit, as well as several wall sconces."

"Very good. We have dined, but if my decanters in the study haven't yet been replenished, send up a maid with a bottle of brandy, and a pot of tea. And we shall need the slate board returned to the room. I trust you did not dispose of it entirely?"

The butler slid a look in Kendra's direction, but his expression remained impassive. "I shall supervise its return. Tonight, Your Grace?"

"Tonight," Aldridge confirmed, and glanced at his nephew. "Alec, if you will escort the ladies upstairs, I shall join you shortly."

The Duke left to seek out his sister while they ascended the grand staircase to the study. A meager fire was burning in the hearth. Alec crossed the room to throw another log into the fireplace before snatching up the poker, coaxing the flames into a greater blaze.

Cozy, Kendra thought, as her gaze traveled to the windows that had been distorted with melting snowflakes running down the glass. She moved to the rosewood table, putting down her reticule and spreading out the three drawings she'd made.

Rebecca joined her, and picked up the crudely drawn figure of a man. "I could have helped you with this."

"I only needed to depict the wounds."

"What's this?"

Kendra glanced over to see that she'd picked up the other paper with the symbol that had been painted on Sir Giles. She asked curiously, "What does it looked like to you?"

"A cross."

"You mean a crucifix?"

"Of course. Although . . ." She tilted her head to the side as she studied the mark. "It could be a simple cross marking—an *X*. Except I see one line is a little shorter."

"Which makes it a crucifix. Or a lowercase *t*. At the moment, I'm leaning toward a crucifix, since Sir Giles was discovered in a church." She told Rebecca about the marks that had been drawn on the body in invisible ink.

Rebecca's lips parted in amazement. "Dear heaven. What can it mean?"

"I don't know. But it does mean something to the killer."

Rebecca's brows drew together, and her gaze returned to the drawing. "But surely this oddity would eliminate Mr. Holbrooke as a suspect in his father's murder? Even if he is such a monster as to cut out his own father's tongue, why would he do *this*?"

Alec strode over to them. "I have never met Mr. Holbrooke, but I agree with Becca. I'm having a difficult time imagining such a thing."

"It would depend on what kind of man Mr. Holbrooke is," Kendra said, tapping her chin as she considered it. "Based on what Mr. Muldoon told us, he seems to be immature for his age. Drinking, gambling, womanizing."

Rebecca made a sound of derision. "Mr. Holbrooke is no different from any other of the young bucks in town when it comes to maturity."

They glanced around when the door whispered open and a maid came through, carefully balancing a tray that held a bottle of brandy, glasses and teacups, and a pot of tea, accompanied by sugar and cream. As the servant deposited the tray on the table, the Duke arrived.

"Ah, excellent," he said, and smiled his approval as he hurried over to the table. "You may go," he told the maid when she lifted the teapot. He took over when she set down the pot and quietly left the room.

"Brandy or tea?" the Duke asked, raising an eyebrow in their direction.

Having had two glasses of the potent blackcurrant wine at the Lantern Tavern, Kendra joined the Duke in choosing tea, and she wasn't surprised when Alec and Rebecca went for the brandy. The quality of the water in this era would make anybody leery. While her 19th-century counterparts might not understand it, they were protecting themselves against dysentery and cholera and God knew what else by boiling water in the form of tea and coffee, or drinking alcoholic beverages in place of a simple glass of water.

The Duke was passing the brandy glasses to Rebecca and Alec when there came a smart rap at the door before it opened again, and Harding ushered in two footmen, carrying the slate board.

"Put it down over there," Aldridge directed, and the footmen eased it down in the corner of the room.

"Will there be anything else, sir?" the butler asked after dismissing the footmen.

"No, thank you, Harding. That will be all."

Kendra picked up a jagged piece of slate, but instead of making notes, she jiggled it in her hand as she walked over to the slate board. The Duke retreated behind his desk with his cup of tea while Rebecca and Alec settled in opposite chairs, near the fire.

"Tomorrow morning, I think Rebecca and I should call upon Lady Holbrooke," Kendra said carefully.

"Morning calls are not done in the morning, my dear," the Duke reminded her.

"Yeah, I remember." For no reason that Kendra could discern, morning calls were actually done in the afternoon. It was one of those strange, illogical quirks that continued to annoy and baffle her. "But this isn't a social visit. It's a murder investigation."

"Point taken." The Duke pursed his lips. "I suppose it would be less awkward for a woman to approach Lady Holbrooke during her time of mourning."

"*Two* women," Rebecca corrected, sipping her brandy.

Kendra smiled at her. "Yeah, you're the calling card." As the daughter of an earl, Rebecca ranked higher than the wife of a baronet. Lady Holbrooke probably wouldn't turn Rebecca away.

Alec was skeptical. "Even if she gave you an audience, you can't expect her to confide in you. You have no acquaintance with her."

"We still need to interview her," Kendra pointed out. "And you'd be shocked at what people confide, if asked the right way. Besides, there are other questions that need to be asked that are less personal. Mr. Kelly said that she couldn't recall any threats against her husband, but she'd just learned of his death. She needs time to process that. Maybe tomorrow she'll have remembered something, or recall something else that could help."

Memories, Kendra had always found, were like slivers under the skin; they might need a little time to work their way to the surface.

"I agree, my dear." Aldridge raised his teacup and peered at her over the rim. "Tomorrow morning—late morning, say, eleven o'clock—you may take the carriage. You can pick up Rebecca en route. Would that be agreeable to you?"

Since she'd anticipated more of an argument, she smiled. "Very."

"While you visit Lady Holbrooke, I plan to ride over to Dr. Munroe's. He ought to be finished conducting the autopsy." He swallowed some tea and then set the cup back on the saucer with a soft clink. "I would very much like to have another look at the secret ink on Sir Giles. It really is quite remarkable." He looked at Kendra. "Have you ever seen anything like it in your America, my dear?"

It occurred to Kendra what they were doing was a verbal form of secret ink, talking in code to hide the truth from Rebecca. She felt a pinch of guilt at the deception, but pushed it away. "I can't say that I ever came across anything like that," she said slowly. She'd worked for the Bureau, not the CIA. She wasn't sure if invisible inks were completely obsolete, but she suspected that sophisticated encryption codes and microchips were more the norm in her timeline.

Alec said, "I hope to learn something from my intelligence contact."

"Good." She lifted the piece of slate and began making notes on the board. *Victimology*. She listed only the basics: *height—five ten; weight—estimated 180 pounds*. She looked at Alec. "How old was Sir Giles?"

"I believe fifty-seven or fifty-eight. I can find out."

"Okay. It's not entirely important, because I don't think this was a stranger killing. The unsub wasn't drawn to Sir Giles because he was a certain type. I think he was targeted by someone he knew."

She created another column on the details of the crime. *Garroted. Tongue removed. Body marked with invisible ink. Symbol resembling a crucifix. Naked. Dump site: a church.*

It was a grisly list, one that would probably give most civilians nightmares if they ever came upon it.

The last column was titled *Suspects*. Underneath the header, she wrote Gerard Holbrooke's name and age.

"There are a few characteristics associated with patricide involving males," she told them. "Usually the son is relatively young, and lives at home. They have substance abuse issues. Sometimes they have mental disorders." She wrote as she talked. "The father is often an authoritarian figure. Often abusive." She paused, then glanced at Alec. "Did you get that impression of Sir Giles?"

Alec frowned. "He was an authoritarian figure, certainly. His position in government, as a spymaster, demanded it. He had considerable responsibility on his shoulders. Men's lives were at risk. But I never considered him abusive. Then again, I was not acquainted with the man outside of our work, and even then, our association was at the most minimal level."

The Duke studied the slate board. "Mr. Holbrooke seems to fit much of what you've written, my dear. He is relatively young, and lives at home—although that is not unusual for someone who is not wed. Sometimes young bucks rent rooms, but if Mr. Holbrooke's financials are in disarray, he might have had difficulty in that area. Given what we know of the incident at Tattersalls, he appears to have substance abuse issues. Perhaps he is mad. Certainly, what was done to Sir Giles indicates that we are dealing with a madman."

"Maybe, or it was just good, old-fashioned greed," Kendra said. "Maybe he wanted to speed up the timetable for when he'd get his hands on the family fortune."

Rebecca frowned. "But that is where I cannot believe it could be Mr. Holbrooke. The crime is too bizarre."

"That might depend on whether Mr. Holbrooke took after his father." Kendra jiggled the slate again as she considered that angle. "Think about it. The more bizarre elements in the crime might be a strategy."

Rebecca looked at her. "I don't understand."

"There are a couple ways to view this. Let's say we have a son who is deeply in debt, estranged from his father, even attacks him in broad daylight. A couple weeks later, the father is found stabbed to death on a lonely road one night. The son inherits a fortune. Would suspicion fall on the son?"

"As abhorrent as such a possibility is, I think that would certainly raise suspicion against the son," the Duke allowed.

Alec added, "Even if nothing could be proven, the son may find himself shunned, doors closed. Society has a way of making its own judgments. Right or wrong."

Kendra nodded. "In other words, even if the son doesn't end up charged and convicted, he could be made very uncomfortable in society. His quality of life would be affected."

"Yes," Alec agreed.

"Okay. So, same scenario. The son attacks his father, is deeply in debt, but two weeks later, the father is found garroted, his tongue cut out, left naked with symbols painted in invisible ink on his body. Now would you suspect the son of being behind the father's murder?"

No one said anything for a moment.

"I take your point," Alec finally said. "And when it is known that the father is also a spymaster, it would make more sense to look to the intelligence community for his killer."

"Classic misdirection," Kendra murmured.

Rebecca raised her eyebrows. "Do you really think Mr. Holbrooke could be so fiendishly clever?"

Kendra looked at Alec. "Do you think Sir Giles would have been smart enough to do something like this?"

"Yes," he said immediately.

"Then maybe Mr. Holbrooke learned a few spy tricks from watching his father. He would probably be familiar with invisible ink." Kendra swung back to study the slate board. "My problem with this scenario is the killer left Sir Giles naked."

"Forgive me, my dear," the Duke said, "but that seems the least of the evils visited upon the poor wretch."

"No, but it's an act of humiliation," Kendra said. "If the father and son relationship had disintegrated into hatred, it could play, maybe. It's a thread that needs to be followed."

The Duke sipped his tea before lowering the cup. "There may be a simple answer, my dear. Sir Giles's clothes had to be removed in order for the killer to apply the invisible ink," he pointed out. "I assume it would have been too difficult to dress the man after he was dead."

"It would be awkward, especially after rigor mortis had begun," she conceded. "But the killer didn't need to leave Sir Giles exposed the way he was. He could have draped Sir Giles's greatcoat over the body or even put a blanket on him. I think the unsub wanted him to be found that way."

"An act of humiliation," the Duke repeated with quiet horror. "My God. If it is Mr. Holbrooke, he truly is evil."

"There is another possibility," Alec spoke up. "A blanket or coat could have been thrown over Sir Giles, or he could have been left there fully dressed, but someone stole his clothes or the coat or blanket. It wouldn't be the first time thieves have taken from the dead."

"You're right." Kendra's gaze traveled back to the slate board. "At this stage, we only have speculation. Hopefully, Mr. Holbrook will have an alibi, and we can eliminate him."

Of course, that would also mean eliminating their only suspect on the board.

She stepped forward to make a timeline. "We know that Sir Giles's coachman dropped him off at his club at around 6:30—half past six. He was found at around 8:30 the next morning." She stared at the line she'd drawn. There was a lot of space between 6:30 on Wednesday evening and 8:30 on Thursday morning. "We should be able to add more to the timeline after Mr. Kelly talks to the night porter at the club."

A quick knock at the door had the Duke rising from behind his desk. Before he could take a step, the door opened, and Lady Atwood came into the room. Her eyes flicked to the slate board, her lips tightening into a thin, disapproving line. Then she switched her gaze to Rebecca.

"The boy has returned with news that your parents are at home, my dear. I have taken it upon myself to have Coachman Benjamin bring the carriage around."

"Oh." Rebecca looked briefly disappointed. She set down her brandy glass and pushed herself to her feet. "I suppose I ought to go to them. Thank you, your ladyship."

"You shall accompany Rebecca, Sutcliffe." Lady Atwood fixed her nephew with a steely look. "The carriage can then take you to your residence. I have sent several servants already to prepare your home for you." With studied casualness, she picked a piece of lint off her sleeve. "Naturally, they shall stay with you until you can summon your own staff from your estate in Northhamptonshire."

Kendra saw the trap that the Countess had laid, and could almost admire it. She'd maneuvered her nephew neatly out of the Duke's house. There would be no sneaking into Kendra's bedchamber in the dead of night. While she and Alec had always been careful about keeping their relationship secret, Kendra had wondered what the Countess suspected. For whatever reason, she'd clearly turned a blind eye to their nocturnal activity at Aldridge Castle. Apparently, that was going to end in town.

"I don't know how to thank you, my lady," Alec said, his expression inscrutable.

If the Countess heard the razor-sharp edge in her nephew's voice, she chose to ignore it. Instead, she smiled. "Always know that I have your best interests at heart." She gave him a pointed look before saying, "Now, off with you. Both of you."

"I'll walk with you to the door," Kendra said, and put down the piece of slate.

Once they were out of the study and away from Lady Atwood's eagle eye, Alec put a hand on Kendra's arm, slowing her stride. Rebecca glanced over her shoulder at them, but kept walking.

Alec muttered, "My aunt is an interfering biddy."

"I think she's probably as good a strategist as Sir Giles. If she had worked for your War Department, Napoleon would probably have been defeated a lot sooner." She gave him a poke. "See what happens when you ignore the contributions and skills of half the population?"

"If you married me—"

"Sh-sh. That's not possible."

"It's entirely possible if you weren't so bloody-minded."

"You have a unique way of trying to win me over."

"Kendra," he said, and she could hear the frustration in the way he said her name, in the heat in his green eyes as he looked down at her.

Because she didn't know what to say, she said nothing. They walked in silence, and it wasn't until they began descending the stairs that he tried again. "Perhaps I can come back later tonight. I have a key—"

"No," Kendra said sharply, and quickly lowered her voice. "It's too dangerous. I don't want some footman shooting you thinking you are a bloody housebreaker."

They'd reached the bottom of the stairs. The butler was waiting ahead of them with Alec's coat, hat, and gloves. Rebecca was pretending to have a sudden fascination for the pink and gray marble floor.

Jaw clenched tight, Alec took his greatcoat from Harding and shrugged into it. Afterward, he offered Kendra a mocking bow. "Good evening, Miss Donovan. I hope you sleep well."

Kendra chewed on her lower lip as she watched Alec offer his arm to Rebecca, and they swept out the door into the snowy night. Briefly, Rebecca shot her a quick, assessing glance, but Alec never looked back.

She sighed. When she became aware of Harding's eyes on her, she made an effort to pull herself together, and retraced her footsteps to the stairs.

Guilt assailed her. Lady Atwood's manipulation to remove Alec had surprised Kendra, but she was also relieved. Because a plan had come to her, and she knew that if Alec found out what she was going to do, he would do everything in his power to stop her.

12

S am Kelly hunched his shoulders against the cold and the steadily falling snow as he waited outside the servant's entrance of the most exclusive gentleman's club in town. Ten minutes ago, he'd knocked on the front door of White's, and had been directed to go to the back entrance to wait for the night porter.

For a club that could trace its roots back to Italian immigrant Francesco Bianco, who'd served hot chocolate to folks under the banner of Mrs. White's Chocolate House, Sam found it ironic that few of those early patrons would have been allowed through its exalted doors today. Of course, Mrs. White's Chocolate House had vanished long ago, when its owners recognized that catering to London's elite was more profitable than serving up cups of cocoa to the well-off masses and, if the rumors were true, a few highwaymen whose nocturnal habits had given them plump pockets.

In the last century, the newly christened White's had moved from Chesterfield Street to the fashionable St. James's Street. After being burnt down, rebuilt, and remodeled, the current club boasted three stories of Portland stone and a Palladian façade with its famous street-level bow window. Sam wasn't an avid follower of the fashionable set, but even he knew that the table in front of that particular window was reserved for the Ton's arbiter of style, Beau Brummell. From that coveted perch, Brummell could observe the parade of stylish pedestrians walking on the pavement outside the window. And probably even more important, Sam thought, it allowed the Beau Monde to observe Brummell.

Sam's lip curled. He'd long since given up trying to figure out the peculiarities of his betters.

A noise made Sam turn. It was only rats scurrying inside an open barrel, probably trying to get warm. God's teeth, it was cold. Colder now than it had been an hour ago. His feet had gone numb, and he stomped them to regain feeling. Where was the bloody porter? He had half a mind to go around again to the front entrance and pound on the fancy black door. The only thing holding him back from being so raggedy-mannered was the fear that such an action would be reported to his superior, Sir Nathaniel.

Hell, it might not even have to be reported to him. The Bow Street Magistrate could be in White's at this very moment, dining on smoked eel or roasted grouse.

Before Sam could fully envision such a nightmare, the back door opened, and a tall man wearing an old-fashioned powdered periwig and dark gray livery stepped outside. He'd taken the time to toss a multilayered greatcoat over his shoulders, wearing it like a cape.

"Mr. Kelly?" the man inquired in lofty tones. "I am Mr. Durst."

Sam had to bite back a nasty reply. Who else did the man think had been waiting out here in the dark and cold for him? For some reason, the porter's elegant cravat and starched collar points grated on Sam's nerves. Maybe because he felt disheveled in comparison.

"Aye, I am Sam Kelly of Bow Street." He managed to keep a civil tongue, and yanked out his baton. The gold of its tip caught the light from the nearby gas lamppost and two gas lamps bolted on either side of the back door. "Good evening ter you, sir. I have a few questions regarding Sir Giles, if you don't mind."

"Yes, I was informed. Shocking. I heard someone strangled him. Is that true?"

Even though the information would probably be in the *Morning Chronicle*, Sam was reluctant to confide such a detail to the night porter. "I'm not at liberty ter say. We're lookin' into Sir Giles's activities last evening. His coachman said that he left his master here at half past six. Is that correct?"

"Yes. He dines at the club on Tuesday and Wednesday. Sometimes on Thursday nights as well."

Sam noticed that the night porter was referring to Sir Giles in the present tense, but he didn't bother correcting him. It took some folks a little more time to absorb the truth. He asked, "When he arrived, how was his mood? Did he seem concerned, preoccupied, or worried about anything?"

Durst frowned. "I did not notice him overly worried, but Sir Giles is a deep man. He's never been inclined to wear his emotions on his sleeve, as it were."

"If you don't mind, tell me what happened after he got ter the club. Did he speak to anyone in particular?"

"He came right into the dining room and was seated near the west wall. He nodded at the other patrons, but he did not speak to them, nor did they approach him. Our members are respectful of each other's privacy. He sat down and ordered his meal." The night porter hesitated. "He was joined by a gentleman."

Sam raised his eyebrows. "He had a dinner companion? Who?"

Again, Durst hesitated, and his obvious reticence was long enough to annoy Sam. "I am not a curiosity seeker, Mr. Durst," he snapped. "This is a murder investigation."

"I am aware, Mr. Kelly," the night porter said stiffly. "The gentleman in question was Lord Cross. He did not dine. He did order a brandy, but seemed more interested in speaking to Sir Giles. They appeared to be engaged in a rather intense discussion."

"I see." As Sam watched, the snowflakes fell and melted into the night porter's periwig. "An intense discussion. Are you saying that they were arguing?"

Durst's nostril's flared in annoyance. "No, I did not say that. It was an intense discussion. Lord Cross appeared to be agitated."

"What was their relationship like?"

"I don't understand what you mean."

"Did they often dine together, or engage in conversation? Did you notice if they have ever had similar intense discussions in the past?"

"No. They have exchanged pleasantries, I believe, but nothing more. Sir Giles is considerably older than Lord Cross. I cannot imagine that they would have much in common, and until last evening I had not noticed any connection between them. Although . . ."

"Although?" Sam controlled his impatience.

"Lord Cross only recently came into his viscountcy. Prior to that, his elder brother held the title. I believe Lord Cross served in the military for several years. He may have known Sir Giles through that connection."

Sam made note of that, and asked, "Do you know what they discussed?"

"That I cannot say." The night porter straightened, and looked down his long nose at Sam. "We do not make it a habit of eavesdropping on our members, Mr. Kelly."

"How did they end their discussion?"

"Lord Cross departed—barely having touched his brandy, I might add. Sir Giles remained to finish his dinner, and a very fine port. But one could plainly see that he was wool gathering, not responding when other members offered him a greeting."

"Lord Cross left before Sir Giles?"

"I believe I did just say that, yes."

Sam ignored the sarcasm. "What time was that?"

"I think it was around eight."

"When did Sir Giles leave?"

"Nine o'clock, I believe. After he received the note."

Sam's brows shot upward. "Note?"

"A young boy delivered a message, requesting that it be given to Sir Giles." The night porter drew his greatcoat closer as snowflakes snuck past his collar. "I delivered it to Sir Giles personally, and he left shortly afterward."

"Who was the note from?"

"I do not know."

"Did you see what was written on it?"

"Of course not! Only the most uncouth would dare open a message meant for someone else."

There was enough outrage in the night porter's voice to convince Sam that he was being sincere. "How did Sir Giles react when he read the contents of the note? Did you notice?"

Durst was silent as he considered it. "I told you that he is—forgive me, *was*—not the type of man to wear his feelings on his sleeve. But he appeared . . . disturbed. He left immediately."

"Did he seem afraid?"

"Certainly not." The night porter sounded offended by the idea. "Sir Giles was not a man to be afraid. I offered to hail him a hackney, but as luck would have it, a hackney had only just pulled up when we stepped outside. It was very fortuitous."

The back of Sam's neck prickled. *It wasn't fortuitous if the killer was driving the hackney*, he thought.

He asked, "Did Lord Cross have his own carriage?"

"No. I offered to secure him a hackney, as well, but he chose to walk. If you remember, last evening was clear, compared to tonight." He turned his face upward, and grimaced when he was struck by the lightly falling snow. He wiped a quick hand across his brow. "Will that be all, Mr. Kelly? I have duties to attend to inside."

Sam pressed his lips together to stop himself from pointing out that he'd been freezing in the alley as he'd waited for the stiff-rumped night porter; the man could spare him a few more minutes. But he swallowed the words, asking instead, "What do you know of Sir Giles's relationship with his son, Gerard Holbrooke?"

Durst eyed him warily. "Why would I know anything about their relationship?"

"Because even though you don't listen deliberately ter conversations between club members, you're not deaf, Mr. Durst. Did you happen ter overhear any gossip about them?"

Durst's mouth puckered. "There *was* talk of their . . . estrangement," he finally admitted. "I believe wagers were being placed on the outcome. Gentlemen tend to gamble on everything."

Sam snorted. He may never have been through the hallowed doors of the club, but Sam had heard about the outrageous betting that went on inside. There was a rumor that some nobleman had bet twenty thousand pounds over whether one raindrop would hit the bottom of the window-pane before another. Most of the wagers, though, were centered around marriage, whether a lord or lady would get leg-shackled. A few of the more outrageous bets ended in bankruptcy, sometimes resulting in the nobleman blowing his brains out.

Sam asked now, "What were people wagering?"

"The odds were that Sir Giles would cut off Mr. Holbrooke come summer."

"Is Mr. Holbrooke a member here?"

Distaste crossed the other man's face. "No. I believe he considers this club far too sedate for his taste. And . . ."

"And?" Sam pressed.

"I got the impression that Mr. Holbrooke had no interest in joining any club of which his father would be a member."

Sam took off his hat, knocked the snow off its brim. "Did you hear about the incident where Mr. Holbrooke attacked his father?" he asked, settling his hat back on his head.

For a moment, Durst looked confused. Then his brow cleared. "Ah, you are referring to the incident at Tattersalls? Yes. Outrageous behavior. Word is the young man was as drunk as a wheelbarrow." He suddenly stiffened, eyes widening. "You cannot possibly believe that Mr. Holbrooke killed his own father, Mr. Kelly!"

"Is that so impossible?"

"Well, certainly. Mr. Holbrooke is like so many of the other young pups in town. Good heavens, if every one of the scapegraces killed their father over an argument on gambling and poor behavior, you would be a very busy man, Mr. Kelly. Very busy indeed."

As far as Sam was concerned, he was already too busy. He touched the tip of his hat. "Thank you for your time, Mr. Durst. Please send word ter me at Bow Street if you should think of anything else regarding Sir Giles."

"I have told you everything. Good evening."

Sam waited until the night porter turned and slipped back through the door into the club. Slowly, he pivoted, and made his way down the alley to the street. The evening's chill was seeping into his bones, which had him contemplating a hot whiskey at the Brown Bear or Pig & Whistle, or any of the many establishments that would accept the likes of him through their front doors.

13

The scullery maids were the only ones moving about when Kendra rolled out of bed the next morning. Hurriedly, she slipped out of her nightdress, and pulled on chemise, stays, and silky white stockings. Shivering—the fire in the hearth had gone out sometime in the middle of the night, and the temperature in the bedchamber would've kept an ice sculpture from melting—she shrugged into her robe and went about the task of tying the garters below the knee and rolling down the stocking to secure the ribbons. Straightening, she crossed the room to grab her half boots, pausing by the window.

At six A.M., Grosvenor Square appeared otherworldly. In the early morning light, fog was scuttling across the snow-covered ground. Last night's snowfall clung like crushed diamonds to dead branches and evergreens in the park on the other side of the street.

It was peaceful. But Kendra knew the peace wouldn't last. In another hour, the silence would give way to the clatter of wagons delivering milk and coal to the households along the square. Servants would be the first to emerge, striking out for the city's various markets and shops and bringing back fish, meats, and vegetables for the kitchen staff and chefs to chop, marinate, boil, and broil for the meals throughout the day.

In the 21st century, fresh, organic food had become big business. Here it was everyday life.

Everything old is new again.

By noon, the world would change again, when the Beau Monde woke in their canopied beds, demanding their cocoa, coffee, or tea.

The Duke did not follow the Ton's ritual of lying in bed all morning. She needed to get moving.

Tying the sash of her robe more securely around her waist, she crossed the floor to the dresser. Last night, she'd laid out her reticule, muff pistol, and a handful of coins.

Kendra scooped up the coins, dropping them into the pouch with quiet satisfaction. She'd earned this money herself by investing in the Exchange. It wasn't quite the fortune she'd anticipated when she'd borrowed money from the Duke to invest. To her surprise, she'd learned that being from the future didn't necessarily give her the advantage that she had thought it would. Macroeconomics versus microeconomics—she was aware of the bigger picture. Diesel engines would be huge—but not for another fifty-plus years. You couldn't invest in technology that hadn't yet been invented.

And knowing about an upcoming trend wasn't quite a sure bet, either, because the stock market wasn't about trends—it was about *companies*. And a company may survive, even continue to thrive in the 21st century, but that didn't mean that same company didn't go through highs and lows along the way.

Still, she'd managed to earn enough to pay back the Duke, and save a tidy sum for herself. Her sense of accomplishment and her need to earn her own money baffled the Duke and Alec. It was an area in which they would probably never see eye to eye.

Like now. They'd never understand what she was about to do. And when they did find out . . . well, she would deal with it then.

She slipped the muff pistol into the reticule and left the bedchamber. The soles of her half boots barely made a sound against the runner as she moved down the shadowy hallway.

The servant's staircase was tucked down a corridor at the back of the mansion. There was no rug to muffle her footsteps here, and she winced at the click her heels made against the wood floor. She let out a breath when she opened the door to the stairwell, but found herself staring with consternation at the pitch-black interior. *Shit.* She hadn't thought to bring a candle with her. For a moment, she debated about going back to her bedchamber, but she didn't want to waste the time. The household was waking up. And really, how hard could it be to go up a flight of stairs?

She left the door open to give her some light, but that quickly disappeared as she climbed the narrow stairs. Halfway up, she was also assailed by memories of another dark stairwell. These stairs angled straight upward, whereas the stairs hidden in the Duke's study at the castle spiraled around, but, oh, God. Her skin tingled at the memory of that darkness, the plunging temperature, the sensation of being ripped apart and knit back together again.

Despite the cold—natural, not supernatural this time—she was sweating, her palm slippery as it touched the wall for guidance. She could hear her raspy breath, too loud in the enclosed space. Her heart pounded. Her own version of PTSD. She lifted her robe and pelted up the remaining stairs, her knees turning to Jell-O when she finally thrust open the door at the top, nearly hitting a scullery maid. The young girl leapt back and gave a frightened squeak, her breath nearly blowing out the flame of the candle she was holding. Her eyes were as big as moons as she regarded Kendra above the gyrating flame.

"Shit. Sorry. *Sorry,*" Kendra apologized as she fought to control her racing heart.

"Gor, miss! Ye scared the livin' daylights outta me, ye did," the maid whispered, and her free hand fluttered to cover her heart. "W'ot are ye doin' 'ere?"

Kendra had the lie ready. "I need my maid. I woke up with a headache."

"Do ye want me ter fetch ye a tonic?"

"You have your own duties to perform. Molly will be able to help me." Kendra peered down the long, narrow corridor. Early morning light streamed in from the small fan window set high on the wall, thinning out the shadows. There were at least a dozen closed doors in the hallway, six on each side. Kendra had never ventured up here before, and realized that she had no idea which bedchamber the former tweeny occupied. "Ah . . . which room is she in?"

"That one." The maid pointed toward the second door at the end.

"Thank you." Kendra hesitated. "I'd appreciate it if you didn't mention this to anyone."

The young girl stared at her, then shrugged. "Aye, miss."

Kendra was aware that the maid continued to watch her as she walked down the hall. When she stopped at Molly's door and glanced back, the maid had disappeared into the servant's stairs. She released a long sigh. There wasn't a snowball's chance in hell that the maid would keep silent about encountering the Duke's ward in the servant's quarters. As soon as she hit the kitchen, she'd be telling the belowstairs staff, and it would spread like a contagion to the stables, then upward to the abovestairs servants. Eventually, it would reach the top echelon of that chain—Mr. Harding, Mrs. Danbury, Lady Atwood's lady's maid, and the Duke's valet. And they would report it to the Duke and his sister.

Kendra winced. She could already hear Lady Atwood's lecture.

There was nothing to be done about it. She had a mission to accomplish. This was why she hadn't wanted Alec to spend the night. He would have tried to stop her.

Or, worse, tried to accompany her.

She didn't knock on Molly's door; she opened it and ducked inside. Another small window bathed the tiny room in the gray light of early morning. Two single beds flanked a nightstand. A small wardrobe was shoved against the wall. A washstand peeked out from behind a privacy curtain. There was probably a chamber pot near there, or under the beds. The occupants of both beds were buried beneath blankets and heavy quilts. It was as cold up here as it was in her bedchamber.

Kendra hadn't considered that Molly would be sharing the room, but it made sense. The staff was large, but, unlike the sprawling Aldridge Castle, the space in Number 29 was limited.

"Molly?" she whispered.

A blanket-covered lump shifted in the nearest bed.

She tried again. "*Molly?*"

"W'ot?" A head covered in a wool nightcap popped out from under the covers. Molly's pale freckled face looked up at her, eyes squinting. She pressed a hand to her mouth as she yawned. "Miss? W'ot's 'appening?"

"Sh-sh," Kendra whispered. But it was already too late. The head of Molly's roommate emerged from the blankets, staring at her owlishly. Kendra recognized her as one of the tweenies from the castle. Berta was her name, she remembered.

Kendra looked at Molly. "I need to borrow a few clothes."

That jolted the maid fully awake. This wasn't the first time Kendra had made such a request. "Oh, nay! *Nay*, miss, not again!" she cried. "'Is Grace will be ever so angry!"

"His Grace doesn't need to know about this." She saw the skepticism on Molly's face. Instead of arguing, she slid her reticule off her wrist, and set it on the nightstand. "I'm just going to borrow a few things," she said as she opened the wardrobe. "Stop whimpering. You won't be punished."

Kendra surveyed the meager offerings. Damn. She'd forgotten that Molly wasn't a tweeny anymore, and had been allowed to abandon the simple blue-and-white uniform in favor of plain cotton and wool gowns in respectably muted colors. At least the style and quality still indicated servant class, and that was what Kendra was looking for.

Except . . .

She tapped her chin as she slid a speculative glance at the two uniforms hanging on hooks. A tweeny was even more invisible than a lady's maid.

She pulled out one of the uniforms and measured it against her body.

"But, miss, those ain't Molly's clothes!" the tweeny protested, shoving herself into a sitting position.

"It might be a little short, but I think it will work." Kendra tossed the uniform on the end of Molly's bed, then peeled off her robe, shivering again as the cold air of the attic hit her body. She clenched her jaw to keep her teeth from chattering and snatched up the uniform. "You don't mind if I borrow this . . . Berta?"

"Abigail."

"Oh, yeah. Thanks, Abigail," she said, yanking the uniform over her head. "Molly, I need you to button me up. Hurry."

"But . . . but . . ." Abigail floundered, bewildered. "W'ot are ye gonna do, miss?"

"Oi'll come with ye," Molly said, scampering from the bed to do Kendra's bidding. "Oi'm yer lady's maid. 'Tis me job ter chaperone ye."

"No." Kendra presented her back to Molly. "This is something that I need to do alone."

"But—"

"No, Molly." Kendra's tone was sharp enough to make the maid subside. Molly tended to take her lady's maid duties very seriously, but Kendra couldn't have the girl traipsing behind her on her current mission. "As of this moment, I'm a tweeny. And tweenies don't need chaperones." Molly pouted, and she added, "I don't need to worry about you."

Molly eyed her nervously. "Is w'ot yer gonna do dangerous?"

"I know how to take care of myself," Kendra said evasively. She went back to the wardrobe to retrieve a mop cap and simple wool cloak. Slipping behind the privacy screen, she stuffed her loose hair into the mop cap, put on the cloak, and peered at herself in the small mirror attached to the wash basin. It would do, she decided.

She returned and picked up her reticule. "How do I look?"

"The reticule ain't right," Abigail observed critically.

Kendra glanced down at the silken pouch decorated with ribbons and embroidery. The girl had a point.

The tweeny scooted out of bed and padded over to the wardrobe. She rummaged through it, emerging with a plain brown wool pouch with a simple corded drawstring, as nondescript as the cloak. "This'd be better, miss."

Kendra grinned. "You're right, Abigail. Thanks." She made the transfer of the muff pistol—which elicited a shocked squeak from Abigail—and coins. She looked at the two girls. "I'll be back in an hour or two."

Or three. It would depend on how fast she could track down her quarry. She only prayed that she was back at Grosvenor Number 29 before the Duke and his sister woke.

It took her forty-five minutes to track her target. It would have been less, but Kendra had been forced to walk outside the residential Grosvenor Square in order to hail a hackney. The driver wasn't thrilled when she told him her destination, but became more agreeable when she added another coin to his fare. The sun was making a fast ascent, the sky already a queer yellowish haze when he dropped her off in Cheapside, a busy area of London filled with merchant shops and the gamey scent of cattle from nearby holding pens.

It took another twenty minutes before she found the man she sought in the dining room of the Toad Inn.

She stood for a moment in the doorway, scanning the room and the hard-faced men inside. Most of their attention was focused on eating and drinking, but her skin prickled when a few narrowed, suspicious eyes fell on her. Her pulse began to race. She slid her hand into the wool pouch, closing over the muff pistol, one finger on the trigger. You can never be too careful.

The next part could get a little tricky. She needed to sit close, but not too close. And she wanted her eyes on the room. This was just the type of crowd who'd enjoy sticking a knife in her ribs.

Aware that she was drawing too much attention, Kendra moved forward. She kept her stride brisk as she wove through the tables and the heavy odors of greasy meat, potatoes, eggs, and ale blended with the more earthy smells of unwashed bodies.

"Hello, Bear." Shoving a chair against the wall, she dropped down onto the seat. "I think we left each other on good terms, but just to be clear, I've got a pistol pointed at your most prized possession. I'd hate for it to go off accidentally." She forced a smile, showing teeth. "But I'm pretty sure you'd hate it even more."

The man opposite her had been shoveling bread dripping with yoke into his mouth, but now he froze. Slowly, never taking his eyes off her, he lowered his hand.

She kept the smile on her face, even though her mouth felt uncomfortably dry. Bear might have been sitting, but that didn't diminish him in any way. He was gigantic, bigger than she remembered. Six foot, seven inches, with muscles the size of boulders. His nearly bald pate gleamed;

his gold earring winked. He'd grown a beard since she'd last seen him. His brown eyes were the same, though, as flat as a shark's. A scar was puckered near his left eye. He was wearing a workman's smock beneath a wool jacket—triple XL—and Kendra knew that beneath his sleeves, his arms were tattooed. She'd seen them last year when he'd taken off his jacket and rolled up his sleeves when he'd vowed to beat Alec to death.

"Ye're still a bloodthirsty wench, I see," he said slowly, his voice a rumble like distant thunder inside his massive chest. He picked up his tankard of ale and sat back to regard her. "Have ye left yer tulip?"

It took Kendra a moment to remember that was the name he called Alec. She ignored the insult—assuming he meant it as an insult. She wasn't quite clear on that. "I'd like to talk to Snake."

The giant lifted his eyebrows. "And why might that be, eh?"

"He found a body yesterday. Have you heard?"

Something that might have been amusement flickered behind the deadpan expression. "Aye. The gentry mort in the church. Ye're lookin' inter the swell's murder?" His eyes narrowed. "Why?"

"Why not?"

"I'll be damned, but ye're an unnatural female."

Kendra pressed her lips together. She didn't need a criminal like Bear calling her a freak. "I just want to talk to Snake."

"He didn't see nothin'."

That was probably true, but Kendra shrugged. "I'd still like to talk to him. The watchman didn't see anything, either, but from my understanding, Snake was running ahead of him."

"W'ot's in it for me?"

"A sense of your civic duty."

Bear laughed, the booming sound causing heads to turn. "Ye're a peculiar piece of baggage, ter be sure. Aye then. If I see Snake, I'll see w'ot I can do for ye."

"If?" Kendra arched a brow at the giant.

He smiled. "When."

Kendra nodded. "Okay. I'm at 29—"

"I remember where ye are." His smile turned predatory.

Kendra studied him for a long moment. Bear was a thug, but he was at the top of a very vicious pecking order. A crime lord. And if Bear was anything like his 21st-century counterparts, he had a pipeline of information on what was going on in his city.

"What do you know about the dead man?" she asked.

"He's dead."

"Any idea who might have put him in that state?"

Bear hefted the tankard, drank deeply, and then set it down. "He's a nob in government," he said, wiping his mouth with the back of his hand. "Plenty of folks would wanna stop his claret, I'd imagine."

"Would his son be in that group?"

Bear scratched his beard, and a gleam came into his eyes. "Gerard Holbrooke."

Kendra leaned back in the chair to regard the giant. "You know him." It wasn't a question.

"Not personal-like. But he's a frequent customer in the gaming hells. And the more inventive academies."

"Yours?"

"I might have an interest. The cove's an elbow shaker—dice," he clarified, grinning at her obvious bewilderment. "He owed a few people."

"Your people?"

"Nay. People ain't so beetle-headed ter tip me the double."

Kendra lifted a finger. "Can you speak English?"

Bear laughed. "No one is stupid enough ter not pay their debt ter me."

Now that she could imagine. "What about his relationship with his father?"

He shrugged his massive shoulders. "Word's gone around that he and his da had a fallin' out."

"And did word go around before or after Holbrooke tried to punch his fist into his father's face?"

Bear smiled. "Before."

"The way I heard it, Sir Giles was unhappy with the debt his son was running up. Even if Holbrooke paid your people, he might not have been so conscientious elsewhere. You wouldn't happen to know anything about that, would you?"

This time Bear's smile was sly. "I might."

"I'm not really in the mood for games, Bear."

Bear sighed. "The young pup couldn't stay away from the gaming tables. He was in Dun Territory, but that's not why the old man was nettled. I heard the bloody fool gave a Jack in the box to one of their housemaids."

Kendra had to think about that one. Jack in the box. *Bun in the oven?* "He got a maid pregnant?" she guessed.

He grinned. "Aye."

"What happened to her?"

"The maid? Suppose they sent her packin'. Can't have a maid servin' ye tea with a swellin' belly."

An unmarried maid who'd become pregnant couldn't stay in a respectable household—even if the father of her child was a member of that respectable household.

Bear went on, "She'll probably end up in the poor house or a brothel after she's had the brat." He shrugged, not sounding too concerned about the girl's plight. "But the old nob flew into the boughs about it all the same. Blamed his son for tossin' up the wench's skirts and havin' his way with her." Bear picked up his knife and fork and cut into the sausages now congealed in grease on his plate. "Word was his da was gonna take care of the problem," he added as he chewed.

Kendra kept her gaze on the giant. "What does that mean?"

"He was gonna buy a commission for his son in the army. Send him off ter some post in India. That's the rumor, anyway."

"I suppose that's one way to solve the problem."

"For the old man, maybe. But India's a hot, nasty place, ain't it? Might be worth killin' ter not get shipped over there."

She tilted her head, regarding him. "So you think Holbrooke could have killed his father?" she asked again.

"Snake said the cove's tongue was cut outta him." Bear lifted the tankard and washed down the sausage. He belched as he set the stein down. "Seems ter me that a son wouldn't do that. Why would he, when he could've just slit the old man's gullet?"

Kendra said nothing.

"But like I said, the nob was in government," Bear continued. "Foreign Office or Home Office. Word is that he traded in secrets. The way I see it, maybe someone told him somethin', then cut out his tongue so he wouldn't be sharin' any confidences."

"He was murdered first," Kendra pointed out.

Bear smirked. "Aye. Ter my way of thinking, that's a fine way of keepin' someone quiet too."

14

Alec was still irritated as he cantered Chance across Hampstead Heath early the next morning. His aunt's high-handed interference the night before had annoyed him enough to cause him to toss and turn most of the night. Of course, she wasn't the only source of his foul mood. Oh, no, much of that he could lay at the foot of one bloody-minded American.

What was *wrong* with the woman? How many times would she refuse his offer of marriage? Would he be forever consigned to sneak around like a thief in the night to be with the woman he loved?

Kendra Donovan was the most amazing, mesmerizing, brilliant, courageous, and frustratingly stubborn woman he'd ever known. Were all the females so blasted contrary in the future? And were all the men in lunatic asylums for dealing with them?

He laughed as he imagined his future counterparts, which loosened the knot of anger inside of him. Around him, icy wind rattled the blades of brown, brittle grass poking through a thin crust of snow. Alec let his gaze travel the rural landscape. Located on the outskirts of London, Hampstead Heath had become pitted from excavations of its prized sand. The larger quarries had been transformed by natural springs and rainwater into ponds, now iced over. It was ruggedly attractive, and slightly eerie, with thin patches of fog crawling across the ground.

The *clip-clop* of horse's hooves sounded in the distance. Alec's hand went to the pistol he had tucked in his pocket. Highwaymen preferred the cloak of night for their nefarious deeds, but it never hurt to keep up one's guard. A rider appeared on the horizon, a dark silhouette against the light, but Alec recognized him and sent Chance galloping in his direction.

"Fiend seize it, Sutcliffe. This is an ungodly hour for a meeting, don't you think?" the man complained when they pulled up their reins next to each other. His big bay skittered a bit, but he controlled his horse expertly.

"Town life has made you soft," Alec remarked.

The man snorted. "*Age* has made me soft."

Alec smiled at Lieutenant-Colonel Lucius d'Ambray. He was a tall, lean man with dark hair liberally streaked with silver, a weather-beaten face from hours spent outdoors, and cynical hazel eyes, all of which made him appear older than his forty-three years. Alec had been introduced to the military man during his two years of intelligence gathering, when d'Ambray's role was to ferry correspondence from the agents in the field back to Whitehall. Sir Giles had been d'Ambray's superior during the war. Today, the older man worked for the Home Office.

"This is about Sir Giles's murder, isn't it?" d'Ambray said, fixing Alec with a steady stare.

"Yes."

Something that might have been regret passed over the older man's stern features. "'Tis a damn shame. England lost a good man. I know Bow Street is investigating." He hesitated, and the corners of his eyes crinkled as he gazed at Alec. "I heard that your uncle and his ward are assisting Mr. Kelly. May I assume you are involved in the matter as well?"

"You may."

The lieutenant-colonel raised an eyebrow, a gesture of amusement rather than surprise. "'Tis not the usual thing for the Beau Monde to become involved in something so base as criminal matters."

"No."

The older man smiled a little at Alec's monosyllabic response. "It appears as though His Grace is making a habit of it, though. I am aware that he involved himself last year with Lady Dover's murder. But given that suspicion had fallen on you, his interest was understandable." His saddle creaked as he leaned forward, his gaze locked on Alec. "I hope you realize that I would have testified to your character if the House of Lords had charged you."

Alec inclined his head. "Thankfully, the matter never rose to that level."

"I was in Switzerland at the time, and only learned about the incident when I returned to London. I heard the Duke's ward was also intimately involved in the investigation. Miss Donovan—she's an American, is she not?"

Alec's stomach tightened, and he knew a moment of concern. The last thing they needed was for Kendra to come under scrutiny by the Home Office. The fact that there was no trace of the American before last August would raise too many questions for which they had no answers. And, God help them, if the government ever found out the truth—if they ever *believed* the truth, that Kendra was from the future . . . Damnation, he didn't even dare contemplate such a thing. A woman who held secrets of the future in her head would be a valuable asset for any country.

The lieutenant-colonel was watching him. "She is," Alec said, "but someday I hope to make her my wife."

The lieutenant-colonel had been in service too long to show much emotion, but Alec sensed his surprise. "Ah, is that the way the wind blows then? Congratulations."

If I can get the bloody woman to agree, he thought. Out loud, he said, "Thank you. However, I'm not here to discuss Miss Donovan."

"No, you are here to talk about Sir Giles's murder. Lord Sidmouth is naturally interested, as well," he said, referring to the Home Secretary.

Alec had expected nothing less. "What is the measure of Lord Sidmouth's interest? We have heard nothing from the Home Office."

The other man smiled slightly. "You have no reason to fear that his lordship will take over the investigation, if that's what you are inquiring.

Your Bow Street man has an excellent reputation. For the moment, Lord Sidmouth is satisfied with the chain of command. Sir Nathaniel is keeping him apprised of what is happening."

Alec seized on the one phrase that concerned him. "For the moment?"

"One never knows when it comes to politicians," d'Ambray said. "I think Sidmouth fears there may be a Catholic component to the crime. Given the volatile state of affairs in Ireland, he most likely feels more comfortable keeping an eye on the investigation from afar." He straightened in his saddle, lifting his reins. "I know a hostelry in the area. Have pity on my old bones, my lord, and let us have the rest of this conversation in comfort."

"Do you know who murdered Sir Giles?" Alec asked bluntly, once they were settled into worn leather wingback chairs before the fire crackling in the taproom of the Stag Head hostelry, drinking coffee.

"If we did, don't you think the man would be in Newgate?"

"Not necessarily. It would depend on who the man was, and if the Home Office had use for him."

D'Ambray smiled briefly. "There is always the greater good when one is dealing with politics and the security of one's country. But I am being sincere, my lord. We do not know who killed Sir Giles."

"What about suspects?"

"There are always suspects, especially for a man in Sir Giles's position. As I mentioned earlier, there is worry that Irish radicals may be behind the murder. There are some whispers about the Scots, as well, although those are not as forcible or loud. Both countries have a predilection for violence."

Alec was of the mind that their predilection for violence was the same as in any other country, including England, but he remained silent.

D'Ambray frowned, his gaze searching Alec's face. "I am aware of the invisible ink on the body, my lord. A spy trick."

"Garroting is also considered a spy technique."

"Yes."

The other man took a long sip of coffee, and Alec sensed that the action was meant to give him time to consider something. The lieutenant-colonel let out a sigh as he lowered the mug. "There are no official suspects, you understand, but one person came to my mind when I heard of Sir Giles's murder—Mr. Silas Fitzpatrick."

"I don't believe I am acquainted with Mr. Fitzpatrick," Alec said. "Who is he?"

"No, you wouldn't be. He doesn't exactly travel in your circles, my lord. He's an Irish immigrant who opened a coffeehouse—the Liber—in Mayfair about two years ago." He paused. "You must be aware of how coffeehouses and taverns are often used as rendezvous points for radicals and spies."

"Sir Giles thought the Liber was such a place?"

"Yes. Mr. Fitzpatrick has been vocal on his support of Irish emancipation."

"So are most respectable Whigs," Alec said with a shrug. "There is no shortage of men and women voicing such sentiment. What is it about Mr. Fitzpatrick that makes you think he killed Sir Giles?"

"Sir Giles confided in me that he thought Mr. Fitzpatrick and his men were following him."

Alec arched a brow. "Following him? For what purpose?"

"Possibly because Sir Giles had the Liber under surveillance as well."

"So they were spying on each other?"

D'Ambray smiled slightly. "'Tis the way the intelligence community works. Although I always got the impression there was something more that Sir Giles was not telling me."

"Like what?"

"Perhaps I'm being fanciful. But if Mr. Fitzpatrick is the Irish spy that Sir Giles suspected him of being, there may be a reason for the invisible ink."

"Are you aware that the symbols drawn on Sir Giles appear to be crucifixes?"

"Yes, I had heard. I thought perhaps a taunt? The madman left Sir Giles's body in what had been a Catholic church."

"Did Mr. Fitzpatrick ever threaten Sir Giles?"

"Not to my knowledge." D'Ambray picked up his mug again and frowned. "There are also aspects to this murder that are . . . troubling. Cutting out his tongue. From my understanding, it wasn't done for torture, which would be more typical. I can't imagine why Mr. Fitzpatrick would do such a thing—spy or no."

Alec thought about what Kendra had said. "Someone who wants to send a message?"

"But what message, and to whom?"

Alec could only shake his head. He switched subjects. "What about Sir Giles himself? Did you notice anything peculiar in his mood or behavior?"

D'Ambray's gaze dropped to his coffee mug. Alec watched something ripple across the older man's face, too subtle for him to discern. Finally, the lieutenant-colonel sighed. "I no longer worked directly for Sir Giles, and my current duties take me away from the country for long spells. However, we did meet on occasion, at his club or elsewhere."

He fell silent. Alec waited.

D'Ambray continued, "About a month ago, I noticed that he appeared unnerved about something."

"Unnerved? How so?"

He looked up at Alec. "Perhaps that is not the right word, and I really don't know how to explain it. Sir Giles was normally the most unflappable of men."

"I remember."

"I had a meeting with Sidmouth, and literally ran into Sir Giles. I apologized profusely, but he . . . he simply stood there for a moment, as though his wits had fled. Not usual at all for a man like Sir Giles. He was obviously distracted, but there was something more. He seemed deeply troubled. Naturally, I asked him if all was well."

"And how did he respond?"

"At first, he brushed off my inquiry, but then he confessed that he'd recently received information that had disturbed him." D'Ambray shook his head. "I asked, of course, but he said that he wanted to keep his own counsel. At the time, I confess that I put his distraction down to his work in the Home Office and his responsibilities there."

Alec paused before trying, "Did Sir Giles speak of his son?"

D'Ambray's grimace was enough to give Alec his answer.

"Not often," D'Ambray elaborated, "but when he did, I must confess that I was grateful that I've avoided the parson's mousetrap. I got the impression that Lady Holbrooke doted on the boy. Sir Giles blamed himself for not taking him in hand when he was younger, and failed to recognize that he'd turned into a scapegrace until too late. It's ridiculous, of course. Sir Giles had enormous responsibilities. The very existence of England was at stake. He could hardly leave Whitehall to coddle a child!"

"And not really a child. Gerard Holbrooke is, what? Five and twenty?" Alec lifted his mug, regarding the lieutenant-colonel over the rim. "Did you know that they had engaged in a public fight at Tattersalls?"

"Good God, no. When?"

"Two weeks ago. Apparently, Mr. Holbrooke was foxed enough to strike out at his father."

"The fool." D'Ambray shook his head, appalled. "That would have been humiliating for a stoic man like Sir Giles. In all the years that we were acquainted, I only saw him openly distraught once, and that was when he lost one of his intelligence agents in Spain."

"'Tis the price of war," murmured Alec. He'd been aware of that steep price when he'd worked for Sir Giles in Italy. As he lifted his coffee mug, he saw something change on the other man's face. "What?"

D'Ambray pursed his lips. "Nothing, truly. It's just that Sir Giles mentioned the young man's name recently—Evert Larson." He hesitated. "I'm not certain. It may be a coincidence, or perhaps I am conflating the two issues, but as I reflect back on my encounters with Sir Giles in the last month, it seems like Evert might have something to do with his recent state of mind."

Alec frowned. "How so?"

"I think he must have said something . . ." His eyes grew distant, as though he were trying to recapture the memory. But then he shook his head, sighing. "Forgive me. I cannot recall the specifics. Though I believe it's near the anniversary of Evert Larson's death, so that may account for Sir Giles's troubled mood. The loss of the young man weighed heavily on him."

"It would be difficult to lose someone you recruited," said Alec. "No doubt Sir Giles felt a sense of responsibility."

"Yes, but there was more. Evert Larson wasn't only a man he recruited; he was the son of an old friend. Unfortunately, their friendship did not survive the young man's death."

Alec took a slow sip of coffee. "Who is his father?"

"Mr. Bertel Larson. He owns an apothecary shop on Cromwell Road in Kensington."

That surprised Alec. "An apothecary? Pray tell, how did Sir Giles form a connection with such a man?"

The lieutenant-colonel smiled. "Perhaps I should have said that Mr. Larson is a very *successful* apothecary? But that is not how the two men were connected. Sir Giles once told me that they'd been boys together in Hammersmith, and fought in the same regiment against the colonist uprising in America."

"A very old friendship, indeed."

"They maintained their connection, even though Sir Giles's military career outmatched Mr. Larson's, and His Majesty granted Sir Giles a baronet title." He blew out a breath. "The man really was a brilliant strategist. Such a terrible loss."

Silently, Alec agreed. He'd had only a handful of encounters with the man himself, but he'd admired Sir Giles's keen intelligence. "How did Mr. Larson's son die?"

"I heard that he was attempting to save captured English soldiers from the Fifty-Second Regiment of Foot. If you wish to know more, you ought to speak to Lord Eliot Cross or Captain Hugh Mobray."

"They know the details?"

"They should. They were the only two survivors."

Alec frowned. "How many men died?"

"Ten or twelve. I'm not certain."

"When did this happen?" asked Alec.

"Unfortunately, in the final days of the Peninsular campaign, near the Maya Pass. Early 1814."

An apple-cheeked maid approached with a coffee pot. Alec waited while she replenished their mugs. After she departed, he remarked, "You said that Mr. Larson blamed Sir Giles for his son's death. But surely he understood that was a possible outcome when his son signed on?"

"It is my understanding that Mr. Larson blamed Sir Giles for persuading his son to sign on in the first place. As you know, I was assigned Italy as my territory during the war, not Spain, but I met Evert in his early days. I understand why Sir Giles brought him on. He was an impressive young man. He had been training as a barrister, and his intelligence was quite formidable. He also had a talent for languages." He smiled at Alec. "Much like you, my lord. Anyhow, Sir Giles and Evert were quite close, almost like father and son. I think Sir Giles was quite proud of him."

Unlike his own son, Alec thought, but remained silent.

D'Ambray went on, "I was under the impression that Sir Giles had been keeping his eye on the boy for quite some time."

Alec lifted an eyebrow. "Keeping his eye on him . . . in order to persuade Evert to serve England by becoming an intelligence agent?"

"Or work in government. Sir Giles never confided in me his plans for the boy. Then Evert was dead, and the families became estranged. I heard a rumor that Mr. Larson even had challenged Sir Giles to a duel."

"Christ." Dueling was not unheard of, but it was discouraged by Polite Society. Maybe because it was so often done by the hot-headed youths of Polite Society. "What happened?"

"To the best of my knowledge, nothing," D'Ambray replied. "Dueling is about honor, not vengeance. I cannot fault Mr. Larson for his rage at losing his son."

"No," Alec conceded slowly. But rage could be twisted into revenge. Alec made a mental note to follow up with Mr. Larson. He returned to Sir Giles's son. "Do you think Mr. Holbrooke could have killed his father?"

"In such a manner?" The lieutenant-colonel frowned, then shook his head. "No, I should think not."

Alec said nothing, but wondered if that was true, or if, like Mr. Muldoon, the lieutenant-colonel simply could not fathom a son slicing out his father's tongue. "You have given me a great deal to consider, sir," he said, and drained his coffee mug. He set it down and stood. "Thank you for meeting me."

The older man rose as well. "I pray you find this madman. He's obviously a dangerous individual. Sir Giles is—was—not a man to be taken by surprise. So for that to have happened . . ." D'Ambray shook his head, and his eyes were grim as he met Alec's gaze. "I wish I had pressed Sir Giles over what was troubling him. Maybe if he would have shared his concern, things might have been different."

"Even if he had confided his troubles, I don't think that would have stopped the killer."

The lieutenant-colonel sighed. "I suppose we'll never know."

15

Kendra never had to sneak past her parents' bedroom after breaking curfew. For the first fourteen years of her life, she'd never had any friends to break curfew with. The irony was not lost on her that now, at the age of twenty-six, her stomach was knotted in anxiety as she slipped into the mansion through the servants' entrance. The household was fully awake, and Kendra held her breath when she spotted Mrs. Danbury through the doors that opened to the kitchens. Thankfully, the housekeeper's attention was fixed on the Duke's temperamental French chef, Monsieur Anton, who was complaining loudly in his native tongue and gesturing wildly toward the two footmen who stood stiffly nearby.

For some reason that Kendra had never understood, Monsieur Anton was paranoid that the English footmen were out to sabotage his culinary masterpieces. From the furious diatribe she overheard, the chef was accusing the two footmen of putting sugar in the salt cellar.

Kendra forced herself not to hurry as she moved past the kitchen doorway. She kept her head angled away, though, just in case Mrs. Danbury happened to glance her way.

Once she cleared the door, she released her breath, and hurried quickly toward the servants' stairs. Along the way, she passed two maids who were sweeping and dusting in the hall. They recognized her, but didn't say anything or stop in their duties. The staff had become inured to what they viewed as her peculiarities.

Instead of returning to Molly and Abigail's room, Kendra let herself into her own bedchamber. Inside, Molly was unpacking an enormous trunk.

"Oh, thank 'eavens, miss!" the maid declared, dropping the silvery beaded evening gown she'd been holding, and coming forward to take the wool cloak from Kendra. "Oi was ever so worried about ye!"

"There was nothing to worry about." Kendra dragged the mop cap from her head, tossing it on the bed alongside the reticule. "Did anyone realize I was gone?"

"Nay." Molly bit her lip. "At least, Oi don't think so. No one inquired about ye. 'Is Grace is 'aving breakfast in the mornin' room. 'Er ladyship is still abed."

Kendra turned so Molly could undo the buttons of the dress. She glanced at the dainty porcelain clock on the fireplace mantel. It was ticking toward 9:30.

"But 'Is Grace will probably find out," Molly warned. "'E always does."

"I'm not planning on hiding it from him." She dropped the gown, letting it pool around her ankles. She stepped out of the homespun uniform. "In fact, I'll be telling him about it."

Molly looked suspicious. "Then why didn't ye tell 'im about it afore ye went out?"

The maid had her there. "'It's better to beg for forgiveness than to ask for permission,'" she quoted with a smile.

"W'ot?"

Kendra sighed. "There are times when His Grace is more protective over me than he needs to be. You don't realize how lucky you are, Molly, to be able to come and go as you please."

Molly frowned as she picked up the garment off the floor and draped it across a chair. "Oi can't go about without the say so from Mrs. Danbury, miss."

"Still, once you're outside, nobody notices you."

The maid gave her a strange look. "Ye don't want anybody ter notice ye?"

"There are times when I don't want to call attention to myself . . ." Her gaze fell on the maid's uniform, and a possibility began to take shape in her mind. "Is there a place where I could buy a maid's uniform?" she asked.

This was not a world of ready-made clothes. At Aldridge Castle, the head laundress/seamstress, Mrs. Beaton, was responsible for sewing the maids' dresses and aprons. Still, there were secondhand shops around that sold used clothing, much like in the 21st century.

Molly asked, "Why would ye wanna buy such a thing?"

"It might come in handy."

"So ye can run about with no one noticing ye," the maid surmised with a disapproving look. "Maybe ye should buy a bonnet with a veil ter conceal yerself. Ye'd still be a lady then."

Kendra decided not to point out that being a lady was the least of her concerns. And a bonnet with a veil wasn't a bad idea either. "You might be right," was all she said.

Molly shook her head, a resigned look on her face as she went to open the wardrobe. "Will ye be staying in the rest of the mornin', miss?"

"No. I plan to visit Lady Holbrooke."

That, of course, meant Molly would choose a different kind of dress—more fitted than the comfortable morning gowns. Kendra went into the dressing room to wash her face and brush her teeth while Molly shuffled through the wardrobe. By the time she came out, the maid had selected a pretty moss-green cambric gown with a triangle pattern embossed across the material. Ivory lace trimmed the long sleeves and ran along the modest neckline. A ruffle of the same fabric was sewn along the hemline.

"Will this do?" Molly asked.

The question was a mere formality, as Molly had learned a while ago that Kendra had little regard for fashion. Kendra tugged it on, waited for Molly to button her up. Once finished, Kendra sank down to the seat before the mirrored vanity and Molly styled her hair into a simple chignon. After trading her half-boots for a pair of wedge-heeled green silk shoes, Kendra made her way down to the morning room.

The Duke was sitting at the table, remnants of breakfast on his plate, sipping tea and reading a newspaper—the *Morning Chronicle*, she noticed, as she stepped into the room.

He glanced up. "Good morning, my dear."

"Good morning." She crossed to the sideboard, which had a breakfast buffet laid out in silver warming trays. She loaded her plate up with the full English breakfast: eggs, bacon and sausage, mushrooms and grilled tomatoes. She was starving, she realized. "Did Muldoon write about Sir Giles's murder?"

"Yes. He didn't mention about the invisible ink, so we can assume he hasn't yet been able to ferret out that piece of information. And he only mentioned our involvement in the vaguest of terms."

"*What?*" Kendra whirled around so quickly that only her quick reflexes saved a plump sausage from rolling off her plate. She set the plate on the table and wiped her fingers with a linen napkin, eyes on the Duke. "He actually wrote about us?"

"Not specifically." Aldridge raised his teacup. His blue eyes twinkled as he took in her aghast expression. "But I do believe I am the high-ranking nobleman that he references, and you are the young lady who has taken a unique interest in uncovering the truth."

Kendra scowled. She circled back to the sideboard to pour herself a cup of coffee from the tall silver pot. "You don't sound angry," she finally said as she brought her cup back to the table and sat down opposite the Duke.

He sipped his tea slowly before putting down the delicate china cup. "It's pointless to be angry, my dear. Mr. Muldoon is not revealing anything that is not already known or whispered about among the Ton. Our involvement in Lady Dover's murder was certainly remarked upon." He smiled at her. "I do not fear that invitations will suddenly become scarce. It's not as though we were in trade."

"God forbid," she said dryly. She added lumps of sugar from the small Wedgewood bowl, and stirred her coffee with the minuscule silver spoon.

"Caro may view this article in a different light, of course." He paused to take another swallow of tea. "But I believe we can trust Mr. Muldoon to continue to be discreet about our involvement in the investigation."

Kendra was reserving judgment on Muldoon's trustworthiness. In her own dealings with the Fourth Estate, journalists usually fell into two categories: the ones you could trust, and the ones who would stab you in the back and climb on top of your corpse to be closer to the spotlight. There was rarely a middle ground.

"I think he might be useful," she allowed.

"Still, we do need to be careful," the Duke said. "It wouldn't do to tell Mr. Muldoon about your predilection for wearing servant's attire, and racing about London alone."

His tone was so mild that it took Kendra a moment to realize what he'd said. Slowly, she set down her coffee cup. "You know."

He regarded her steadily. "Did you think I would not find out what is happening in my own household?"

Twenty-six years old, and I'm feeling as guilty as a child caught playing hooky. "I was going to tell you."

He lifted his eyebrows to telegraph his doubt.

She picked up her coffee again and studied it for a long moment before she finally let out a frustrated sigh. "You know, where I come from, women don't have to ask for permission to step outside. And they don't require chaperones to follow them around. I miss my freedom."

"I am aware we come from different worlds, my dear. But these rules are in place to protect ladies from harm."

They were at an impasse. The Duke belonged in a different era. *This* era. She was the one who didn't really belong.

"Who did you visit this morning?" he finally asked.

"Bear."

"*Bear!*" The Duke set down his teacup with a rattle. "Good God. Are you speaking of the ruffian who had you and Alec kidnapped last year? Who beat Alec? Who threatened to molest you?"

Kendra smiled weakly. "Now you know why I didn't tell you."

"This is not amusing, Kendra." A steely note sharpened the aristocrat's voice. "The man could have killed you this morning."

"I had my gun."

Aldridge pressed his fingers to his eyes and shook his head. "Dear God in heaven."

She forked up egg and tomato. "You know that I know how to use it."

"I am aware." He dropped his hand and looked at her. "Do you realize that if he *had* murdered you and dumped your body in the Thames, Alec and I would have been none the wiser? We may have concluded that you had disappeared through another wormhole or vortex, or whatever phenomenon had brought you to us in the first place."

She hadn't thought of that.

The Duke said softly, "It would have broken our hearts. And, I think, Alec would have been driven mad not knowing what had become of you."

Kendra had never had anyone truly worry about her before. Her parents had been concerned about how she'd performed academically, and of course her superiors at the FBI had been concerned for her welfare, just as they were for the welfare of every agent in the field. But worry that came from a place of love and caring was something else entirely.

She must have looked disturbed, because the Duke reached over to squeeze her hand. "I am aware that you often feel chafed by the restrictions in this world, my dear." He hesitated. "And I must admit that there are certain aspects to your world that I have difficulty with as well."

Kendra had a feeling he was talking about her relationship with Alec. In the Duke's eyes, she'd been compromised and, if this were the normal course of events, he'd demand Alec marry her. Instead, he looked the other way. She'd never realized that he might be bothered about their relationship, though.

"Do not fret, my dear."

She looked up at him to find the twinkle had returned to his eyes, and that there was a small smile on his face. That was one of the things she liked about him; he wasn't the kind of guy to stay irritated for very long.

He patted her hand. "We shall figure out a way to rub along with both our sensibilities intact."

Kendra didn't know how that was possible, but she nodded.

He withdrew his hand and lifted his teacup again, a wry glint in his eyes. "And for both of our sakes, let us pray that my sister never finds out about your early morning adventure or we shall never hear the end of it."

16

Kendra and the Duke had moved to the study by the time Alec and Sam arrived within minutes of each other. The Duke ordered breakfast trays sent up for the men, with new pots of coffee and tea. After replenishing her cup, Kendra took up a position before the slate board, while the Duke settled behind his desk, picking up his pipe. He went through the ritual of packing the bowl with fresh tobacco, but Kendra had noticed that he rarely smoked it anymore in her presence. Alec and Sam sat down at the table, tackling their hearty breakfast.

Kendra looked at the Bow Street Runner. "Did you manage to get a hold of the night porter, Mr. Kelly?"

"Aye," he confirmed, spreading marmalade on a buttered bun. "Mr. Durst said that Sir Giles arrived at White's at half past six on Wednesday evening. It was his custom to dine at the club on Tuesday and Wednesday evening."

"It was a routine then," Kendra said thoughtfully, sipping her coffee. *Not hard for the killer to find his victim.*

"It would appear so." He bit into the bun, chewed, and swallowed. "Mr. Durst said that Sir Giles appeared solemn, but that wasn't unusual for a man like him. He was joined by a gentleman. A viscount by the name of Lord Cross. Accor—"

"Lord Cross?" Alec interrupted sharply.

"Aye." Sam peered across the table at Alec. "Do you know him, milord?"

"Not personally, no. But I heard the name mentioned just this morning. Forgive me, Mr. Kelly. Please continue." Alec stood and walked over to the sideboard to refill his coffee cup.

Sam eyed the marquis closely, but continued, "According ter Mr. Durst, Lord Cross appeared agitated and sought Sir Giles out. The porter said they had an intense conversation, and then Lord Cross left."

Kendra raised her eyebrows. "They argued?"

"Nay. At least, Mr. Durst wouldn't say that it was an argument—and I pressed him on the matter. Unfortunately, he didn't overhear what was being said."

Kendra set down her coffee and picked up a piece of slate. "What time did Lord Cross leave?"

"Eight o'clock. After he left, Mr. Durst said that Sir Giles finished his meal. Then he received a note, and left."

Kendra gave Sam a sharp look. "A note? From who?"

"Mr. Durst didn't know who it was from, only that a street urchin delivered it and said it was to be delivered ter Sir Giles. Mr. Durst said that Sir Giles appeared disturbed after he read the note and left the club immediately."

"What time?" she asked as she added Lord Cross's name to the board.

"Nine, or close ter nine. Mr. Durst offered ter hail a hackney, but luckily one had already arrived. That was the last time Sir Giles was seen. Alive, that is."

The Duke frowned. "You suspect the hackney driver of being the killer, Mr. Kelly?"

"More like the killer being the hackney driver," Kendra commented. *And hackney drivers, like maids, often became invisible.*

Sam grinned at her. "Aye, lass. That's my way of thinkin'."

"Hackneys are common near clubs such as White's," Alec pointed out. "Having one pull up in such a timely matter is not all that odd."

The Bow Street Runner shrugged. "I've got me men askin' around, just ter see if any hackney drivers can recall pickin' up Sir Giles. And if someone did, where he might've let him off."

"I cannot imagine Sir Giles voluntarily stepping off at Trevelyan Square at such an hour," the Duke murmured. "From what you've said, Mr. Kelly, it is in an unsavory section in London."

"It is, that."

"I'd say it depends on what was in the note," Kendra said.

"Sir Giles wasn't a feeble old man," added Alec. "If someone asked him for a meeting in an unsavory area, he would have thought he could handle himself."

For a moment, they fell silent, no one wanting to voice the obvious: if Sir Giles thought he could protect himself, he'd been wrong.

Kendra broke the silence. "He was found naked, so we don't know if he carried a weapon of any kind on him. If he did, it would add weight to the hackney driver being our killer."

Sam frowned. "How so, miss?"

"I'm speculating here, but think about it. Sir Giles gets into a hackney for an unknown destination because of a note he received—a note that disturbed him enough to lure him out immediately. I'd think that when he arrived at the destination, he'd be prepared, his hand on his weapon . . ." She thought of how she'd approached Bear that morning. Her finger had been on the trigger of the muff pistol the moment she'd entered the taproom. "He paid off the hackney driver, dismissed him. He would be looking ahead of him, thinking of who he was supposed to meet. The evidence shows that he wasn't facing his killer. He was attacked from behind."

The Duke said, "And the hackney driver would have been behind him."

"Assuming the hackney driver didn't leave," Alec argued. "If he did, someone else could have easily snuck out of the shadows and attacked him."

"I don't think so," Kendra said slowly, shaking her head. "A trained military man? A spymaster? Sir Giles would have been attuned to his surroundings. He would have turned if he heard approaching foot-steps. Of course, the attacker *could* have snuck out of the shadows, if he was also trained in the art of subterfuge. But Sir Giles was caught by surprise."

"Hmm." Sam scratched his nose as he considered. "In this cold weather, they're all bundled up somethin' fierce, with scarves, hats, gloves, and greatcoats. Makes a clever disguise. Sir Giles would never have recognized him . . . even if it was his own son."

The Duke drew in a breath. "Terrible to think of a son doing some-thing so sinister, but you make an excellent point, Mr. Kelly."

Kendra thought of what she'd learned from Bear about Gerard Holbrooke, but decided to wait before imparting that information. *I'm procrastinating.* Because she knew Alec wouldn't be happy about her visit with Bear any more than the Duke.

She looked at the marquis as he polished off the rest of his breakfast, and asked instead, "Did you manage to get a hold of your contact in government?"

"This morning." He set his fork and knife on his plate and pushed it away. "Lieutenant-Colonel d'Ambray mentioned Lord Cross's name."

"He thinks Lord Cross might be the killer?"

"He actually had another suspect in mind. An Irishman by the name of Silas Fitzpatrick. He owns a coffeehouse called the Liber in Mayfair. Sir Giles believed he was using his establishment as a meeting place for likeminded individuals to sow radical thoughts on Irish emancipation and covertly pass information on."

"The free one," Kendra translated. "Mr. Fitzpatrick isn't exactly subtle for a spy, is he?"

Alec shrugged. "I got the impression that he's not trying to hide his position on Ireland. I thought to introduce myself to Mr. Fitzpatrick today." He looked at Sam. "Do you fancy a cup of coffee, Mr. Kelly?"

The Bow Street Runner grinned. "As a matter of fact."

"Why does your contact think Mr. Fitzpatrick could have murdered Sir Giles? Aside from the possibility that he's a spy. I'm not familiar with the political climate here"—*in this era,* she added silently—"but I think there're probably more spies in London besides Fitzpatrick."

A ghost of a smile crossed Alec's lips. "I believe you are right, Miss Donovan. But Mr. Fitzpatrick was the only spy that Sir Giles mentioned might have been following him. Mr. Fitzpatrick, or one of his associates."

Kendra lifted her eyebrows. "Well, that changes things. If Fitzpatrick had Sir Giles under surveillance, he'd know Sir Giles's routine. Know where he would be on Wednesday night." She wrote the name on the slate board, then stepped back, jiggling the piece of slate as she considered the fresh angle. "An Irish spy would know something about invisible ink, I'd think. The Irish conflict has a lot to do with Catholicism, or the Irish refusing to convert to the Church of England, right?"

"In its most simplistic form, yes," the Duke said. "But religion and politics tend to be intricately linked, where it is impossible to see where one ends and the other begins. The head of England's monarchy is also the head of the Church of England. By refusing to convert, the Irish are essentially rejecting the monarchy, which is treason." He leaned back in the chair, clearly troubled. "Needless to say, the conflict goes back centuries. But I see your point, my dear. The crucifix drawn on Sir Giles certainly appears to cast a religious light on his murder."

"And he was left in a Catholic church," Alec reminded them.

Kendra began to pace. "It's a thread. We'll know more after you talk to him, but on the surface, Fitzpatrick checks a few boxes. The crosses, if tied to Catholicism. The invisible ink ties to intelligence work. Even the method of the murder tends to be military. But cutting out the tongue, leaving the body naked? That's more personal.

"Intelligence work isn't personal," she continued slowly. "You can be passionate about king and country and all that, but it's more about strategy. Outsmarting the other side. If Sir Giles had discovered something that endangered Mr. Fitzpatrick's operation, I can see one operative killing the other. But what was done to Sir Giles . . . that doesn't fit for me."

Alec said, "D'Ambray seemed to think there was something more between Sir Giles and Mr. Fitzpatrick. But that was an impression, nothing more."

"Okay," Kendra said, nodding. "We'll need to find out more about Mr. Fitzpatrick's background. Did d'Ambray say anything about Sir Giles's behavior recently?"

"He thought he was troubled, and confided that Sir Giles had received information that disturbed him."

"What sort of information?"

"Sir Giles didn't say, and d'Ambray wasn't certain the two—Sir Giles's mood and the information he'd received—were connected."

The Duke frowned. "How could they not be?"

"D'Ambray said that Sir Giles's mood may have had more to do with the anniversary of the death of a recruit—Evert Larson, the son of a friend. Apparently the friendship died with Evert."

Aldridge asked, "How did the boy die, Alec?"

"I'm not sure. An incident in Spain, near the end of the war."

"Seems like a long time ago ter have anything ter do with Sir Giles's murder," said Sam.

"I would have said the same thing, except for Lord Cross. He and another man, Captain Mobray, were the only two survivors from the incident in Spain."

The back of Kendra's neck prickled. "That's a little too coincidental." She strode back to the slate board to write down the new names. "We'll need more information on what happened in Spain. Who's Evert Larson's father?"

"Mr. Bertel Larson. He owns an apothecary shop on Cromwell Road in Kensington."

"Larson & Son!" Sam snapped his fingers. "I'm familiar with the shop. Even have a few of its remedies at home."

Alec nodded as he stood again. "Apparently the man is a successful merchant."

Kendra looked at him as he wandered to the window. "And he blames Sir Giles for his son's death?"

"From my understanding, Mr. Larson blamed Sir Giles for persuading Evert to join his network of spies in the first place. Evert was reportedly a brilliant man."

"I can understand Mr. Larson blaming Sir Giles for his son's death," said the Duke. He tapped the bowl of his pipe against his palm, his gaze traveling to the slate board. "I would say that would be very personal."

Kendra nodded, jiggling the slate. "I agree."

"Aye, but why now?" Sam said. "Not ter make light of the young man's death, but the war was over last year, and the Peninsular campaign before that. If Mr. Larson was harboring ill will toward Sir Giles, wouldn't he have done something before last night?"

"There is no time limit on grief, Mr. Kelly," Aldridge said softly.

No one said anything. In the hushed silence, Kendra turned back to the slate board to add the new information, acutely conscious of the scrape of slate against slate as the only sound in the room. She cleared her throat. "We're probably dealing with a recent trigger," she said finally. "Maybe whatever happened a month ago. It's something to pursue."

Her gaze shifted to the name she'd written last night. Gerard Holbrook. A nervous knot twisted in her stomach. She couldn't put off sharing her information.

"I've learned that the estrangement between Sir Giles and his son might have been more severe than we realized," she said, turning to face her audience. "Holbrooke may have impregnated a housemaid."

Sam's eyebrows shot up. "Where'd you learn that, lass?"

Kendra ignored the question, continuing, "That might have been the last straw for Sir Giles. He was making plans to send Holbrooke to India."

Sam's eyebrows were already high, but now they practically disappeared into his hairline. "India?"

"Apparently that's motive right there," she said dryly. She looked at the clock, deliberately avoiding eye contact with Alec. "I have to go. With any luck, Lady Holbrooke will be able to clear up some of our questions."

"One moment."

Alec didn't raise his voice, but there was a lethal bite to the two words that sent a shiver of apprehension dancing down her spine. *Shit.* "I really don't have a moment—"

"I'm curious how you came by this information, Miss Donovan?" he cut in.

Reluctantly, she looked at him, and had to control a wince. His expression was enigmatic, but she recognized the temper that brightened the flecks of gold in his green eyes. He lifted a silky brow as he regarded her. "'Tis morning," he pointed out unnecessarily. "How did you acquire this sordid gossip since we last spoke? I cannot imagine anyone in the Duke's household having that information, much less imparting it to you."

She drew in a deep breath and reminded herself that she had done nothing wrong.

The Duke pushed himself to his feet. "I think that Mr. Kelly and I shall give you both a moment of privacy."

"Aye." Sam stood hastily.

Kendra chewed on her bottom lip as the two men departed. "Okay. Promise me you won't go crazy?"

"What did you do?"

"Snake discovered the body," she reminded him, and was pleased that she sounded calm. *Never let them see you sweat.* "This is how investigations work, Alec. An investigator needs to interview the first person on the scene." *Too defensive.* "I needed to talk to Snake, but it's not like I have his address."

Alec stared at her. Kendra's gaze was drawn to the muscle jumping in his jaw. She swallowed, and waited. The sudden quiet scraped across her already raw nerves. She could hear her own breathing, the pulse throbbing through her veins, the clock ticking. That was why silence was so effective as an interview technique. She had to stifle the desire to continue to talk, to beg for forgiveness, to fill the quiet. Christ, civilizations could have fallen and risen again as Alec simply looked at her.

She sucked in another breath, then said, "Here's the deal. I spoke to Bear this morning so he could pass on a message to Snake."

"You spoke to Bear."

Kendra pressed a hand to her stomach, realized what she was doing, and dropped it. "Yes."

"You spoke to Bear—an underworld criminal."

"Look, I know that you're upset. But you don't have to worry about my reputation. I dressed as a maid. No one noticed me." She attempted a smile, but Alec stared back at her stonily. Hell, she'd seen happier expressions on death row inmates.

"Do you think that is what I'm upset about?" he finally said. "Your *reputation?*" He raked agitated fingers through his hair as he paced across the room, then stopped and swung around to face her. "Are you *mad?*

Bear is *dangerous*. He could have—" He swallowed, his gaze locking on hers. "My God, he threatened to rape you last year. Did you forget that?"

"And I threatened to blow off his balls," she shot back. "The way I look at it, we're even." She threw up her hands. "Look, I don't want to argue with you, Alec. The Duke already lectured me." And those words still stung. "Let's focus on what's important."

Green fire leaped in his eyes. "Bullocks to that! Let's focus on you trying to kill yourself. Or driving me to Bedlam!"

Kendra pressed her fingers to the bridge of her nose, frustration welling up. "I wasn't trying to kill myself. How many times do I have to tell you, I'm not a child! I knew what I was doing. Bear and I have an understanding of sorts."

"God in heaven," Alec muttered, and raised his gaze to the ceiling. "What understanding could you possibly have reached with that ruffian?"

"If I cross him, he'll try to kill me, and if he crosses me, I'll try to kill him. Mutually assured destruction."

"Christ." Alec scrubbed a hand across his jaw like it ached.

"Did you take your valet with you when you met your contact this morning?"

He glared at her. "Don't be stupid. My contact isn't a three-hundred-pound madman who has previously threatened me with grievous injury."

She sighed, and then they were both silent for a long moment. Slowly, Kendra closed the space between them. She reached out and touched his arms, the muscles rigid beneath her fingertips. "I'm sorry if I scared you," she said carefully. "That was not my intention."

His lips twisted. "But you're not sorry for disguising yourself as a maid and sneaking off to see a crime lord?"

She opened her mouth, then closed it, thinking. "I'm not sorry for needing a little bit more freedom than most women here," she finally said.

"Married ladies have more freedom."

"Only if their husbands permit it." She cocked her head. "Widows have probably the most freedom."

His jaw relaxed enough to allow his mouth to curve into a slight smile. "So if I ever do get you to the altar, I will have to sleep with one eye open?"

She huffed out a laugh. "Let's not get ahead of ourselves." Beneath her hand, she could feel his arm relax. "Alec." She slid her hand down to link her fingers with his. "We'll figure it out."

"Before or after I'm thrown into the lunatic asylum?"

She smiled. "Hopefully before." She let go of his hand to reach up and smooth down the collar of his jacket. She fixed her gaze on his. "Are we good?"

He blew out a breath. "I should lock you in some tower somewhere."

"That's very medieval of you. But you forget that picking locks is a skill of mine."

"I haven't forgotten," he said, his tone gruff. His gaze searched her face as his arms came around her. "I missed you last night."

"I missed you too." She flicked a glance at the closed door. "I think we've got about five minutes before the Duke returns."

He lifted a dark eyebrow, and his green eyes brightened between spiky lashes. "Oh? Do you have indecent designs upon my person, Miss Donovan? Maybe I need the chaperone."

She laughed, her mood suddenly light. "Oh, I most definitely have indecent designs upon your person, my lord. I don't think we can make up for last night, but let's see what we can accomplish in five minutes."

17

Kendra's lips were still numb when the carriage swung around to pick up Rebecca at her parents' residence on Half Moon Street. She smiled at Rebecca as she climbed into the carriage and settled into the seat opposite Kendra. "Good morning."

Rebecca eyed her closely. "Pray tell, why are you so cheerful?"

"What? I'm not." But she wanted to squirm as Rebecca continued to study her.

"Hmm. You are . . . glowing."

"Oh, for God's sake, don't be ridiculous," Kendra muttered, and was relieved when the carriage jerked forward.

The vehicle's wheels made a slushy sound as it advanced down the street. The sun had chased away the earlier fog, and brought the temperature high enough to melt the previous evening's snow, leaving London soggy and muddy. An army of street sweepers—mostly young children—were busily clearing the guck off the cobblestones with brooms, seeming to make a game out of leaping out of the way so as not to get hit by oncoming traffic.

Sir Giles's residence was located in the upscale Berkeley Square area of London. Kendra used the journey to update Rebecca on the investigation. She didn't mention her meeting with Bear. Not because she didn't feel justified in approaching the criminal, but because she damn well didn't need another lecture on the matter.

"Do you think that whatever happened to disturb Sir Giles has anything to do with his murder?" Rebecca asked when she finished.

"I don't like coincidences, but it's also a mistake to make assumptions. It's an avenue that we need to pursue." She chewed on her lower lip, her gaze traveling to the window. They'd entered Berkeley Square, and, as always, Kendra felt a queer sense of déjà vu. She'd driven through this area in the 21st century. It would continue to be upscale, but many of the old buildings had been—*would be*—converted into commercial spaces, for offices and retail stores. Now, though, the square was lined with grand Georgian houses and terraces. Sir Giles's home was a stately four-story redbrick mansion detailed with white cornices, tall window frames, and dormer windows jutting out near the pitched roof. A flagstone path, wet from melting snow, led to the steps and a wide portico. Yew shrubbery and dead rosebushes surrounded the porch. A black sash had been tied to the lion's head door knocker to signify a death in the household.

When Benjamin halted the carriage and came around to fold down the steps, Rebecca handed him her card. She looked at Kendra. "Our visit is rather unorthodox. Lady Holbrooke could be laid low with grief. She may not be receiving anyone."

They didn't have to wait long. Benjamin returned moments later with Lady Holbrooke's "at home" status. An elderly butler held open the door. As they swept inside, Kendra scanned the foyer, which was festooned in black crepe. A maid stepped forward to take their coats, bonnets, and gloves. Kendra kept hold of her reticule, mainly because she hadn't thought to remove the muff pistol.

The butler led them up the stairs and down the hall to a large, airy drawing room with pale green silk walls, and furniture styled in the Grecian period, with feet carved into serpents. More black crepe hung from paintings and mirrors. A coal fire blazed in an elegant fireplace with an intricate marble chimney piece, providing a modicum of warmth against the chill of the day.

Lady Holbrooke stood near one of the long windows, a petite, fragile-looking woman with tawny-colored hair tucked under a matron's lace cap. She'd donned an unadorned black gown, the symbol of widowhood. In her hands, she held a cup of tea. Kendra let her gaze travel over the woman's perfectly composed features. At forty-six, Lady Holbrooke was a decade younger than her husband, but she looked another dozen years younger than that. The only lines marring her flawless complexion were two vertical indentions between her winged eyebrows, as though she spent a great deal of her time scowling.

Or worrying, Kendra amended.

Still, her brown eyes were clear. If she'd spent yesterday weeping over her husband's death, she'd done an excellent job covering it up.

Rebecca moved toward the matron, her cornflower blue eyes sympathetic. "Thank you for agreeing to see us, Lady Holbrooke. We know this is a difficult time for you. Please accept our condolences." She turned, and lifted a hand to indicate Kendra. "This is my friend, Miss Donovan."

Lady Holbrooke inclined her head in acknowledgement. "I am slightly acquainted with your parents, Lady Rebecca."

"I had not realized," Rebecca murmured.

The older woman was already shifting her gaze to Kendra. "But I do not think this is a condolence call, is it? I am aware of your connection to the Duke of Aldridge, Miss Donovan. I am also aware of the rumors that you and His Grace assisted Bow Street last year. Such gossip seemed too unbelievable to be true. Yet here you are." She paused, her gaze fixed on Kendra's face. "I read the *Morning Chronicle*," she said simply. "You are here about my husband's death."

"Yes." Since she didn't seem angered by that, Kendra continued, "I realize that Mr. Kelly has already spoken to you, but it would be helpful if you could answer a few more questions."

Lady Holbrooke turned, gliding over to the table that held a porcelain teapot, and replenished the cup she held. "I have ordered more tea," she told them, calmly adding sugar from the sugar bowl. The small spoon clinked against the china teacup as she stirred. She looked over at them. "Shall we be seated?"

They were settling into the chairs when a young maid arrived with a tea tray. Kendra noticed that the girl's eyes were red, and wondered if she'd been crying over her master's death—and then wondered about the widow who obviously had not.

"When did you last see your husband, ma'am?" Kendra asked once the tea had been distributed and the maid had left.

Lady Holbrooke's brows drew together, deepening the lines between them. "I spoke to Mr. Kelly about this. We had breakfast together on Wednesday morning before my husband left for his office in Whitehall. I never saw him again." Her gaze dropped to her teacup, her lips pursed. "I did not realize anything was amiss until yesterday morning, when he was not at the breakfast table. I sent Stevens up to my husband's bedchamber, and then Mr. Kelly arrived . . . with the news."

Rebecca gave her a sympathetic look. "I'm sorry. It must have come as a shock."

Lady Holbrooke raised her eyes to Rebecca. "Yes. Yes, it was."

Kendra asked carefully, "Can you tell me if your husband's behavior changed recently? Did he seem troubled? Upset?"

The widow appeared to think about it. "My husband was a man with enormous responsibilities, Miss Donovan," she said finally. "He was not a frivolous sort of man, and tended to keep his own counsel."

Which was another way of saying the guy didn't talk much, Kendra supposed. "Still, a wife knows when her husband is upset, doesn't she?" she pressed. "You didn't notice Sir Giles's behavior changing in, say, the last month or so?"

Lady Holbrooke looked away. Kendra couldn't tell if she was trying to remember or trying to come up with a suitable story. "He may have been quieter than usual," she conceded softly. "I assumed he was preoccupied with governmental matters and had no wish to pry."

"Do you know if your husband received any threats recently?"

The widow turned back to look at Kendra. "He may have, but he did not confide in me. Undoubtedly he did not wish to worry me."

Kendra asked, "Did he ever mention a man named Silas Fitzpatrick?"

Her frown deepened. "No, I don't recall the name. Why?"

"What about Lord Cross?" Kendra asked, and saw Lady Holbrooke's eyes widen in recognition.

"I know Lord Cross. We've been introduced at social events, and I am aware of . . . of a long ago incident involving the viscount."

"What incident?" Kendra asked, interested to see what the older woman would say.

Lady Holbrooke was silent for a moment, her gaze dropping back to her teacup. "He is connected to a tragic event during the war. A young man serving under my husband was killed," she said quietly.

"Evert Larson."

Lady Holbrooke's eyes flew up and she drew in a swift breath. "You know of Evert?"

Kendra nodded. "I was told your family and the Larsons were close."

"Yes. We were all devastated when we learned of his death."

"We?"

Kendra saw Lady Holbrooke's hands tremble, rattling the teacup she held. Hastily, she set the cup aside, and laced her thin fingers together, resting them in her lap.

"I am referring to Bertel and Astrid Larson, Evert's parents. Sir Giles and Mr. Larson were boys together, and for many years, our families enjoyed a friendship."

Kendra pretended surprise. "And Evert's death changed that?"

Something flickered in Lady Holbrooke's brown eyes. "Yes."

"How was Lord Cross involved exactly?"

Lady Holbrooke frowned. "The viscount—he was not a viscount at the time, you understand—"

"Yeah, I realize he hadn't inherited the title at that time." Kendra had to control her patience. Maybe it was because she was from the 21st century, or maybe it was because she was an American, but the laws governing inheritance and titles struck her as arbitrary and archaic.

"Yes, well. Lord Cross's regiment was captured by the French. They were held in a prison camp for months near some maggoty mountain village in the Pyrenees. It sounded quite dreadful." She gave a delicate shudder. "We were told that Evert discovered the camp while he was working as an agent in Spain. Somehow, his identity became known, and he was taken captive." She pressed her lips together and shook her head. "I don't know what happened, except there was a fire or an explosion of some kind. Evert perished in it."

"How terrible," murmured Rebecca.

"Lord Cross and another man—I don't know his name—managed to escape."

Kendra looked at her. "How did they get away?"

But Lady Holbrooke could only shake her head. "I'm not certain. But as horrible as the incident was, it happened two years ago. How can it possibly have anything to do with my husband's death?"

"It might not," Kendra admitted. "But Lord Cross was seen having an argument with your husband on the night he died. Do you know why?"

"I can't imagine."

"And Sir Giles didn't mention Lord Cross recently?"

"No."

Kendra searched the other woman's face, but saw only genuine puzzlement. She changed the subject. "What was the relationship like between your husband and your son?"

Lady Holbrooke's gaze narrowed on Kendra. "What do you mean? It is the same as any other father and son."

Defensive, thought Kendra. She kept her eyes on the widow when she said, "Most fathers and sons don't get into public fights." At least, she didn't think so.

"That was an unfortunate incident," Lady Holbrooke snapped, her delicate features suddenly hardening. Then she bit her lip, as though regretting the impulsive rejoinder. When she spoke again, she seemed to weigh her words. "Gerard was not himself at the time. You must understand how young gentlemen can be . . ." She lifted a delicate hand and waved it, as though dismissing the topic.

"Inebriated?" Kendra was curious to see whether Lady Holbrooke would deny it.

The widow's lips thinned. "I'm afraid Gerard is too easily influenced by his friends."

"Is that why Sir Giles was sending him to India?"

Lady Holbrooke's nostril's flared. "I do not know who told you such a Banbury Tale, but you are mistaken, Miss Donovan. My son has no interest in that filthy, disease-ridden country. My husband would certainly never send him to such a place. The very idea is ridiculous."

The lady doth protest too much, Kendra thought. "Where was your son on Wednesday night, from nine P.M. to yesterday morning?"

"You cannot possibly be insinuating that Gerard had anything to do with what happened to his father?" Lady Holbrooke pushed herself to her feet in an abrupt, agitated movement. Her gaze slewed over to Rebecca. "I agreed to see you in my time of mourning, Lady Rebecca, in deference to your parents. But this inquiry is beyond the pale."

Kendra stood as well, and set the tea that she hadn't touched to the side. "I'm sorry you feel that way, Lady Holbrooke, but these questions need to be asked. Either by me or Mr. Kelly."

Rebecca spoke up. "Please forgive what must seem like a tactless inquiry, my lady, but we really do have your best interests at heart. Better to clear all suspicion from your son so that your husband's killer can be found."

Something flickered in Lady Holbrooke's eyes. "My son was at home," she finally said, and locked eyes with Kendra. "He was at home all evening, Miss Donovan."

"All right. I'll need to speak to your son."

"No. He's mourning his father." She clasped her hands together, the tension revealed in the white knuckles. "I must ask you to leave."

"Lady Holbrooke—" Kendra began.

"Please."

Rebecca leaned forward to set her teacup and saucer on the table. Slowly, she stood, catching Lady Holbrooke's gaze with her own. "We truly did not mean to upset you, ma'am."

"I shall show you out," was all she said, and started to cross the room.

Kendra and Rebecca followed, but before they reached the door, it swung open, and a young man strode in. He was easy enough to identify. Gerard Holbrooke bore more than a passing resemblance to his mother, with dark brown eyes and gold-streaked tawny hair artfully arranged in the trendy Brutus style. Twenty-five or twenty-six, Kendra thought, with a tall, athletic figure that was shown to advantage beneath the navy cutaway coat, black waistcoat, and buff colored pantaloons tucked in gleaming black hessian boots. Attractive in a boyish way. Except there was nothing boyish about the gleam in his eye or the curl of his lip as his gaze traveled over them. If he hadn't been wearing black armbands to signify his loss, no one would have known he was in mourning.

"I was told that we had guests. You should have informed me at once, Mama." His tone was gently chiding. His eyes flicked over Rebecca, dismissed her, then traveled over Kendra in a once-over that made her skin crawl. "You must introduce us."

"Lady Rebecca and Miss Donovan came to offer their condolences, but they are ready to take their leave," his mother said stiffly.

"Oh, no. Please stay. We rarely have such charming company." He wandered to the side table that twinkled with the various crystal decanters. He pulled out a stopper to one, and poured what looked like brandy into a glass.

"I can call for another teacup, darling," Lady Holbrooke said, her brows pulling together as she eyed her son.

"You know I detest tea."

"I'm sorry about the loss of your father, Mr. Holbrooke," Kendra offered.

He looked at her as he lifted the glass to his lips and took a slow sip. "Did you know him?"

"No."

Holbrooke's lips twisted. "Well, he was a bit stiff-rumped."

Lady Holbrooke gasped. "Gerard, darling, do not tease."

Something ugly flashed in his eyes, but then was gone. "Forgive me, mama. I *am* teasing. I'm certain the ladies are aware."

"Everyone reacts to grief in different ways," Kendra murmured drily.

Holbrooke appeared surprised, then he laughed appreciatively. "Quite so. And now I have shocked and dismayed my mother again. But my father and I were not close."

"Gerard, Miss Donovan has been here inquiring into your father's death," Lady Holbrooke told him, and there was no mistaking the warning note in her voice. "I explained that we were at home on Wednesday night."

Kendra's jaw tightened, irritated. This was why suspects were always kept separate during interviews, to stop them from feeding each other information or possible alibis.

Holbrooke looked at Kendra in surprise. "That's a devilishly odd thing for you to do. Pray tell, what does my father's death have to do with you?"

"He was murdered. Finding the murderer should be of interest to everyone," she said, and braced herself for what he was going to say next.

"But you're a woman!"

"Believe it or not, I figured that out a long time ago." She kept her gaze on his. "What were you and your father arguing about at Tattersalls?"

His expression closed down. He lifted a shoulder in a half shrug. "I can scarcely recall."

"Can you recall Sir Giles finding you a position in India? I heard you didn't want to go."

Lady Holbrooke's brown eyes flashed as she rounded on Kendra. "I told you, Miss Donovan, that you were given faulty information. My husband would never have sent my son to such a horrible place."

"I can speak for myself, Mama."

"Of course, darling," Lady Holbrooke said quickly.

Holbrooke studied Kendra for a long moment. The boyish charm had leached away. "My father and I quarreled often, Miss Donovan," he admitted. "We did not see eye to eye on a great many things. He may have mentioned finding me a position in India, but I had no intention of traveling to that godforsaken land, so it was a moot point."

"Would he have given you a choice in the matter?" Kendra asked bluntly.

Holbrooke's lips twisted. "I guess we shall never know."

Kendra paused for a heartbeat, then switched the subject. "Does the name Silas Fitzpatrick mean anything to you?"

Holbrooke frowned. "No."

"What about Lord Cross?"

"Eliot Cross—Viscount Cross? We attended Eton together, although we were barely acquainted. Why?"

Kendra glanced at Lady Holbrooke. "You didn't mention your son was in school with Lord Cross."

"I didn't think of it. It never occurred to me."

"It wouldn't," Holbrooke said easily. "We were not in the same class. He was a year behind me, and not a friend. Do you have any idea how many boys attend Eton? I would have no reason to speak of him."

"What about at parties, social events?"

He shrugged and took a sip of his drink. "I'm certain we have attended the same social events, cricket matches, whatever. But we had no dealings with each other. As I said, he was not a friend. What is this about?"

"Lord Cross was seen talking to your father at White's on Wednesday night. Arguing. Do you know what that could have been about?"

"I can't imagine. I didn't realize my father even knew Cross, except for Spain."

"When Evert Larson was killed," Kendra added.

Holbrooke's eyebrows rose. "Yes. You know about Evert?"

"Yes." She caught the speculative gleam in his eyes.

"If you want to know who had vengeance against my father, I suggest you take your questions to Bertel Larson," he said. "Evert's father."

Lady Holbrooke drew in a quick breath. "Gerard, do not tease so."

"I am not teasing. Not this time." He glanced at his mother. "If you recollect, Mr. Larson threatened to kill Father."

"Two years ago! Bertel had only learned his son was dead. He said that in his grief."

"Sometimes the past has a funny way of resurrecting itself," Kendra said softly. For just a moment, her mind circled back to Yorkshire, where the past, present, and future had tangled dangerously for her. "Did Sir Giles say anything about Mr. Larson recently? Was there any indication that maybe Mr. Larson made recent threats?"

"If there were any, I doubt my father would have said. Despite everything, he was always protective of the Larson family."

Kendra heard the strange note of anger in Holbrooke's voice. "I heard that your father and Evert were very close."

His lips curled into a sneer. "Oh, quite close. He treated Evert like a prince. But then he *was* descended from the Norse gods themselves."

"Norse gods?" Kendra wondered if she was missing some sort of 19th-century catchphrase.

"My son is joking," Lady Holbrooke said quickly, casting a worried glance at him before shifting her gaze back to Kendra. "The family claimed that they could trace their lineage back to the kings of Norway. A silly fantasy, of course. They are as English as anyone."

"Evert and David would boast of the gods. They were quite taken with the Scandinavian legends."

Kendra looked at him. "David?"

"Bertel and Astrid's youngest son," identified Lady Holbrooke.

The son in Larson & Son, Kendra realized. "I wasn't aware there was another son. I had only heard of Evert."

"Of course." A nasty edge came into Holbrooke's voice. "Whenever Evert was around we all faded away."

"Darling—"

"Do you know that Evert spoke five languages by the age of ten, Miss Donovan? Father was impressed. So impressed that I sometimes thought Evert hadn't been boasting, and he was descended from the gods after all! Even our headmasters at Eton admired him."

"You were at school together?"

"Naturally. Evert and I were the same age, but he had advanced to the class ahead." He tossed the remainder of his brandy back, but not before Kendra caught the glow of rage or resentment in his eyes. Probably both. He went back to the side table to set his empty glass down. "Father cultivated Evert, convinced him to become a barrister and then work for him in the Home Office. They had much in common."

Kendra didn't need to be a psychiatrist to recognize Holbrooke's jealousy or understand the root of it. Everything she'd learned about Sir Giles showed him to be a workaholic, dedicated to his job and devoted to his country. But when he hadn't been working, he had apparently been more interested in cultivating a relationship with Evert over his own son. If Evert had been the one murdered, Holbrooke would have been at the very top of Kendra's suspect list.

"Evert was brilliant, but so are you, darling," Lady Holbrooke interjected, her gaze on her son, almost pleading. "Your father was very proud of you, Gerard."

This time Kendra recognized the glow in Holbrooke's eyes as contempt. His jaw tightened and he gave a jerky shrug. "If you will excuse me, ladies, I must return to the study. I am now the head of this household, and there are many matters to which I must attend."

Kendra watched him move to the door. "If you discover anything in your father's papers that might be relevant to the investigation, you will send word to the Duke of Aldridge's residence, won't you?" Without a badge, Kendra was forced to use the next best thing—name dropping the Duke.

Holbrooke paused, glancing back at her. "I shall most assuredly be keeping you in my thoughts, Miss Donovan." He sketched a mocking bow in their direction, and left the room.

Kendra let her gaze drift back to Lady Holbrooke. The widow had been composed when they'd first arrived, but now her face seemed older, her features strained.

Rebecca took it upon herself to end their visit. "Thank you so much for seeing us during this difficult time, ma'am." She eyed the other woman, and perhaps saw the same tension in the fine-boned face that Kendra had, because she added, "Please sit . . . we shall see ourselves out."

"Mr. Holbrooke may be wearing armbands, but his grief for his father was noticeably absent," Rebecca murmured once the elderly butler had closed the door behind them. She glanced at Kendra as she tied the ribbon of her bonnet into a bow beneath her chin. "He has considerable hostility toward Sir Giles."

"Yeah, I noticed. And Lady Holbrooke is very protective of her son."

"'Tis natural, I suppose, for a mother."

"She's in a difficult position," Kendra conceded, and then frowned. Her attention was drawn to the Yew shrubs on the side of the portico. There was no breeze, and yet the branches were trembling. Curious,

Kendra walked to the edge of the porch and peered down. Big brown eyes peered back at her through the greenery.

Kendra smiled at the little girl. "Hi, there."

The child frowned up at Kendra. "That is a very odd thing to say," she commented with surprisingly crisp enunciation. "I am not up high at all. I am standing on the ground."

Kendra blinked, then studied the girl more closely. "You must be Ruth." She remembered what Sam had said about finding her behind an urn. "Are you hiding from your nanny?"

The brown eyes widened. "How did you know?"

"A little bird told me."

Ruth looked puzzled. "That would be quite impossible. Birds do not have vocal chords. They have a syrinx. Do you know that is located down in the birds' throat, near their lungs?"

Kendra exchanged a surprised glance with Rebecca, who'd joined her. Rebecca pointed out, "Parrots can talk."

"Some birds can mimic speech," Ruth allowed. "They do it by expelling air in the syrinx. Lady Watley has a parrot. Whenever Mama and I visit, it screams, 'Blast you, you cocky wench!'"

"Good heavens," Rebecca said, startled. "Lady Watley has this bird, you say?"

"Yes." Ruth abandoned her camouflage, dropping to her knees and crawling out of the shrubbery. "Lady Watley's nephew brought the parrot back from his travels," she said as she leaned over and began swatting the snow and dried leaves off her skirt and coat with her mitten-covered hands. "Parrots are supposed to be terribly clever, you know."

"The cleverest of all birds," Kendra said, eyeing the strange little girl. She wasn't a pretty child. Her face, framed by wispy blonde curls and a floppy wool beret, was too thin. In contrast, her brown eyes appeared disproportionately enormous. Kendra asked, "Do you like studying birds?"

"I have no interest in ornithology, but I've read several books on the subject. I am now reading Sir Newton's *Philosophiae Naturalis Principia Mathematica*. It is ever so much more interesting than birds. Have you read it?"

"It's on my reading list," Kendra murmured.

A shadow passed over the little girl's face. "I don't know if I shall be able to finish it now. Mama doesn't approve of too much reading for girls." She puffed out her chest and quoted in a perfect mimicry of her mother, "'A dusty book has never gotten a young lady a husband.' Mama is not keen on mathematics either." That was said with a wistful sigh. "She says it's a dull subject that no one wishes to discuss. She says I would do better to concentrate on my embroidery and watercolors. The thing is, I don't have much interest in embroidery. Although I do enjoy painting."

Rebecca's lips twitched. "I enjoy painting as well. And there have been brilliant women mathematicians who have married, so their husbands must have been interested in the subject. Émilie du Châtelet, and Elena Cornaro Piscopia."

Ruth nodded, hoisting herself onto the porch steps in an agile move to stand next to them. "Yes, I know. Hypatia of Alexandria as well. But she was killed by a mob of Christians."

"Oh." Rebecca didn't seem to know what to do with that information. "Well, that is absolutely dreadful."

The little girl asked suddenly, "Who are you? You know my name, but I don't know yours."

Rebecca smiled and did a playful curtsy. "I am Lady Rebecca, and this is Miss Donovan."

Ruth frowned. "I should be the one curtsying. You are my elders, and higher up in society. Although I may be higher than you." She turned her gaze on Kendra. "Are you an American?"

"Yes."

Ruth nodded, apparently satisfied. Then, in the way children had, she abruptly returned to the earlier subject. "I enjoy mathematics, but I would much rather become an architect like Mr. John Nash and build grand homes and parks." Her small face lit up, but then dimmed just as quickly. "But Mr. Nash is a Whig, and Papa would not approve." She dropped her eyes. "But Papa is dead now."

Rebecca let out a sigh, her eyes softening. "I'm so very sorry, my dear. You must be very sad about your papa."

The child gave a slight nod, her mouth pulling down. "He wasn't at home very much, but he let me read his books and never told Mama or

Nanny." She stared out into the street for a long moment, her small face pensive. Then she lifted her serious gaze to Kendra and Rebecca. "He didn't just die, you know. He was killed. Mama said that it was probably an enemy of Papa's. He was a very important man who worked in government."

"Yes, I know." Kendra squatted down so she was eye level with the little girl. "I'm trying to find out who might have wanted to hurt him."

Ruth cocked her head like an inquisitive bird, and Kendra found herself being thoroughly studied. "Why? What business is it of yours?"

"I think that when someone is injured, it's the business of everyone in society to find out who did it and why, and make sure that person never does it again. Don't you?"

"I suppose so," the child agreed slowly. "Mr. Kelly from Bow Street is investigating."

Kendra smiled slightly. "You might say I'm assisting Mr. Kelly with the investigation."

That seemed to intrigue the little girl. "You are an American, but you are still a lady. How can you find out who might have hurt my papa?"

"By asking questions. That's how investigations are conducted. Even ladies can ask questions." She regarded the child. "Maybe you can help me. Did you notice anything different about your father lately? Was he upset about anything in particular?"

Ruth's small teeth chewed on her lower lip as she thought about it. "Well, Papa was very vexed with Gerard because Mama had to let Betty go."

"Betty?" But Kendra knew.

"She was our downstairs maid. Marie has been crying something fierce because Betty is gone. Marie is our upstairs maid," she said, obviously anticipating the next question.

Kendra thought of the maid with the red eyes who'd served them tea. Not crying over the death of the master of the house, after all, but her friend, who'd been let go because she was pregnant. "Ruth, do you remember what you were doing on Wednesday evening?"

"What time on Wednesday evening?"

Kendra smiled. "Let's say from seven o'clock to midnight."

"Oh, that is simple to remember. From six to half past seven Nanny made me practice the pianoforte."

"I'll bet your mother enjoyed listening to you play."

"You would have lost your wager, Miss Donovan. Mama was in her bedchamber dressing to go to Lady Beaumont's ball. Her bedchamber is too far from the library, where the pianoforte is. She could not have heard me play."

"You're right," Kendra nodded, and asked, "When did your mother leave for Lady Beaumont's ball?"

The small face scrunched up in concentration. "I think it was half past eight. Mama says that you do not want to be the first to arrive at a ball, but you do not want to be too late either. There are many rules in society, are there not?"

"I've thought the same thing," Kendra admitted with complete honesty. She regarded the girl closely. "Did your brother escort your mother to the ball?"

Ruth wrinkled her nose. "Oh, no. Gerard says those affairs are full of starched shirts and young chits looking to get you leg-shackled. He doesn't mean actual shackles, though, because I asked him. He means marriage."

Kendra kept her voice casual when she asked, "Did he stay at home with you, listening to you play the pianoforte?"

"Gerard doesn't care for the pianoforte. And he rarely stays home in the evening. Nanny and I were the only ones home on Wednesday evening. Oh, and the servants, of course. After I practiced, we had dinner. Afterward, Nanny allowed me to toast cheese in the fire. It was quite nice."

Kendra stared at the strange little girl. Still a child, and yet oddly adult. "It sounds very nice."

"Do you believe in ghosts, Miss Donovan, Lady Rebecca?"

The non sequitur startled Kendra. "No."

Ruth nodded, and looked like she was about to say something more when the door swung open, and a stout, middle-aged woman in a black bombazine gown peeked around the wooden panel. "Ah! There you are, you naughty miss!" she said when her gaze landed on Ruth. "I've been looking for you all over the house! 'Tis past time for your lessons." Her gaze swung toward Kendra and Rebecca, her face full of apology. "Oh dear, I hope she hasn't kept you out here all this time. Talking about Sir Newton or Mr. Nash's latest extravaganza." She clucked her tongue, wagging a finger at the little girl. "How many times have I told you that such subjects have little interest to gentle folks?"

Ruth looked up at her nanny. "Miss Donovan is a Bow Street Runner."

"Ack," the older woman rolled her eyes. "The imagination on you! Come along now." She grasped Ruth's elbow, pausing to give Kendra and Rebecca a quick nod. "Good day."

Briefly, Ruth resisted her nanny's hand, pivoting to look back at them. For the first time since they'd discovered her lurking in the bushes, her mouth curved in a small smile. It didn't erase the somberness of her expression, but Kendra found herself oddly affected by the gesture. Then her nanny took a firmer hold of Ruth's arm, pulling her young charge into the house and closing the door behind them.

"Such a peculiar child," Rebecca noted with a shake of her head. "Being an architect is an unusual dream for a little girl. I only know of one—Mary Townley."

"If anyone can accomplish her dream, my money's on Ruth." Still, history was against the little girl, Kendra knew. She'd never read about an architect named Ruth Holbrooke in any book. Of course, she'd never read about Mary Townley either. So maybe . . .

Kendra stifled a sigh as she wondered how many girls like Ruth had dreams that withered on the vine because the system and society was against them. It was depressing.

They retraced their steps to the carriage, and Rebecca said, "Lady Holbrooke and Mr. Holbrooke lied about their whereabouts on Wednesday evening."

"I caught that too." Kendra pushed aside the troubling thoughts of Ruth Holbrooke's future, or lack thereof. "I think it's interesting that Lady Holbrooke feels the need to lie for her son. That tells us something."

She paused. Benjamin was holding open the door to the carriage. "We need to go to Trevelyan Square," she told the coachman, and wasn't surprised when he scowled at her.

"The Duke ain't gonna like that."

"The Duke gave me his permission," she lied, and met Benjamin's doubtful gaze squarely. It wasn't like he could pull out his cell phone and call the Duke to verify her story. "If you won't take us, I'll find a hackney. His Grace will like that even less."

"Oi'll take ye," he muttered, and slammed the door with more force than was necessarily after they'd climbed inside.

Rebecca looked at her. "What do you think to find at Trevelyan Square?"

"I don't know, but that's where the body was dumped. I need to see it myself."

Rebecca nodded, leaning back into her seat. "Lady Holbrooke may have only lied because she wants to avoid her son coming under suspicion, you know. A mother's protective instinct."

"Possibly. Or maybe she lied because deep down a part of her believes that her son is quite capable of murder."

18

Trevelyan Square was a narrow enclave located in the London Borough of Tower Hamlets, which was part of the larger, much grittier East End. Benjamin maneuvered the carriage on a thoroughfare jostling with hackneys, wagons, and cattle. A noxious stench strong enough to sting the eyes seemed to seep up from the muddy streets. Part of it was the area's lack of a sewage system, Kendra knew. But the other part she recognized as the sharp, coppery smell of blood, which could probably be traced to the local slaughterhouses. *At least I hope it's from the slaughterhouses.*

"Rats! Oi'll catch yer rats!"

"Tallow candles—two for six pence!"

The cries of peddlers drifted through the window as Benjamin turned the carriage onto one street and up another twisty lane. Slowly, the masses of people fell away, leaving only the odd echo that came from the clip-clop of the two horses pulling the carriage, and the rumble of the carriage's wheels. The street they were rolling down belonged to a different era, narrowing to a point where the modern carriage couldn't go further, and Benjamin was forced to draw to a stop near a curb. He leapt off his perch and came around to open the door.

"This ain't a good area," he warned them. His hand inched to the blunderbuss that he always carried, shoved through his wide leather belt. His gaze darted uneasily to the crumbling, soot-smeared stone tenements on either side of the street.

"Now that's an understatement," Kendra said under her breath. She didn't wait for the coachman to unfold the steps, but hopped down. Benjamin scowled at her, clearly affronted by her initiative, and quickly unfolded the steps for Rebecca to descend like a proper lady.

"Oi can't leave the horses," he growled.

"I can see the church up the street. We can walk from here." Kendra caught the worried look in Benjamin's eyes. "I have my reticule," she assured him.

He stared at her. "An' w'ot are ye gonna do, miss? Hit someone with yer tiny pouch?"

She grinned. "It's what's inside the pouch that matters." She paused to make sure that the strings were loose enough so she had ready access to the muff pistol.

"At least the air is a little fresher here," Rebecca said as they began walking.

"Probably because this area appears to be uninhabited." Kendra lifted her skirt as she leapt over a muddy puddle. There were still piles of grungy snow in the shadowy corners of buildings, but much had melted into slop around the broken cobblestones. She scanned the edifices of decaying stones and blank, broken windows. "Appearances can be deceptive, though," she said softly, the hairs on the back of her neck going up with the sensation of watching eyes.

Rebecca shivered, and glanced back to where Benjamin waited beside the carriage. "Maybe we should return with Mr. Kelly and Sutcliffe."

"It's probably nothing. Or just harmless squatters." Still, Kendra allowed her hand to dip into the reticule, her fingers closing over the pistol. "Come on."

She quickened her pace to the church, sprinting up the two steps. The heavy oak door was already ajar. Her entrance into the vestibule disturbed the two pigeons that had been drinking from a river of ice and water that snaked across the floor. The birds immediately took flight, arrowing through the door that opened into the nave of the church. Cautiously, Kendra moved forward, her gaze following the birds as they flew upward. Bits of feathers rained down as they landed in one of the many crooks and crevices along the vaulted ceiling. Given the many layers of white bird droppings and gray feathers on the floor below, the church had been the pigeons' home for a very long time.

Kendra continued to scan the large, gloomy room. Daylight streamed through the stained-glass windows, though there wasn't anything to see. The church had been stripped bare.

"Why are we here?" Rebecca crossed her arms in front of her chest and looked around nervously.

"Mr. Kelly thinks the killer used the church to dump the body," Kendra replied, moving to the door of the sacristy. She opened it and peered inside the shadow-filled room. Empty.

"You doubt that?"

Kendra shrugged, closing the door and turning back to the nave. "Not necessarily, but he's basing his assumption on the lack of blood. The tongue was cut postmortem, so there wouldn't have been much blood." She frowned as she studied the floor. "And the minimal flecks of blood would have been scuffed away."

What would I be able to see if I had a spray bottle of luminol and a black light? She tried not to let that bother her, her gaze on the boot marks churning up the thick layer of dirt and grime.

"And what do you see?" Rebecca asked.

Poor police procedure, Kendra wanted to say. "Right now? Nothing much," she admitted instead. "But sometimes you can determine if a body was dragged or carried by the marks on the ground. Unfortunately, this scene is too contaminated."

Rebecca's eyes flickered with interest. "I suppose that would indicate the physical strength of the killer. If the body was carried, the fiend would have to be very strong."

"There are ways to carry a body that would allow someone of lesser strength to do it." Kendra thought about the fireman's lift, which was designed to allow a smaller person to carry a dead-weight body fifty feet without stopping. She looked at Rebecca. "But overall, yes, if the victim was carried, that would help narrow the profile toward the unsub being male. If the victim was dragged, it widens the profile."

"But if Sir Giles was dragged, wouldn't his body have shown that?"

"He wasn't dragged naked down the street. If the unsub painted the marks on the body and cut out his tongue somewhere else, he might have wrapped Sir Giles's body in something to transport him here. Or if he strangled Sir Giles down the street—the area is out of the way enough to do it without attracting attention, and the murder itself was relatively quick—he didn't need to wrap him up. He could have just dragged him the rest of the way, undressed him in here, and done the rest of what he needed to do."

Kendra's eyes were drawn to the stained-glass windows. Sunbeams caught dust motes floating in the air. "It would have been night . . . so pitch black in here. Did the unsub plan for that?" Kendra thought of how she hadn't planned for the darkness when she'd gone up the servant's stairs earlier that morning.

"I think he did," Rebecca said, and lifted her shoulders in a quick shrug when Kendra swung her gaze back to her. "He planned for everything else, didn't he?"

"Yeah, you're right." Kendra nodded. "The unsub is organized. None of this appears to be impulsive. Which means he chose this site. Why? It's out of the way." She paused. "But there must be other abandoned buildings in the city that would be easier to access. So why here?"

Rebecca said, "The drawings on the body suggest a religious overtone. Catholicism certainly has its rituals and symbols." She paused, frowning. "Although I suppose the same argument could be made for many religions. Still, this church is abandoned, which was necessary. He could hardly bring the body into an active church, where he could be seen by a priest or the parishioners."

"You're assuming the symbols are religious."

"They are crosses. How could they not be religious?"

"They *look* like crosses." Kendra shook her head. "We're dealing with too many variables. We can't even be certain that the unsub wanted Sir

Giles found. He was only discovered because Snake was trying to outrun a watchman."

"But he must have thought Sir Giles would be found eventually. Why else go through the trouble of doing what was done to the body?"

"I'm not sure." *Variables*, Kendra thought again. "Maybe the unsub planned to bring attention to the body in some way, but it was preempted by Snake and the watchman."

Kendra let her gaze travel across the empty chamber. Above them, the pigeons' throaty coos and fluttering echoed off the high ceiling. She'd hoped to find something here that her 19th-century counterparts had missed. Was that hubris on her part? Maybe. But they sure as hell didn't understand the concept of preserving a crime scene. If there had been physical evidence left behind, it was gone now.

"I think the killer is familiar with this area," Kendra said, circling back to the earlier point. "The square is isolated from a main thoroughfare. It's not something you stumble across. That's a thread to pull. Maybe Mr. Kelly can find out more about this square, this church. Or—" She stopped abruptly, a chill racing down her arms.

"What?" Rebecca demanded, casting a fearful glance around.

The silence seemed profound. Then they heard it. The soft scrape, like the sole of a shoe against stone.

Plunging her hand into her reticule to close over the muff pistol, Kendra began to run for the door.

"Kendra!"

She caught sight of a dark shape moving beyond the door that led into the vestibule. There came the sound of running feet, and then the outside door banged shut. Kendra's heart accelerated as she ran through the vestibule, and she lost a moment shoving the outside door open. Once through, she leapt down onto the pavement, her gaze sweeping the dilapidated square. It took only a second for its emptiness to register. *Shit! Where did he go?*

Kendra struggled to control her breathing as she let her gaze roam over the crumbling abandoned buildings and broken windows. Tattered gray curtains curled like banshee fingers around an open window frame. More curtains flapped in the breeze, which had grown stronger. The sun was still out, high in the sky, but this desolate section of the city seemed darker somehow. An urban canyon created by the surrounding tenements. The lack of people was eerie, giving it the feel of a postapocalyptic world.

"Kendra." Rebecca panted as she came running up behind her.

In her peripheral vision, Kendra thought she saw something. She spun around.

There. A movement inside the entrance to the building across the street, a shifting between light and dark.

Or a figment of my imagination?

Rebecca said anxiously, "I think we should get Benjamin."

Kendra ignored her, jogging across the street. The door was broken and left askew. She drew her weapon as she approached the front steps. Behind her, she heard Rebecca let out an exasperated hiss. She strained to listen for other noises. *Something . . .*

Kendra climbed the steps, ready to duck through the door, when the creature lunged at her, gnarled hands waving.

"Go away! Go away! *Go away!*"

Rebecca gasped.

"*Shit!*" Startled, Kendra fell back down the steps, just managing to not land on her ass or accidentally shoot the old crone. Her heart beat hard in her chest, her blood thrumming wildly in her veins as she stared at the screeching woman.

She wore a filthy black dress and clutched a moth-eaten knitted shawl around her skinny shoulders. The linen cap that covered her wiry gray hair might have been white at one point, but was now a grayish brown. The old woman's face was so deeply lined that it looked as though it had been cut apart and sewn back together again. Her eyes were sunken into her head, but Kendra caught their dark blue glitter as they fixed on her.

"Sh-sh! Sh-sh!" The old woman lifted her knobby finger to her thin lips, and her mouth twisted into a smile, revealing approximately six crooked, rotting teeth. "Go away! *Sh-sh!*"

"She's harmless," Rebecca murmured, pity in her eyes.

The woman cocked her head to the side as she regarded Rebecca with her mad eyes. "She's 'armless," she repeated, and released a dry cackle. "Sh-*sh*. She's 'armless!"

Kendra edged back as the old woman shuffled forward. Not because she was afraid—Rebecca was right; the crone was mad, but harmless—but because she was certain the old woman was infested with lice or God knew what parasite. Kendra's nose wrinkled with distaste as she caught a whiff of the transient as she continued to hurry past them, muttering and laughing, "Sh-sh! She's 'armless! She's 'armless! *Go away!*"

"Jesus," Kendra muttered, and shook her head.

They watched the old woman hobble down the street, passing Benjamin and disappearing around the corner.

Rebecca cleared her throat. "Are we finished here? Shall we return to Grosvenor Square?"

"Yeah," Kendra said, but her gaze continued to roam the square. Her skin prickled. She listened intently, but heard nothing beyond the noise of nesting pigeons and the breeze as it moved through the urban canyon, fluttering rotting curtains. "Yeah, we're done here." She shoved the pistol back into her reticule. "But there's one more stop we need to make."

19

Even though London coffeehouses were not as popular as they had been twenty years ago, the Liber was doing brisk business when Alec and Sam arrived. The clientele was well-heeled, running the gamut from merchants, bankers, office clerks, and young dandies to Corinthians, the last being easy to spot in their fashionable riding habits, the men carrying just the tiniest whiff of horseflesh.

As his gaze skimmed across the crowd, Alec wondered which individuals were Irish spies or French agents. The war with Napoleon had ended with the dictator's exile on St. Helena, but intelligence gathering never ended. *On both sides*, he thought, remembering how d'Ambray had suggested that more than a few of the Liber's coffee drinkers were probably British operatives sent by Whitehall to listen in on discussions and report any seditious thoughts that might be going around.

By mutual agreement, Alec and Sam wove their way across the room, and slid into a high-paneled booth in the corner.

Three gentlemen in the next table were engaged in a lively debate about how the Prince Regent would destroy the monarchy with his extravagant spending. A few heads were cocked in that direction. *And there are the British spies*, Alec thought with some amusement.

Another conversation rose above the more measured murmur of the room, one man at a nearby table opining that it was time for women to be given the right to vote. His companion clearly didn't share his opinion, chortling heavily and declaring that it was a scientific fact that women with their smaller brains did not have the intellectual capacity to become involved in politics. Briefly, Alec had the entertaining vision of Kendra boxing the fellow's ears.

A pretty maidservant approached with two earthenware mugs and a silver pot of coffee. "Do ye want somethin' ter eat?" she said with a smile as she set down the mugs and filled them.

"No, thank you. But we would like to speak to the proprietor," Alec told her. "Silas Fitzpatrick."

She eyed him through her lashes. "And who wants ter talk ter him?"

Alec smiled. "Alec Morgan, the Marquis of Sutcliffe."

She looked at Sam.

"Sam Kelly, Bow Street Runner."

The maid's brow wrinkled. But if she thought it odd that a marquis was sitting with a Bow Street Runner, she kept her thoughts to herself. Without another word, she left their table. They watched her as she circled the room, replenishing coffee mugs. She stopped at one table across the room, leaning down to whisper in a man's ear. Alec saw the other man's head come up sharply, and swivel around to look in their direction. Alec lifted his coffee mug in acknowledgement as he met the other man's stare.

Silas Fitzpatrick scraped back his chair and stood up. He was of average height, with a body that was lean and tough beneath his white shirt, brown tweed jacket, and buff-colored pantaloons. His cravat was carelessly tied. Alec's valet would have been horrified at the slipshod manner, but Alec suspected that it was deliberate, with Fitzpatrick wanting to give the impression of rakishness. Or maybe it was a way to signal his identity to spies coming into the Liber. Such tricks were done in the intelligence world, Alec knew.

Alec judged him to be a couple years older than himself, in his mid-thirties. He wore his black hair long enough to brush his collar. His face was narrow and ruggedly handsome with sharp planes, his skin browned by the sun. Which might be a little odd for an owner of a coffeehouse, Alec reflected, but not all that odd for a possible spy.

The Irishman's mouth curved in a smile, but his dark gray eyes were hard and assessing as he sauntered up to their table. "You wanted to speak to me?"

Alec knew the Liber had opened two years ago, but Silas Fitzpatrick's Irish accent was muted enough for him to suspect that the man had been in England much longer.

"Yes." Alec returned the man's smile with a careful one of his own, and gestured to the space across from him in the booth. "Please, join us."

Fitzpatrick hesitated, then jerked his shoulders in a rough shrug. He sat and asked, "What's this about? I don't suppose either of you lads are wantin' the name of my coffee bean supplier."

Sam said, "Maybe later. Right now, I'd like ter know what you were doin' on Wednesday evening."

Fitzpatrick didn't pretend surprise. "Ah. This has to do with Sir Giles's death."

Sam looked at him closely. "You know about that, do you?"

Fitzpatrick snorted. "Everybody in town knows about it, I'd say." He made himself comfortable, lifting his arms to stretch across the top of the booth, legs spread. He grinned across at them. "Heard he got garroted in a church."

"You seem to be real pettish about his murder," Sam remarked.

"I'm not gonna pretend that I'll miss the bastard. Me da would be turnin' over in his grave if I told such a bouncer. Sir Giles was an opponent of Irish emancipation."

Alec said, "Half of England is against Irish emancipation."

Fitzpatrick shifted his gaze back to Alec. "Well, seeing how you are a lord and all, I don't suppose you would understand the suffering of us wee folks."

"Save your blarney, Fitz," Sam snapped. "And answer the question. Where were you Wednesday evening, after nine P.M.?"

The proprietor's face hardened. "I know why you're askin', but I can't help you. I was at home."

Sam raised his eyebrows, not bothering to hide his disbelief. "A man such as yourself was at home alone at nine in the evenin'? 'Cause I know this here coffeehouse stays open until eleven o'clock."

"I left Pru over there to lock up. Trust her with me life—and me cash box. And I didn't say I was alone." Now he gave a self-satisfied smile.

Alec studied him. "Then if you give us the name of your lady bird, we can be off."

"Well, now, I would." He stretched a bit, scratched behind his ear. "Truly I would. But she wasn't exactly a lady. I met her when I was doing business in Covent Garden. 'Tis cold, in case you haven't noticed. Can't blame me for wantin' a wench to warm me bed at night."

Sam said, "We'll need the lass's name ter confirm your account."

"Dorothea . . . Diana . . . or was it Dora?" The Irishman shrugged, still smiling. "We didn't do a lot of talkin'. If I see her again, I'll be sure to send her down to Bow Street."

Sam's mouth tightened. "Were you causin' Sir Giles trouble?"

"Now why would I be doing such a thing?"

Alec leaned forward, fixing his gaze on the other man. "Maybe because he'd become a threat to you."

Fitzpatrick did a commendable job of exhibiting bewilderment. "How so?"

Alec said, "We know that the Home Office is aware of your establishment. Maybe Sir Giles learned that you were passing confidential information to your likeminded countrymen, or stoking traitorous rhetoric and rebellion. Men have been jailed for sedition." He allowed his eyes to travel over the other man. "I don't think you'd fancy a stay in Newgate."

"I'd be an odd sort of fellow if I did fancy that, wouldn't I?" The Irishman rubbed the side of his nose, and grinned. "You're correct that Sir Giles thought my humble establishment was a front for the most nefarious sort of criminal activity. But despite his spies and such . . ."

Fitzpatrick made a show of studying his clientele. "He had no proof," he said, bringing his gaze back to Alec. "And because he had no proof, he threatened me—not the other way around. He owed me an apology."

Sam glowered at the other man. "Seein' how he's dead, I guess that's not gonna happen, eh?"

"I guess not," Fitzpatrick agreed. "I suppose I need to be satisfied that the bastard is dining with the devil. Now, gentlemen . . ." He stood up in a swift, athletic motion.

"One moment," Alec said mildly. The Irishman had started to turn away, but now he paused, arching one eyebrow as he waited for Alec to continue. "If you didn't kill him, do you have any idea who did?"

Alec half expected a glib response. But the charm that the Irishman wore as casually as his cravat suddenly vanished. "I'd think any of the poor wretches whose lives were made miserable by his strategies could have done the deed." The gray eyes brightened, and Alec recognized the emotion as rage. "It wasn't me, but, by God, I'd buy the man who stopped his claret a cup of me finest coffee. Now, if you'll pardon me, I have a business to run. Good day."

They paid for their coffee and left the shop, unaware of the man who slid from his booth and followed.

"I'll have me men go ter Fitzpatrick's neighborhood and ask around ter see if anyone saw him on Wednesday night," Sam said.

"Why do I get the feeling that you won't find anyone?"

"Aye. I think he was lying about his whereabouts and the convenient doxie. But it's a thread ter follow."

Alec shot the Bow Street Runner an amused smile. "Now you're starting to sound like Kendra—Miss Donovan."

"Aye, the lass has a way of speaking. And making sense."

Alec nodded. His smile faded as his thoughts returned to the Irishman. "Fitzpatrick didn't bother to hide his hatred for Sir Giles."

"That's because everyone knows about it," said a new voice from behind them.

Alec and Sam both gave a jerk and swung around.

"Muldoon." The Bow Street Runner said the name like it was a curse. "Eavesdropping again?"

The reporter grinned. "I told you, 'tis the best way of gathering information. Unfortunately, I was too far away to hear what Fitzpatrick was telling you gentlemen. Care to share?"

"Will we be in tomorrow morning's newspaper?" asked Alec. He pivoted again and began walking briskly in the direction he and Sam had been heading. Both Sam and Muldoon hurried to catch up.

"I don't have to identify you," Muldoon said.

Alec cast the man a narrow-eyed glance. "Just as you didn't identify the Duke of Aldridge and Miss Donovan?"

"I didn't! Town is filled with high-ranking noblemen, in case you haven't noticed, milord."

"Involved in murder? With a young lady? Do you take me for a flat, Muldoon?"

"Never. But you have to admit His Grace and Miss Donovan's interest in murder *is* peculiar."

"All the more reason not to have it written about," Alec said tersely.

"Of course," the reporter agreed readily. "What were you doing at the Liber? It appeared that you and Mr. Fitzpatrick were involved in a heavy discussion."

Sam scowled. "What were *you* doing there?"

Muldoon grinned at him. "Following up on information I'd been given."

"What information?" Sam demanded. "And remember, you gave your word that you'd share any information pertaining ter Sir Giles's murder."

"I imagined an equal exchange of information," Muldoon remarked, but lifted a hand as though to ward off the glower Sam shot him. "All right. See now, everyone knows that Sir Giles believed Mr. Fitzpatrick's coffeehouse was a meeting place for foreign spies. It's called the Liber, after all. You'd have to have cotton for brains not to know where Fitzpatrick's sympathies lie."

"I don't have to struggle too mightily to see where your sympathies lay in that regard, either, Mr. Muldoon," Alec countered dryly. "Fitzpatrick's allegiance to Irish independence would have drawn Sir Giles's regard, but Fitzpatrick's vitriol against Sir Giles seems out of proportion.

I understand that politics and patriotic fervor can inflame one's passions, but this—this seems like something else."

Muldoon nodded. "Mr. Fitzpatrick's animosity toward Sir Giles is well-known enough for me to make inquiries. As an Irishman myself, you might say I have connections to the Erin émigré community." The reporter huffed a little in an effort to keep up with Alec's long stride. "You are correct, milord, in thinking this is personal. At least for Fitzpatrick."

That stopped Alec, who spun to face the reporter, and only Muldoon's quick reflexes saved him from crashing into the marquis. "How so?" Alec demanded.

Muldoon's affable expression disappeared. "Fitzpatrick believed Sir Giles was responsible for his sister's death."

Sam blew out a breath. "That would certainly cause animosity. What happened?"

"The story is that three years ago, the Irish village of Clondalkin had been causing a wee bit of trouble with their protests against English rule. Sir Giles ordered British troops to stop any rebellion in its infancy. There was a lass in the village. From what I heard, a pretty little thing." Muldoon's mouth thinned as he continued, "She was set upon by one of the British soldiers. He ravaged her, then murdered her. Strangled her with his bare hands."

Alec stared at the reporter. "Strangled . . ." he murmured, and wondered at the parallel between the girl's murder and Sir Giles's. By the suspicious glint in Sam's golden eyes, Alec knew the Bow Street Runner was thinking the same thing.

"The lass was Fitzpatrick's sister," Alec said slowly. "And Fitzpatrick blamed Sir Giles for giving the order to send the troops to the village."

As Muldoon nodded, Alec wondered if he was imagining another parallel. *Speak no evil.* If Fitzpatrick was the fiend, had he cut out Sir Giles's tongue as a bizarre sort of retaliation against the man who'd given the order to send British troops to Clondalkin, which had resulted in his sister's savage murder?

Sam shook his head. "Then Fitzpatrick is mad, because Sir Giles couldn't have foreseen what would've happened ter the lass."

Alec's shadowed gaze met the Bow Street Runner's eyes. "What was done to Sir Giles is a little insane, I think."

"There's more to the story," Muldoon said. "The villagers demanded a trial for the soldier—his name was Sergeant Robin Clay. I'm certain he would have been found guilty and sent to the hangman's noose."

"Was there evidence that he did the deed?" Sam asked.

Muldoon's eyes flashed. "Two witnesses. And the lass's locket that she always wore around her neck was found in his quarters."

"God's teeth," Sam muttered. "What happened?"

"Sir Giles happened. He ordered the Sergeant back to England to allegedly face justice here. Said he didn't think the young man could get a fair trial in Clondalkin, or the whole of Ireland, for that matter." Muldoon sounded bitter. "So Sergeant Clay came back to England. I was told the trial lasted less than an hour before he was acquitted. I'm looking into his whereabouts now."

The reporter's face seemed to arrange itself into long, somber lines. He said softly, "The lass was only twelve, milord. If you're looking for motivation, I can't think of anythin' better than avenging the death of your little sister. Can you?"

20

Benjamin didn't want to take her to the Larsons' apothecary shop on Cromwell Road in Kensington—no surprise there—so it took a few minutes of haranguing to convince him to make the additional stop. And even then, Kendra suspected it was Rebecca's quiet intervention that finally forced the coachman into agreeing.

Unfortunately, the journey took longer than expected—and undoubtedly had Benjamin silently cursing her from his perch on top of the carriage—when they got stuck behind an accident. A wagon had hit an icy patch and overturned, spilling kegs of ale. It was weirdly similar to many of the 21st-century traffic jams Kendra had been stuck in, including the impatience thrumming in the air around them. There were no horns for irate drivers to honk out their displeasure, but curses filled the air and several men looked on the verge of road rage.

When they finally arrived at Cromwell Road, Kendra thought they'd have to make inquiries to get directions to the apothecary shop. Luckily, though, Bertel Larson was a man who took pride in his family name.

LARSON & SON APOTHECARY was emblazoned on a banner sign across a Jacobean redbrick building. Kendra was a little disconcerted to observe that the sign was also decorated with two large swastikas. She had to remind herself that the symbol had been around for thousands of years in almost every country and culture before Hitler had co-opted and corrupted it into a mark of pure evil. Before the Third Reich, the symbol had represented eternal life, good fortune, and a supreme being.

All things that suited an apothecary shop, she supposed.

Below the sign was a large bow window. Like modern-day retailers, the window was crammed with products and advertisements to lure in potential customers. Kendra paused outside to study the collection of pretty blue-and-white-painted delft earthenware jars before her gaze moved to one of the larger signs that someone had leaned against a pyramid of pots. *HAMILTON'S HARMLESS ARSENIC WAFERS. WHITENS SKIN! RID YOURSELF OF REDNESS, BLEMISHES, AND BLOTCHES. ONLY 4 SHILLINGS!*

She'd forgotten that it had been a popular practice for women to ingest small quantities of the deadly arsenic to brighten their complexion. The trend would become even more popular in another thirty years, when women in the Victorian Age actually wanted to look like they were on the verge of death—not unlike the heroin chic trend popularized by models in the 1990s. Of course, the irony for women in the Victorian era was that by taking the poison, many of them actually were killing themselves.

Aware that Rebecca was waiting, Kendra turned away from the window display, and moved to the red door. Once inside the shop, she had to stop again, taking in the large room. It appeared smaller than its true size, because the shelves and countertops were jam-packed with a wide variety of merchandise. It was part pharmacy and part oddity shop. *Very odd*, she decided, her gaze landing on a stuffed five-foot alligator displayed on a shelf next to a stuffed parrot. Kendra thought of Ruth's story of Lady Watley's cheeky parrot, and smiled.

The air was heavy with a collision of scents, from spicy to floral. Four women—two obviously gentlewomen, the others their maids—and one gentleman were wandering around the store, checking out merchandise ranging from lavender lotions to herbal remedies that promised to invigorate a person, from cough syrups to—*holy crap*—live leeches.

Curious, Kendra picked up a lumpy package. Mrs. Middleton's complexion soap listed among its ingredients animal oils, rosewater, lye, and mercuric chloride. Shaking her head, she put the package back on the shelf. Mercuric chloride was a poisonous form of mercury. And in this era, people were washing their faces with it.

Then again, Kendra had to remember that she'd come from a time when people paid a bundle to inject themselves with Botox—derived from Clostridium botulinum, one of the most lethal toxins known to mankind. Who was she to judge?

"Have you ever bought Mrs. Middleton's soap?" she asked Rebecca.

"No. Our stillroom maids make our soaps," Rebecca said.

Thank God for the self-sufficiency of large estates. "Good," was all she said before moving toward the shopgirl working behind the long counter. She was in her late teens, with chestnut hair peeking out from her mop cap. Her attention was focused on carefully spooning what looked to be bath salts into a dish on an old-fashioned balance scale. She glanced up as they approached, and set down the spoon. "May I help you?" she asked, turning to give them a smile that showed off her dimples.

"We're looking for Mr. Larson."

"Oh. He's in the laboratory. But I'm certain I shall be able to assist you." Her gaze slid to Rebecca's face. "We have an excellent paste to help settle the complexion."

In her peripheral vision, Kendra saw Rebecca stiffen at the unintended insult. She said coolly, "No, thank you. We just need to speak to Mr. Larson." After a beat, she added, "Please tell Mr. Larson that Lady Rebecca Blackburn and Miss Donovan would like a word."

Rebecca's title and upper-class accent appeared to do the trick. "I'll inform Mr. Larson that you wish a word with him, your ladyship." The girl walked down the length of the counter to the swinging doors near the end and pushed through.

Kendra turned to Rebecca, wanting to apologize for the shopgirl's insensitivity, but Rebecca deliberately turned away to study a display of herbal teas. She'd had a lifetime of dealing with unkind, cutting remarks.

The shopgirl reemerged from the swinging doors, followed by a tall, broad-shouldered man with brown hair, intense, arctic blue eyes, and a strikingly handsome face. Early to mid-twenties, Kendra estimated. Not the Mr. Larson she'd been expecting. It had to be the youngest son, David, that Lady Holbrooke had mentioned.

"Good day," he said, coming forward. "Sally says that you wish to speak to me. Lady Rebecca?"

"No. I'm Kendra Donovan. This is Lady Rebecca."

"I see. How can I be of assistance?"

Kendra said, "I'm sorry. We were actually hoping to speak to Mr. Larson—Evert Larson's father."

The man's face changed subtly. "My brother is dead."

"I know. I'm sorry. Is your father here?" She shot a glance at the swinging doors.

"No. He is . . . he is at home." The brilliant blue eyes dimmed. "I am a trained apothecary. My name is David Larson. What is this about?"

"Sir Giles." She said the name and watched the emotions flicker across the gorgeous face. "Did you hear that he was murdered the other night?"

His jaw tightened. "Yes. What does that have to do with my father?"

"I was told that your families were quite close until your brother's death. Your father blamed Sir Giles."

"My father was naturally filled with grief." His eyes went hard. "Evert had trained as a barrister, and had only just begun to practice law. He had no business in war, but Sir Giles persuaded him to put aside everything to work for him as an intelligence agent. He charmed Evert with dreams of honor and glory."

Kendra studied the man. It occurred to her that there was more than one member of the family who might want to see Sir Giles dead. "You and your brother were close?"

"Yes," he said simply.

"I've heard that your brother was an exceptionally brilliant man."

"He was." He looked away, but not before Kendra saw the sheen of despair in his eyes. He was silent for a moment, composing himself. "Evert was . . . everything," he finally said. "He was extraordinarily intelligent. We could see that even when he was a boy. He was my senior by two years, and I undoubtedly made quite a pest of myself trailing after him and Gerard." A small smile curved David's mouth at the memory, quickly gone.

"You are referring to Sir Giles's son, Gerard Holbrooke?"

He nodded. "Yes. Evert and Gerard were of the same age. They were friends, for a time."

"For a time?" Kendra prompted.

David hesitated, and something flashed in his eyes. "As they grew older, it became quite clear that Gerard began to resent Evert."

"Because of the attention Sir Giles gave your brother?"

"Yes, among other things." His lips thinned. "I wish to God that Sir Giles had developed more of an interest in his own son. Maybe if he had, my brother would be alive."

Kendra studied him for a long moment. "You must have resented Sir Giles as well," she finally said.

"Evert died—viciously," he snapped, loud enough to cause one of the ladies who was browsing nearby to glance in their direction. Aware of the attention they were drawing, David gestured for Kendra and Rebecca to follow him to the corner of the shop where there were no customers. He fixed his gaze on Kendra again. "Why are you asking these questions, Miss Donovan?"

"My guardian"—that still stuck in Kendra's throat; she was twenty-six years old, for Christ's sake—"the Duke of Aldridge and I are assisting Bow Street with their investigation into the murder of Sir Giles." She held up a hand when she saw his eyebrows lift in surprise. "And, yes, I know that I'm a woman."

His eyebrows lowered into a frown, but he said nothing.

"Where were you on Wednesday evening, from nine to midnight?"

David stared at her.

She spread her gloved hands. "If I don't ask the question, Bow Street will."

He glanced away. Across the room, the gentleman who'd been shopping approached the counter with his selections. The shopgirl, Sally, hurried over to help him. The door opened, and a matron swept inside the shop, trailed by a harried-looking maid carrying boxes and a straw basket.

"I was here, if you must know," he finally said.

Kendra kept her gaze on his. "From nine to midnight? Will anybody be able to verify that?"

"No. The shop closes at half past five, but my duties often keep me working late in the laboratory. We are an apothecary, Miss Donovan. Larson & Son mixes our own proprietary remedies. We fill many prescriptions for our loyal customers."

"So you would say working late is usual for you?"

"I believe I just said that." He glanced at the matron approaching the counter. "I must take care of one of those customers now. I trust we are done here?"

Kendra nodded. "For now."

Something flickered in his eyes, but was gone before Kendra could decipher what it was. He gave an abbreviated bow. "Ladies."

Kendra and Rebecca were silent as they watched David Larson approach the new customer. She was an older woman with graying brown sausage curls framing a pleasantly plump face. The velvet bonnet she wore was a little excessive, Kendra thought, ornamented with lace ruffles, flowers, and silk ribbons. Her dark blue pelisse was fur-lined, to suit the weather. Beneath that was a pale primrose-and-white-striped carriage dress that boasted three golden ruffles along the hem.

Kendra knew the lady's affinity for ruffles; she'd been introduced to Lady St. James the last time she'd been in London, when she'd been investigating the murder of Alec's former mistress, Lady Dover. The countess was a friend of the Duke's sister. And one of the most notorious gossips in London. And nosy people were always valuable sources of information in murder investigations.

As they watched, Lady St. James gave David a flirtatious smile, never mind that he was at least thirty years her junior. "Mr. Larson, good day to you. I have immediate need of having my tonic prescriptions refilled." She snapped at her maid, who shifted the boxes she was carrying to open the woven-straw basket hooked over her arm. Glass clinked as the maid deposited three amber-colored medicine bottles on the counter.

David offered the countess a polite smile, picking up one of the bottles to inspect the label. "Certainly, my lady. May I inquire how you have been sleeping with the cordial?"

"Your father's cordials have ensured a dreamless slumber, thank you." She tilted her head and her bright, curious eyes fixed on his face. "And, pray tell, how is your father? Will he be returning to his place of business soon?"

If she hadn't been watching so closely, Kendra might have missed the way David's broad shoulders tensed. "At the moment, no," he told Lady St. James. "My father has his own maladies to contend with."

"Oh, dear." The countess made a sympathetic tut-tutting sound with her tongue. "Well, he is most fortunate to have you."

"You are very gracious, ma'am." He bowed slightly before gathering up the bottles. "If you will pardon me, I shall take care of your order now." He flicked a quick look at Kendra and Rebecca, aware of their surveillance. His lips tightened, and then he swiveled on his heel, moved around the counter, and disappeared through the swinging doors.

At the end of the counter, Sally finished up with the gentleman, and began dealing with one of the ladies who'd been waiting. Kendra noticed that the woman held a green- and amber-colored glass bottle in each hand, and wondered if she, too, was buying a sleeping potion, which no doubt was laced with opiates—all perfectly legal—to ease her into a dreamless slumber.

Kendra moved toward Lady St. James, who was examining a display of charcoal tooth powders which promised to help the user keep their natural teeth.

"Lady St. James?" Kendra waited until the other woman set down a jar and turned to look at her.

Recognition dawned. "Miss Donovan. And Lady Rebecca! This is a serendipitous surprise. How do you do?"

Rebecca bent her knee for a quick curtsey. "Very well, thank you. And you?"

"I'm quite well, thank you." She regarded them with the same bright curiosity that she'd bestowed on David when asking after his father. "Pray tell, what brings you to London?"

By the way Lady St. James was regarding her, like a cat waiting outside a mouse hole, Kendra suspected the matron knew the answer. "Have you heard about the murder of Sir Giles?"

"Oh, yes!" Her lips curved into a knowing smile. "And you must be the young lady I read about in the *Morning Chronicle*. I must say, it is most odd, this interest that you and His Grace have taken in our criminal element. It is not at all the thing. However . . ." She leaned forward, her voice dropping to a whisper. "It is also *quite* exciting. What have you learned, Miss Donovan?"

"We're only at the beginning stages of the investigation," Kendra said, aware that whatever she told the countess would be passed along to the first acquaintance she encountered. "We couldn't help but overhear your conversation with Mr. Larson. Do you come here often?"

"To Larson and Son?" Lady St. James seemed surprised by the question. "Yes, for years. My doctor recommended Mr. Larson the Elder for my lesser complaints. At the time, I was quite vexed with him for doing so. I am not a commoner to be passed off to an apothecary!" She sniffed, and some of her previous indignation surfaced. But then she waved it away. "However, I quickly realized that Mr. Larson the Elder is not some lowbrow apothecary, and I have been enormously satisfied with his service and tonics. I highly recommend him—and Mr. Larson the Younger. They are both excellent chemists."

Kendra said, "It sounds as though Mr. Larson the Elder has become ill."

Lady St. James made another sympathetic *tsk*ing sound in her throat. "Oh, my, *yes*, the poor dear."

"How long has he been sick?"

"Oh, let me think." She pursed her lips as she considered the matter. "I last spoke with him around Christmastime, when I needed a cordial to calm my nerves. I was traveling to my son's estate in Gloucestershire. I love my grandchildren dearly, but I confess the incessant wailing of the twins quite shatters my nerves. During my last two visits, Mr. Larson the Elder has not been here. However, as I mentioned, Mr. Larson the Younger is as skilled as his father."

"So Mr. Larson has been ill for at least a month," Kendra said slowly. The same time that Sir Giles had begun to appear troubled.

"Yes." Lady St. James eyed her closely. "Is that significant?"

Kendra evaded answering truthfully with, "It just seems like a long time to be sick."

"Oh, I agree. Especially a man such as Mr. Larson the Elder. He is such a robust, *attractive* gentleman." Her eyes held a surprisingly lascivious gleam.

Kendra wondered if Lady St. James's patronage of Larson & Son had more to do with Mr. Larson the Elder's attractiveness than his skills as a chemist.

The countess went on, "Really, my dear, what *is* this about? Why are you so interested in my apothecary?"

Kendra ignored her questions, asking instead, "Did you know Mr. Larson's son, Evert?" When the other woman stared at her blankly, she added, "He was killed in the war."

"I knew *of* him, of course, but I was never introduced to him. Why should I be? We hardly travel in the same social circles." She gave a slightly condescending laugh. "As an American, I daresay you are still unfamiliar with society, Miss Donovan."

"Did Mr. Larson speak of his son?"

"No, I only learned of him when he died. Two, two-and-a-half years ago, I believe. That was the first time Mr. Larson the Elder stopped coming into the shop." She leaned forward to whisper, "Melancholy, you know. It was fortuitous that he had Mr. Larson the Younger to take over the apothecary business until he returned."

"How long was he gone the first time?" Kendra asked.

Lady St. James wandered to the next display, pyramids of bath salts in jars and perfume bottles. She picked up a bottle and sniffed. "Oh, several months. I believe Mr. Larson the Younger said that his father left London for Bath for a time." She set down the bottle. "The waters in Bath are quite therapeutic for one's nerves."

Kendra and Rebecca followed her. "Were you acquainted with Sir Giles?" asked Kendra.

The countess gave her a sly smile. "I have been introduced to both Sir Giles and his wife, Lady Holbrooke. The king granted Sir Giles his baronetcy fifteen—mayhap twenty?—years ago, which allowed them entry into the Beau Monde. Lady Holbrooke and her son often attend functions."

"Not Sir Giles?"

Lady St. James picked up another perfume bottle. "He was forever working at Whitehall. Understandable, of course, given the war with that little tyrant Napoleon. There were rumors that Sir Giles was on his way to becoming the next prime minister, so no one was likely to deny him an invitation." She wrinkled her nose. "Well, mayhap the most radical of Whigs. But even those scapegraces would think twice, considering the close connection Sir Giles enjoyed with the Prince Regent."

Lady St. James waved her maid over and handed her the bottle of perfume.

Kendra waited until the maid slipped back a few paces before asking, "What was your impression of Sir Giles's son, Mr. Holbrooke?"

"He seemed a charming enough young man when I met him, but I have heard things . . ."

Kendra willingly took the bait. "What sort of things?"

The countess leaned closer, dropping her voice again into a conspiratorial whisper. "The young pup had a row with his father, and attacked him at Tattersalls. I could scarcely believe the story, but it is true."

Kendra said, "Yes, we heard."

"Oh." Lady Atwood looked momentarily crestfallen not to be the first one to impart that information. She rallied. "Well, the on-dit was that Sir Giles was quite out of temper with his son, and was making plans to send him to India."

"How do you know?" Kendra asked, impressed that the countess had managed to learn that nugget of information. Although she supposed if Bear knew about it, there was a good chance Lady St. James knew too.

The matron smiled. "Oh, one hears such things here and there."

Lady Rebecca spoke up. "But was it true?"

The dark eyes danced. "*Yes.* Lady Holbrooke was not happy about it, but I have it on excellent authority that Sir Giles had not only made inquiries, but was on the verge of booking passage for the rogue. In fact, Sir Giles was supposed to do that next week."

Kendra lifted her eyebrows. That was news. "So soon?"

The countess nodded. "I imagine Mr. Holbrooke is in an odd position. Despite the obvious troubles between him and his father, he must mourn Sir Giles. And yet I daresay he is relieved that his banishment to India is no more."

They fell silent as they considered that. Kendra changed subjects. "Do you know Lord Cross?"

Lady St. James pursed her lips. Kendra could almost see the wheels turning. "Lord Eliot Cross. He is the second son of the Earl of Cambay. The earl has a smallish country seat in one of the west counties. Devon, I think. Or was it Dorset? Well, no matter. He rarely comes to town, but is known to be close-fisted. His son came into the viscount title when Cambay's eldest died in a carriage accident last year. A modest annual income—two thousand pounds." She tapped her chin, thinking. "They say the viscount will soon be on the hunt for a wife of more considerable means."

Kendra stared at the woman, impressed. Who needed Facebook when you had Lady St. James?

The countess took a breath, and continued, "I have been introduced to the viscount in society, but nothing more. He seemed a pleasant enough chap." Her eyes narrowed on Kendra. "Why? What does he have to do with Sir Giles's murder?"

"Maybe nothing," Kendra said, earning an unhappy frown from the older woman, who undoubtedly was hoping to add some new bit of gossip to her arsenal.

Kendra was relieved when David Larson emerged from the swinging doors with the now-filled medicine bottles. Attention drawn, Lady Atwood hurried over to the counter, her bored-looking maid in tow.

"Is there anything else that I may assist you with, madam?" David asked as he transferred the bottles to the countess's maid and added the purchase of the perfume. He kept his gaze fixed on the countess, ignoring Kendra and Rebecca, who had followed in Lady St. James's wake.

The flirtatious smile was back on the older woman's face. "Thank you, no. You have positively *saved* me, Mr. Larson."

"Your servant," he said, inclining his head. He finally looked at Kendra, unable to disguise his wariness. "I must tend to my business, Miss Donovan. I believe I have answered all your questions."

Kendra found herself mimicking his gesture by inclining her head. "Thank you, sir."

Lady St. James cut her a sideways glance. "If you are done here, Miss Donovan, Lady Rebecca, perhaps you'd walk with me?"

They left the shop, falling into step with the matron while her maid trailed behind. They didn't have to walk far. If Kendra wasn't mistaken, the bright canary-yellow carriage parked in front of the Duke's more understated carriage belonged to Lady St. James. Benjamin and the other coachman were chatting, but now broke off their conversation. Lady St. James's coachman hurried over to unfold the carriage steps, open the door, and gallantly take the straw bag and boxes from the maid.

The countess paused. "I was remiss in not asking whether my dear friend Lady Atwood is with you in London?"

Kendra said, "She's here."

"Ah, I must call upon her. I'm certain Lady Atwood has been sent an invitation for Lord and Lady Smyth-Hope's ball tonight. It promises to be quite the crush."

"Hmm," was all Kendra could muster. Unless there was a reason, she didn't feel the need to have to socialize with the Ton. But if Lady Atwood had received an invitation, she knew it might be hard to get out of it.

Lady St. James's lips curled in a catlike smile. "I would urge you to attend as well, Miss Donovan. In all likelihood, Lord Cross will be there. If I'm not mistaken, there is a connection between the Earl of Cambay and Lady Smyth-Hope. A distant relation, but still. It would be churlish for Lord Cross to refuse an invitation."

"Thank you, my lady. The Smyth-Hope ball is sounding better and better."

The countess laughed. "I thought so." Her smile vanished in the next moment, her eyes narrowing on Kendra. "Now why are you here, Miss Donovan? I do not mean in London. I mean *here*—in this particular shop? I do not believe for a second that you needed bath salts or tooth powder. You were obviously quizzing Mr. Larson the Younger about something when I arrived. And quizzing me about Mr. Larson the Elder."

The woman wasn't stupid, Kendra knew, and so she chose her words with care. "The two families are acquainted. Mr. Larson and Sir Giles have known each other since childhood, and Mr. Larson's son, Evert, worked for Sir Giles during the war."

The countess raised her eyebrows. "Indeed? I was not aware of the connection." She seemed to mull that over. "You cannot imagine that Mr. Larson had anything to do with Sir Giles's murder?"

"The Elder or Younger?"

"Don't be a cheeky puss," she murmured, amused.

Kendra shook her head. "Honestly, we're only asking questions, trying to figure out who might have wanted Sir Giles dead."

"Hmm. Given his high position in the Home Office, I daresay all the enemies of England would want him dead. In fact, you ought to look at those Irish radicals."

"We've got inquiries there as well."

"Good." She nodded, then fixed her gaze on Kendra. "I shall be frank with you, Miss Donovan. You'll catch cold if you think Mr. Larson—Elder or Younger—has anything to do with what happened to Sir Giles. For heaven's sake, they are *apothecaries*. If one can't trust an apothecary, who can you trust?"

Kendra laughed. "I'm not sure any American would agree with you, my lady."

Lady St. James had been turning away, one foot on the steps of her carriage, but now she looked back at Kendra, her brows arched in a haughty expression that seemed at odds with her ruffled attire. "Pray tell, why would Americans dislike apothecaries?"

"Not dislike. But they might not trust one—Benedict Arnold was an apothecary."

"Ah." The matron inclined her head, and smiled. "Well, that is a matter of perspective, Miss Donovan. Mr. Arnold *was* trustworthy—to the English."

21

D r. Munroe found cockles and langoustine, asparagus, and beetroots in Sir Giles's stomach," Aldridge informed the group seated around the table in his study.

Kendra thought it was a little ironic that she, Alec, Rebecca, Sam, and the Duke were picking through a light luncheon of thinly sliced ham and roast beef, Somerset cheddar and Swaledale cheeses, brown bread, and churned Epping butter while discussing Sir Giles's last meal. No one else seemed to notice, though, so she kept her mouth shut.

The Duke added, "The contents were easily identifiable."

"Ah. That's good." Kendra nodded, making a sandwich out of the cheeses and ham.

Rebecca frowned. "Why is that good?"

"It means that Sir Giles died not long after he ate his dinner at the club," Kendra explained. "We're dealing now with a window of approximately two hours. After two hours, stomach contents become . . . less identifiable." She picked up the water that she'd asked to be boiled, and took a slow sip as she considered the timeline. "This helps us," she said, setting the glass down. "We know that Sir Giles received a note around nine P.M. and left his club shortly afterward. Now we know that he was killed within two hours after that. That means he was dead by eleven P.M."

The Duke's eyes brightened as he looked across the table at Kendra. "We include the time that the hackney driver drove him to his destination. If we find out that the hackney driver is the killer—"

"He *was* the killer," Sam spoke up between bites of ham. "Pardon me, Your Grace."

The Duke lifted his eyebrows at the Bow Street Runner. "So certain, Mr. Kelly?"

"Aye." He chewed and swallowed. "Me men found the hackney driver—Mr. Richardson. He was tending ter his business just off Brompton Road, but had ter stop his hackney 'cause there were a couple of crates blocking the street. He got down ter move them when he said he was clouted. He said he came ter in a nearby doorway an hour later, with a bump the size of a goose egg and feelin' like he was as drunk as an Emperor. He reported that his hackney was stolen to the local watch. Mr. Richardson said he was mighty relieved when his nag was found wandering about Spitalfields, pullin' the carriage. He knew it wasn't a robbery, because his coins were still in his purse. Figured it was some young bucks well into their cups who was havin' a bit of a lark."

"Since he was struck from behind, we can learn nothing from our unfortunate hackney driver then," Aldridge murmured, disappointed.

"That's not exactly true. Mr. Richardson might not be able to identify the killer, but we *have* learned something," Kendra said. "The absence of action tells us something about the unsub. He didn't kill the hackney driver, even though he could easily have done so. He didn't leave him in the street where he could have been run over in the snow and the dark. He carried Richardson into a doorway. Is Richardson a big man?"

"Nay. I'd even say he was on the smallish side. Maybe ten stone or so."

Kendra converted that in her head to 145 to 150 pounds. "Okay. That doesn't eliminate anyone. We're still dealing with someone roughly the same height as Sir Giles, and reasonably strong."

"But if the hackney driver is the killer," Rebecca said, "didn't the night porter see him?"

Kendra had forgotten that Rebecca hadn't been a part of their earlier discussion. "Almost everyone working outdoors is wearing coats, scarves, gloves, and hats that can be used to conceal a person's identity."

"Ah, yes. I hadn't thought of that."

They spent a few moments focused on their lunch. Kendra polished off her sandwich and then pushed herself to her feet. She crossed the room, snatched up the piece of slate, and began to write the new information down on the board. "Sir Giles was targeted," she said, stepping back to review the notes. "We know that. But the unsub didn't want to kill unnecessarily to get to his target. That indicates a level of compassion."

"I'm not so certain," Alec disagreed. "Head injuries are precarious. The hackney driver could have died from such a wound. And the fiend could have moved him to a doorway so he wouldn't be found so quickly and raise the alarm."

"Okay, that's possible," she conceded, jiggling the piece of slate in her hand as she reconsidered. "However, he could still have killed the driver, and dumped his body in the doorway to keep it out of sight. The fact that he didn't says something. Compassion might be the wrong word. He's obviously calculating, but maybe he isn't as cold-blooded as we originally thought."

"At least not for anyone other than Sir Giles," murmured the Duke.

She nodded, meeting his eyes. "Exactly. You'd be surprised at how many killers have no qualms about taking out other people in order to get to their target." At the Bureau, she'd studied John "Jack" Gilbert Graham, who in 1955 had blown up an airplane with forty-four people onboard in order to kill one passenger—his mother. Obviously the unsub that they were currently dealing with wasn't quite the psychopath Graham had been.

Kendra became aware that everyone was staring at her. "Sorry, my mind was elsewhere," she muttered. She could hardly share the story with Sam and Rebecca, who had no clue what an airplane was.

She cleared her throat, and looked at Sam. "Did Richardson mention anything about being followed, or feeling like he was being watched?"

Sam shook his head. "Nay. Maybe the fiend just got lucky."

Organized, Kendra thought again. "This isn't a crime of opportunity. Our unsub isn't going to leave something like that to chance. This is about strategy. It was a setup."

The Duke picked up his teacup, surveying Kendra over the rim. "So you believe the murderer followed Mr. Richardson. Do hackney drivers have established routines?"

"Aye," said Sam. "They have certain territories they stay in and routes that they follow."

"The unsub probably shadowed several hackney drivers," Kendra said. "Richardson was the one he chose because his routine or route worked for him. To set up the crates and block the road, he had to be sure that Richardson was the only one driving down the street at that time. This takes planning."

Alec said, "And planning takes time."

"Well, he didn't need ter waste time with Sir Giles," Sam pointed out. "His routine was consistent."

Kendra nodded. "All he had to do was send in a note, and Sir Giles would come out to him."

"Clever, isn't he?" Aldridge mused, taking a long sip of tea.

"He's not an idiot," Kendra agreed, and shrugged when the Duke grinned. "You're right. We're dealing with someone with above average intelligence or cunning."

"Do you really think Mr. Holbrooke is that clever?" Rebecca asked.

Kendra stopped pacing to look at her. "You don't?"

Rebecca spread her hands. "I confess he struck me as an arrogant, spoiled young man, which is very typical of the Ton, but not terribly clever. You think differently?"

"I think I'd like to keep an open mind," Kendra said. She jiggled the slate in her hand as she thought about it. "Sir Giles had a high IQ. The daughter as well. There's no reason to think that Holbrook isn't just as intelligent."

Sam smiled slightly. "She's a peculiar lass, ain't she?"

Kendra nodded, but didn't say anything. She'd been called that too often for her to think it was funny. *My issue*, she thought. Instead, she said, "As far as facts go, we know that a week ago, Holbrooke was in debt and his father was going to ship him off to India. But with his father's death, Holbrooke is now the head of the household, which includes controlling the purse strings. Nobody can tell him what to do anymore. And he sure as hell isn't going to India."

"Put like that, Mr. Holbrooke certainly has motivation to kill his father," said the Duke.

Kendra shrugged. "People have killed for less."

Sam ate the last bit of bread on his plate before pushing his plate away. "If I may ask, what's an IQ?"

Kendra blinked, and had to think about it for a bit. "Oh. It's just how Americans refer to individual intelligence."

Of course, "IQ" was actually coined by a German psychologist working at Poland's University of Breslau. Ironic, really, given all the Polish jokes about intelligence.

"Lady Holbrooke lied about her and her son's whereabouts on Wednesday evening," Rebecca told the group as she got up to retrieve the teapot.

Alec frowned. "You can't be suggesting Lady Holbrooke may have had something to do with her husband's death?"

"No," Kendra said. "I'm still not ruling out a woman as the killer, but Lady Holbrooke is petite. Physically, she couldn't have caused the type of laceration on Sir Giles's throat unless she was standing on a stepladder."

"She lied ter protect her son," Sam said flatly.

"I'd say so, yes. But she was too hasty. Ruth told us that her mother went to a ball that night. Why did Lady Holbrooke think her son needed an alibi?"

The Duke eyed her closely. "Because she believes her son could have killed Sir Giles."

It wasn't a question, but Kendra nodded. "She certainly has imagined the possibility. Otherwise she wouldn't have been so quick to give him an alibi."

"What do you think?" Alec asked Kendra.

"As I said, I'd like to keep an open mind. Holbrooke is everything Rebecca says—spoiled, arrogant. But I think he's smart. I'd like to interview him again without his mother around. Sometimes young men like him are a bit too smart for their own good."

Aldridge said, "Garroting is one thing, but painting the symbols on the body? And what was done with the tongue? I know we discussed this, but it is still difficult to imagine a child doing such a thing to their parent."

Kendra bit her lip, her mind conjuring up a picture of the savage serial killer Ed Kemper, who'd bludgeoned his mother to death before ripping out her voice box, which he then stuffed into the garbage disposal. Maybe Sir Giles's tongue carried the same sort of symbolism for Holbrooke.

Looking at her audience now, she decided to spare them the horror of Kemper's atrocities. She asked, "Did you learn anything from Silas Fitzpatrick?"

"He hated Sir Giles as well. For good reason," Alec said, and told them the story that Muldoon had uncovered about the murder of his little sister.

Rebecca let out a breath. "Oh, that poor girl. Sir Giles may not have been responsible for her death directly, but his actions were deplorable."

Kendra looked at Alec and Sam. "Did he have an alibi for the night of the murder?"

Sam opened his mouth, then looked at Rebecca. "Ah, well . . . he said he was occupied."

Rebecca's eyes sparked. "I assume you mean he was with a Bird of Paradise. I am not a child, Mr. Kelly. I insist that you stop treating me like one!"

"Pardon me, milady," he mumbled.

Good for you, Kendra wanted to tell Rebecca. But she needed to focus. "You don't believe Fitzpatrick?"

"I can't say, but Mr. Fitzpatrick seems like a slippery fellow. I've got me men talkin' ter the businesses around the Liber. Maybe someone saw somethin'."

"Good idea. Can you spare a few men to talk to the businesses around Larson & Son Apothecary, and the Holbrooke residence? See if the neighbors noticed anything unusual in the last month."

"Like what?" asked Sam.

"I have no idea," she admitted.

The Duke pushed himself to his feet, looking troubled. "I have the same problems with Mr. Fitzpatrick as I do with Mr. Holbrooke. The garroting is the only part of the murder that makes sense, as ghastly as that sounds. Why would he cut out the tongue, paint the symbols on the body?"

"Both acts are about symbolism," said Kendra. "He could have cut out the tongue of the man who ordered his sister's murderer be set free. The crosses are maybe a Catholic thing. It's a theory.

"The same theory goes for the Larsons," she added. "We visited Larson & Son's to speak with Bertel Larson. He wasn't there, but his son was. David."

The Duke settled behind his desk. "And?"

"My impression is that David holds a lot of bitterness for Sir Giles for his role in persuading Evert to become an intelligence agent." Kendra thought of the anger and despair that she'd glimpsed on David's face. "We did learn something odd," she said. "Bertel Larson stopped coming into the shop about a month ago."

"He is ill," Rebecca clarified.

Kendra looked at her. "Maybe."

"A month . . ." Sam's eyes went to the timeline on the slate board. "Around the same time Sir Giles began acting in a peculiar manner. That's mighty suspicious."

"I agree. Mr. Larson—the Elder—needs to be interviewed. David didn't have an alibi for the night of the murder. It will be interesting to see if his father has one."

The Duke said, "You and I shall call upon Mr. Larson tomorrow."

"It's not a social call," Kendra warned.

"Meaning you wish to call in the morning?" guessed Aldridge.

"I'd rather not waste time." She hesitated. "Speaking of which . . . we ran into Lady St. James at Larson & Son. She said the Smyth-Hopes are having a ball tonight."

Alec raised his eyebrows. "*You* aren't angling for an invitation, are you?"

"Lady St. James believes Lord Cross will be there."

"Ah." He nodded. "Now your sudden desire to socialize becomes clear."

Kendra smiled. Social events were not the best places to conduct interviews, but she had learned to make do.

Sam was still staring at the slate board. "Do you think there's any significance between Lord Cross's name and the symbols drawn on Sir Giles?"

The Duke drew in a sharp breath. "My God, I hadn't even considered that." He met Kendra's gaze. "But you have."

"I have," Kendra admitted. "It would be a pretty bold statement to actually sign your name to a murder victim. I'm reserving judgment until I meet him."

"It was written in invisible ink," Rebecca spoke up. "Mayhap he never meant it to be discovered."

"Possibly," Kendra said.

The Duke stood. "I shall speak to Caro. She is the one who has been sorting through the invitations. I imagine the Smyth-Hope fete is in there, but, if it is not, I don't think it will be too difficult to procure an invitation."

Kendra had to smile. Being associated with someone as powerful as the Duke of Aldridge had its perks. As unlucky as her involuntary time travel experience had been, she'd been fortunate to end up here. God only knew what would have happened to her otherwise.

"I must go home." Rebecca jumped to her feet. "I'm certain I can persuade Mama to attend the Smyth-Hope ball as well, but if they have other plans, would it be ill-mannered of me to foist my presence on your party tonight, Your Grace?"

"I would be cast down if you did not, my dear," he said, smiling at his goddaughter with his pale eyes twinkling. "I shall escort you to the door, and have Harding order the carriage brought around."

"I must be off as well," Sam said, rising.

Kendra and Alec watched them leave, and whether it was by design or not, the Duke closed the door, allowing them the privacy that most unmarried ladies did not receive in the presence of an eligible bachelor. A protection that Kendra knew cut both ways—saving the maid from being ravaged and saving the man from being forced into an unwanted marriage.

She and Alec weren't in need of such protections, since she didn't mind being ravaged by Alec, and he would love it if she forced him into marriage.

"What's so amusing?" he asked as he advanced to where she stood before the slate board.

"I was just thinking of the rules," she said with a smile, and then caught her breath when he ran a caressing hand down her arm. Beneath her sleeve, her skin tingled with the warmth of his palm. God, would she ever get used to it?

Her smile widened, and she slid her hands up his chest to loop around his neck. "Let's break some rules."

Alec gave a husky laugh as his arms encircled her, drawing her into a tight embrace. Her blood surged in a way that never failed to amaze her. She tipped her head back so she could gaze into the green eyes, the gold flecks flaring.

"Last time we were alone, we managed to do quite a bit in five minutes, if I recall," he murmured softly.

"Yeah, I seem to recall that as well. Let's try to break that record."

22

Aldridge had seen Rebecca off in his carriage and was about to seek out his sister regarding the Smyth-Hope affair. He couldn't imagine that she'd voice any objection. Caro enjoyed scolding him about doing his duty as the Duke of Aldridge, which meant putting in the occasional appearance at society's many soirees.

"Your Grace."

The Duke paused, one foot on the bottom step, and turned at Harding's quiet approach. He lifted an eyebrow in inquiry as he searched his butler's carefully composed face. "Yes?"

"There is a young . . . person at the back entrance. He is requesting to speak to Miss Donovan. I believe he is the same child who was here during last year's distressing upheaval."

"Ah, yes. Snake."

"Unfortunately, that is his name."

Aldridge's lips twitched, but he quickly suppressed his amusement. "Show him up to the study."

Like most majordomos, Harding took great pride in maintaining an impassive expression in all circumstances. But the idea of bringing a street urchin through the Duke's mansion to the study made the butler's nostrils flare in horror. "But, *sir*. Are you absolutely certain? Perhaps Miss Donovan would meet him in the kitchens? Or better yet, the stables?"

"I'm afraid I must insist on the study. Why don't you bring him here, and I shall escort the boy the rest of the way."

Harding's lips parted in shock, but he immediately firmed them as he grappled with his dignity. "As you wish, sir," he finally said, with utmost formality, and retreated.

It took a few minutes, but Harding returned, marching the boy ahead of him. Somehow, he managed to do it without actually touching Snake. Aldridge couldn't blame him. The child was utterly filthy, from the top of the shapeless brown wool cap he had squashed on his head to the knit scarf he'd wound around his neck, his brown coat—so threadbare that Aldridge could see his jacket and smock beneath—his patched pantaloons, and boots. Snake's eyes darted around the entrance hall, and Aldridge caught the crafty gleam in his gaze.

"Good evening, Snake," he greeted the boy, and frowned as he examined the small face. The child seemed much thinner than their last encounter.

"Gov'ner." Snake shot him a cheeky grin.

At least his bold attitude was the same, the Duke thought, suppressing a smile. He glanced at his butler, who stood nearby like a disapproving sentry. "Have Cook put together another tray of roast beef, ham, cheese, and bread to send up." He noticed Snake's eyes light up. "And a glass of milk."

The boy grimaced, appalled. "Oi don't want no cow's juice!"

Harding scowled at him. "You'd best mind your tongue around your betters, boy."

Unfazed by the reprimand, Snake shot the butler an impudent smirk.

"Come along." Aldridge turned to the stairs. He glanced at the urchin as they began to climb the steps. "By the by, what is your name?"

"Snake."

"I am referring to your Christian name." He already knew that Snake was a derivative of "little snakesman," an appellation given to criminals—mostly children—who were small enough to crawl through tight spaces into houses, where they would then unlock doors to allow entry for the adult housebreaker.

"Oh." Snake frowned. "Oi don't rightly remember. Me ma was shipped off ter Botany Bay after she was caught filching a loaf of bread. Oi was jest in little breeches." The boy's gaze ogled the paintings and vases as they rounded the top of the stairs. "Me sister 'ired me off ter Bear, and that's where Oi learnt ter be a little snakesman."

"Your sister?"

"Aye. Didn't want me under 'er feet when she was doin' 'er business."

The Duke's lips tightened. He had a pretty good idea what kind of business Snake's sister had been involved in. "What about your father?"

"Ack!" Snake snort was dismissive. "Jack Ketch got 'im even before me ma was transported."

Aldridge said nothing, but he knew that Snake's story was typical. England's harsh legal system had made orphans out of thousands of children just like Snake. Even though he preferred the country to town life and had no interest in politics, he had signed countless petitions to change the laws. Nothing, however, ever seemed to get done.

Snake looked up at him. "Bear says the gentry mort—Miss Donovan—is wantin' ter see me on account of that cove cocking up 'is toes."

"That's correct." The Duke put his hand on the boy's bony shoulder to steer him to the door of the study. He made a show of rattling the knob longer than usual before he pushed open the door, and pretended not to see the way Kendra and Alec broke away from each other. "We have a visitor," he announced.

Kendra's rosier than normal lips broke into a genuine smile as she hurried forward. "Snake!" Her gaze assessed the boy carefully. The Duke thought Kendra's brown eyes, already as dark as onyx, darkened even more with concern. "You've grown," she finally said.

"Aye." He grinned back at her. He'd been involved in kidnapping her, but the Duke suspected Kendra had earned the scamp's respect when she'd bloodied another lady's nose.

He said, "I've ordered a tray prepared. Snake could probably grow a little more."

Snake's features twisted in obvious horror. "Oi'm almost ter big now ter do me job."

Kendra frowned. "Why don't you sit down. Do you know why I wanted to talk to you?"

They moved to the table, and were settling into the chairs when the door opened again, and a maid arrived with the lunch tray. Snake's eyes went round as he stared at the plate filled with food. As soon as the maid set the tray down, he reached for the thickly sliced bread, but then he snatched his hand back at the last minute, looking at the Duke.

"Go on," the Duke urged. "You must be hungry."

"Gor! Oi'm gutfoundered." Having been given permission, Snake didn't waste time, tearing apart the bread, buttering it, and stuffing it into his mouth, before he eagerly moved on to the meat and cheese. His gaze fixed on Kendra. "Ye want ter ask about that buff mort in the church," he said with his mouth full.

"Yes," Kendra said. "I know that the watchman was chasing you. He said that when he got to the church, he didn't see anything. But you were ahead of him. Did you see anything?"

A sly look came into the child's face. "Well, Oi'm gonna 'ave ter think on it."

"Will a shilling jog your memory?" Kendra asked drily.

Snake's cheeks looked like a greedy chipmunk, but he managed to grin anyway. "Aye, that might 'elp."

"I don't have my purse on me—"

"Here." Alec dug inside his jacket, producing a coin. As soon as he put it on the table, Snake snatched it up with his grimy hand and shoved it into his coat pocket.

"Um, well . . ." He chewed. Before he even swallowed, he was shoveling more food into his mouth, as though he feared it would be taken away. "Let me think . . ."

"If you didn't see anything, I don't want you to make up something," Kendra warned. "Lying would be more detrimental to the investigation than saying nothing. You can keep the coin regardless."

Something that might have been relief flickered across the boy's face. "Aye, then. Oi didn't see nobody. Jest the nib."

Alec regarded the boy curiously. "Did you recognize Sir Giles?"

"Nay," Snake mumbled around the food in his mouth. "Never laid me peepers on 'im before."

Alec asked, "How did you know he was a gentleman?"

"'Cause 'e was clean, weren't 'e? 'E 'ad a soft look about 'im, even with 'is tongue bein' cut outta 'is 'ead."

Aldridge was surprised. "That's very observant of you, Snake."

The boy shrugged. "Oi got me peepers; Oi use them."

And he's probably counted every valuable in the hallway and this room with those peepers, Aldridge thought wryly.

"Besides," the boy went on, "Ye ain't gonna find common folk in Trevelyan Square these days, it being 'aunted and all."

Kendra raised her eyebrows. "Haunted?"

"Why'd ye think Oi ran in there? Thought the bloody Charley wouldn't be followin' me."

Aldridge searched Kendra's face. "What, my dear?"

"Nothing really. Ruth Holbrooke asked me if I believed in ghosts."

"Why would she ask such a question?"

"I don't know." Kendra looked at Snake. "You weren't afraid when you ran into Trevelyan Square?"

An uneasy expression crossed Snake's face. "Well, it was still mornin'. And Oi didn't plan on stayin', jest reckoned Oi'd slide on through."

Kendra frowned. "Why do people think Trevelyan Square is haunted?"

Snake finished polishing off the plate. "Oi ain't exactly sure w'ot 'appened. Couple of years ago, folks began leavin'. There were still some poor folk around, but 'eard tell they fled cause they'd seen a demon. No one goes there now."

"Some people still go there," said Kendra. "We ran into an old woman."

"Bah! That's old Annie, Oi reckon." He tapped his temple. "She be dicked in the knob. Normal folk don't go there."

"Unless they're running from the law," murmured Kendra.

Snake grinned at her and pulled out a small silver flask from his inside coat pocket.

Kendra snatched the flask away. "Uh-uh."

"Oy!"

She pushed the glass of milk toward him. "You are not drinking whiskey at the table. You will drink your milk, or I will pour it down your throat."

The Duke had to suppress a laugh as he watched the battle of wills play out between the American and the thief. He wasn't altogether sure who'd win until Snake capitulated, his small face twisting in a grimace, and picked up the glass of milk, loudly slurping it down.

"What are you going to do when you get too big for your job, Snake?" Kendra asked.

Snake's naturally impertinent expression faded, and he jerked his thin shoulders in a quick shrug. "Oi reckon Bear'll find me somethin' else ter do." His gaze fell on his empty plate for a long moment, then he shoved himself to his feet. He jutted out his chin as he regarded them. "Oi 'ave ter go. Can Oi 'ave me drink back?"

Kendra said nothing, her gaze pensive as she studied the boy. Snake shuffled his feet, clearly uneasy under the intense regard.

"What would you do if someone offered you a job, Snake?" she asked. "A legitimate job."

"W'ot kinda job?" Snake asked suspiciously.

"I don't know. Stable hand, maybe. Your Grace?"

Aldridge was rendered speechless when Kendra shot him a pleading look. He thought of the reaction his head groom, Hadley, would have if he were asked to take charge of the young criminal. And Caro . . . good God. It was probably best not to think of his sister. He said slowly, "Well, I imagine we ought to be able to find the boy a position at Aldridge Castle, or one of my other estates."

Snake's mouth pulled down. "Leave London Town?"

He shifted his gaze to the urchin. "Perhaps." *Most definitely.* "And there will be standards that you shall be required to obey."

The boy eyed him narrowly. "W'ot sort of standards?"

"Cleanliness," Aldridge stated firmly. "You'd have to bathe on a regular basis. At least once or twice a week." In fact, Aldridge wondered if he should douse himself in whiskey to rid himself of any of the invisible insects that the boy was most likely carrying.

"Gor!"

Aldridge continued, "No more thievery and criminal activities."

"Bloody 'ell!"

"And no cursing—at least not in a lady's presence," Aldridge said, although he didn't need Alec's quick grin to recognize how absurd that stipulation was, given the fact that the only lady present had a tendency to swear in a most unladylike manner.

The boy stared at him, aghast. "Are ye Quakers?"

Aldridge had to smile. "No. Why don't you take some time to consider my proposal?"

Snake chewed on his lower lip, his gaze flicking to his empty plate. "Aye, gov'ner . . . Oi'm gonna 'ave ter think on it. Oi gotta go."

"I must take my leave, as well," Alec drawled, and there was a glint of amusement in his green eyes. "I shall escort you to the door, Snake. Good evening, Duke, Miss Donovan."

Aldridge suspected his nephew was ushering the boy out of the house to make sure the silver candlesticks didn't go missing.

Alec paused at the door, his gaze traveling back to Kendra. "You are much more kind-hearted and generous than you let on, Miss Donovan."

After they left, Kendra looked to the Duke. "Yeah, I'm being kind and generous with your money and food, Your Grace. I'm sorry. I don't know what came over me."

"Do not fret, my dear. My purse can afford it."

She shook her head, then pinched the bridge of her nose, clearly frustrated. "That's not the point! Christ."

He wondered if should remind her of the rule of no cursing, but decided she looked too upset to tease her.

"It was impulsive," she continued, dropping her hands. "I am *not* impulsive. And this is the second time I've done this."

Aldridge knew Kendra was referring to Flora, an abused farm wife that she'd rescued in Yorkshire, and who was now assisting the cook in his skeletal staff at Monksgrey, his Lancashire estate.

"Bloody hell, maybe I *am* turning into a Quaker," she muttered.

Now he laughed. "I don't think so." *Not with that sailor's mouth.* "I think you are aware that soon Snake will outgrow the position that he holds in Bear's criminal organization. And when that happens, either

Bear will cut the child loose or he will train him to do something far worse than housebreaking." He laid a comforting hand on her shoulder, searching her troubled expression. "Why are you so upset that you were being kind, my dear?"

She said nothing for a long moment, then sighed heavily. "I can't explain it without sounding stupid. Doing things out of character . . . I feel like I'm losing myself, like I don't know who I am anymore. Who I'm becoming. And it's not fair to you. I'm not providing Snake with a job—you are. I'm not being generous. I'm forcing *you* to be generous."

"You worry too much. I might not be able to take in all of London's homeless, but I ought to be able to take in one small boy, my dear." He gave her shoulder a squeeze. "Of course, if Snake accepts our largesse, I think we ought to send him to Aldridge Castle, or somewhere else far away from his current associates."

She was still frowning, but nodded. "You're right. Thank you, Your Grace. I suppose I need to get ready for tonight." She crossed the room, hesitating when she reached the door. She glanced back at him. "I really don't know why I interfered. Next time I do, maybe you should hit me over the head with a rock or something."

"I don't believe we need to resort to violence," he chuckled.

"If I can't control my suddenly quixotic impulses, you may have to buy another estate to house all the new servants I find on the streets."

He lifted his eyebrows. "I hadn't thought of that. Maybe I do need to find a rock, after all."

This time, Kendra was the one who laughed.

He smiled as he watched her leave. Then he walked to his desk to retrieve his pipe. He went through the ritual of filling the bowl with tobacco, tamping it down, and lighting it with a stick he set on fire from the blaze in the hearth. Sinking down into his chair behind his desk, he puffed gently on the stem as he contemplated what had happened.

When Kendra had first arrived from the future—and, by God, he still marveled at that—she'd been careful to keep herself detached from this world. Oh, she'd participated in murder investigations, and he knew that she had formed attachments. Deliberately, he shut his mind to the one she'd formed with his nephew. Society would change, he now knew, but he was a part of *this* society. Was it wrong for him to wish his nephew and ward would seek their pleasures in the marital bed?

He leaned back in his chair, his gaze on the curling gray smoke as he thought about how skittish Kendra had always seemed about becoming more involved with life around her. She'd talked about butterflies flapping their wings in one part of the world, causing hurricanes in another part of the world, or some such nonsense.

Something had changed in Yorkshire, though. For the first time, Kendra had moved beyond her position as an observer. She'd become actively engaged when she'd helped Flora.

And now here was Snake.

He smiled slowly. It was a slow process, but his world was becoming Kendra's world.

She just didn't know it yet.

23

Lady St. James had been right in her prediction; the Smyth-Hope ball was indeed a crush. The Beau Monde was packed so tightly inside the Belgrave Square mansion that Kendra was certain a few of the guests would be sporting bruised ribs and smashed toes the next morning. Lady Atwood, who'd accompanied the Duke, Alec, and Kendra, took one look at the crowded entrance hall and declared Lady Smyth-Hope an unqualified success as a hostess.

As they joined the humanity surging toward the grand staircase, Lady Atwood glanced over at Kendra. "Remember, Miss Donovan, you must not dance with the same gentleman more than twice this evening."

"I don't plan to dance at all. I'm here to find Lord Cross."

"I hope the waltz has infiltrated the Smyth-Hope ballroom," Alec murmured, his mouth curving into a small smile. There was enough heat in his green eyes to ignite warmth in Kendra's belly.

Lady Atwood sniffed. "Let us hope that scandalous thing has not reached so far into decent society.

"If you *do* dance, you must remember to have more than one partner, Miss Donovan," Lady Atwood continued with a hiss. Unfurling the ivory fan dangling from her wrist, she used it to combat the oppressive heat in the hall. "You cannot dance only with Sutcliffe. Do you understand? You do not want to make it look as though he were singling you out for his attention."

Kendra wondered why the condemnation should fall on her if Alec was the one singling her out.

"However," Lady Atwood went on with dogged determination, "if you refuse one gentleman, you must refuse *all* the gentlemen who request a dance. It would be bad ton to deny one gentleman and dance with another."

Crap. Kendra hated the rules in this era. She had a nearly eidetic memory and yet even she had trouble remembering the rules that were countless, many contradictory and often idiotic.

"Why don't I turn down Sutcliffe now, so I can avoid dancing altogether?"

Lady Atwood's lips compressed into a thin line of disapproval. "That is not amusing, Miss Donovan."

Kendra wondered if she should admit that she hadn't been joking when the Duke intervened. "Miss Donovan shall be perfectly fine, Caro," he said, and shot Kendra a grin. "She has been in . . . England long enough to understand these matters."

"This is *serious*, Aldridge," Lady Atwood whispered, and pinned Kendra with her gaze. "Your manners shall be under observation. Do *not* embarrass yourself or the Aldridge good name."

"Yes, ma'am." Kendra had to curl her hands into fists to stop herself from saluting.

Lady Atwood narrowed her eyes, obviously trying to figure out if there was sarcasm in her quick agreement.

"Come, Caro." The Duke cupped his sister's elbow and tugged her forward. They'd reached the bottom of the grand staircase, where only two people at a time could ascend. Kendra had the whimsical thought that they were all a little like exotic animals climbing the steps of Noah's Ark.

Alec caught her gloved hand and brought it around the crook of his arm. He leaned toward her to murmur against her ear. "Have I told you that you look beautiful this evening, Miss Donovan?"

Her gown was a sheer, shell-pink gauze over a cream satin under slip, with long-sleeves and a square neckline that was dangerously low. Tiny rosettes and seed pearls were scattered across the high bodice, catching the candlelight, while the skirt seemed to froth around her ankles with each step. While there were many days when Kendra desperately longed for the easy stride of Levi's jeans, the comfort of a cotton T-shirt and knit cardigan, or even the cotton and spandex blend of trousers and a blazer, tonight she did feel elegant in her long white kid gloves, with her dark hair pulled up high in an elaborate bouffant that Molly had decorated with a netting of pearls.

"Thank you," she murmured, and her lips curved in a slow smile as she gave Alec a provocative look from beneath her lashes. "You don't look so bad yourself, my lord."

Actually, that was an understatement. Alec looked drop-dead gorgeous in his dark blue evening coat, layered over a silver-embroidered waistcoat, and cream breeches. His valet had done his snowy white cravat in a style with folds and knots that would have looked fussy and effeminate on anybody except Alec, she decided.

At her comment, Alec's green eyes widened in a brief moment of surprise, and then he huffed out a laugh. His aunt craned her head around to frown down at him. Kendra half expected Lady Atwood to reprimand her, *And you must not make a gentleman laugh*.

Lord and Lady Smyth-Hope stood outside the door to their ballroom, regal sentries greeting their guests. Kendra murmured something polite and innocuous when they were introduced, aware that she was inspected thoroughly by both of her hosts. Then she and Alec surged through the tall double doors, into the ballroom where—thank God—they had more breathing room.

The ballroom had ice-blue silk walls decorated with gilt-framed paintings and mirrors. Two enormous diamond drop chandeliers were blazing with candles, their light reflected back in the glittering jewels that adorned a few gloveless fingers, encircled throats, and dangled from ears. An orchestra, tucked near the French doors, was already playing a Scottish reel for those on the dance floor. On the sidelines, a group of matrons were seated together, gossiping from behind fans, their eagle eyes observing the dancers as well as the single girls stuck on the sidelines and couples who strolled the outer perimeter of the dance floor.

The familiar odor of beeswax from the candles wafted across the ball-room, mingling with the heavier perfumes and colognes of the guests. As the evening wore on, Kendra knew from past experience, the floral and musky scent would become even more overpowering, with ladies making trips to the withdrawing rooms to douse themselves with perfume to combat the stench of sweat. Kendra only hoped that Lady Smyth-Hope would be smart enough to open a window.

Lady St. James, puce evening gown billowing with her trademark ruffles, barreled toward them. She was accompanied by a young gen-tleman, probably no more than twenty-five, with an affable, unremark-able face framed by golden curls already going limp in the heat of the ballroom. Kendra's gaze skated over his elaborate cravat and decided that she'd been right. Alec could carry it off without being fussy; this man could not.

"Good evening, Your Grace, and my dear Lady Atwood!" Lady St. James gave a quick curtsy. Rising, she said, "Miss Donovan, Lord Sut-cliffe. I am so *pleased* that you came. May I introduce Mr. Humphrey." She turned a sly smile on Kendra as the young man executed a perfect bow. "Mr. Humphrey is the son of Lord Colter. He was *most* interested in making your acquaintance, Miss Donovan."

Before Kendra could wonder about that, the man offered her a shy smile and said, "I would be most honored if you would dance the next set with me, Miss Donovan."

Kendra could feel her lips part in surprise. "What?"

"Of course, Miss Donovan would be delighted to dance with you, Mr. Humphrey," Lady Atwood accepted in a rush, even as she threw a steely look in Kendra's direction, as though daring her to contradict her. "Aren't you delighted, Miss Donovan?"

Hell. But Kendra managed to summon a smile. "Of course. Thank you, sir." She shifted her gaze to Lady St. James, and asked, "Have you seen Lord Cross?"

The other woman's smile broadened. "Yes, he's in attendance. Although I don't know where he is at the moment."

Kendra was thinking about grabbing Alec and doing a room by room search, but it was too late. The music that the orchestra had been playing died away, finishing the current dance set, and the smiling Mr. Humphrey stepped forward to offer his arm. She tried not to scowl when he led her out onto the floor in one of the popular longways. Two rows formed, segregated by sex, dance partners facing each other. For a moment, Kendra was glad that she wore gloves because she could feel her palms dampen as the orchestra struck up a new melody. The men bowed, and she joined the women in curtsying. Then they were gliding toward each other, and her memory of the dance lessons that she'd endured over Christmas kicked in. Slowly, she relaxed.

She looked at Mr. Humphrey as they clasped hands and moved in a circle. She asked, "Did you hear about what happened to Sir Giles?"

He blinked, startled. Murder probably wasn't the normal topic of conversation on the dance floor. But, damn it, if she had to dance, she didn't think it was unreasonable for her to utilize her time. Two birds, one stone.

"Yes," Mr. Humphrey said after he'd recovered. He pursed his lips together in a way that conveyed sympathy and horror. "A terrible tragedy."

"Did you ever meet him?"

"No, I never made the man's acquaintance. However, I am familiar with his son, Gerard. We attended Eton together."

Kendra wasn't really surprised. The so-called Polite Society sent their male offspring to many of the same schools to be shaped and molded like wet clay to one day lead the British Empire. She asked, "Were you friends?"

"Not friends, no."

"What's your impression of him?"

Before he could answer, though, the steps of the dance changed, forcing them to separate. Impatiently, Kendra waited until she circled back to him again. It took a moment to get into their rhythm. She was about to repeat the question when he said, "Holbrooke was a year ahead of me, but I found him to be a likeable enough fellow, I suppose. As long as one didn't get in his way."

"Did you get in his way?"

"There was a time or two." Mr. Humphrey's lips twisted into a wry smile. "Let's just say he could make life unpleasant if he were vexed enough by you. But we were children. Thirteen is a difficult age for boys.

I have two older brothers, and they relished torturing me and my two sisters when we were children."

She kept her gaze on his. "You're saying that you think he's changed?"

Again, she had to wait for his answer when the dance broke them apart. "We travel in the same circles, but we are not friends," he finally said, then laughed. "I must say, Miss Donovan, this is not the conversation I imagined when I asked you to dance. You are a most unusual woman."

Kendra tried not to wince. He hadn't said it with any censure or mockery, and his affable expression remained. "What conversation did you imagine?"

"Oh, the typical. Lady St. James said you are an American, so naturally I would inquire about your home there, and your journey to England. I would ask you of your opinion of England, and if you have enjoyed your stay." He smiled at her. "This is much more interesting. Less . . . rehearsed."

She returned his smile. "Well, then . . . what do you know about Lord Cross?"

His eyes flickered. "Not very much. We went to school together as well, but he was also a year ahead of me."

"Were he and Holbrooke friends?" she asked before they parted.

"I don't recall that they were especially close," he said when they were back together, clasping hands and strolling forward. "That's not to say that they were not, only that I had not noticed. I ran with a different set."

"What about David and Evert Larson?"

He laughed. "Are you going to ask me about everyone I went to school with at Eton?"

"I'll finish with them." She smiled at him, and was a little surprised that it was a genuine smile, not for politeness's sake.

"I remember David as being a serious student, and Evert . . . even though he has no pedigree, most of the boys hero-worshiped him. But I can't say I was friends with either of them. Different groups. Different interests. I must say, I haven't really thought about them in years. Don't know where they are."

The music was changing, coming to an end. "David is helping his father with his apothecary shop," Kendra said.

"Ah, that's right. I remembered he was a merchant of some kind."

"Evert died in the war."

Shock crossed Humphrey's face, followed by sorrow. "Ah, there's a pity." They drew to a halt when music ended. He bowed, and she curtseyed.

"I didn't mean to finish on such a depressing note," she apologized as he led her back to where Alec, Lady Atwood, and the Duke waited.

"Not at all. You are a refreshing change to the insipid debutantes. In fact, now I am depressed, knowing all other dance partners will pale in comparison." He took her hand, and bowed over it, his gaze on hers. "I hope I may see you again soon, Miss Donovan."

"I don't see why not."

He grinned, then left her.

"You did *quite* well, Miss Donovan." Lady Atwood practically beamed at her.

Kendra thought about saying something snide, but decided it wasn't worth it. She'd rather have the countess happy with her.

"You seem to be in a congenial mood." Alec eyed her closely, unsmiling. "Was Mr. Humphrey to your liking as a dance partner?"

"Actually, he was nice." *And informative*, she thought, but didn't reveal that before Lady Atwood. "It wasn't as bad as I thought."

"Mayhap I need to request your hand for the next dance before you are too occupied with your new beaux."

There was an edge in Alec's voice. She glanced at him in surprise. "I rather think Mr. Humphrey will be the last man to ask me to dance tonight," she said. "Except for you and the Duke, of course."

She was wrong. Much to Kendra's utter shock, other men asked to be introduced to her, and she found herself dancing three more sets consecutively. Unfortunately, her partners were much less agreeable than Mr. Humphrey. The first dance was with a portly man, whose face was nearly scarlet from his exertions, making Kendra afraid that she'd be forced to do CPR on him by the end of the dance. The second was a middle-aged lord whose gaze seemed transfixed by her bosom. The last dance was with Mr. Allen, who couldn't quite hide the glint of avarice in his eyes as he quizzed her about her connection to the Duke of Aldridge.

While she was fielding those questions, Kendra allowed her gaze to drift around the room. She wondered if Lord Cross was among the crowd. Across the ballroom, she noticed Rebecca and her parents had arrived, with Rebecca and her mother joining Lady Atwood and Lady St. James's social circle while Lord Blackburn moved off to where Alec and the Duke were conversing with several gentlemen.

By the time Mr. Allen brought her back to Lady Atwood, who, along with the Duke, was her chaperone for the evening, the Duke was leading Rebecca out onto the dance floor. Kendra grabbed Alec's arm before anyone else came up to her.

He lifted an eyebrow in inquiry. "Do you wish to dance?"

"God, no! How do we find Lord Cross?"

Alec turned to his aunt. "Miss Donovan is famished. I'm escorting her to the refreshment room."

"I should never have learned to dance," Kendra muttered as they moved into the hallway.

Alec gave her a strange look. "You are not thrilled by your success? You have been declared a diamond of the first water. London beaux will soon come calling."

She searched his face. "Are you angry?"

Alec said nothing, but his jaw tightened.

"You saying that beaux will be calling is probably the scariest thing you've ever said to me."

He gave a reluctant laugh. "Most women would be thrilled with your success," he said, steering her around a knot of young men in the hallway. "You know, there is one way you could stop the young bucks from competing for your favors."

"How?"

He leaned close to whisper in her ear. "Marry me."

"Okay, *that* is the scariest thing you've ever said to me." She saw his features tighten in anger and frustration, and knew she'd made a mistake. "I was *joking*."

He said nothing.

She sighed. Marriage was the one topic that she and Alec would never agree on. "I've wasted too much time dancing, and all I was able to learn is that Gerard Holbrooke was a bully," she muttered.

He cut her a sidelong glance, frowning. "How did you learn that, pray tell?"

"Mr. Humphrey went to school with him. Eton."

"Good God." Alec jerked his head around to stare at her. "Never say that you quizzed Mr. Humphrey about Sir Giles's murder on the dance floor."

"I didn't know what else to talk to him about."

He laughed, and Kendra sensed his annoyance with her was over. He said, "I'm not certain that Gerard Holbrooke's unappealing character is a new revelation."

"No, but it confirms the picture that's building." Kendra glanced around in surprise when she realized that Alec had maneuvered her into the card room. "I thought we were getting refreshments."

"And I thought you wanted to speak to Lord Cross." Alec grabbed two champagne flutes from a silver tray carried by a passing footman.

The Smyth-Hopes had transformed one of their drawing rooms into a card room, with at least a half-dozen green baize tables. Both gentlemen and ladies were playing games of hazard, baccarat, and whist. Kendra was sure the games were meant to be entertaining, the wagers small, but there were a few tables where the participants appeared tense, their laughter carrying a razor-sharp edge.

"The gentleman with the unfortunate whiskers is Lord Cross," Alec murmured as he handed her a flute.

Kendra's gaze drifted over the faces as she sipped the champagne, until she found the man in question. Alec was right about his facial hair being an unfortunate choice. Cross looked to be in his mid-twenties with a thin, pallid face and light brown hair that had been curled and carefully arranged. The side whiskers flared out, too bushy for his narrow face. His nose was long and thin, his pale blue eyes small. Kendra thought that he had the look of a ferret. Of course, that could have been the side whiskers.

"Now what?" Kendra asked.

"Now we wait."

It took twenty minutes before Lord Cross finally shoved back his chair and declared that he was done. Alec and Kendra intercepted him as he stalked out of the card room.

"Lord Cross? A moment of your time?" Alec smiled at the younger man. "I am Sutcliffe—Alexander Morgan, the Marquis of Sutcliffe. This is Miss Donovan, the Duke of Aldridge's ward."

Recognition flickered in his small eyes. His face tightened, telling Kendra that he probably would have come up with an excuse to get away from them, if he could. "My lord, Miss Donovan," he acknowledged with an abbreviated bow. "I am at your service."

"Walk with us," Alec directed, and, taking Kendra's arm, began to move in the direction of a withdrawing room, forcing Lord Cross to fall into step beside them. "You may be aware that my uncle is looking into the death of Sir Giles."

Cross's mouth knotted with tension. "That is a peculiar pastime for a duke. Unless you are referring to another uncle?"

"No, he is the one. We are assisting him in the investigation."

"What has any of this to do with me? I did not know Sir Giles."

Kendra kept her gaze steady on him as they came to a halt in an alcove across from the card room. "Really? You had dinner with Sir Giles on Wednesday night—the night of his murder," she said bluntly, watching the emotions flit across his narrow face. Fear. Panic. "Odd for you to do if you didn't even know him."

Cross adopted an outraged expression. "You are being deliberately provocative, Miss Donovan. I meant I did not know him as a close connection. And I did not have dinner with him. I joined him at his table for a moment. That is all."

"Why did you join him at his table at all? What did you have to say to this man who was not a close connection?"

"I don't recall. It was a trifling subject."

"What is it? You don't recall or it was a trifling subject?" Kendra pressed.

He frowned at her. "A trifling subject."

She said coolly, "What would you say if I told you witnesses have reported that you and Sir Giles were involved in a heated discussion? One might even call it an argument."

His bushy side whiskers quivered. "I can't imagine who could have said such a thing."

Alec raised an eyebrow at the man. "As the last person to have seen Sir Giles alive, I would think you would want to help us in our investigation, my lord, lest you give the impression that you have something to hide."

Cross blinked four times in rapid succession. "I have *nothing* to hide."

"Then you shouldn't have a problem telling us why you sought Sir Giles out at his club to speak with him," Kendra said, and watched Cross gaze at the doorway to the card room, probably regretting ever having left the table.

He exhaled. "It was a private discussion. He outbid me on a horse that I had my eye on, if you must know."

"Your argument was over a horse?" Kendra didn't bother to hide her skepticism.

Cross nodded quickly. "I told you it was a trifling."

"Okay," Kendra allowed with a nod. "What horse? Where did you bid on it? I'll make sure I ask Lady Holbrooke about this horse that her husband purchased as well."

"And Sir Giles's man of affairs," Alec put in smoothly. "Unless you've finished with your Banbury Tales, and are ready to tell us what you really argued about with Sir Giles?"

Cross's narrow jaw clenched. "I have nothing to say on the matter."

"Was it about Spain?" It was a shot in the dark, but Kendra thought it was interesting to watch the horror flicker across his face.

"Spain?" he said faintly. "What does Spain have to do with anything?"

She said, "We know you were involved in the incident in Spain."

"*Involved*? What are you suggesting? I was held captive by the French for months." A shudder rippled over him. "It was a terrible time. A terrible time. I do not wish to remember it."

"That's understandable," she said. "Most of your regiment was killed, along with a young man. Evert Larson. Did you know him?"

Cross blinked. "No."

Alec spoke up. "That is curious. He was killed while rescuing you and another soldier."

"Of course, I know the name," he said quickly. "I only meant that I did not know Mr. Larson personally."

"Not even from Eton?" Kendra asked mildly.

"I did not associate with Mr. Larson at school. He is . . . was the son of a merchant."

Kendra changed subjects. "What happened in Spain? How was Evert killed?"

"What can that have to do with Sir Giles's murder?"

"It's come up, and we're following all leads." She eyed Cross. He looked like a man who badly wanted a drink, his upper lip dotted with sweat. "Where did you go once you left White's?"

"Lord Cross," someone hailed.

Kendra observed the relief that washed over the viscount's face before he faced the newcomer. She shifted her gaze to the stranger as well. He was tall and broad-shouldered, with russet hair and chiseled features. Good-looking, and confident with it, Kendra decided.

The man said to Cross, "I thought you only stepped out of the card room for a moment, my lord, but would be returning for another hand." He smiled, flashing even, white teeth. His eyes were dark gray, and despite the smile, curiously flat when he turned to look at Kendra and Alec. "Will you introduce me to your friends?"

"Certainly. Lord Sutcliffe, Miss Donovan, this is Captain Mobray. Captain Mobray, this is the Marquis of Sutcliffe, and Miss Donovan."

Alec said, "This is a fortuitous meeting. Miss Donovan and I were speaking to Lord Cross about Sir Giles's murder."

Mobray lifted one eyebrow in a languid movement that seemed practiced. "That hardly seems an appropriate conversation in such a frivolous setting as a ball, my lord."

"Perhaps . . ." But Alec shrugged in an equally lazy gesture to telegraph how little he cared about what was or was not appropriate. "I understand that you and Lord Cross served together during the Peninsular war."

"Yes." Mobray shot Cross a hard look. "My lord, I hope you were not regaling them with our war stories. 'Tis not fit for ladies' ears."

"My ears have heard a lot of stories," Kendra assured him, summoning a slight smile. "I don't necessarily believe everything I hear."

"Indeed," was all he said.

"Did you know Evert Larson?" Maybe if she hadn't been watching him so closely, she would have missed his slight hesitation.

"Yes, but only by reputation," Mobray said finally, reaching inside his breast pocket and fishing out a small, delicate porcelain container that Kendra recognized as a snuffbox. He flicked open the lid with his finger. "I know that I owe my life to him."

"How?"

Mobray glanced at Cross. "Did you not tell them?" He took a pinch of snuff from the container, dabbed it into his nostrils, and inhaled sharply. "Lord Cross and I were in a regiment that came under attack in the mountains of Spain. We were captured by the French. It was . . . not a pleasant time. Two of our men died from battle wounds immediately, and the French officers shot one for sport."

Cross drew in an unsteady breath, but he said nothing.

"Mr. Larson found us," Mobray continued. "He was in a nearby village, pretending to be a peddler, I think. He worked his way into our camp." His gray eyes darkened. "I don't know what happened exactly, but the French realized he was a spy, and he was captured." He snapped the snuffbox closed and tucked it back into his pocket.

"How long was he around before he was captured?"

"I'm not sure. Two days, perhaps."

Kendra looked at Cross. "Is your memory clearer?"

The viscount's mouth pinched. "He may have been in the camp for longer. I don't know. I barely recognized him. He'd darkened his hair and was quite unkempt."

Kendra nodded. There were regions in Spain with naturally blond citizens, but it made sense that Evert had disguised himself to blend in more fully with the majority of the Spanish population. She asked, "What happened next?"

"I think Mr. Larson attempted to escape, but, again, I cannot be certain. There was an explosion and a fire. In the confusion, Lord Cross and I managed to escape."

Alec's lips thinned. "You left your men behind."

For the first time, something hot glinted in Mobray's eyes—anger maybe. "It was too late for them, sir. Would you have us sacrifice ourselves for dead men?"

No one said anything.

Mobray smiled in a way that revealed his teeth to Alec. "As I said, my lord, it was not a pleasant time. And not a memory I care to revisit." He paused. "What does Spain have to do with Sir Giles's murder?"

Kendra ignored his question, asking instead, "Were you well acquainted with Sir Giles?"

"Yes. Not during the war, but after. I work in Whitehall, in the Home Office. I have never worked for Sir Giles directly, but he was a presence one couldn't ignore."

"Do you know why anyone would have a reason to kill him?"

He seemed to ponder that for a long moment, but finally released a sigh, shaking his head. "I can't imagine anyone doing such a thing, especially in the manner that it was done."

Kendra switched her attention back to Cross. "You never said where you went after White's, my lord."

"Didn't I?" Cross blinked. "I didn't have a particular destination. I wandered for a bit. There are other entertainments to be had in London. Then I went home."

"What time?"

"I don't know. Two, I think."

"Did anyone see you at those other entertainments? Someone who can verify your whereabouts?"

"Speak to Mr. Huntley—his father is Lord Winthrop. And, oh, there were countless men at—" Cross suddenly stopped, flushing. He glanced at Kendra, and she guessed he had visited a brothel, or some other sordid establishment not for a lady's ears.

"You'll need to say the name of the place, my lord. I won't faint," she promised drily.

He stiffened, glaring at her.

The captain laughed, though his eyes remained watchful. "If you met Huntley there, it's probably the Blue Boar. Isn't it?"

"Yes," Cross said reluctantly.

"There you go." Mobray smiled, and straightened. "As interesting as this discussion is, I must take my leave. There is more to London than the Smyth-Hope ball as well. Cross, will you join me?"

"What? Oh, yes. Good evening, my lord." He looked warily at Kendra. "Miss Donovan."

Kendra's gaze followed the men as they wove their way through the people loitering in the hallway. "Well, Mobray was right—it was an interesting discussion," Kendra murmured. Despite Cross's higher pedigree, she noticed that the captain seemed to exude the most confidence. His stride was long and easy, while Cross scurried to catch up.

"We need to have Sam check out the Blue Boar and Mr. Huntley, see if Cross was there and how it works with the timeline," she said. Realizing she was still holding the champagne flute, she lifted it and drank. "Overall, though, I thought Cross was a very bad liar."

"And Captain Mobray?"

She met Alec's gaze. "He's much better."

24

W hat did you tell them?"

Cross glanced uneasily at Mobray. The captain never raised his voice when he was in a fury. He lowered it, like the whisper of a blade before you found it embedded in your gut. He couldn't quite control his shudder as he met Mobray's flat gaze in the dim light of the carriage as it jolted down the street, the coachman maneuvering the vehicle in the evening's heavy traffic and winding streets.

"Nothing, I tell you." Cross swallowed against the hard lump of fear that had risen in this throat. "They are inquiring into Sir Giles's death."

"I'm aware of that. I read the *Morning Chronicle*. No names were given, but I was in town last year when the most interesting rumors came to light about the Duke of Aldridge and his ward investigating the death of Lady Dover."

"I recall the rumors," Cross said. "But I didn't give it any credence for a peer of the realm to be pursuing such matters. And a female. Who would believe it?"

"Miss Donovan is a bold piece of baggage," Mobray agreed as he took out his snuffbox.

"An American." Cross allowed his lip to curl. "If she is an example of womanhood in that dreadfully backward country, the men ought to gird their loins."

The captain dipped a finger into his snuffbox, added a pinch to each nostril, and inhaled. Cross regarded him somewhat enviously. He'd never been able to take snuff without a fit of sneezing.

"I agree, but I think it would be folly to underestimate the creature," Mobray said, returning the snuffbox to his inside pocket. "There was something about her pointed inquiries regarding Spain."

"She cannot know—"

"She would not know anything if you had stayed away from Sir Giles," Mobray snapped. Cross flinched. "I specifically recall telling you to stay away from him."

"But . . . I *had* to see him. He called upon me. He asked me about Spain." Cross pressed a finger near his right eye, which had begun twitching. "I-I had to make him see reason. Nothing can be changed of the past."

Mobray regarded him with contempt. "You sodding fool. What did you say to him?"

"Nothing. I swear!"

"Sir Giles called upon me, as well, but I had the situation well in hand."

Cross drew in a sharp breath as he stared at the man seated across from him. "My God—did you kill him?"

Mobray stared at his companion for a long moment. "Don't be absurd," he said finally.

Sweat broke out on Cross's palms, and he wished that he could believe the other man's denial. His mind drifted back to Spain. He'd been a coward, he knew. But Mobray . . . Mobray had been . . . *evil*. A chill raced down his arms.

Cross forced himself to laugh, aware that the captain was watching him with hooded eyes. "Of course, even if you had," he said, licking his suddenly dry lips, "it would be completely understandable. You are highly regarded in Whitehall, and in political circles." He was talking too much, but he couldn't seem to stop. "I have heard you may soon be sitting in the House of Commons."

Mobray said nothing, merely looked across the carriage at him. Tension prickled along Cross's spine, and he nearly sagged in relief when Mobray finally spoke.

"You are correct, my lord," the captain said slowly. "I have much to lose if what happened in Spain ever comes to light. But your position is equally tenuous, I believe. Soon you will be hunting for a wife from a respectable family. If your actions ever became known, the doors to Polite Society will close. Your shame would extend to your family." He paused, his gaze fixed on Cross. "I wonder, how would your father react to such a thing?"

Cross had to suppress another shiver. His father would give him no quarter, he knew. The only reason he'd been in Spain in the first place was because his older brother had been alive, and his father had bought him a commission. The earl had declared that no son of his would become an idle popinjay, pursuing the pleasures of Town.

Now he lifted a hand in supplication. "We are on the same side, Captain. I have no more desire to see the past come to light than you do." *But did you take action to stop that from happening?* he wondered. "We have no quarrel," he assured the other man.

Mobray fixed his gaze on him. Cross had the unsettling thought that he could see right into his skull. "Good," Mobray said, and leaned forward slightly to rap on the ceiling, signaling his coachman to pull aside. "I must beg your leave now."

Cross gaped at the other man, jerking forward to glance out the window. They'd pulled up on the curb near the Bath Hotel at Piccadilly. "You are leaving me on the street?"

"There are plenty of hackneys for you to hail in the area. I have other appointments that I must see to. And you . . . you need to relax, my lord. Go and find yourself a wench. You are much too tense."

Cross opened his mouth to deny it, then pressed his lips together. He *was* tense. He grasped the leather strap and hoisted himself up. The coachman had come around to open the door.

"And my lord?"

Cross paused to look back at Mobray. "Yes?"

"In the future, have a care with your tongue . . . lest someone be tempted to cut it off."

25

The next morning, Kendra and the Duke tossed aside all social proprieties in favor of old-fashioned police work, which meant knocking on the door of Mr. Bertel Larson at the unseemly hour of 9:30. Or, rather, having Benjamin knock on the door, with the Duke's calling card.

The early morning visit was apparently unusual enough for the Larsons' butler to not immediately accept the card, but rather poke his head out the door so he could study the crest on the Duke's carriage with his own eyes. Kendra got the impression that he was assuring himself that he wasn't the object of some strange prank.

Kendra surveyed the five-story, redbrick Georgian mansion. Above, the sky was the color of denim washed a hundred times, with just the faintest sepia tone. The air quality in the morning always seemed better, with the yellowish smog building up by late afternoon. The cooler temperatures helped, too, Kendra thought, and a light breeze. The day was starting out much like yesterday, cold but pleasant. But she'd been in England long enough now to know that the weather was mercurial, and by the afternoon they could be dealing with rain or snow. Without the cheerful TV meteorologist and satellite maps, there was no way to predict it. And even in the 21st century, predicting the weather was still a toss-up.

"The apothecary business must be doing very well," she said, continuing to eye the house.

"'Tis not that surprising. More people can afford apothecaries than doctors," the Duke replied. "And given Lady St. James's patronage of their shop, we can assume they have an affluent clientele."

Benjamin returned with news that the Larsons were at home. The butler met them near the door, and after dealing with their outerwear, ushered them down a wide hallway, past a grand staircase, and through tall doors that opened into a spacious, interesting drawing room. Not English, although Kendra recognized a few English pieces in the Chippendale sideboard and tables. Most of the furnishing had been appropriated from ancient Rome, their scrolled arms and legs carved into lion head footings. Kendra also noticed pieces that paid homage to the Larsons' Scandinavian ancestry: side cabinets with traditional Rosemaling, drawers and doors hand-painted in stylized geometric-like flowers and leaves.

A tall, statuesque woman stood in front of one of the drawing room's large Palladian windows, gazing outside. When the butler announced them, she turned and surveyed them with eyes as cool and blue as the fjords that her ancestors had no doubt once sailed. She wore a pale linen cap, but a few stray curls, the color of ripe wheat, brushed against alabaster cheeks. Kendra estimated Astrid Larson to be in her mid-forties. She was beautiful, but hers was an intimidating beauty, with a long nose and high, sharply sculpted cheekbones that could have been carved by Michelangelo himself. Her full mouth was unsmiling. Kendra recalled Gerard's mockery that Evert had claimed that his kin had descended from Norse gods. Looking at Astrid Larson now, she could believe it.

"Forgive us for intruding upon you at such an indecent hour, Mrs. Larson," the Duke began with quiet courtesy.

"Do not trouble yourself, Your Grace. My husband and I have always been unfashionably early risers. Although, I confess, entertaining a duke—morning or afternoon—is something of a novelty." Her lips curved into a faint smile, which disappeared when her gaze slid back to the window. "My husband will be joining us momentarily. Let us sit by the fire. I have ordered tea. Unless you prefer ale?"

Glancing outside, Kendra was surprised to see an enormous glass-paned building attached to a wing of the house. "You have a conservatory," she remarked, stepping over to the window.

"My husband and son are apothecaries," Astrid said. "We grow many medicinal plants and herbs that we use in our proprietary blends."

It was actually ingenious, thought Kendra. She suspected that when the back gardens weren't covered in snow, they were also less ornamental than the Larsons' neighbors.

In the distance, she noticed a solitary figure, his back to the window, facing a long slab of stone. He wore a greatcoat, but no hat, and his brown hair fluttered in the cold breeze. For a second, Kendra wondered if the man was David. But she realized her mistake when a young maid ran out to him, and he turned around. Despite the distance, she could see that he was an older man, with deep lines etched into his handsome countenance.

"That is an interesting sculpture," the Duke observed. The slab was painted red and covered in patterns.

"'Tis a runestone, Your Grace. My husband thought to erect it in memory of our son, Evert," Astrid said quietly, and turned away, walking toward the sofa and chairs in front of the fireplace. Kendra followed, her gaze lifting to the enormous oil painting above the fireplace. It was a family portrait, with Astrid sitting on a gilt carved chair, looking magnificent and imperial. Her husband, Bertel, stood on one side, resting one hand on her shoulder. On the other side were their two sons, Evert and David. Visually, the entire family was stunning.

"We had that painting commissioned five years ago," Astrid said, following Kendra's gaze. "In happier times."

"Good morning." Behind them, Bertel Larson entered the room, bringing with him the fresh scent of snow and cold. He'd shed his greatcoat, and wore an expertly tailored jacket, waistcoat, and pantaloons, the last tucked into scuffed Hessian boots. David took after his father in the planes of his face, chiseled mouth, the cut of his chin. Bertel's brown hair was lighter, woven with silver. His blue eyes, paler than his wife's and son's, reflected a haunting melancholy.

Kendra thought of how he hadn't been in to his shop for about a month. His illness wasn't of the body, but of the soul.

"The Duke of Aldridge and Miss Donovan have come to call," Astrid said. Unnecessarily, Kendra thought, since the maid had most likely told him.

"My apologies for the early visit," the Duke said.

Bertel regarded him steadily. "This is about Giles, isn't it?"

Astrid spoke before they could answer. "Please, let us be seated." She sank down onto the sofa, arranging her burnished brown skirts around her legs as she waited for her husband to join her. The door opened just as Kendra and the Duke settled into chairs and a young maid entered, carrying a tea tray. She carefully deposited the tray on the table next to Astrid, and waited silently as Astrid inquired on her guests' preferences. After Astrid filled each teacup, the maid passed them around.

Astrid waited for the servant to leave before she looked at Kendra. "David told us that you were at the shop yesterday, Miss Donovan. He said that you were investigating Sir Giles's murder."

"Yes." Kendra glanced at Bertel. "When was the last time you saw Sir Giles, Mr. Larson?"

A muscle jumped in Bertel's jaw. "We had words after I received news that Evert had been killed. Two years ago."

"You haven't seen him since then?"

He hesitated. "He has attempted to see me, but I have . . . had little to say to the man."

"When did he try to see you? Recently?"

Astrid laid her hand over her husband's. "Sir Giles came to this house several weeks ago, but we were not at home to meet him," she said.

"So you never spoke with Sir Giles then?" Kendra asked.

"No," Astrid said.

Kendra looked at Bertel. "You blamed Sir Giles for your son's death?"

His expression hardened. "He *was* responsible."

Kendra's gaze drifted again to the portrait hanging above the fireplace. Evert and David could have practically been twins, but the artist had added a certain vibrancy to Evert's features compared to David's sober composure.

"Evert was provided for," Bertel continued. "He did not need to join the military like someone from an impoverished family or a second son. Giles was the one who persuaded him to risk his life on the Continent."

Kendra brought her gaze back to Bertel's face. "How did you and Sir Giles know each other?"

His brows pulled together, as though confused over why that should matter, but he answered, "We were lads in Hammersmith together. When the colonists revolted, we signed on." His lip curled in self-mockery. "It was a burst of patriotic fervor, which I discovered faded rapidly with the blood on the battlefield. Although Giles . . . Giles came into his own, proving to our superiors that he had a talent for stratagems. He rose through the ranks quickly."

"And was rewarded with a title," remarked the Duke.

Bertel nodded. "Giles continued his service to the government. He was always ambitious." His gaze fell to the teacup he held, his expression softening at the memory. "There was a time when I admired that, was proud of him."

Kendra waited. The only sound in the drawing room was the crackling of logs in the hearth. She finally prompted, "But that changed when he recruited your son?"

Bertel lifted his eyes, and Kendra saw the glow of rage in the pale depths. "He didn't recruit Evert; he *dazzled* him. He played upon my son's honorable nature, his thirst for adventure and natural curiosity. I tried to convince Evert that his zeal was misplaced. But he would hear none of it." The hand that held the teacup shook, rattling the china. He hastily put it aside.

Astrid laid a hand on her husband's arm. "It was not your fault."

He didn't seem to hear her. His handsome features twisted in pain. "God help me, I encouraged their association. When Evert was a boy, it seemed of little consequence. And as he matured, Giles was in a better position to introduce Evert to connections beyond my social circle." He clenched his hands. "I did not know my good *friend* would persuade my son to put himself in harm's way. I had always thought he regarded Evert as his own."

"Even more than his own son?" Kendra asked curiously.

Bertel looked startled at the question. "Not more than, no. Gerard is his flesh and blood." He paused, then pushed himself to his feet. Astrid's comforting hand fell away. Kendra saw the concern on her beautiful face as she watched her husband wander to the window to stare outside. Kendra wondered if he was looking at the runestone he'd put up in his son's memory. "Evert and Gerard were of the same age," he said slowly. "All the boys played together, even David. David idolized the boys."

Happier times, Kendra thought.

"But it soon became apparent that Evert excelled in many subjects." Bertel turned away from the window to look at them. "Giles took notice. He began to spend more time with him. Evert dreamed of becoming a barrister, and Giles fostered that dream."

Kendra asked, "How did Gerard react to his father's interest in your son?"

"I think there may have been some resentment. Gerard could be a petulant child, with a tendency to be spiteful. Some boys are that way." Bertel shrugged dismissively.

"Unfortunately, Jane—Lady Holbrooke—indulged the boy," Astrid said quietly, sipping her tea.

An uncomfortable silence fell. Kendra said, "Your son is a hero. We heard he died trying to save captured soldiers."

"And is that supposed to comfort me?" Bertel snapped, his nostrils flaring in his anger. "My son died alone, tormented."

Astrid set aside her teacup and rose, hurrying to her husband's side. "My love," she murmured, touching his arm, as though to steady him.

He ignored her, his gaze fixed on Kendra. "You are still a maiden, Miss Donovan. You do not know what it is like to have your child taken from you. Evert was full-grown, but he was my child. And to not even be able to give him a decent burial . . ." He spun away, a shudder wracking his body. "You do not know."

The Duke frowned. "Your son's remains were not returned to you?"

Emotions, too quick to identify, flickered over Astrid's striking face. "There was an explosion and a fire," she said simply.

"I understand your anguish." Aldridge's blue eyes darkened, and Kendra knew he was thinking of his six-year-old daughter, Charlotte, who'd died in a boating accident with his wife. Arabella's body had been found ashore, but his daughter had been swept out to sea. "I, too, have lost a child, and have no gravesite to visit." He let out a shaky breath. "I have only my memories of what had been, my yearning for what can never be."

Bertel slowly pivoted to look at the Duke. "Was your child sacrificed because of a good friend's ambition, Your Grace?"

"No. It was a dreadful accident."

"Then you really cannot understand my anguish, sir. My son's death was no accident."

The Duke appeared at loss on how to respond to the bitterness in the other man's voice.

Astrid filled in the silence. "Evert's death could have nothing to do with Sir Giles's murder. What do you want from us?"

It occurred to Kendra that the other woman could have committed the murder. She was tall, and appeared strong enough. Staring at Astrid's formidable beauty, Kendra recalled the stories of shield-maidens—Viking warrior women—and had no difficulty imagining Astrid in that role, striking down her enemies—or cutting out Sir Giles's tongue and painstakingly painting crosses on his dead, naked flesh.

"It would be helpful if you could tell us where you both were on Wednesday night." Kendra asked, watching them closely.

Astrid drew herself up to a majestic five feet, ten inches as she regarded Kendra coldly. "We were at home, Miss Donovan."

"Can your servants confirm that?"

The other woman stared down her nose at her for a long moment. Kendra had never felt more like a peasant in the presence of royalty. Hell, even Lady Atwood hadn't been able to make her feel this boorish. Kendra felt at a disadvantage sitting, so she set the teacup and saucer aside and stood as well.

"I'm certain they could, but I will not have them quizzed like common criminals," Astrid said. "My husband did not kill Sir Giles. That is what you are really demanding to know, isn't it?"

"What is happening here?" David Larson suddenly loomed in the doorway. He shot Kendra an angry look, before hurrying across the room to join his parents at the window. Concern darkened his eyes as he scanned his father's face. "How are you feeling?"

Bertel raised his hand, waving it in a dismissive gesture. "I'm fine. Do not fuss, boy."

David spun around to lock eyes on Kendra. "What is this about? I told you that my father is unwell."

"I'm sorry, but we still need to make inquiries."

As she looked at the family, Kendra realized they had unintentionally assumed the same positions they'd held in the family portrait. Astrid was standing, but she was flanked by her husband and son in a show of family unity. Evert might not be standing with his family, but Kendra felt that he was still there. Not a ghostly presence, but something stronger, forged in the memories of his loved ones.

Were those loving memories of a dead son and brother now laced with unhealthy rancor and a thirst for revenge? *Before and after*, she thought suddenly. Before, these people were united as a family, untainted by tragedy. And now, after, they were broken.

Astrid looked at her. "I think we are finished. There is nothing more we have to say about Sir Giles or the Holbrooke family."

"What about Lord Cross?" Kendra asked, her gaze moving back to David. "Do you know him?"

David's eyes narrowed. "We were in school together."

"Friends?"

"No. He was older than me." He hesitated. "I know my brother gave his life for Lord Cross and Captain Mobray."

She regarded the family. "Do you have any idea why Lord Cross would have met with Sir Giles on Wednesday night?"

Bertel frowned, but said nothing.

David shook his head, his eyes guarded. "No, but I haven't seen Eliot Cross since we were boys. We don't exactly travel in the same social circles," he added drily.

"What about Captain Mobray? Do you know him?"

"No," David said, his mouth tight. "I have never met the man, but I have read about him occasionally in the newspapers. He has high political ambitions, I believe."

Astrid put her hand on David's arm, linking them together. Her eyes narrowed on Kendra. "We do not know him," she repeated coldly. "I think we are done with this inquiry, Miss Donovan." She glanced at the Duke as he rose to his feet. "Your Grace."

211

"Thank you for seeing us, Mrs. Larson, Mr. Larson," said the Duke. "We truly do not wish to cause you more pain. Our only desire is to find out the truth. Sir Giles's murderer is still out there."

Astrid moved to the bell-pull. "I shall have Wyman show you out."

"That won't be necessary," Kendra said, and walked with the Duke to the door. When they reached the threshold, she paused, looking back at the family. "One more question. Do you know a formula for invisible ink?"

There was a sharp silence. "We know several formulas for secret ink," Bertel finally said, frowning heavily. "What of it?"

Kendra studied him, wondering if it was her imagination or if he looked more strained than when he first came in from the garden. She said, "I was just curious. Thank you."

This time, she allowed the Duke to escort her out of the room.

"Well, that was more distressing than I thought it would be," the Duke admitted as he sank back against the velvet tufted seat of his town carriage. His eyes were troubled when they met hers. "I am fully cognizant that inquiries must be made, my dear. Murder was done. But it was difficult not to be affected by their pain over the loss of a son, a brother. Didn't you feel it?"

"Yes. But that pain might have turned one of them into a murderer."

The Duke said nothing for a long moment, then he sighed heavily. "You are correct, but . . . the poor man. I know what it is to lose a child in such a way. 'Tis a wonder that he didn't go mad with grief . . ." His voice trailed away, and he looked out the window.

Kendra was surprised to find a lump rising in her own throat as she saw the haunting sadness on the Duke's face. She remembered when she'd first arrived in the 19th century and had been put to work in the kitchens. She'd been told then how the Duke had gone temporarily mad when he'd lost his wife and child.

Someone had stripped Sir Giles and spent hours marking up his body with invisible ink, before cutting out his tongue.

'Tis a wonder that he didn't go mad with grief . . .

She replayed the Duke's words in her mind and thought: *Maybe he—or she—did.*

26

Kendra inhaled deeply, stretching her arms straight overhead, fingers linked. She exhaled and bent her body sharply to the right. Normally, she did yoga in her bedchamber in the early morning, so she could wear the more loose-fitting shift and stays, with only Molly observing what the maid believed was an odd American practice. But she hadn't had time to do anything that morning before leaving for the Larsons, and upon returning, she'd spent fifteen minutes updating the slate board and murder book, a file that included her drawings and observations. It was standard law enforcement practice to keep such a book, and she'd started doing so recently to track her work here.

The Duke had left for a lecture at the Natural History Society, where American abolitionist and Quaker Elias Hicks was scheduled to speak. The name rang a distant bell, but Kendra couldn't place him. She'd declined the Duke's invitation to join him. The last thing she needed was to be introduced to a fellow American, she thought, forcing her arms and torso to stretch a little further. What if he tried to talk to her about their homeland? Elias Hicks's America was not *her* America. They would have very few reference points. Her apartment complex in Virginia was probably some plantation owner's cotton or tobacco field right now. And she didn't even want to contemplate the sickening horror of what was happening right now with slavery. *Definitely not my America.*

She closed her eyes. *Breathe in. Breathe out.*

Opening her eyes, she slowly drew herself upright, stretching toward the ceiling for the count of three, and then dropped to the left.

She was adjusting to this new life—she *was*—but she couldn't stop the panic from tightening her chest whenever there was a possibility of meeting someone who'd once only existed for her in the history books. Part of her still feared that she might say something, do something, to inadvertently change the course of history. But another part of her thought that any meeting would be just plain weird. Better to not develop any connections between herself and these random figures from history. Even if she was now living that history.

Connections . . .

From her sideways stretch, she moved her gaze back to the slate board. She needed to think about the connections.

"Whatever are you doing?"

Kendra twisted her head around to watch Rebecca and Alec come into the room. A beam of sunlight teased out the fiery highlights in Rebecca's auburn hair, which had been swept into a topknot, woven with a peach ribbon that matched the color of her simple cotton muslin dress. Alec had clearly been out riding; the hunter green riding jacket was taut across his broad shoulders, his long legs encased in doeskin breeches tucked into black Hessian boots that his valet had most likely spent considerable time buffing into a rich gleam.

"Thinking," she said, and drew herself upright. She moved her shoulders, gratified that stretching had helped relieve the knots of tension.

Rebecca arched a dubious brow at her. "If you say so. Where's His Grace?" she asked, moving toward the sideboard, which held a tray with coffee and teapots.

"Natural History Society."

"Ah." She lifted a teapot and poured herself a cup. "Papa is attending that as well."

Alec pulled a scrap of paper from his inside breast pocket. He moved toward Kendra, handing it to her.

"What's this?" she asked, scanning the note.

"I intercepted a boy delivering a note from Mr. Kelly. Apparently he's managed to locate the Holbrookes' disgraced maid, and is hoping to have a word with her."

"Good. Disgruntled ex-employees are the best source of information."

"What sort of information do you think the maid will tell Mr. Kelly?" Alec asked.

"I'm hoping she'll tell him what was happening in the Holbrooke household before she was let go. She was still working there when Sir Giles's mood reportedly changed."

"If the maid is disgruntled, can she be trusted to speak the truth?" Rebecca asked. She glanced at Alec. "Sutcliffe, do you want tea or coffee?"

"Coffee, thank you, Becca."

Kendra shrugged. "People lie for various reasons. Mr. Kelly is a good cop—ah, Bow Street Runner. I trust him to figure out whether she's credible or not, if she's got an axe to grind against her former employer and is being less than truthful." She was only vaguely surprised to realize that she'd spoken the absolute truth. Sam Kelly *was* a good cop.

She set the scrap of paper aside, and picked up a nearby rag, dampening it with water from the carafe. Slate boards were almost identical to chalkboards with the exception that you needed to use a wet rag to erase whatever was on it.

"What are you doing?" Rebecca asked, handing a steaming cup of coffee to Alec.

"Rearranging things a bit." She wrote down Sir Giles's name again. To the right, she jotted down Silas Fitzpatrick's name, and ran a line connecting the Irishman to the victim. "Okay. We know Fitzpatrick has a motive to kill Sir Giles. But why now?"

Alec took a long sip of coffee, his gaze on the slate board. "Maybe it has less to do with his sister's death, and more to do with what's happening at the Liber now. Sir Giles was keeping the coffeehouse under surveillance. Maybe he discovered something incriminating against Fitzpatrick, and Fitzpatrick found out about it and killed him."

Kendra jiggled the piece of slate. "How'd Fitzpatrick learn about the incriminating evidence?"

"Who says he doesn't have his own spy network?"

She looked at Alec. "You think Fitzpatrick was spying on Sir Giles?"

He shrugged. "It's hardly unusual to have both sides spying on each other."

Really, it wasn't unlike what was happening in the 21st century. Intelligence and counterintelligence games were the bread and butter of the military and special ops. "You're right," she said. "But cutting out the tongue, the invisible ink . . . I don't know. That doesn't seem like a political assassination."

"Why can't it be both?" Rebecca asked. "If Mr. Fitzpatrick realized that Sir Giles needed to be . . . eliminated, maybe he added his own embellishment as revenge for what happened to his sister."

Kendra looked at her in surprise. "That's possible." And because it was possible, Fitzpatrick's name stayed on the board. She added another name, and drew a line to Sir Giles. "Gerard Holbrook has obvious reasons to commit patricide. Whether he has the temperament to plan this out, though, I don't know."

Rebecca shook her head. "I cannot see it."

"It stands to reason that Sir Giles would have been troubled by his son's behavior in recent weeks, and could account for his own mood," said Alec.

Kendra nodded. "The idea of being sent to India would have been an obvious trigger for Holbrooke. He knows his father's routine. It wouldn't take much planning on his part to set up Sir Giles. And just as Fitzpatrick could have embellished, so could Holbrooke. But for Holbrooke, it's about misdirection. Maybe people could believe a son would commit patricide, but cutting out his tongue, using the invisible ink? That points to someone else, doesn't it?" She gave Rebecca a look. "*You* don't believe Holbrook could have done it for those reasons."

"Not only those reasons. I am thinking of the man I met yesterday," Rebecca argued. "He did not strike me as evil. Spoiled, arrogant, but not evil. And he would have to be evil to do what was done to his own father!"

"What does evil look like? I think you know more than most that evil can hide behind a normal face." She met Rebecca's eyes, saw the glimmer of awareness, and knew she was remembering the two times she'd personally encountered evil lurking behind normalcy. "Evil is an emotional description," Kendra continued briskly. "Let's stick to the facts. Holbrooke had motive. And he lied about his whereabouts the night his father was murdered."

"He actually didn't lie—Lady Holbrooke lied when she provided him with an alibi," Rebecca countered.

"Okay. Lie by omission. He didn't correct her."

Kendra moved forward and added Lord Cross's name, then a new line connecting him to Sir Giles. "The connection between Cross and Sir Giles is a bit more ambiguous."

Alec said, "Cross sought out Sir Giles before he was murdered, and was seen having a heated discussion with the man. That's not ambiguous. And he was evasive about their conversation. I certainly didn't believe his assertion that Sir Giles outbid him on a horse."

"He's definitely hiding something," Kendra agreed. "But does it have anything to do with the murder?" She tapped her chin with the piece of slate as she considered it. "To be honest, he didn't seem to have the temperament to commit the murder."

Rebecca lifted a brow in her direction. "Because he doesn't look evil, perchance?"

Kendra laughed. "Touché. However, I really do mean his temperament. He was visibly nervous, and when he lied, he lied poorly. The unsub we're dealing with is more cold-blooded and calculating. Someone like his friend, Captain Mobray." She added the captain's name to the list, and drew another line. "Mobray's connection to the victim is even more ambiguous—at least at this stage. He and Sir Giles knew each other. They both worked in government. We need more information about him. Maybe our reporter friend, Mr. Muldoon, can help us there."

"Why is the captain's name up there at all if his connection to Sir Giles is so tenuous?" Rebecca asked.

This was where things got tricky, Kendra realized, because she was relying more on instinct than solid facts. "I got the impression that Mobray was rescuing Cross from our interview," she said slowly.

"Why would he do such a thing?" Rebecca asked.

Instead of answering, Kendra leaned forward and wrote another name on the slate board.

"Evert Larson," Rebecca read, and looked at Kendra. "How can a man who died two years ago have anything to do with what happened to Sir Giles two nights ago?"

"Connections," Kendra said softly, and drew a line from Evert to Cross and Mobray, and then from Evert to Sir Giles. "Evert connects the men together."

Alec said, "And according to my contact, Sir Giles had mentioned Evert's name recently."

Kendra added Bertel, David, and Astrid to the slate board. "Your contact also said a month ago Sir Giles became upset over something."

"Unnerved by information he'd received," Alec clarified.

"And a month ago, Bertel Larson also seemed to have some sort of setback. A malady of some kind. At least that was how it was described. It's too much of a coincidence." Kendra shook her head. "I don't like it."

"And you think the information has to do with Evert Larson?" Rebecca guessed.

"I don't know, but Evert is the one person that links everyone together, except for Fitzpatrick. His family, of course, had ties with the Holbrookes that go back years. But their estrangement can be traced to Evert's death." She thought of the rage she'd seen in Bertel's eyes. "Mr. Larson regards Sir Giles's decision to persuade Evert to become an intelligence agent as a betrayal that led directly to Evert's death. It may be two years since his son died, but his anger hasn't abated." She began pacing. "There needs to be a more recent trigger."

"The information that Sir Giles learned a month ago," Alec said.

She nodded and retrieved her coffee cup, then went to the sideboard to replenish it. It was the seventh cup she'd had that morning, but who was counting? "Evert also has a strong link to Cross and Mobray. He died trying to save them. Cross became visibly nervous when we questioned him about Evert. He initially lied about knowing him, even though they were at Eton together. He's hiding something."

Rebecca asked, "What?"

"I don't know. That's what we need to find out." She sipped her coffee. "I find it interesting that Cross and Mobray appear to still be friends. They're from different social circles."

"They were prisoners together in a French camp. They are the only survivors," Alec pointed out. "Such experiences have a tendency to forge very strong bonds."

"True . . . except that's not what I saw last night."

Rebecca regarded her. "What did you see?"

"Control," Kendra said. "Mobray knew who we were, and what we were talking to Cross about. He stopped it. Why?"

"He was afraid what Cross might say," Alec said.

"Yeah," she agreed with a nod. "Cross gave us an alibi for where he was after he left Sir Giles. We'll need to check it out, of course. And I'd like to interview Cross again. Without the possibility of being interrupted." She thought of his blinking and the sheen of sweat on the viscount's upper lip, and didn't think she'd have to apply too much pressure to break him.

Rebecca frowned, her gaze on the slate board. "You have Mrs. Larson's name up there as well. You can't possibly imagine she killed Sir Giles?"

"I saw nothing that would rule her out. She's tall enough to have been the unsub. Garroting is more a matter of leverage. As I said before, it requires some strength, but not above average."

"And to strike the hackney driver and carry him into a doorway?"

"Nobody said he was carried into a doorway. He could have been dragged. Just as Sir Giles could have been dragged after he'd been strangled. The killer's identity was concealed by the outerwear. It could have been a woman." She looked at Alec, but he shook his head.

"I'm afraid I cannot agree. I don't think a woman could have done this."

Kendra decided to let it go for now. "It's too bad we can't verify Evert Larson's death," she murmured.

Rebecca looked at her, shocked. "But you cannot believe he fabricated his death! For what purpose?"

Alec raised an eyebrow at Kendra. "That is a rather incredible notion."

"I'm not saying he did. I'm only saying that it would be nice to verify." She shrugged. "It's a loose thread."

"But do you believe it's a possibility?" Rebecca pressed.

Kendra considered it for a long moment. "Not really," she finally said. "It doesn't fit what we know. The Larsons are a loving family. Evert's death traumatized them." She remembered the sorrow that had etched deep grooves in Bertel's face. "Still traumatizes them. I can't imagine Evert would allow his parents and brother to suffer in such a way."

"He would have to be a monster," said Rebecca.

"Not exactly the description we've been given."

Kendra turned back to the slate board, then glanced around when the study door opened and Lady Atwood sailed in with such a quick gait that her lace cap looked in danger of flying off. Her eyes were bright as they fixed on Kendra, and without the usual censure that Kendra associated with the countess.

The older woman actually smiled at Kendra. "Miss Donovan, you must ready yourself. You have callers."

Kendra felt her lips part in surprise. "What?"

"You have callers," she repeated. "*Gentleman* callers."

Kendra stared at her.

Lady Atwood went on, "Despite my misgivings, you did not embarrass our family at last evening's ball. Mr. Humphrey and Mr. Roland have come to call. They are in the morning room. Tea and cakes are being served. Now, you must go and change at once!"

"What?"

The countess's blue eyes sharpened. "Will you stop saying that in such a ridiculous manner, Miss Donovan? And close your mouth. It is most unbecoming for you to stand there looking as though you are about to catch flies. *You have callers.* Mr. Humphrey's father is Lord Adder, but as he has two older brothers, he is not in line for the earldom. Mr. Roland, however, is in line to inherit. His father is a viscount, and one day will be Lord Oglethorpe. Unfortunately, the on-dit is that the family's estate is impoverished. Undoubtedly he is on the hunt for an heiress, so we shan't encourage his suit any more than necessary."

We? thought Kendra, dazed. *Suit?*

Lady Atwood glanced over at Rebecca. "What is wrong with the creature?"

"I believe she's in shock at the notion of gentleman callers, ma'am."

"I confess I have been taken by surprise as well." The countess's hand fluttered to her bosom. "She isn't exactly a young maid. Now go and tidy yourself up, Miss Donovan. I expect you to be downstairs in ten minutes."

"I shall help her," Rebecca promised, earning a bright smile from Lady Atwood.

"Bless you, child." She shifted her gaze toward Alec, and frowned. "Mayhap you ought to take yourself off, Sutcliffe."

"I don't think so."

"Yes, well." His aunt appeared to realize she wouldn't get her way. "Then you must behave yourself." She hurried toward the door, but paused to throw Kendra a stern look. "Ten minutes, Miss Donovan!"

"Shit," Kendra muttered after Lady Atwood left. "I don't have time for this." She really didn't. She could feel the muscles in her neck knot again.

Rebecca laughed. "It won't take that much time. It would be ill-bred for any gentleman to stay longer than thirty minutes."

"*Thirty minutes?* What am I going to talk to them about for thirty fuc—ah, minutes?"

"Pleasantries—without any profanity. And it might only be fifteen minutes. Come along. You must prepare for your London beaux."

Shit, Kendra thought again. She allowed Rebecca to tug her toward the door, but shot a look back at Alec, who didn't look any happier at this unexpected development than she did. If she wasn't so afraid of what Lady Atwood would do, she'd be inclined to send a note down to the morning room to tell her callers to go home.

She let out a long sigh. "Okay. Let's get this damn thing over with then."

27

There were rules—of course, there were rules—for this strange ritual. With impatience thrumming in her blood, Kendra listened to Rebecca tell her that the gentleman waiting for her in the drawing room must have been introduced to her last evening. "Gentleman do not call upon ladies with whom they have not been introduced."

"So you're saying that I brought this on myself by dancing last night," Kendra grumbled from the dressing room as she quickly washed her hands, splashed water on her face, and patted both dry with a towel hooked on the arm of the washstand. She hurried back into the bedchamber, plopping down in front of the vanity to allow Molly to tidy her hair by pinning up stray tendrils. "I knew that was a mistake—*ow!*" She jolted when Molly reached down and pinched her cheeks. "What the hell? What was that for?"

"Her ladyship said Oi was ter do it, seeing 'ow it will give ye roses in yer cheeks, miss."

"It will give me bruises in my cheeks."

"Come along," Rebecca said, and tried to stifle her laughter as she hauled Kendra out of the chair, dragging her into the hallway. She continued, "It shan't be too long. As I told you, calls by gentlemen last from fifteen to thirty minutes."

"Got it."

"There are topics that can be discussed, and topics that cannot be discussed."

"Figures."

"Do not flatter the gentlemen in their appearance."

"What if they are looking especially fine today?"

Rebecca cut her a sidelong look as they walked down the hallway. "I believe you are joking, so I shall ignore that. If they remark upon your looks, that is also considered ill-mannered."

"So if they tell me *I* look nice, that is actually rude?"

"Yes. Compliments are only for intimate friends and family. And one should not comment on any public scandal or gossip that's making the rounds."

"Got it. Nothing fun."

Rebecca laughed. "And please do not discuss bodily functions, like pregnancy, childbirth, or disease."

"I'm not sure why I'd discuss any of those, but it might be easier for you to tell me what we *can* talk about." They'd reached the stairs, and started down.

"Well, if you wish, you may retrieve your embroidery hoop to do a little fancy work to occupy yourself."

"Look at you joking too."

Rebecca smiled. "Maybe a little."

"Well, at least one of us is finding the situation funny," Kendra muttered as they approached the morning room. A footman had been standing nearby, and now leapt forward to open the door.

At their entrance, Mr. Humphrey and Mr. Roland set aside their teacups and plates and stood. Alec was already standing, having taken up a careless pose against the mantel of the fireplace. Kendra felt a jolt of warmth when she met his eyes from across the room, a strangely intimate moment despite the distance and their audience. Then Lady Atwood broke the spell when she introduced the gentlemen to Rebecca and insisted that everyone sit down. Kendra noticed that the countess had brought her embroidery to do fancywork.

Kendra pulled her gaze away from Alec and responded to the men's abbreviated bows with a brief curtsy. Mr. Humphrey had the same affable expression on his face that he had the night before. Mr. Roland was the gentleman she'd pegged as a fortune hunter. At least she'd been spared the lascivious attentions of the lord who'd stared at her bosom throughout their dance, and the Heart-Attack-Waiting-To-Happen guy.

"Is His Grace well?" Humphrey made the first stab at conversation as they sat down, smiling at Kendra.

"Of course." Kendra frowned. "Why wouldn't he be?"

Humphrey's face went blank.

"His Grace is very well, thank you," Rebecca put in. Her lips trembled suspiciously, then cleared her throat. "He is currently attending an engagement at the Natural History Society. One of Miss Donovan's countrymen is speaking."

"Are you acquainted with the speaker, Miss Donovan?" Mr. Roland asked, his oily gaze settling on Kendra.

"No." Kendra racked her brain for something more to say, but came up blank.

After an awkward beat of silence, Humphrey said, "How are you enjoying London, Miss Donovan . . . Lady Rebecca?" His gaze turned to include Rebecca.

"I confess I prefer the country," Rebecca said politely. "But London has much to offer."

"And you, Miss Donovan?" Mr. Roland pressed. "Is London to your taste?"

Kendra thought of Sir Giles laid out on the autopsy table. "It's certainly interesting," she said. She snuck a veiled glance at the clock and was dismayed to realize only a couple of minutes had ticked by. At this rate, she was going to want to jump out a window in another five minutes. Unfortunately, they were on the ground floor. Kendra envisioned excusing herself to go upstairs, and *then* tossing herself out of a window.

"Miss Donovan!"

Kendra realized Lady Atwood had been saying her name. "I'm sorry. What did you say?"

"Mr. Roland asked you a question," she said, and her eyes fixed on Kendra with unmistakable warning.

"Sorry." She turned to look at the fortune hunter. "What did you say, Mr. Roland? I'm afraid I was thinking about something else."

His lips stretched into a smile that could only be described as condescending. "Not at all. I realize that females have more delicate constitutions."

Kendra raised an eyebrow. "You realize that, do you?"

"Exactly how do you view a woman's delicate constitutions, sir?" Rebecca put in with a sweetness that was belied by the dangerous glint in her eyes.

"To be protected, of course!" Mr. Roland turned his patronizing smile on Rebecca. "And guided in the more taxing decisions of life."

Lady Atwood cleared her throat loudly, apparently recognizing the hazardous turn the conversation had taken. "Tell me, Mr. Humphrey, how is your father, Lord Adder?" she inquired with a practiced smile, steering the conversation to safer topics.

"Ah, as robust as ever."

"And Lady Adder?"

"My mother enjoys good health as well." He slid a look at Kendra. "Would you care to ride with me tomorrow in Hyde Park, Miss Donovan? If the weather holds, of course."

Kendra blinked. "On a horse?"

"Well, ah . . . yes."

"Unfortunately, riding is not a skill that Miss Donovan has acquired yet," Alec drawled from his position by the fireplace. "Pray tell, are you a Corinthian, Mr. Humphrey?"

"Oh, no, I wouldn't dare align myself with that set. They are superb whips. However—" He paused when a soft knock preceded Harding's entrance. He carried a bouquet of flowers, and a small box wrapped in white tissue paper tied together with a silky black ribbon.

"Forgive me for interrupting," the butler said, his eyes on Lady Atwood. "These have just arrived for Miss Donovan."

"Oh, *my*. How lovely." Rising, Lady Atwood shot a glance at Humphrey and Roland that made Kendra wonder if the countess was behind the unexpected gifts. Lady Atwood set aside her embroidery and moved toward the butler. "Miss Donovan has many admirers," she proclaimed to no one in particular.

"I can well imagine," Humphrey said, smiling at Kendra. "There is much to admire about Miss Donovan."

Kendra liked Humphrey, but it took an effort not to roll her eyes at him.

"Please find a vase for the flowers, Harding, and put them in the foyer," Lady Atwood instructed.

"Very good, ma'am." The butler handed her the gift box, inclined his head, and glided out of the room.

"'Tis rather forward to send gifts, and not call themselves," Roland said, with a disapproving frown. "Very brazen."

Alec straightened, his dark brows pulling together in a scowl. "Who sent them?"

Lady Atwood turned the box over. "I do not see a note."

"Perhaps the note is inside the box?" Rebecca suggested.

"There's only one way to find out," Kendra said with some asperity. The very *last* thing she needed was another admirer. As far as she was concerned, there were two too many in this room already. "Why don't you open it?"

The countess didn't need any more encouragement. With quick fingers, she pulled at the silk bow, allowing the tissue paper to fall away. "It is most likely a posy or perhaps some sweets," she said, smiling as she pried open the box lid to look inside. "Marzipan, or . . ." Her eyes widened in shock, her features quivering in horror. She reeled backward, dropping the box as she gave an ear-splitting screech.

"What the hell?" Kendra leapt up from her seat.

Alec bolted forward and caught his aunt before she crashed to the floor in a dead faint. "What the devil is it?" he demanded, swinging Lady Atwood around and dumping her in the nearest chair.

Everyone was on their feet, staring at the overturned box. "Don't touch it!" Roland ordered as Kendra bent down. She ignored him, carefully lifting the box and tissue paper to stare down at the object that now rested on the Persian carpet. It was roughly two-and-a-half inches long, squared off on its thicker end, tapering down and rounded on the other end. There had been a time when it had been a healthy pink, she knew. But it was now blackened and slightly shriveled, curling at the sides.

Beside her, Humphrey gave a yelp, backpedaling away from the object like it might suddenly leap up at him. Roland stayed where he was, but his face twisted in horror and revulsion. "Good God, is that . . . ?"

Kendra nodded slowly. "I think we may have just found Sir Giles's tongue."

28

Dark clouds had begun to knit together in the distance, a dire promise that London might be in for either sleet or snow. But for now, Sam considered himself a lucky man. The sun was still shining above, and his visit to the Holbrooke stables earlier had borne unexpected fruit. He'd anticipated a long day of hunting for the Holbrookes' dismissed maid, Betty, but the stable lads had been surprisingly forthcoming, and given him directions to her new address. Apparently, the maid had been fortunate enough to be taken in by her sister and brother-in-law.

After he dashed off a note for the Duke and Miss Donovan to let them know about his good fortune, Sam made his way to Betty's new home with her relations on Earl Street, and was directed by Betty's sister to the King's Arms in Chatham Square, about ten paces from the Blackfriars Bridge, where Betty now worked as a barmaid.

At least a dozen customers were in the pub's low-ceilinged, darkly paneled interior. Wherrymen and dock workers, Sam identified by assessing their coarse dress. But he wouldn't be surprised if there was a smuggler or two in the crowd as well. They had that look, rough and ready for a brawl. Devious, too, given the cagey way they regarded him. In public rooms, he was inclined to sit with his back against a wall and his eye on the room, but he decided that with this crowd, it wasn't just a preference, but a necessity.

As he made his way across the room, the aroma of eggs and greasy bacon and frying onions assailed him, along with the less pleasant smells of stale beer, smoke, sweat, and urine. He slid into an empty booth, his gaze drawn to the comely barmaid working the tap. Her hair was so pale it was almost white, and caught up in a colorful red, yellow, and green handkerchief that showed off both the graceful curve of her long white neck and the rounded shoulders revealed by the peasant smock she wore. The wall lamps and crackling fire in the hearth transformed much of that ivory flesh into gold.

The barmaid flashed him a bold smile when she caught him staring. After sliding the tankard she'd been filling to a bulky fellow standing at the end of the counter, she came around, crossing the room toward Sam with an indolent roll of her hips. She was winsome enough in face, Sam thought, to distract from the slight swell of her belly.

"What'd ye want, good sir?" she said, and her eyes widened in appreciation when he laid a crown on the table.

"Are you Betty?"

Her smile faded, and the pretty face suddenly hardened. "Who wants ter know?"

"Sam Kelly." Carefully, he brought the tip of his baton out of his pocket to allow her to see it.

Her eyes widened again, but this time not in appreciation. He recognized fear. "What're ye doin'?" she hissed. "Put that thing away!" She glanced quickly behind her to see if anyone had noticed.

"They don't have their peepers on *me*, lass," Sam assured her. He didn't have to tell her where a few of the men's eyes were trained. "I just want a word with you."

"What about?"

Sam pushed the crown a bit forward with his index finger, watching her gaze narrow in on the movement. She looked around again, then shrugged, sliding into the booth. Her small hand swept the coin up to be held clenched beneath the table. "I don't peach on anybody," she warned.

"You were the downstairs maid at the Holbrooke residence before you were dismissed?"

Betty's puckered brow smoothed out in relief. "Is this what yer about then? Aye." She regarded him steadily. "I heard the master done cocked up his toes the other day. I ain't got nothin' ter do with it. Her ladyship dismissed me a fortnight ago. Refused ter give me a reference too. Bloody bitch!"

"She didn't like findin' out she was gonna be a grandma?"

The barmaid snorted. "Ack, that Mr. Holbrooke was a bold 'un, always tryin' ter turn me head with his flummery."

Sam raised an eyebrow. "Looks like some of that flummery might've worked."

Surprisingly, Betty grinned at him. "Well, as ter that, Mr. Holbrooke weren't me only beau."

Sam grunted. "What was his relationship like with his da?"

"Ack, it was peculiar, it was. Don't know why he hated the master. It weren't like Sir Giles was home most of the time." She shrugged. "Suppose it was the master's threat ter send him off ter some foreign place because Mr. Holbrooke was a tats man."

"His game was dice, eh?"

"Aye. But he weren't good at it. Fallen inter the River Tick, he did."

Even though he knew all this, Sam decided to continue. He'd always found he got more information by gentling a possible witness into the conversation rather than asking bold questions immediately. "That must've troubled Sir Giles."

"Well, it bloody well didn't make him happy. That's why he was gonna send him away ter some foreign place."

"How did Mr. Holbrooke react ter that?"

"He said he weren't gonna go." She looked at the wall behind Sam, her expression thoughtful. "Reckon he was the most angry I've ever seen him. But what's he gonna do, eh? Gerard—Mr. Holbrooke was always one fer a soft bed and food in his belly."

"Bets!" The publican behind the bar yelled, glaring at Betty. "Stop wit yer prattling, wench. Ye got folks 'ere wit parched lips!"

Betty rolled her eyes. "'Tis me sister's husband's brother that owns this place. I got hired on as a downstairs maid, hopin' one day ter become a lady's maid. But that's not looking bleeding likely. Still, I gotta do me job, or me sister will box me ears." She placed her palms on the table, fingers splayed, and began to shove herself up. Sam stopped her by laying a hand over one of hers.

"A moment, lass." He fixed his gaze on hers. "Do you think Mr. Holbrooke could have killed Sir Giles?"

"Gor, what a thing ter say! Maybe he weren't nobility, but he was a nob." But her response was automatic, and as he watched, something changed in her face.

"Even nobs have been known to kill," Sam said quietly.

She bit her lip, but shook her head. "Nay. I can't imagine it."

Sam let her hand go and leaned back in his seat. "Did he ever mention ter you about wishing his da would cock up his toes?"

"Well, maybe, but it was more talk when he was in his cups. It weren't like he was makin' plans ter do the deed. More like he was *wishin'* fer it to happen." She lowered her eyes for a moment, then she slid a sideways assessing look at him. "Do ye think he did it?"

"It's something we're looking into."

"Bets!" the bartender roared.

She ignored him, still staring at Sam. "He won't know I talked ter ye, will he? I don't want no trouble."

Sam raised an ironic eyebrow, shifting his gaze to the other men in the pub.

She recognized the look in his eyes, and waved a hand impatiently. "They don't give me no trouble. And if they did, 'tis regular folk trouble. I don't want trouble with me betters."

Sam nodded, understanding. "What about Sir Giles?"

Confusion puckered her pretty forehead. "He's dead. He ain't gonna give me no trouble."

"I mean, did you notice anything different about him? I heard that somethin' upset him about a month ago. Did you see anythin' unusual?"

He was watching her carefully, and observed the flicker of her pale eye-lashes. "What did you see?"

Betty shrugged. "I don't remember the exact date, mind you, but it could've been a month ago. It was a bit before her ladyship realized I was increasin' and sacked me . . . The master got all in a dither about somethin'. Even the little one, Ruth, noticed it. She's a queer one, ain't she? Do you know what the last thing she said ter me was?"

"What?"

"That her papa was anxious about ghosts." She gave a little laugh.

"Ghosts?"

"Aye. I told you she was a queer one. I said ter her, 'Your papa is too tough ter be afraid about ghosts.' I said, 'Your papa will give those silly old ghosts a facer, so you needn't fret about it, dearie.' Do you know what she says ter me? She says that ghosts ain't corporeal—that's what she said. Cor-por-eal." Betty enunciated each syllable carefully. "She said that means a body, and if they ain't got a body, no one can give them a facer! Don't that beat all?" She shook her head. "I asked her why she was talkin' about ghosts and such, and she said it was her papa who'd been talkin' about them."

Sam wondered aloud, "What can it mean?"

"It means the gal's touched in the attic, that's what it means. The master's trouble weren't no ghosts. It was a woman. A foreign lady."

Sam stared at her. "How do you know that?"

Betty leaned forward with a conspiratorial look on her face. "One of me duties was ter dust around the house, ye know. I came inter the master's study ter do some tidying up, but he were there, sitting behind his desk, burnin' a piece of paper on that silver tray the old butler used ter bring the letters in on."

"He was burning a letter?"

"Aye."

"*BETS!*" the publican bellowed again.

"Bleeding Mary and Joseph," she breathed, then glanced around. "I'm *coming*! Ye don't need ter shout so!"

Sam retrieved another coin and slid it toward her. "I could use a hot whiskey."

She grinned at him. "Aye."

He sat back, thinking, as Betty jumped up and hurried back to the tap. He could hear sharp words exchanged between her and the publican. A moment later, she returned with his hot whiskey.

Sam prodded, "Tell me what happened next."

Betty didn't sit down. "Oh, well, not much ter tell, really. The master slapped out the flames—they weren't much—and got up and left the room without sayin' a word."

"Was that odd for him ter do?"

"I don't expect him ter talk ter me. But he did look . . ." She thought about it for a moment. "I don't know. Not hisself, that's for sure. Kind of like he was gonna cast up his accounts. He was ill, but not ill, if ye know what I mean." She grinned suddenly. "Maybe like he had seen a ghost, and all."

Sam kept his eyes on the maid. "What did you do then?" he asked, although he suspected.

"I gotta admit that I was curious, on account the master looked so . . . queer-like." She had the grace to blush as she said, "I sort of sifted through what was left on the tray. Most of it was burnt up, but I saw a word or two."

Sam paused in lifting the hot whiskey, surprised. "You know how ter read?"

Insult flashed across her pretty face. "Me sisters and me were taught ter read by our vicar's own wife when we were half-grown."

"My apologies," he offered, and tipped back the glass, enjoying the warm whiskey as it slid smoothly down his throat. He sighed, setting down the glass on the scarred table with a soft thud. "What did you read?"

"I already told you. A foreign lady's name—Magdalena, it was. I think it was right around that time that the master began havin' his troubles." She nodded sagely, and for some reason, Sam found his gaze lowering to the swell of her belly. When he jerked his gaze up, Betty gave him a sly smile, almost as though she knew where his mind had wandered.

"Aye," she nodded as though they shared a dark secret. "The master wasn't havin' ghost-troubles. He was havin' women troubles."

29

There was something absurd about having only a tongue resting on the autopsy table while Munroe, Barts, Alec, Kendra, and even Rebecca—although she held a hankie firmly to her nose—stared down at the damned thing.

An hour ago, after her gentleman callers, Humphrey and Roland, had fled, and Lady Atwood had been revived with smelling salts and taken to her bed, declaring that her nerves were now shattered, Kendra had used the tissues that had been scattered across the floor to shove the pulpy organ back into the box. The only thing she could think to do was whisk the package to Dr. Munroe's anatomy school to have him look at it.

"I suppose it could have belonged to Sir Giles," Dr. Munroe said slowly, his black brows drawn together in a frown as he stared down at the severed tongue.

"Suppose? Is anyone else running around London without a tongue? Or have you had any dead corpses come your way that were missing their tongues?" asked Kendra. She dropped her gaze back down to the grotesque bit of flesh.

Behind his round spectacles, Munroe's eyes gleamed with amusement. "As you know, I am a thorough man, Miss Donovan. Last evening, I released Sir Giles's body to his son, Mr. Holbrooke, for burial, so I no longer have it to make a visual comparison, and therefore cannot say with one hundred percent certainty that this tongue belonged in Sir Giles's head. However . . ." He brought up the magnifying glass to study it. "This appears to have been cut with the same type of knife. If you note, the flesh has been cleanly excised. We're dealing with a very sharp blade; the removal was swift—which matches with what had been done to Sir Giles."

Rebecca suddenly made a gagging sound. "Forgive me, I . . . I . . ." She turned and bolted to the door, and let out a soft cry when she ran into the hard body that had materialized in front of her.

Muldoon placed his hands on her shoulders to steady her. "There now, Princess, is the devil himself after you?"

"Oh, you . . . *oaf*!" Rebecca jerked out of his arms and continued her flight out of the autopsy chamber.

With a concerned frown, the reporter stared after her for a moment, then turned to look at them. "What has happened?"

Kendra frowned at him. "What are you doing here?" she asked in return.

Muldoon whipped off his battered tricorn hat as he came into the room. "I've been calling upon Dr. Munroe every afternoon to see if there's been any new development regarding Sir Giles."

"That he has." Munroe gave the reporter a disgruntled look. "Despite me telling him that the dead can speak for only so long, and Sir Giles gave up his secrets when I conducted the autopsy."

"And yet here I find you with a sizeable audience, doctor," the reporter pointed out with an impudent grin, his gaze drifting to the autopsy table. As Kendra watched, Muldoon's eyes widened, and he hurried across the room to gape at the blackened muscular organ on the table. "Sweet Jesus, is *that* what I think it is?"

Kendra said, "If you think it's Sir Giles's tongue, then yes."

"Most likely," Munroe corrected, and bent forward again, training the magnifying glass on the wider part of the tongue. "As I was saying, the blade used was sharp enough to make a clean cut. And the decomposition matches Sir Giles. I'd say as of three days ago, this tongue was still attached to its owner."

"How did you find it?" asked Muldoon, fascinated.

"You might say it found us," Kendra murmured.

A muscle pulsed on Alec's jaw, his green eyes dark with temper as he fixed his gaze on Kendra. "Not *us*—you. Someone sent it to *you*."

Muldoon's reddish blond eyebrows rose as he looked at her. "Why would the fiend feel the need to send you Sir Giles's tongue, Miss Donovan?"

"That is what I'd like to know," Alec said.

Muldoon answered his own question. "Obviously he is attempting to frighten you," he murmured. "But why? What do you know?"

Kendra found herself being thoroughly examined, his gaze shrewd. She shook her head. "I don't know anything. Not at this stage."

"Ah, then I suppose the killer is worried about the next stage." He scratched behind his ear. "You must be making somebody nervous."

Kendra said nothing. He was right. Sending her the tongue was as much of a message as it had been when the killer had removed it. While she didn't know what was behind the invisible ink symbols or even cutting off the tongue, Kendra had a pretty good idea what *this* message meant: *Stay away.*

"Are you going to let this go, Miss Donovan?" Muldoon asked, and again Kendra felt his gaze on her like a physical weight.

Alec glared at the reporter. "This is your fault, Muldoon. If you hadn't been trying to be clever by putting Miss Donovan in your damned newspaper—"

"I didn't—"

"Don't take me for a simpleton. You did everything but spell out her name."

Muldoon cocked his head as he returned Alec's hostile gaze. "And here now I was thinking this little gift might have more to do with the lass running about, quizzing everybody about the murder. The killer might take exception to having his identity exposed," he said sarcastically.

Alec advanced on him, and the reporter took several prudent steps back.

"Enough!" Kendra slid in front of Alec and slapped a hand on his chest. "Stop it. Both of you." She shot a brief warning look at Muldoon, then dropped her hand. "Let's stay focused. Muldoon's right—I must be making someone nervous. And that's good for us."

The reporter's eyebrows sprang up in surprise. "It is?"

"The killer inadvertently helped us narrow down the pool of suspects. We can cross Silas Fitzpatrick off the list. I never interviewed him, never met him. He has no reason to send this to me."

Alec scowled. "He probably reads the *Morning Chronicle*."

Kendra said, "It's a warning, but it's *personal*. It's a warning specifically for me."

"This does not comfort me," Alec muttered.

Kendra decided to ignore that, turning to look at Muldoon. "I've wanted to talk to you. Do you know Captain Mobray?"

"By reputation only. His stock in Whitehall has been rising in the last year, and there's talk that he may run for political office. At the moment, he works in the Home Department." Muldoon seemed to consider the matter. "His record is exemplary."

"What about Spain?"

"He served in the Fifty-Second Regiment of Foot during the campaign in Spain and was captured by the French. He managed to escape. I don't recall the specifics. Why? What does that have to do with Sir Giles?"

Kendra asked a question of her own. "Can you find out more about Captain Mobray's capture and his escape?"

"I might be able to get my hands on the official reports. But the war is over. What could that possibly have to do with Sir Giles's murder three nights ago?"

"I'm not sure—yet," she admitted. "Have you heard of Evert Larson and Lord Cross?"

"Evert Larson . . . the name sounds familiar. Lord Cross, I don't think so. Who are they?"

Kendra said, "Evert Larson worked for Sir Giles in intelligence. Lord Cross served with Captain Mobray, and was captured with him."

"And escaped with him," Alec put in, his expression brooding. "Evert Larson wasn't so lucky. He died while trying to rescue the captured British soldiers."

Muldoon frowned. "I seem to recall the incident. All the soldiers perished, didn't they?"

Alec nodded. "Except for Captain Mobray and Lord Cross."

"Hmm." The reporter rubbed his chin, his expression thoughtful. "I'll see what I can do about getting ahold of the report. But I have to ask again, what could an incident so long ago have to do with the killing of Sir Giles?"

"Two years isn't very long," Kendra said softly.

She thought of the Larson family with their grief and rage, and Gerard Holbrooke with his festering resentment—a lifetime of bitterness. And Captain Mobray and Lord Cross? Where did they fit in? She thought of Lord Cross and his tense conversation with Sir Giles before Sir Giles was murdered, and Captain Mobray's cool, watchful gray eyes.

Something had happened in Spain besides the death of Evert Larson and the British soldiers. She was sure of it. But whether that tragedy had anything to do with Sir Giles's murder, she didn't know.

30

Kendra, Rebecca, and Alec arrived back at Grosvenor Square at the same time the Duke was stepping out of his carriage. "Good afternoon," he greeted them with a smile. "Your countryman, Mr. Hicks, gave an impassioned speech against the abomination of slavery."

"I would hope so," Kendra murmured as they walked up the steps together, where Harding held open the door.

"My father was quite horrified when he inherited the sugar plantation in Barbados from his uncle and learned that it was run by slave labor," Rebecca put in as she untied the bow to her bonnet and handed it over to Harding. "It took longer than he realized it would, but he managed to free them. Still, Papa was upset to realize his uncle had engaged in such a practice, and had even kept a Negress mistress."

The Duke didn't seem surprised by the admission. "Your father and I discussed it. It was bad ton of his uncle to be part of such an abhorrent practice. I hope America will soon follow Mr. Hicks's lead and overthrow the bonds of slavery. What say you, Miss Donovan? Will your countrymen end this ugly arrangement?"

Kendra met his keen gaze, and knew he was asking her what *would* happen, not her take on what *might* happen. "It may take a while, but I'm certain those who share Mr. Hicks's viewpoint will be vindicated," she said carefully.

"Very good," he said, smiling, and patted his breast pockets. "I spoke with Mr. Hicks at some length after his lecture, and he gave me this." The Duke produced a gray stone, roughly one inch in length, that had been hammered and honed to a sharp point.

"An arrowhead," Kendra said, tugging off her gloves.

The Duke nodded, his gaze on the stone. "We have found our own arrowheads from primitive men, but to think this simple stone was plucked from the earth and fashioned into a weapon by a noble savage as a way to feed and protect his family . . . it is quite remarkable, really."

Kendra handed the waiting maid her pelisse, gloves, and bonnet. "You got an arrowhead. I got a tongue."

"Yes. Wait. *Pardon?*" The Duke glanced at her sharply. "Is this a joke?" Then comprehension flashed in his grayish blue eyes, and he stared at her in shock. "Good God, you are not saying *Sir Giles's* tongue?"

"The household has been in quite an uproar, Your Grace," Harding said as he took the Duke's greatcoat, folding it over his arm. His tone was grave as he flicked a brief, accusatory look at Kendra. "Her ladyship is in a terrible state."

"Good God," the Duke said again. "Where . . . is it?"

Alec said, "We took it to Dr. Munroe and left it with him."

Aldridge nodded. "I suppose that was wise. But what does it mean?" Then he shook his head. "Forgive me, this is not a discussion to be had in the middle of the entrance hall. Harding, send up a tea tray—and coffee—to my study."

They were near the stairs when someone knocked at the door. Harding, who'd been on his way to the kitchens, immediately swung around to answer it. "Mr. Kelly, sir," he announced, and stepped aside to allow the Bow Street Runner to come inside.

Harding made an effort to school his features into impassivity, but he couldn't quite conceal the look of resignation on his face. Kendra knew that Bow Street Runners and severed tongues had never been the norm, until she'd come into their lives.

Sam's eyebrows went up as he surveyed everyone standing in the entrance hall. He must have seen something on their faces, because his golden gaze narrowed into a flat cop stare. "What's happened? What's amiss?"

"Let's make ourselves comfortable in the study," the Duke said, glancing at Kendra. "I have a feeling this might be a long story."

It wasn't that long of a story, but Kendra did have to pause a time or two for the Duke and even Sam to absorb their shock.

"God's teeth," Sam muttered, shaking his head when Kendra had finished. He looked at her and asked, "Why would the fiend send you such a thing?"

"Muldoon—we met Muldoon at Dr. Munroe's—thought the killer was sending me a warning, that he's nervous about the investigation."

Sam pursed his lips. "Aye, seems that way, lass."

"Then I'm missing something," she murmured. She lifted the cup she held, her gaze on the slate board as she took a swallow of coffee. The notes were starting to look like hieroglyphic script, and she didn't have the Rosetta stone. She looked at Sam. "Did you speak to Holbrooke's former maid?"

"Aye, I did. She's working as a barmaid for the brother of her sister's husband in Chatham Square. The lass wasn't as disgruntled about her dismissal as I thought she'd be."

Kendra asked, "Was she forthcoming?"

"Aye. Didn't believe Mr. Holbrooke could have killed his da at first, but then she seemed ter think on it, and reckoned it wasn't such a peculiar idea, after all. Said that he'd mentioned it, but it was more of a wish than a plan."

"Wait a moment." The Duke lifted his hand, appearing to be shocked. "You are saying that Mr. Holbrooke actually voiced a desire to have his father murdered?"

"It would seem so," said Sam. "Or at least wished him ter conveniently cock up his toes."

"Dysfunctional family," Kendra murmured. "Wishing something and actually doing it are two very different things. Go on, Mr. Kelly."

"Well, I asked if she'd notice Sir Giles acting strange or preoccupied before she'd been dismissed."

"And?"

"And aye, she'd noticed that he'd been preoccupied. Said the wee lass—Ruth—noticed it, as well, and said the most peculiar thing. Ruth said that her da was anxious about ghosts."

"Ghosts?" The Duke's brows shot up. "Whatever can she mean? It couldn't possibly be taken literally."

Kendra said, "I think Ruth takes a lot of things literally. Sir Giles must have said something to her to give her that impression. She asked me if I believed in ghosts too."

"I don't understand. Sir Giles thought he was being *haunted*?"

"Not necessarily. Ruth may have taken the words literally, but that doesn't mean Sir Giles meant them that way." Kendra let her gaze travel to the slate board. "I wonder if there's any way that I can talk to Ruth alone."

"You want to quiz the little girl?" Rebecca asked.

"I'd like to hear what she has to say."

Sam rubbed his chin. "I found the lads in the Holbrooke stable ter be a friendly sort when I asked after Betty. If the lass has a routine outside of the house, they might tell me."

"I wouldn't be surprised if her nanny takes her to the park for outings," Rebecca said.

Kendra glanced at the window. It might have been her imagination, but she thought she saw a couple of raindrops fall past. Damn. "She won't be taking Ruth to the park if the weather gets worse."

"Not necessarily," Rebecca said. "Many doctors encourage children to participate in outdoor activities in such weather, as cold air is invigorating for the body, and excellent for young lungs."

Sam said, "I'll make inquiries. But there's something else. The maid didn't think Sir Giles was worried about ghosts." He hesitated, looking at Kendra. "Betty thought Sir Giles might've been concerned about a woman. Magdalena. She came across Sir Giles burning a letter from her."

"Magdalena?" Kendra echoed with interest. "Who's she?"

Sam scratched the side of his nose. "I reckon she was someone he didn't want Lady Holbrooke ter know about, which is why he burnt her letter."

"This woman might not have anything to do with Sir Giles's murder," Alec pointed out. "It could be about another matter entirely."

"Aye. But Betty thought this happened right around the time Sir Giles began ter be more troubled."

"Alec might be right," Kendra acknowledged, "but we need to follow up on that anyway." She thought about how too many leads were dismissed because they didn't look like they were connected to the crime, only to turn out to be something that cracked the case. Hindsight could be an embarrassing bitch, often involving a reporter shoving a microphone in your face asking why no one had considered following the lead from the beginning.

Her gaze drifted back to the slate board. "Magdalena. Is it just a coincidence that Evert Larson died in Spain, and the woman who wrote to Sir Giles has a Spanish name?" she wondered softly. "Or is it another connection?"

31

Ella Browne's gait had been much steadier two hours and twelve customers ago. For every gentleman that she'd taken into the alley behind the Bell & Swan, she'd rewarded herself with a shot of gin. Although her mind was now soaked in a comfortable golden haze, on some level she knew that she should be squirreling away a few of the coins she'd earned so that she could rent her own room rather than be forced to share with Peggy and Esther. Not that she minded sharing, but it meant that once a week they drew lots for who could use the room to entertain. This was not Ella's night.

If she could only save enough blunt, she'd have the warmth and comfort of a bed for the coves who came looking for whores on Haymarket Street. But Ella had been servicing the bucks for three years now, and couldn't resist the sweet temptation of gin. The Quakers and likeminded folk called it the blue ruin. Ella considered it an alchemist potion, for a shot of gin had the power to chase away dark memories from long ago and transform her present into something that shimmered in a most pleasant way. When Ella was sober—a state that was growing less and less frequent these days—the world was an ugly, brutal place. Was it any wonder that she sought out a better reality with the sweet elixir?

Now she wove unsteadily through the tables at the Bell & Swan, ignoring the stray hands that slapped and groped at her along the way. She smiled mistily at the burly man behind the tap, tossing down her latest coin. "'Ere ye go, George. One more, if ye please."

He snorted. Ella preferred to think the sound was jovial rather than contemptuous. She braced her hands, encased in fingerless gloves, on the bar, and leaned forward. A mistake, she realized, when the world tilted madly around her. "Gor," she muttered, pushing herself upright and nearly falling over. She caught herself, and for some reason, her situation struck her as uproariously funny, and she almost tipped over again, laughing.

"Ye're as drunk as an emperor, Ella," George said, taking the cork out of the bottle.

"Nay. Only drunk as a lord," she chuckled good-naturedly.

"Speakin' of lords." He splashed gin into a glass and pushed it toward her. "There's a couple o' swells over there, if ye care for more business. Selena's already got her hooks into one, but the other . . ."

Ella grabbed the glass as she turned to look in the direction George had indicated. Her eyesight had become a little blurry, but she spotted Selena's golden curls. The whore was at a table with two gentlemen, sitting on one of the cove's laps, an arm looped around his neck, a hand caressing him beneath his greatcoat and jacket. Her other hand was free to lift her glass of gin. Ella narrowed her eyes at the other gentleman. Gad, what was on his face?

"Bleeding 'ell," she muttered to George as she identified the side whiskers. "Thought a couple o' rats crawled up on 'is face."

George laughed.

Ella tossed back the gin and slammed down the glass. Straightening the velvet bonnet that she wore, she put as much swing into her hips as she dared given her inebriated state, strolling over to the gentleman with the puffy whiskers. "'Ere now, gov'ner, it looks like yer friend is 'aving all the fun. Do ye wanna bit o' pleasure?"

The gentleman holding Selena grinned over at his friend. "Have a bit of fun, Cross," he urged. "You've been blue-deviled all evening."

"Aye," Selena joined in. "Go off wit ye, sir! Ella will show ye a good time. Won't ye, Ella?"

"Aye, that I will," she assured him, and slid her hand flirtatiously along his shoulder. "C'mon, love. I'll make it worth yer while, I will."

The man named Cross ran his eyes over her. Ella knew she wasn't a diamond of the first water—her red hair and green eyes weren't fashionable—but apparently the swell didn't have any complaints, because he shoved himself to his feet and grabbed her arm. "Where's your room?" he asked, yanking her close enough to smell the brandy on his breath.

"Ah, now, as ter that . . ." She allowed her fingers to toy with his cravat. "We can go out back."

His brows twitched together. "It's cold out!"

"We'll keep each other warm," she promised, and slid her hand down, intertwining her fingers with his to tug him to the door. She didn't mention that she didn't expect their coupling to take very long.

"C'mon," she said when he hesitated outside the door, squinting into the swampy fog that had rolled in from the Thames. At least the sprinkling rain had stopped. Lamps had been lit along the street, their glow muted by the mist.

Fearing the loss of the coin, Ella pressed herself against the gent and kissed him. Just when he started to respond, she pulled back with a breathless laugh. "C'mon, love," she said, smiling at him as she pulled him toward the mouth of the alley. Light spilled from nearby windows, limning the empty crates and barrels shoved against the stone walls, but much of the alley was pitch black.

"This is far enough," the gent growled, his fingers tightening on hers and yanking her to a stop when she would have led him down farther to her usual spot. Grabbing her roughly by the shoulders, he pushed her against the wall. Despite the layers of her clothing, she could feel the cold emanating from the stones.

Ella huffed out a laugh. "I weren't gonna rob ye, ye know."

He gave a grunt, occupied with unbuttoning his pantaloons.

"But this 'ere transaction ain't free," she warned.

"I'll give you a farthing."

"Bleeding 'ell, w'ot do ye take me fer? A shilling!"

"Fine," he snapped.

Ella smiled, and reached over, swatting away his fumbling fingers in order to take care of the rest of his buttons. He didn't waste time, his hands going to her skirts to ruck them up above her knees.

"'Ere now, slow down a bit," she huffed.

He groaned when she finally freed him, but then gave a harsh cry, jerking against her.

"Oy, gov'ner, if ye're done without me, ye still pay," she began, then realized something was wrong. He was pulling away from her, clutching wildly at his throat, gagging and thrashing.

Ella gasped. Panicked, she tried to shove against him, but remained trapped between the wall and his oddly jerking body. The air in her own lungs seemed to evaporate when she saw the shadow looming over the gent. *The face* . . .

Panic turned to terror. Squealing, she made an attempt to escape by diving to the side, but her foot caught in her skirts and she went crashing down, her hip hitting the pavement with an agonizing crack. The coppery tang of blood filled her mouth, but the pain from her bitten tongue barely registered. She was already scrambling to her feet, her heart hammering so loudly that it roared in her ears.

A scream tore out of her as she exploded out of the alley. She kept screaming long after she ran through the doors of the Bell & Swan.

32

Kendra stared down at the sprawled body of Lord Eliot Cross in the gloom of early morning. At least half a dozen men from the tavern had crowded into the alley, many of them holding hissing torches that cast a golden light across the dead man. Beyond the press of men, fog and darkness swirled.

"He was found exactly like this? No one moved him?" she asked.

"Nay. No one touched 'im," one of the men said from behind her.

Kendra heard the revulsion in the man's voice. Understandable, she supposed. The viscount wasn't looking so good. In the flickering light, she could see that his eyes were open, reddened from petechiae and glassy with death. His features were swollen, his mouth open. His tongue would probably have protruded, but it had been cut out.

Kendra continued her visual inspection of the body. Cross wore a greatcoat, jacket, waistcoat, pantaloons, and boots. The cravat was torn. She imagined the killer standing behind him, looping the hemp rope around Cross's throat before yanking tight. Like Sir Giles, he would have clawed at his throat, ripping his cravat, scratching at his own skin before losing consciousness. Kendra noticed the front flap of Cross's pantaloons was unbuttoned. No need to guess at what he'd been doing in the alley; the traumatized sex worker he'd been with was inside the Bell & Swan. Kendra's eyes shifted to the waistcoat and shirt, where the fabric had been cut, the two sections pulled together so they overlapped, the material slightly askew. *Interesting.*

"They ain't laid a finger on him," Sam added quietly.

The Bow Street Runner was standing on one side of her, holding a lantern; on the other side was the Duke. She knew the *they* Sam referred to was George Bell, the burly owner of the Bell & Swan, the first watchman who had been called to the scene, and the constable who'd been called after that. The remaining spectators, mostly Bell & Swan customers, were roughly dressed men. Kendra had a feeling there'd been more people before she and the Duke had arrived, but watching a dead man wasn't all that entertaining, and the crowd had thinned considerably.

The constable who'd been summoned by the watchman read the *Morning Chronicle*, and thought it was a strange enough coincidence to have another man garroted with his tongue cut out that he'd sent word to Sam. While Sam admitted that he'd hesitated to contact them given the lateness of the hour—nearly two A.M.—he'd finally done so, knowing Kendra's penchant for seeing the crime scene with the body still in it. Sam had also sent for Ethan Munroe, but the doctor had yet to arrive.

Kendra squatted down for a closer look. "Can we get more light here?"

She heard movement, and then someone swung a lantern closer. She didn't realize the Duke had grabbed a nearby lantern until he spoke. "How is that?"

"Yes, that's good, thank you." She leaned over, and carefully inserted a gloved finger between the overlapping material of waistcoat and shirt, and flipped open the material to reveal Cross's thin, pale torso.

"Well, this is new," she murmured. Someone gasped and there were murmurings from the men close enough to see the body. She ignored them, her attention focused on what appeared to be a large cross carved into the dead man's flesh, beginning at the base of Cross's sternum and ending just below his navel. Blood, dark as oil, had seeped out of the wound. Not much, though, given the man's heart had stopped pumping when the cut had been made.

She said, "I guess the unsub didn't have time for the invisible ink."

"In all's holy, w'ot's that?" asked a rough voice.

Sam ignored the bystanders. "The killer didn't have time ter do much at all, on account of Ella Browne. The lass is lucky the fiend didn't stop her claret as well."

"The killer obviously has a target, and isn't interested in killing beyond that target."

Kendra shoved herself to her feet just as a voice ran out, "Clear the way! Pardon me—clear the way!"

Munroe pushed through the knot of people to where the body was sprawled. He'd already put on his spectacles, and the flames from the lanterns and torches danced in the twin lenses as he assessed the situation. "Your Grace, Miss Donovan. I shouldn't be surprised to see you here, but I am. Who is this unlucky devil?"

"Lord Eliot Cross," Kendra told him, pulling the collar of her pelisse closer to her throat. The weather had changed yet again. The earlier sleet had stopped, but now the temperature was cold enough to turn everyone's breath into icy puffs of steam. "He was one of the murder suspects on my list."

Munroe's black brows quirked. "I guess he's off that particular list."

"Yeah. There are easier ways to get off it, though." She shook her head, and looked over at Sam. "Let's go and find out what our witness has to say."

They stepped into the shabby interior of the Bell & Swan. Lanterns hung from the low, beamed ceiling to cast a warm light over the heavy wood chairs, tables, and long bar. A coal fire was burning in the stone hearth, but that couldn't chase away the damp cold in the room. Only a handful of customers lingered, mostly men, mostly hunkered around the bar. They'd been talking in low voices, but that came to an abrupt stop when Kendra, Sam, and the Duke entered. Kendra could feel the weight of their eyes on her as she moved into the room. Ignoring their scrutiny, she let her gaze drift over them to the heavily rouged blonde at the end of the bar. The only other woman in the room was slumped over a table, one arm stretched out, revealing a hand with fingerless gloves. Those fingers loosely clutched at an empty glass.

"Don't expect much outta the lass," Sam warned Kendra, moving toward the woman.

"Ella!" The Bow Street Runner grasped her shoulder and gave her a shake. "Ella, lass. Wake up!"

Kendra caught the strong piney scent of gin as she approached the table.

The woman's face was pressed to the table, her velvet bonnet crushed and tipped to the side of her head. Most of her red hair had escaped her hairpins, falling in front of her face. "Sard off!" she muttered, jerking her shoulder away from Sam's hand.

"C'mon, lass!"

"Bloody 'ell!" she groused, and came awake with a start. Straightening suddenly, she took a wild swing at Sam, which he blocked easily.

"Ella! Calm down, lass. I mean you no harm."

"Oy! Pardon!" Green eyes blinked owlishly through the snarls of red hair. She pushed the mess out of her face, dislodging her bonnet. "Yer the thief-taker, ain't ye?"

"Bow Street man," Sam corrected, his lips thinning. "Wake up, lass. You need ter answer questions on account of what happened in the alley."

"I told ye. I didn't do it!"

Kendra scanned the thin face with its light dusting of golden freckles. The woman looked like she might be in her thirties, but Kendra suspected her lifestyle choices had aged her beyond her biological years, and she was probably only in her early twenties. "We know that you didn't do it, Ella," she assured. "But you were with the victim when he was murdered. We need to ask you a few questions."

The girl frowned bleary-eyed at Kendra. "And 'oo the bloody 'ell are ye? Where's George?" She turned to look at the bar.

Sam told Kendra and the Duke, "George is the publican. He's the big fella out in the alley."

Kendra nodded, and pulled out a chair, the legs scraping against the floor, so she could sit next to the girl. "Ella, I need you to tell me what happened with Lord Cross."

"Gawd! Me 'ead feels like a fokking mule stomped on it." She rubbed her temples, cutting Kendra a sideways look. "'Oo's Lord Cross?"

"The man you were with in the alley."

"Oh. Aye. I think 'is friend called 'im somethin' like that, now that I'm remembering properly. And George 'ad said 'e was a lord."

"His friend? He didn't come here alone?"

"Nay. Selena was wit the other bloke. The coves were out caterwauling, so I went ter see if 'e wanted a bit o' fun. Fer a shilling. Wasn't gonna tup fer less! Cheeseparing nob wanted ter only give me a farthing!"

Sam said, "Selena's the yellow-haired Haymarket ware over at the bar. I spoke ter her. She said Lord Cross's friend was named Wentworth. A viscount. He was gone by the time I got here."

"Lord Wentworth," murmured the Duke. "I'd have to ask Caro, but I believe he is Lord Standish's heir."

Kendra nodded. "We'll need to interview him, see if he saw anything." She shifted her gaze back to the woman. "What happened, Ella?"

The sex worker smacked her lips together. "Can I get meself a drink? Me throat is as dry as cinder, it is."

"All right." Kendra glanced at Sam, who gave a grunt. He pivoted on his heel and crossed the room to the tap.

"Gin, if ye please!" Ella called after him.

Kendra was of the mind to order her a strong cup of coffee, but let it go. "Ella, look at me. Look at me. You need to tell me what happened."

The thin face convulsed, and Kendra saw horror shine in the green eyes. "I didn't 'ave a room ter take the cove, so I-I took 'im inter the alley." She swallowed hard, rubbed her mouth. "I do that with the blokes, never 'ad no trouble."

Ella brightened when Sam returned and set the glass on the table. Before the woman could snatch it up, though, Kendra put her hand over it. She said calmly, "Talk first, then you can drink." *And pickle your liver.*

Ella scowled, but Kendra met the other woman's eyes squarely. "Talk."

She hesitated, then shrugged. "I told ye. I brought 'im out back and . . ." Her breath suddenly hitched. "'E began ter twitch somethin' fierce against me. I-I reckoned he was, ye know . . . but it weren't that.

And that's when I looked up, and I seen 'im . . ." She licked her lips before whispering, "The devil."

Kendra frowned. "What did this devil look like? Describe him to us."

"Nay, ye're not understandin', miss." Ella shuddered, and her eyes went glassy with the memory. "It weren't a man. I *told* ye. It was the devil 'isself." She reached for the glass, and her hand trembled violently. "Please, miss."

Kendra met Sam's flat cop gaze. His face was impassive, and she suspected that he'd already coaxed this story out of the woman. "Describe what this devil looked like," she said to Ella.

"Like the *devil*," Ella hissed, sounding both exasperated and fearful. She lifted her hands to her face, made a circular gesture as she grimaced. "'Is face wasn't right, red and all scaly-like. 'Is eyes were black as pitch, they were. And *evil*. That's when I knew . . ." Her voice dropped to a whisper, choked off by fear.

Kendra found herself leaning toward the woman, her gaze intent. Ella's eyes were almost black, her pupils dilating to the point where they swallowed up the green.

"What did you know, Ella?"

"That's when I knew that 'e weren't a man," Ella whispered. "'E was a demon straight from 'ell."

"Her wits are addled by gin," Sam said as he and Kendra stepped outside back into the fog and cold.

"Hm," was all Kendra said in reply.

A wagon had arrived, and a couple of men were hoisting the remains of Eliot Cross into the back of it. Munroe, observing, now came around to meet them. "I'll begin the autopsy tomorrow. As it is Sunday, I shall wait until early afternoon. One o'clock, if you wish to attend."

"Thank you, Doctor," said the Duke. "We'll be there."

Munroe hesitated, and looked at Kendra. "It appears as though the madman has struck again. Will there be more victims by the time this thing is finished?"

Kendra shook her head. "I wish I had the answer for that."

He let out a pensive sigh, then inclined his head. "Until tomorrow, then." The doctor turned on his heel and strode to a nearby carriage.

The Duke turned to Sam. "Do you require a ride to your home, Mr. Kelly?"

"That would be most kind, sir."

"One minute," Kendra said, and moved toward the alley. The gawkers had vanished, leaving the narrow ribbon that ran between the Bell & Swan and the haberdashery shop next door empty.

"What are you doing, lass?" Sam asked.

"Checking something out."

Slowly, she walked to where Cross's body had been sprawled, and spun so her back was pressed against the stone of the tavern. The alley stunk of decay, urine, and vomit. "Mr. Kelly, if you could stand before me, and Your Grace, if you could position yourself behind Mr. Kelly."

The Duke smiled. "Ah, an experiment."

Kendra studied him carefully as he stood behind Sam. The shadows here were thick, but it wasn't absolute. The glimmering light from the street lamps managed to penetrate the alley, and she could see the pale cameo of Sam and the Duke's face. "Okay," she nodded, and turned. They began walking toward the street. "She saw something."

Sam raised his eyebrows, glancing at her sideways. "A demon?"

"I don't think we need to conduct an exorcism, Mr. Kelly," she said drily. "I'd like to interview Ella again when she's sober to get a better description of the murderer. One that hopefully won't require us to travel to Hades."

33

Kendra took a long, slow sip of coffee, needing the jolt of caffeine to strip away the cobwebs from her sleep-deprived brain. She'd finally tumbled into bed around three A.M., but strange dreams had chased her through what was left of the night. Even though she couldn't remember anything, she got the sense that severed tongues and devils with sly, scaly faces featured prominently in those nightmares.

She'd woken up at 7:30 and contemplated sleeping for another hour, but after tossing and turning a bit, she'd given up. Rolling out of bed, she'd stumbled to the dressing room, where she gave herself a quick sponge bath and then wiggled into one of the more loose-fitting morning dresses. Even though she knew it would cause an uproar among the servants, she ventured belowstairs into the kitchens. Mrs. Danbury was there, her gray eyes cool with disapproval—what else was new?—but Kendra wanted coffee more than she feared the housekeeper. She managed to snag a cup on the spot, with the promise of a fresh pot delivered to the study.

By 8:30 she was comfortably ensconced behind the Duke's desk, drinking coffee and enjoying the hushed Sunday atmosphere both inside the mansion and outside in the square. Soon the Duke and Lady Atwood would leave for services at the Anglican Church, along with half of the staff. The other half, she knew, would continue their duties after saying prayers in the servants' hall.

She allowed herself a moment to savor the rare silence. Then she got up and moved to the slate board.

Eliot Cross's murder changed everything. Silas Fitzpatrick was already an outlander, but unless something turned up between the Irishman and the viscount, she thought she could knock him off the list completely. She also thought it knocked Gerard Holbrooke down the list, if not eliminating him altogether too. Holbrooke had known Cross while they were boys at Eton, but it didn't look like they'd had a friendship then or now. Their lives may have overlapped a bit—same parties, similar social circles—but as far as she could see, they were virtual strangers.

Unless . . . Unless the two had formed an alliance, with Cross helping Holbrooke kill his father.

But no, she decided, it was too much of a stretch. Nothing in it for Cross, and everything in it for Holbrooke. Besides, Cross had been the last person to be seen with Sir Giles in what appeared to be an argument. Not smart for Cross if there'd been some sort of alliance with Sir Giles's son. If Cross had had a partner, it would've been Captain Mobray.

Her gaze drifted over to the name on the board that, though it was no bigger in size, seemed to dominate the other names she'd written: *Evert Larson.*

The man had been dead for two years but her gut was telling her that he was somehow involved in what was happening now. Instinct wasn't as ethereal as most people believed. It was formed by thousands of tiny moments that processed through the brain and settled into the sub-conscious. Six years as an agent at the FBI, and the years of education and training before that, had made her trust her gut instinct. Logic and looking at the slate board added to that feeling. Evert was the common denominator that connected Sir Giles to Cross and Mobray.

Kendra found herself tapping her index finger against the coffee cup as she considered that. If she eliminated Fitzpatrick and Holbrooke from her pool of suspects, Evert then became the central figure. So what could a dead man have to do with what was happening now?

Evert had died in Spain. It had been wartime, she reminded herself. God knew, atrocities were committed on the battlefield—and in a prisoner of war camp. Human nature was unpredictable. War could transform a modest individual into a hero who demonstrated amazing acts of valor. Or it could unleash a man's darkest impulses. People did things, vile, unspeakable things to survive.

What would they do to keep a secret once the war was over?

An image of Mobray's watchful gray eyes came to mind. There was something implacable about the man, more so than Cross, who'd struck her as . . . weak. Weak enough to spill secrets if pressed too hard? She thought so. She believed she could break him, if she could just get him alone.

If Mobray and Cross shared a secret from their time in Spain, the captain no longer had to fear Cross talking. Dead men didn't talk.

Her gaze drifted to another name. *Magdalena.* Another link to Spain? The name was Spanish, but that didn't mean the woman was. And perhaps Magdalena wasn't a woman at all. What if it was a code for an operation, or another spy? Still, it was a strange coincidence that Evert Larson had died in Spain, and a month or so ago Sir Giles had received a letter from someone with a Spanish name. And if Magdalena was a woman, what were the odds that Sam could find her in a city of more than a million people? They had no last name, no description. Was Magdalena a member of the nobility, gentry, merchant class, or lower classes?

Kendra sighed. Even in the 21st century, it would be like finding a needle in a haystack. But at least she would've had databases to work with. And it was a digital age, with Facebook, credit cards, CCTV cameras on every corner. You could hide, but it was becoming increasingly difficult to hide forever. In the 19th century, the search for Magdalena seemed hopeless.

She turned her mind to the letter itself. Sir Giles's decision to burn it suggested that it must have held some incriminating or dangerous information. On the other hand, Sir Giles was a spymaster. Maybe this was his common method of disposing of letters.

Somehow, Kendra didn't think so.

She glanced around when the door opened, and a maid came into the room, carrying a tray with the promised pot of coffee, a plate of hot cross buns, and small dishes of churned Epping butter and marmalade. "Do ye need anything else, ma'am?" she asked after depositing the tray on the table.

"Thanks, no. Is His Grace awake?"

"Aye. He and the countess ought ter be leaving for church in a bit." She dipped into an abbreviated curtsy and left the room.

Kendra splashed more coffee into her cup, added sugar, and stirred. Her stomach growled as she reached for a bun, still warm enough to be steaming as she tore it in two. She slathered butter and marmalade on the bun before taking a bite, and nearly moaned. Modern life had put anything with carbs on the Do Not Eat list—unless the carb in question tasted like tree bark. She'd certainly been cautious about her carb intake. Now she wondered how she'd ever live without fresh, made-from-scratch buns and bread.

Chewing, Kendra resumed her position before the slate board. She shifted her gaze to the other names written there. Bertel, Astrid, and David Larson. Each member of the Larson family had a direct link to Sir Giles, but only Evert and David had a direct connection to Lord Cross through their time at Eton.

She dismissed the boarding school. It was too long ago, and they'd been boys at the time. That left the more recent connection between Evert and Cross in Spain.

The rattle of carriage wheels and the clomp of horses' hooves interrupted Kendra's thoughts, drawing her to the window. Below, she saw the purple plume of Lady Atwood's bonnet before she ducked into the carriage, followed by the Duke. Benjamin slammed the door shut and folded up the steps, and then the coachman hurried around to climb back onto his perch. He picked up his lines, and the vehicle began to roll away. Kendra surveyed the square. The fog had lifted, and the sky was a soft pale blue, lightened by sunshine. Whether it would still be that way in two hours or more was anybody's guess.

Polishing off the bun, Kendra moved to the coffee pot, replenished her cup, and grabbed another bun. Pacing, she ate and drank coffee, her mind circling back to Spain again. Two years was a long time. There had to have been a recent trigger. *The mysterious Magdalena?* she wondered. The timing certainly fit.

She was wide awake now, pumped up on caffeine and a sugar-and-carb high from the bun and jam, but she was no closer to figuring out anything. A few suspicions had begun buzzing like annoying insects at the back of her brain—although that could be the caffeine. She needed more information. She needed to find Magdalena.

Kendra finished off the second bun, still pacing. Maybe she needed to take it from a different angle.

Why cut out the tongue? To send a message to someone? Or was it a ritual only to satisfy some impulse in himself?

She paused and closed her eyes. She needed to compartmentalize, to think about the act itself—not the victims. What did it mean when someone had their tongue cut out? In biblical times, it was punishment for crimes like bearing false witness, slander, and perjury. She opened her eyes, lifting her cup to take another swallow of coffee. The Code of Hammurabi allowed a person's tongue to be cut out if they had defamed someone. Did the killer believe Sir Giles and Lord Cross had defamed him in some way? Or borne false witness?

And why the crucifix? A religious symbol, though crosses were symbols that had been found in many non-Christian cultures. Fitzpatrick was Catholic. She assumed the Larson family and Captain Mobray were members of the Church of England. Still, crucifixes were nondenominational. Regardless, it had been important enough to the killer to put the symbol on Lord Cross.

And that brought up another point. Why had the unsub killed Cross so quickly? He hadn't even waited until the viscount had finished with the sex worker.

Kendra's skin prickled. Was the killer escalating? Sir Giles's murder had been carefully plotted and planned. But Lord Cross was more impulsive. Not disorganized necessarily, but—

"Miss Donovan."

She turned sharply. She'd been so deep in thought that she hadn't heard Harding open the door or come into the room. "I apologize for startling you," he said.

"No, that's all right. I was thinking. What is it?"

"Mr. Kelly is downstairs. He said that he has discovered Viscount Wentworth's address, and wishes to know if you and His Grace want to accompany him. Of course, I informed him that the Duke is not at home."

Kendra gulped down her coffee and set the cup down. "Tell him to wait. I'll go with him. I just need to get my coat." *And use the chamber pot.*

Harding's expression was stern enough for Kendra to think that he was channeling Mrs. Danbury. "You will be bringing your lady's maid, will you not? You cannot simply leave unescorted with Mr. Kelly."

"Yeah, yeah." There was no point in arguing. "I'll get my coat *and* my maid."

Viscount Wentworth lived in a small Georgian, white-stucco terrace near Regents Park, off Marylebone Road. The gray-haired butler who answered the door didn't seem inclined to let them inside without a calling card. Apparently saying that she was the ward of the Duke of Aldridge didn't cut it, especially since she said it with an American accent. And Sam's gold-tipped baton only elicited a sneer. Patience snapping, Kendra pushed past the majordomo.

"Now, see here, young lady!" he began indignantly.

She rounded on him. "Lord Wentworth was involved in a murder last night. Either you can bring him here to us or we'll go to him. Your choice."

His mouth fell open. "This . . . this is quite outrageous!"

Sam said, "This is important, Mr.—?"

"Thompson."

"Mr. Thompson, we need ter speak ter your master about the murder of Lord Cross."

"Well, he certainly never . . . *Lord Cross?*" His eyes widened as the name registered. "Lord Cross is dead?"

Kendra watched the butler closely. "Yes. Lord Wentworth didn't say anything to you about it?"

Thompson hesitated. "I have not seen his lordship this morning. It's only half past ten, madam. The master is still abed."

"We'd appreciate if you could wake him so we can speak to him." Kendra watched the uncertainty flit across the butler's face, and added, "We'll wait."

He seemed torn between trying to toss them out, and giving in. He finally let out a put-upon sigh, perhaps realizing that evicting them wouldn't be easy. "Very well. If you will follow me."

Thompson led them into a drawing room decorated in deep green and blue jewel tones and heavy masculine furnishings. Above the carved fireplace hung an oil painting of a naked, golden-haired nymph languishing on a Greek sofa. Kendra didn't need to examine the painting to know that it wasn't a Botticelli. It was, Kendra decided, the 19th century's version of a centerfold. And this room was a 19th-century bachelor pad.

"Gor," Molly said, ogling the nude painting.

"I shall have a footman take your coats."

Kendra turned to face Thompson. "We won't be staying long. We just need to ask Lord Wentworth a couple of questions."

Still he hesitated. "Do you wish tea? Ale?"

"No, thank you," Kendra said.

"Nay," Sam added.

The butler bowed slightly and departed, leaving them to wander the room.

Sam said, "I spoke ter the doxy again before I came ter see you."

Kendra looked at the Bow Street Runner. "Is she sober?"

"As much as she can be, I suppose. But she ain't changed her story. She still says a demon from Hell came up ter kill Lord Cross."

She shook her head. "Our one witness and she's useless."

"Did she really see a demon?" Molly asked, eyes round.

"Of course not," Kendra said.

"Then why'd she say it?"

"'Cause she was foxed," said Sam.

The door opened, and they turned as Lord Wentworth came into the room. The viscount was probably in his mid-twenties, with sandy blond hair limp around a long face with even features. He might have been attractive if not for the deathly pallor and haggard appearance that made him look at least a decade older. His blue eyes were painfully bloodshot. He looked like he was having the mother of all hangovers.

"Good morning," he greeted them carefully. He frowned as his gaze slid over Kendra and Molly, settling on Sam. "This is about Cross, isn't it?"

Sam nodded. "It is."

"God." He raised a trembling hand to press against his brow. "I . . . I wasn't certain, you know. I had hoped that it had been a dreadful nightmare. Please, let us be seated." He didn't so much sit as collapse in one of the chairs.

Kendra and Sam took seats opposite him, while Molly chose to hang back, trying to blend in with the furniture like a good servant.

"Tell me what happened last night," Kendra prompted.

The viscount shook his head, then wished he hadn't, a pained expression crossing his face. "I really do not know. The whore came running in, screaming. It took a glass of gin to calm the creature down. And then she said a demon was murdering folks. I thought it was a joke until we . . ." He licked his lips, revulsion flitting across his face. "Until we went out to the alley. Bloody hell. That's when we saw him, the poor fool. Someone—I don't know who—began shouting for the watch."

Kendra regarded him steadily. "You didn't stay for the watch's arrival?"

"I . . . no. I cast up my accounts." He flushed at the memory, and Kendra recalled the smell of vomit in the alleyway.

He continued. "Afterward, I just wanted to get away. I hailed a nearby hackney and came home. It's not as though I could have done anything for Cross," he added, his voice rising defensively. "What use would I have been to the watch? I didn't see anything!"

"How did you and Lord Cross come ter be at the Bell & Swan?" Sam asked.

"I invited Cross to the theater. My father has boxed seats at Drury Lane."

Kendra regarded him. "How did you know Lord Cross?"

"Our fathers have a connection. And we went to school together."

"Eton," Kendra guessed.

Wentworth's eyebrows pulled together. "How did you know?"

"It's a popular school," she said. "Did you know Evert and David Larson?"

He looked surprised. "At Eton, yes. But they were not people one maintained a connection to outside of school. Their family is in trade, you know. It's odd that you mention them, though. I have scarcely given a thought to either of them, but I believe Cross mentioned Evert's name last night."

Kendra exchanged a quick glance with Sam. The Bow Street Runner leaned forward, his golden eyes narrowing. "What did he say?" he asked.

"Ah, as to that, I'm afraid my memory of last evening is faulty." The viscount lifted his hands, pressing his fingers against his eyes, as though he could force the memory from his skull. After a moment, he dropped his hands, saying, "It had something to do with the war, some complaint that only if his brother had cocked up his toes earlier, he would've been his father's heir and never been sent to Spain . . ." He shrugged. "It was a common grievance for Cross. He was captured by the Froggies, you know. It affected him. Turned him a bit melancholy."

Kendra asked, "Did Cross ever tell you what happened to him while captured?"

"Good God, no. And I wasn't going to pry. Best to get on with life."

"But you said that he complained about being in the military," she pressed.

"Only when he was in his cups. Seemed to think that if he hadn't been there . . . ah, I think that's where he mentioned Evert Larson. Guilt, plain and simple."

"Guilt about what?" Kendra asked.

Wentworth shook his head. "I don't know, really. Can't blame yourself for what happens in war, can you?"

That depends on what you've done, Kendra thought again. Out loud, she asked, "Did Lord Cross ever mention a woman by the name of Magdalena?"

"A woman? You mean, a . . . a doxy?" He colored slightly. It seemed to occur to him for the first time that this might be an inappropriate conversation to have with a lady.

Kendra shrugged. "Maybe."

Normally, she wouldn't have even given him the name Magdalena, preferring the information to come from the witness. False memories could be too easily planted, witnesses too easily manipulated. But Wentworth's altered state the night prior might require a nudge.

"Magdalena," he murmured, a frown behind his eyes. "No, I don't think so."

"What about Captain Mobray?"

"I can't remember if he mentioned him last night, but he's spoken about Captain Mobray in the past. They were in Spain together." Wentworth chewed on his bottom lip for a moment, thinking.

Kendra watched him carefully, and saw when his face changed subtly. "What?" she asked.

"It may be nothing . . ."

"Nothing might turn into something."

"Again, I don't know about last night, but when he's spoken about Mobray in the past, I got the impression that he didn't like the man."

"What else?" Kendra prompted.

He shook his head. "It may be my imagination, but I always thought he was fearful of him."

"Have you ever met Captain Mobray?"

"We've never been introduced."

"Did Cross ever mention Sir Giles?"

Wentworth frowned. "Yes, but I don't remember the context. I know they had a connection. And, of course, he mentioned him last night when we spoke of his murder. The horror."

Kendra kept her gaze on the viscount. "Did he tell you that he'd spoken to Sir Giles on the night he was murdered?"

Wentworth's eyes widened. "Good God, no."

"Did you notice anything different about Cross in the last month? Did his demeanor change at all?"

"No. But I've been out of town at my family's estate for Christmas. I only returned last week." He shuddered. "I'm inclined to go back to the country immediately. There's been talk of establishing a more permanent police force here in London, and I may now agree. Seeing Cross like that . . . dreadful business."

"Murder is always dreadful business," Kendra allowed, and pushed herself to her feet, ending the interview. "Thank you for your time, Lord Wentworth. If you remember anything else about last night—anything at all—please send word to me at the Duke of Aldridge's residence or to Mr. Kelly at Bow Street."

34

W e need to speak to Captain Mobray immediately," Kendra said as soon as they were outside. They'd come by a hackney, so they hailed another. "I want to see if he has an alibi for last night. In fact, we need to run through all our suspects to see if they have alibis. It would be nice to narrow down the list." She glanced at Sam. "And figure out how to find Magdalena."

"I've got me men making inquiries."

"Where?" She remembered her earlier hopelessness at finding the woman, and was honestly curious about the 19th-century detective's strategy. "We don't know anything about her. We don't even know if the letter was posted from London or even England."

"Ah, that would be the rub," he admitted. "Right now, I have some of me men going into the areas of the city where Spanish immigrants live. They'll start with markets and churches. Folks gotta eat, and they usually go ter mass."

It wasn't a bad starting point, Kendra decided. London was a vast metropolis, but it wasn't exactly a melting pot. London's ethnic, racial, and religious groups operated in their own sphere, just as the classes were segregated.

"If the lass is in London, we'll find her. It's just gonna take a bit of time."

Kendra said nothing. Her gaze went to a carriage pulling up next to the curb, and the tall man stepping out of it. It was Alec, carrying his beaver hat in his hand, which allowed the light breeze to ruffle his dark hair as he walked toward them. He looked grimmer than usual, his green eyes intense as they fixed on her.

"I heard about Lord Cross," Alec said in lieu of a greeting when he joined them. "What the blazes is going on?"

"I'm not sure," Kendra admitted. "How did you know we were here?"

"Harding informed me that you and Mr. Kelly went to speak with Lord Wentworth. He was with Cross last night?" He glanced at the residence behind them.

"Yes."

"Did you learn anything?" he asked.

"Not as much as I'd like. You could say that Wentworth and Ella Browne were both in altered states last night."

His grim expression lightened slightly, and he lifted one eyebrow. "Altered states?"

"Completely foxed," Sam put in.

Kendra looked at the carriage. "Would you mind giving us a lift, milord? It will save us from finding a hackney."

"I'm at your service, my lady." Now the well-shaped mouth moved into a crooked smile. He opened the door. "To Grosvenor Square?"

"Actually, Captain Mobray is first up," she said as they piled into the carriage. "Lord Cross, Sir Giles, Evert Larson. What do they have in common?"

"Spain," Alec said immediately. "Mobray has that in common with them as well."

"Yes, he does. Except for one major point."

Sam frowned. "And what's that, lass?"

"They're all dead. And he's alive."

Kendra was surprised by how quickly Sam found Captain Mobray's place of residence. Because of Mobray's background and current employment at Whitehall, Sam's first stop was a coffee house that catered to soldiers and government workers. He returned with information that Mobray rented rooms on Sackville Street, off Piccadilly.

After telling Molly to stay in the carriage, they climbed the stairs to the second story, where the captain's apartment was located. Because he wasn't nobility, landed gentry, or the burgeoning nouveau riche like the Larsons, the captain opened the door himself. Kendra watched him closely. The only sign that he was surprised by his unexpected guests was the slight tightening at the corner of his eyes. Otherwise his expression remained inscrutable. He would be, she decided, a formidable poker player.

Kendra took the lead. "Captain Mobray, may we come in?"

In answer, he stepped back, opening the door wider. "Certainly. May I inquire what this is about?"

They entered a small receiving room. Oddly enough, there was an almost 21st-century vibe to the room, with tufted leather club chairs and a sofa. The side tables and credenza were simple, fluid designs carved out of oak, masculine in feel. The only thing separating this room from a man cave in her era was the lack of a big-ass, 70-inch-screen TV.

Mobray's chestnut hair seemed slightly damp, his jaw a little red, as though he'd recently bathed and shaved. "When was the last time you saw Lord Cross?" Kendra asked.

"Cross? Why?"

She summoned a small smile. "Indulge me."

Mobray indicated the sofa and chairs. "I'm afraid I can't offer you refreshments. I do have a maid-of-all-work, but Sunday is her day of rest. Shall we sit?" He waited until they were seated before lowering himself to a chair. He allowed his gaze to drift over the three of them before focusing on Kendra. "As odd as I find this inquiry, I believe I will indulge you, Miss Donovan. The Smyth-Hope ball. Why?"

"Is there any reason he was upset?"

"Upset? I have no notion. He wasn't upset at the ball."

Kendra pretended to be surprised. "Really? I would say he was troubled. Especially when we spoke of Evert Larson, and what happened in Spain."

"Well . . ." He reached into his jacket, emerging with the porcelain snuffbox. "That is understandable, Miss Donovan. Spain was not a pleasant time for either one of us. It's best forgotten."

"Is that possible?"

"I have done so." He took a delicate pinch and sniffed it into each nostril. His gaze shifted to Alec, dismissing her. "What is this about, sir?"

Kendra leaned forward, catching Mobray's gaze again. "Do you know a woman named Magdalena?" she asked, and wondered if the gray eyes flickered just a bit.

"No."

"Where were you last night, between ten and two?"

He stared at her. "Last night? Why? What's happened?"

Answering a question with another question was a well-known delaying tactic. Kendra wondered if that was what he was doing, and, if so, why he needed the delay. To come up with an alibi? She said, "If you could answer the question, please."

He didn't like that, she could tell. Whether it was because she was a woman telling him what to do, or because he didn't like the question, she didn't know.

"I was here last night, if you must know," he finally said. "What happened?"

"Can anybody verify that?"

Mobray's mouth tightened, irritated that she had yet to answer his question. "No. I was home alone."

"On a Saturday night?" She infused the question with skepticism, knowing it would piss him off.

His gray eyes narrowed. "Why would that matter? I worked yesterday in the Home Office, and spent the evening reading."

Kendra had to remind herself that weekends had little meaning in this era. Even the name *weekend* wouldn't be coined for another sixty-three years. It was strange to her that a concept so familiar in her timeline was unheard of here. The five-day work week would be implemented in the early 20th century, a byproduct of a New England mill allowing their Jewish workers the day off to observe their Saturday Sabbath. Until then, you worked when you worked. Which meant there was no TGIF or lounging around in your bathrobe on Saturday morning.

"What did you read?" Kendra asked.

Amusement flashed in Mobray's flat gray eyes. "Government reports, Miss Donovan. Classified, so I cannot share them with you or his lordship." He flicked a look at Alec, pointedly ignoring Sam. Kendra didn't need the captain to tell her that a Bow Street Runner had a place in this society, and it was way below a captain who worked in the Home Office.

Kendra glanced at Sam. His expression was impassive, but she had a feeling by the way he locked his jaw that Mobray's arrogant dismissal irritated him as much as it did her.

Mobray asked, "Are you going to tell me what this is about?"

"Lord Cross was killed last night," she said bluntly, and watched him closely. "In an alley behind the Bell & Swan. Do you know it?"

For a minute, Mobray froze. Then he shot to his feet, staring at her. "Cross is *dead*? How?"

Kendra rose as well. "Strangled. I'm assuming by a hemp rope. His tongue was cut out, and he was marked with a crucifix."

"A crucifix? Good God. Why?"

His horror seemed sincere. But Kendra was sure that Ted Bundy's sympathy had seemed sincere to the women who'd called into the rape crisis hotline at which he'd volunteered.

Mobray went on, "Maybe it is the bloody papists. They're going to murder us if we don't do something."

She said, "I don't think so. I think this has to do with Spain."

Mobray's face hardened. "Why do you persist in bringing up Spain? 'Tis the past." He drew in a deep breath. "I must ask you to leave. Lord Cross was a friend of mine . . . I am naturally distraught."

Alec and Sam had already risen. Sam said, "My condolences on your loss, sir, but if you should think of anything ter catch this fiend, please send word."

Mobray didn't respond.

Kendra waited a beat before saying, "I'd advise you to be careful, Captain. You may not think this has anything to do with what happened in Spain, but from where I'm standing, that's the only connection you seem to share with Sir Giles and Lord Cross."

He didn't rise to the bait, saying only, "I will show you out."

Sam waited until they were in the carriage before he spoke. "I don't like the man, but he appeared shocked by the news of Lord Cross's death."

Kendra shrugged. "Maybe."

Alec frowned. "Do you really think this has something to do with Spain?"

Kendra hesitated. "It's like I told Captain Mobray—it's the only link between him, Cross, and Sir Giles. And Evert Larson."

"Ghosts," Sam said suddenly. "Like Ruth said. I can't imagine anything that would be more vengeful than the spirit of a young lad I'd sent off ter war, who died far away from home and country."

"I can imagine one thing more vengeful," Kendra said slowly, meeting Sam's eyes. "The family who has been mourning the dead man."

35

Eliot Cross was laid out on Dr. Munroe's autopsy table. Even with the amber glow from the lanterns circling above, his skin still looked eerily pale, blanched of most of its color, except for the petechiae around the eyes, the raw ligature wound at his throat, and the crucifix carved into his torso. Kendra thought the bristly side whiskers looked as incongruous in death as they had when Cross was alive. And as incongruous as the cloth that Barts had hastily draped over Cross's groin area when she'd arrived with the Duke, Alec, and Sam in the subterranean autopsy chambers at one o'clock.

Sam peered down at the corpse. "Not really sure what you can tell us about the crime that we don't already know, Doctor. Had ter have been the same man that killed Sir Giles."

"Yes, and I believe he did it with the same rope, as well," said Munroe. "Like Sir Giles, the killer garroted his victim. This abrasion was deeper than Sir Giles's, though, suggesting more strength was applied."

"Adrenalin," murmured Kendra.

Munroe looked at her. "I'm not familiar with the word."

Oh, shit. How could she explain without opening herself up to more questions that she couldn't answer? "It's when the body becomes overly excited," she finally said. "Adrenalin floods the nervous system. It can give a person more strength than normal."

Behind his spectacles, Munroe's gray eyes held a puzzled frown. He continued to stare at her for several more beats. "I suppose that would make sense," he allowed. "I have witnessed similar behavior when men are in the throes of fury or fear." He returned his gaze to the corpse. "Lord Cross's death was quick and brutal. If the madman had used a wire instead of rope, I think there would have been enough force here to decapitate him."

"Jesus," muttered Sam.

"Instead, we've got a deeper than normal burn mark," Kendra said. "Do you have—" She had to smile when Barts thrust a magnifying glass at her. "Thanks. I need to start carrying around one of these myself."

As Kendra brought the magnifying glass toward Cross's throat, Munroe said, "Before you arrived, I managed to lift several strands of fiber. If you care to look for yourself, they are under the microscope."

The Duke moved to the counter, bending over the microscope. "Hmm. Hemp, I presume."

Munroe nodded. "I cannot swear with one hundred percent accuracy that those match the fiber I found embedded in Sir Giles's throat, but they are most similar."

"Yes, I see that. Hemp, twisted," remarked the Duke.

"Made of double ply yarns, nine yarns per strand," Munroe added.

Kendra suppressed a smile. Munroe and the Duke sounded like any of the laboratory geeks she'd known in her own time.

"I assume the blade's the same, as well," Sam said, his gaze sliding from the mutilated tongue to the cut flesh on the stomach.

"It matches. The blade was wickedly sharp. Straight—not serrated or curved." Munroe pointed to the cross. "This I thought was interesting."

Sam leaned closer. "What?"

But Kendra saw what the doctor was referring to. "Hesitation marks," she murmured, staring at the three small nicks on the sternum. "That *is* interesting."

Alec looked at her. "Why?"

"It's . . ." Kendra had to think of the right word. "An anomaly. We've got a killer who is bold enough to garrote a man in public, while the victim is engaged in sexual intercourse. He didn't know what Ella would do, but I'd say it was a pretty good guess that she wasn't going to stick around and be his next victim. That takes balls."

Sam seemed briefly disconcerted by her description, but then grinned. "Aye."

Alec coughed, which sounded suspiciously like a laugh. "Ah, yes, well, balls aside, the killer was rather occupied with strangling Lord Cross. That was his intended victim, not the doxy. He could hardly kill both of them at once."

"He could have if he'd used the knife," Kendra argued. "But he didn't kill her, even though he must have known she'd run for help. He only had minutes before discovery."

The Duke straightened from the microscope, looking across the room at her. "But we've already established that death by garroting would have taken only seconds, not minutes."

"But then he had to slash through Cross's clothes—waistcoat and shirt." She glanced at Munroe. "As you said, a very sharp blade. Once the torso was exposed, he started to cut, then hesitated. One. Two. Three." She pointed to each scratch. "It took the killer four times before he made the long stroke."

"It's quite deep—at least three inches," Munroe said.

"Adrenalin," she said. At least she wouldn't have to explain it again. "He was pumped up by then. If you notice, there are no hesitation marks in the horizontal cross stroke."

Alec said, "He also knew he was running out of time. He couldn't hesitate any longer."

"True, but I find it interesting that he hesitated at all. He's bold. Aggressive. He's murdered before. He's got a woman screaming bloody murder inside the pub, but still he hesitates? That's odd."

Sam grunted. "I think it's odd that the fiend feels the need ter make this mark at all. Especially when he could be discovered any moment."

Kendra looked at the Bow Street Runner. "Maybe it's a compulsion. Or he wanted to make sure this murder is tied to Sir Giles's murder. That we'd know they were related."

Alec asked, "Why is that important?"

"I don't know. I'm hypothesizing here." She frowned, her gaze on the symbol. "This is a much larger mark than the ones that were done in invisible ink. Amplified like this, it looks more like a lowercase letter *t* than a crucifix. I thought this little curl"—she pointed to the end of the long slash that curved slightly toward the right—"was an errant brushstroke on Sir Giles, caused by the way the killer held the brush. But he's done it here as well, which means it was deliberate."

The Duke joined them at the autopsy table. "Instead of a cross, he's marked both bodies with a *t*? What does a *t* represent?"

"It's the most commonly used consonant in the English language," she said. When they stared at her, she waved her hand. "Sorry. That's the only thing that comes to mind." *Good God, I sound like Ruth.*

"Well, I don't think that the murderer is trying to give us English lessons," the Duke remarked drily.

Kendra huffed out a laugh. "No. He—or she—is doing it for a reason."

"She. You still think Astrid Larson could have done this?" Alec sounded skeptical.

"I haven't found any reason to eliminate her as a suspect. Adrenalin isn't limited to men. It can give women considerable strength too."

Alec said, "I'd think that Haymarket ware who'd been with Cross would have noticed if their attacker was a woman."

"Ella swears the devil came up from the depths of Hell to kill Cross," she said. "Even if we didn't have her eyewitness account that we're dealing with a demon with a red, scaly face, the killer was probably bundled up, and therefore unrecognizable."

Kendra glanced at the clock mounted on the stone wall. "Before we interview the Larsons, I would like another chat with Lady Holbrooke. Woman to woman."

The Duke shot her a look. "What you are really saying is that you would like to speak to Lady Holbrooke alone."

"I think it would be best."

Sam frowned. "You still believe Mr. Holbrooke had something to do with the murder of his father and now Lord Cross?"

"No. Which is why I think another chat is in order." She smiled at the Bow Street Runner. "With her son no longer a suspect, Lady Holbrooke should be a lot more forthcoming. Instead of spending her time coming up with lies to protect her son, she might actually tell me the truth."

36

The Duke insisted that Kendra take Molly with her, unwilling to give the Beau Monde any excuse to shun her. Kendra didn't have the heart to remind him that being the recipient of Sir Giles's tongue had probably already gotten her bumped off the Ton's guest lists.

Without Rebecca accompanying her, though, Kendra wasn't entirely sure if Lady Holbrooke would receive her. Being the ward of a duke was probably a lot further down the pecking order than being the daughter of an earl. It didn't hurt, though, to be delivered to the Holbrooke door in the Duke's plush town carriage with his family crest on the door.

In the end, Kendra had no idea why Lady Holbrooke agreed to see her; she was just happy the woman had. While Molly waited in the foyer, she followed the elderly butler down the depressing hallway decorated with its heavy black mourning crepe and into the drawing room.

"Miss Donovan," Lady Holbrooke greeted as soon as Kendra entered, setting aside the book she'd been reading, and the butler departed, closing the door behind him. Lady Holbrooke didn't stand up or smile, but instead gestured to the chair opposite her.

"Thank you for seeing me," Kendra said as she took the seat, studying the other woman. Lady Holbrooke wore her widow's garb and a simple linen cap. Her face was pale, but composed. Her pretty brown eyes were wary as she regarded Kendra.

"Do you wish tea? I can ring for it."

"No, thank you. I'm sorry to bother you, but I have a few more questions."

"If this is about my son—"

"I don't think your son was involved."

Lady Holbrooke raised her eyebrows, then just as quickly lowered them. Her face changed subtly, softening. "Of course, he was not. The very idea is ridiculous."

Kendra didn't necessarily agree, but there was no point in arguing, not when it looked like she was getting back into the widow's good graces. "I wanted to ask you a couple of questions about your husband. You mentioned before that he'd seemed preoccupied in the last month. I have to ask you again, Lady Holbrooke, did he give you any indication why?"

The older woman frowned, which caused the vertical creases to deepen between her brows. She was silent for a long moment. "I confess that I have given your question considerable thought since your last visit, Miss Donovan, and it occurred to me that my husband did say something odd," she said slowly.

Kendra waited.

"As I told you, my husband spent much of his time at work. He had heavy responsibilities, so it was not unusual for him to be preoccupied, you understand."

"I understand."

"I hesitate even to mention this . . ."

"Lady Holbrooke, your son may not be under suspicion anymore, but your husband's killer is still at large. Anything you tell me could help."

"But that is just it, Miss Donovan. I don't know how this could help." She drew in a deep breath.

"My husband was not an atheist, but he was not a religious man," she finally said, then seemed flummoxed as to how to proceed.

Kendra covered her surprise. Whatever she'd expected the widow to say, this was not it. Then the memory of the symbols painted on his body came to her. "Your husband mentioned a religious matter?"

"No, not exactly." She surged to her feet. "I don't know how to explain."

Kendra stood as well. "Why don't you tell me what you and your husband were doing before he said what he did." Sometimes it was helpful to ground a reluctant witness in the mundane to tease out a memory.

Lady Holbrooke nodded. "We were having breakfast. Maybe that is why it struck me as so odd. I was telling him about a salon that I had attended, and he asked me something about hiding sins and finding mercy. There was no context, you see." She frowned, even appearing to find the recollection baffling. "Of course, I asked him what he could possibly mean, and he said that he was making reference to a quote in the book of Proverbs."

Kendra hesitated. "And that was odd?"

"It was not unusual for Sir Giles to quote text, but he tended to quote philosophers and politicians. But quoting religious text? No. That was very odd."

"What was the quote? Exactly?"

"I'm afraid I cannot tell you that, Miss Donovan. In fact, I had quite forgotten all about the matter until your first visit."

"He was upset?"

"Not upset. Melancholy."

"When was this?"

Lady Holbrooke shook her head. "I cannot give you an exact date, but I think it was about a fortnight ago. I believe it was the morning after Mrs. Braxton's salon."

"Okay." Kendra kept her gaze on the other woman. "What do you think he meant by that? Hiding sins and finding mercy?"

"I truly do not know. I did not pursue the matter." Her brown eyes darkened. "Now I wish I had."

Kendra waited a moment, but when Lady Holbrooke remained silent, she asked, "Did your husband mention a woman named Magdalena recently?"

She watched the widow carefully, but could see nothing deceptive about her behavior. No eyes refusing to make contact or telltale flush.

She shook her head. "Magdalena? No. Who is she?"

"I'm not sure. Someone from Spain, maybe."

"Spain?" Lady Holbrooke's lips parted, awareness rippling across her delicate face. "You persist in thinking this has something to do with Evert's death?"

Instead of answering, Kendra threw out another question. "Did you know that Lord Cross was murdered last night?"

Lady Holbrooke's eyes widened, her hand fluttered to her throat. "Good heavens. No, I have heard nothing. What can this mean? Do you think it has anything to do with my husband's—with what happened to Giles?" she asked, her voice faint. "London is a violent city. The two murders might not necessarily be connected."

"They were killed in the same manner," was all Kendra said.

Fear leapt in Lady Holbrooke's eyes. "You don't think . . . Gerard *is* safe, isn't he? This madman won't come after my son, will he?"

"There's no reason to think that."

Lady Holbrooke was still for a moment, then expelled a sigh. She moved to the window. "I do not understand what's happening," she murmured, staring outside.

"The only thing that links your husband to Lord Cross is what happened to Evert in Spain." Kendra said. "Did your husband ever talk about what happened in Spain? How Evert died?"

"Well, of course he spoke of it at the time. But not recently, no."

"What did he say—at the time? Do you remember?"

Lady Holbrooke frowned. "He died in a fire. That's all I recall," she whispered, and shook her head. "Such a tragedy. I loved Evert—both Evert and David."

Kendra kept her gaze on the other woman. "Do you think any of the Larsons could have killed your husband? And Lord Cross?"

Shock flashed across the delicate features. "No! No, of course not. The very notion is absurd. How can you think such a thing?"

"Is it so hard to believe that one of them might want revenge for what happened to Evert?" Kendra asked softly.

"But . . . I don't understand." Lady Holbrooke shook her head, her brow puckering. "What happened to Evert was terrible, and it drove a wedge between our families that will never be healed. But it was war, Miss Donovan. Evert was captured, and . . ." She lifted a pale hand, then let it fall. "He died. No one can hold my husband responsible for what happened in Spain. And Lord Cross . . . he had been captured by the French as well."

"And survived."

"I don't understand what you're saying, Miss Donovan."

Kendra wasn't entirely sure what she was saying either. But an idea was beginning to take shape, the elusive threads slowly solidifying. She just needed more information.

She asked, "Would you mind if I speak to your daughter?"

"Ruth? Why?"

"Sometimes children see and hear things that adults overlook." *Especially a girl like Ruth.*

Lady Holbrooke thought it over. "Nanny Howe took her to Hyde Park," she finally said. "They ought to be by the lake. They asked for a loaf of bread to feed the ducks."

"Thank you. I'll show myself out."

Kendra left the older woman, staring sightlessly out the window, a troubled look on her face, her book abandoned on the sofa.

Kendra found Ruth and her nanny standing on the banks of the Serpentine, where the manmade lake began to curve to the east. A cold breeze churned the waters, but the scattering of ducks looked content to bob up and down on the choppy waves. Despite the chilly temperature and occasional drift of snow, the area appeared to be a popular hangout for children. Rebecca had apparently been right about doctors urging parents to take their children outdoors and embrace the cold. Although looking around, Kendra didn't see any parents. Instead the dozen or so children who were running across the stiff grass, madly shrieking, were all doing it under the watchful eyes of their governesses.

Ruth was not part of that boisterous crowd of children. Instead, she cut a solitary figure dressed all in black—save her mittens, which were a pale blue. Kendra watched the little girl's gaze track the energetic play of the other children. The stout figure of her nanny stood about five feet away, breaking off crumbs from a loaf of bread to toss at the ducks on the water.

"Why don't you join them?" Kendra asked as she came up to Ruth. "The other children. I'm sure they'd let you play with them."

Ruth wrinkled her nose. "They aren't playing a real game. They're just running about being silly."

Kendra eyed the little girl. Maybe there were similarities between her and Ruth, but this was not one of those areas. She thought back to her often lonely childhood, and knew that given the chance, she'd have been out with the other children, and at least trying to conform to the social group.

"I tell her all the time to go and talk to the other children," Nanny Howe said, trudging over to them. "Better than standing there doing nothing."

"I am doing something. I am looking at the Serpentine," Ruth said, frowning at her nanny. "It is not a natural body of water. It was created when the River Westbourne was dammed."

"Oh, heavens, child, you think too much about things that do not need thinking about!" The older woman all but rolled her eyes. Her expression smoothed out as she smiled at Kendra. "Good afternoon. I'm Nanny Howe. I remember you. You were at the house the other day. Forgive me, but I don't recollect your name?"

Ruth piped up, "Her name is Miss Donovan. She's a Bow Street Runner, although . . ." She turned her solemn face up to Kendra, regarding her with intelligent eyes. "Nanny says you were telling me a Banbury Tale, because there is no such thing as a female thief-taker."

"Ack, now, I said that Miss Donovan was obviously teasing." The other woman's already ruddy face pinkened. She shot Kendra a sideways glance that was half apologetic, half embarrassed. "We know that ladies do not become Bow Street Runners, especially gently bred women."

Ruth's frown deepened. "No, you specifically said Banbury Tale. I have an excellent memory, and I know what you said."

"I'm sure you do," Kendra said quickly, smiling at the other woman to reassure her that she wasn't angry. She shifted her gaze back to the little girl. "In fact, I'm hoping your memory is as good as I think it is, because maybe you can help me."

Ruth's face brightened. "How can I help you, Miss Donovan?"

"The other day, when I met you, you asked me if I believed in ghosts. Why did you ask that?"

"Oh." The little girl's gaze dropped to the ground, and she stretched out a toe to push a rock into the snow.

The nanny looked uneasy. "What's this about ghosts?"

Kendra said nothing, watching Ruth. The little girl kept her gaze on the rock she was nudging with her foot, but finally said, "You wanted to know if Papa was upset by anything. I never believed in ghosts, but Papa believed in them."

"He was upset by ghosts?"

Ruth nodded. "Yes."

"How do you know?"

"Because I went into Papa's study to borrow a book. I didn't know Papa was at home. He usually was not. He was sitting behind his desk, but the room was dark. I asked Papa if he wanted me to light a candle for him, but he said that some ghosts were best dealt with in the dark." Ruth glanced at Kendra. "That is a strange thing to say, isn't it?"

"Why do you think he said that?"

"I don't know, but I told Betty when she mentioned him being vexed. I told her that he was vexed over ghosts. She told me that I oughtn't worry about ghosts, because Papa was strong enough to fight them." She wrinkled her nose in disdain. "It was a stupid thing to say. You can't fight an apparition. They do not belong in the physical world. Isn't that a stupid thing to say?"

"Did your father say anything else?"

"I asked Papa if ghosts were real, but he said it was his dilemma, and that I was not to worry about it."

"He used that word precisely? Dilemma?"

"Yes. 'Do not worry, Ruthie. 'Tis my dilemma,'" she said in such a way that Kendra knew she was repeating her father's words exactly. The little girl cocked her head to the side, her brown eyes regarding Kendra with solemn intensity. "Will this help you find who killed Papa?"

"Possibly," Kendra said slowly. "You've given me a lot to think about. Thank you."

"*Do* you believe in ghosts, Miss Donovan?"

Kendra opened her mouth to say no, but then thought about the more complicated answer, about how ghosts could take on many forms and were not necessarily just the spirits of the dead. But she knew Ruth's literal mind wouldn't understand, so she smiled and gave the child a wink instead. "Let's just say that I'm keeping an open mind."

37

Having control of the carriage gave Kendra a heady jolt of freedom, not quite equal to getting behind the wheel of a Jaguar—hell, any car—and driving herself to wherever she wanted to go, but close. Instead of returning to Grosvenor Square, Kendra directed Benjamin to take her to the Larson residence. It was a victory of sorts that Benjamin didn't argue with the new directive. He scowled—but that was normal for the coachman—and did what might have been an eye roll, eventually shrugging his acceptance. Maybe the Duke's staff was starting to get used to her. Or maybe she was just wearing them down. Whatever worked.

Molly fidgeted nervously when the carriage began rumbling down the road. "We're not goin' 'ome?"

"Not yet. I need to conduct a few more interviews. You can wait in the coach while I go inside. It shouldn't take too long."

Molly looked horrified by the suggestion. "Oh, no, miss. It wouldn't be proper for ye ter go into a 'ouse all by yerself."

Kendra said nothing for a long moment. *Who's wearing who down?* she thought wryly. "Do you think while I'm speaking to the Larsons, you can talk to the servants?" she said finally. "Find out if the family was around last night, after ten?"

The maid's eyes widened, but she nodded. "Aye. Oi can maybe ask for a cuppa tea."

"See if you can also find out how many servants the Larsons employ." She thought of her own attempt to sneak out of the Duke's residence days earlier. The Duke employed an army of servants, but she'd still managed to sneak out of the house.

The carriage drew up outside the Larsons' redbrick mansion. Benjamin unfolded the steps, and Kendra thrust open the door, stepping down. She had no calling card to present, so she went up the path to knock on the door herself. It was probably audacious. She heard Benjamin mutter something behind her, but he made no move to stop her.

The butler's eyebrows rose when he opened the door to find Kendra and Molly.

"I need to speak with Mr. and Mrs. Larson," Kendra told him.

The majordomo hesitated, but then stepped back to allow them into the entrance hall. "If you will wait here, I shall see if Mr. Larson is home," he said, making no move to take her coat and gloves or bring her into a lesser drawing room to wait. "Miss Donovan, isn't it?"

"It is."

She watched as the butler strode off. Because it was Sunday, she expected the Larsons to be at home. Whether they would be at home to *her* was another matter. She wasn't entirely sure what she would do if they declined to see her. Come back with the Duke, she supposed. *And how annoying would that be?*

After several minutes, the butler reappeared. "If you will come with me," he said.

Kendra followed, leaving Molly to linger behind in the entrance hall. The butler still didn't ask to take her coat and bonnet, which she thought was a sign that she wouldn't be staying long, until the servant ushered her down the hall, past the drawing room that she'd been in the other day, and into another corridor that led to French doors that opened to the conservatory.

"Miss Donovan," the butler announced as he opened the doors, stepping aside to let Kendra go through.

Aldridge Castle had a conservatory, an enormous glazed glass structure that was used to grow fresh vegetables in the winter months. The estate also had an orangery for more exotic fruits. Kendra had been in both buildings only twice in the months she'd been in the 19th century, but she'd been impressed at the self-sufficiency of country estates.

The Larsons' conservatory was similar to the one at Aldridge Castle, and yet different. The sloping, glazed glass walls were the same, but this room wasn't for growing asparagus and broccoli. This was serious horticulture, with tables filled with terracotta pots, dirt, and seedlings, and larger pots with full-grown plants and herbs. The air was heavy with the pungent scents of dirt and fertilizer. *And this is how you became a wealthy apothecary in this era,* she thought with a flash of amusement.

It wasn't freezing in the greenhouse, but the air was moist and chilly—hence the butler not taking her coat. Astrid was also wearing a loose-fitting wool coat over her apple-green cotton morning gown as she stood behind one table, carefully cutting off stalks from a potted plant with a small knife. David was the only one not wearing a coat, but he was in the process of hauling a large hemp bag of what looked like dirt over to another table. Several similar bags were stacked up against the wall. Undoubtedly the work he was doing was keeping him warm. Bertel was bent over another table, peering into a microscope. Now he straightened, looking over at Kendra as she entered the greenhouse.

Once again Kendra was struck by the sheer physical beauty of this family. Beneath the physical appeal, though, was one of them a murderer?

"Forgive us for not greeting you in a more proper manner, Miss Donovan," Bertel said, coming forward to join his wife. "We are not gentry, and must work for a living."

"I think your operation is admirable," Kendra said honestly, and lifted a gloved finger to touch a nearby flowering stalk. "What's this?"

"*Actaea racemosa*—black cohosh," Astrid identified. "Used for stiffness of the joints and muscle pain."

"And this?" Kendra shifted to another flowering plant.

"*Aesculus hippocastanum*—horse chestnut. Toxic unless processed properly. But I don't think you have come here to be educated on the medicinal properties of plants and herbs, have you, Miss Donovan?" Astrid said coolly.

Kendra allowed her gaze to travel over the other woman's beautiful, proud face. There was strength of will that she saw beyond the splendor. It was the kind of determination that could garrote a man, she thought, or drag an unconscious hackney driver into a doorway.

Her gaze dropped to the knife Astrid had been using to make the clippings. Too small to be the murder weapon. She shifted her attention to the other table that held bags of dirt, bags tied off with rope that Kendra would bet her paycheck—if she actually had a paycheck—was made of hemp.

"No," she finally said, swinging her gaze back to the Larsons. "This is not a social call. Can you tell me where each of you were last evening, after ten o'clock?" Again, she didn't like doing a group interview, but she couldn't see them agreeing to split up so she could question them separately.

Her inquiry brought on a moment of silence, thick with tension. Slowly, Astrid brushed the dirt from her palms. "Why are you asking about last night?"

Kendra debated her answer, but decided she had nothing to gain by keeping the information to herself. "Lord Cross was murdered last night."

Astrid's frigid blue eyes fixed on Kendra's. "And you think one of us might have killed this man?"

"It would be nice to eliminate you from the list of suspects." She watched them exchange glances. "Or would you rather a Bow Street Runner ask you these questions?"

David was the first to break the silence. "I was in the laboratory until quite late."

Kendra looked over at him. "The laboratory at the shop, or do you have one here?"

"The shop," he answered, and shrugged his broad shoulders. "And I was quite alone."

Kendra kept her eyes on the gorgeous face. "Inconvenient."

"I had no reason to believe that I would need someone to vouch for my whereabouts today," he said simply.

"My son did not kill Lord Cross," snapped Bertel, his handsome face flushing with temper.

"I'm not accusing anyone." *Not yet.* "When did you return home, David?"

"I can't say exactly. Sometime after one, I think."

Kendra nodded, and looked at Bertel. "Where were you last night, sir?"

"My husband and I were at home," Astrid answered, and laid a hand on her husband's arm as she had on Kendra's first visit. Kendra wasn't sure if it was a gesture of comfort or strength. Or caution.

A wife alibiing her husband—or vice versa—was, in general, a terrible alibi. Especially when the wife clearly loved her husband. "Together?" Kendra pressed.

Astrid hesitated. "For much of the evening, yes."

"And from ten o'clock on?"

"I spent the evening in here, Miss Donovan," Bertel said. "Ever since my son died, I have found sleep to be elusive. I told you. We are not gentry. We work for our livelihoods. I find comfort tending to these plants, experimenting with cross-pollination. It keeps my mind occupied. My wife was in bed around that time."

In interviews, one learned just as much from what wasn't said as what was. Kendra thought it was interesting that no one asked her how Lord Cross had been killed. It was usually the first thing out of people's mouths when they learned of a murder. Maybe the Larsons didn't care. Or maybe one of them already knew, and the other two chose to look the other way. A willful oblivion.

Kendra changed gears. "Did you ever ask to see the official reports on what happened in Spain at the time of your son's death?"

Bertel's mouth tightened. "I asked Giles what happened. He would have told me what was in the reports."

"So you never actually saw them?"

"No."

"Did you ever speak to Lord Cross and Captain Mobray about what happened? As the only two survivors, they were the only ones privy to the details."

"After learning of my son's death, I approached both men, but they were remarkably short on details," said Bertel. "They told me that my son was captured by the French while attempting to rescue them. They were held in different areas of the camp." Bertel's lips thinned, his eyes darkening with temper. "There was an explosion and fire. Cross and Mobray escaped amid the confusion. At least, that is the story they told."

Kendra raised her eyebrows. "It sounds like you don't believe them."

David looked at her. "Would you?"

Probably not. She asked, "What do you think happened in Spain?"

David hesitated, but shook his head. "I don't know."

Kendra glanced at Bertel and Astrid.

"I only know my son is dead," Astrid said coldly.

"Do you know a woman named Magdalena?"

Kendra had thrown the question like a sucker punch, and found it fascinating to watch the play of expressions that flickered across each face. Surprise. Fear. Then each of their expressions smoothed out into blank masks. Tension, however, seemed to crackle in the air like electricity.

"No," Bertel said, his voice harsh.

Again, Kendra thought it was interesting there was no follow-up question: *What does this woman have to do with anything?*

When no one else spoke, Kendra nodded. "Okay. Thank you for seeing me. I appreciate it."

"I shall show you out, Miss Donovan," Astrid said abruptly. Even in the drab wool coat, the woman looked like a queen. She came around the table and fell into step beside Kendra as they exited the conservatory.

"Why are you persisting in these inquiries?" Astrid demanded once they were walking down the hall. "They can only cause my family pain. And we have gone through enough of that."

"I'm sorry, Mrs. Larson." Kendra met the other woman's searing gaze. "Two people are now dead. Someone murdered them. I think it ties back to Spain. To Evert. Don't you want answers on what might have happened over there, to him?"

Astrid said nothing. Because she didn't want answers? Kendra wondered. Or because she already had them?

They reached the entrance hall, which was empty. "Goodbye, Miss Donovan," Astrid said. Kendra didn't think she imagined the note of finality in the other woman's voice. With a swish of skirts, Astrid turned and retraced her steps back down the hall.

Kendra didn't have to wait long before the butler and Molly materialized. He opened the door, his eyes guarded as he watched them leave.

Kendra waited until she and Molly were seated in the carriage before she asked, "Did you learn anything?"

"Aye. The Larsons 'ave a staff of five. Mr. Wyman—the butler—is married ter the cook. Then there's two maids, and a footman. Oh, and their coachman and stable boy. Oi suppose they'd be considered staff."

Kendra thought about that. "It's a big house for only five servants."

"Oi reckon."

"Easy enough to avoid five or seven servants. Ten o'clock, they could've been in bed or in the kitchens. Did they mention where the Larsons were at that time?"

"Oi asked if they were around, and they said the young master was at 'is laboratory in the shop, and the old master were workin' in the conservatory. Mrs. Larson was abed." Molly hesitated. "They weren't the most friendly of staff. Oi don't think they liked that ye're pokin' around the family's business."

"Nobody does," said Kendra, and smiled a little as she settled back against the seat. "But that doesn't mean you stop poking."

38

The caffeine high from earlier that morning had tapered off by the time Kendra climbed the steps to the study, so she was grateful to see a new tray carrying a tall silver pot of coffee on the table. The Duke was behind his desk, pipe in hand, a thin tendril of smoke curling through the air, as he studied the estate's financial ledgers. Kendra knew he'd made the decision to install gas lighting in Aldridge Castle, but the project was massive and expensive, and required a great deal of his time. A duke running a dukedom, she'd come to realize, wasn't all servants and parties. It was a Fortune 500 CEO running a multinational corporation.

Alec was lounging on the sofa, long legs stretched out and crossed at the ankles, reading the newspaper. He glanced at her, then was on his feet, moving to the coffee pot.

"Was Lady Holbrooke more forthcoming this time?" he asked as he poured a steaming cup, added a lump of sugar, stirred, and then brought it to her. "You look like you are in need of a refreshment."

"Thanks," she murmured, briefly distracted when their fingers brushed, and she caught the warm light in Alec's green eyes. "Yes."

Alec gave her a crooked smile. "Yes that Lady Holbrooke was more forthcoming, or yes you are in need of refreshment?"

"Both, actually," Kendra said, returning his smile as she lifted the cup and sipped. "Lady Holbrooke admitted that her husband had been more disturbed lately."

"The man had a son who was deeply in debt and had impregnated the maid," Alec pointed out drily. "That would trouble anyone."

Kendra lowered her coffee cup and grinned at him. "You may have a point. But Sir Giles already had solutions to those problems." She took another swallow. "Lady Holbrooke said her husband was quoting Proverbs. She said Sir Giles mentioned something about hiding sins and finding mercy. She doesn't remember the exact quote, but thought it was odd enough at the time. Apparently, Sir Giles was not the kind of man to go around quoting from the Bible."

Alec frowned. "She never mentioned this before."

"Yeah, well, the first time I spoke to her, I put her on the defensive because I thought her son might have murdered his father."

The Duke stood and moved across the room to the bookcases.

She continued, "Without that being an issue, she was more talkative. And she'd had time to think about how her husband was behaving recently."

Puffing gently on the pipe, the Duke ran a finger across the book spines on the shelf. "Proverbs, you say?"

"Yes."

"Ah." Leather slid against leather as he pulled out an ancient-looking Bible. Not the family Bible, though. That was kept at Aldridge Castle, and was as thick as a cinderblock, filled with family marriages, births, and deaths that dated all the way back to William the Conqueror. When she'd first seen it, it had brought home to her the Duke's long and noble lineage more than Lady Atwood's lectures ever could.

The Duke returned to his desk with the book and began flipping through pages.

Kendra said, "I asked if she heard of the name Magdalena, but she hadn't."

Alec crossed his arms, leaning against the fireplace mantel. "Mayhap Sir Giles burned the letter to prevent his wife from reading it. For all we know, she could be Sir Giles's mistress."

"I don't think so. There was no indication that he had a mistress, and I really think any rumor in that regard would have come up. Mr. Muldoon would have mentioned it when he spoke of Sir Giles's character. Speaking of—"

"Here's one," the Duke interrupted, glancing up. "Pardon me, my dear."

"No, go on."

"Proverbs 10:12. 'Hatred stirs up strife, but love covers all sins.'"

Kendra considered it, but shook her head. "It doesn't say anything about mercy. And I think Lady Holbrooke would have mentioned love if it had been part of the quote."

The Duke went back to flipping pages, scanning the passages.

Alec looked at her. "What were you going to say about Muldoon?"

"I haven't heard anything from him, and I want to find out if he has made any progress on getting ahold of the official report of what happened in Spain."

He lifted a dark eyebrow. "You doubt Lord Cross and Captain Mobray's account?"

She shrugged. "Theirs is the only account that we have. Evert Larson was captured, then killed in some kind of explosion and fire. How did the other British soldiers die? How did Cross and Mobray escape? I assume no one bothered following up on their account after the war. No one is going to track down the French who were at the camp to interview them about it, are they? Even if they could find them."

Alec shook his head. "No."

"So, what if there was another account? Something that didn't quite match up with what Lord Cross and Captain Mobray said?"

Alec frowned. "You are speaking of Magdalena."

"It fits."

"To a point. Let's say this woman did contact Sir Giles about a month ago, and told him a different account about what happened in Spain, which contradicted Lord Cross and Captain Mobray's official report. Why didn't Sir Giles begin an investigation?"

"How do you know he didn't? Maybe that's what he and Cross were arguing about at White's."

The Duke lifted a finger to gain their attention. "Here's another quote—'Whoever tries to hide his sins will not succeed, but the one who confesses his sins and leaves them behind will find mercy.'"

Kendra walked over to the desk, reading the passage herself over the Duke's shoulder. "Maybe." She went over to the sideboard and replenished her coffee. "I spoke with Ruth, as well, and she said that she'd come upon her father sitting in his study in the dark. He told her that ghosts were best dealt with in the dark."

She glanced up to catch the Duke's frown. "It does appear as though Sir Giles had something weighing heavily on his conscience," he conceded.

Alec shook his head. "If there was an official investigation, I think we would have heard about it. Muldoon would have heard about it."

"Maybe it was an unofficial investigation," Kendra said. "Regardless, maybe it's not that simple. The truth never is, especially if it's an inconvenient truth. Muldoon said that Sir Giles was the kind of man who would do anything for king and country. Let's say someone came forward with information that turned Mobray and Cross's account of what happened to Evert on its head."

"Magdalena," said the Duke.

Kendra nodded. "And maybe the truth would cast England in a poor light."

The Duke frowned. "How so?"

"I'm not sure. How embarrassing would it be if it came out that two British soldiers, one of whom currently works in government and is looked at as a war hero with a bright future, acted less than honorably in the war?"

Alec said slowly, "It would depend on what you mean by *less* than honorably."

She took a slow sip of coffee. "I don't know, but Sir Giles was a strategist. The end always justifies the means. For him, England is the greater good, and everything else can be sacrificed."

The Duke closed the bible, his uneasy gaze meeting hers. "But we are talking about the son of a good friend, a boy he once loved like his own."

"Maybe that's why he was troubled," Kendra said. "This wasn't some young, faceless Irish girl who'd been murdered by a British soldier. This was Evert Larson. 'Whoever tries to hide his sins will not succeed, but the one who confesses his sins and leaves them behind will find mercy.' I don't know about you, but that sounds like someone with a guilty conscience."

The Duke tapped his pipe against his palm, frowning. "What could have happened in Spain?"

"I don't know, but Sir Giles wasn't feeling guilty over what happened in Spain two years ago. He was feeling guilty over thinking he might have to cover up what had happened in Spain," Kendra corrected. "There's a difference."

"And if he buried the truth about what happened in Spain, he would also be burying the truth about what happened to Evert Larson," Alec said softly. "Justice could not be done—assuming an injustice had been committed."

"Oh, I think an injustice had been committed, and Magdalena brought it to Sir Giles's attention," Kendra said with quiet certainty. "I think that's what the last month was about. He was trying to come to some sort of decision—whether to go public and launch an official investigation, or"—she shrugged—"let it go."

"Or he began his own investigation, as you suggested, questioning Cross and Mobray over their account of what happened in Spain." Alec shoved his hands into his pockets, his eyes brooding. "That would have alarmed them."

Kendra met his eyes. "Yes."

He said, "Cross didn't kill Sir Giles."

"No."

"Captain Mobray?"

Kendra shrugged. "He certainly has motive."

The Duke looked at her. "Whatever happened in Spain, Cross and Mobray were in it together. They supported each other's account."

"It wouldn't be the first time partners in crime or conspiracy ended up killing the other," she murmured.

"You think Lord Cross was going to betray Captain Mobray," said the Duke.

"I think Mobray could have *feared* that Cross would betray him. Mobray has political ambitions. God knows there's nothing worse than someone who has political ambitions and a secret." She shot the Duke a pointed glance. "That doesn't change, no matter the century."

Alec's gaze moved to the slate board. "Why the theatrics with the tongue, the invisible ink? And carving the symbol into Cross's chest?"

Kendra had to take a moment to consider that. "Theatrics might be a good way to describe it," she said finally. "A bit of theater to cause misdirection."

"That is what you said about Gerard Holbrooke," Alec reminded. "Are we certain he is no longer a suspect?"

"Unless something else connects Holbrooke to Cross, I don't think he's good for it." She hesitated. "After I spoke with Lady Holbrooke and Ruth, I went to the Larsons."

Alec stared at her. "You've been busy."

"It seemed like a good idea at the time." She tried not to sound defensive. She wasn't going to apologize for doing her job. "We needed to find out if they had an alibi for last night."

The Duke asked, "And did they?"

"Nothing verifiable. I told them Lord Cross had been murdered, but no one asked me how. And they had nothing to say when I asked them if they knew a woman named Magdalena."

"Odd," the Duke murmured.

"Exactly!" She pointed a finger at him, nodding. "These are natural questions. It's human nature to ask. So, either the Larsons are the most uninquisitive family I've ever met, or—"

"They are hiding something," Alec finished for her.

"They are definitely hiding something," clarified Kendra. "Magdalena contacted them as well."

The Duke threw her a startled look. "How do you know? Just because they didn't inquire about—"

"That's just icing on the cake. It's really about the timing. We know that about a month ago, Sir Giles burned the letter from Magdalena and became troubled, guilty, whatever. At the same time, Bertel Larson stopped going to the shop because he was supposedly ill."

The Duke nodded. "You are right, my dear. But what could have happened in Spain?" he asked again.

Kendra shook her head. "Something Sir Giles thought embarrassing enough to cover up. Unfortunately, I've always found that people in government tend to have thin skins. Their first instinct is to cover up anything that they consider a scandal." It had been a cover-up that was responsible for her being here in the 19th century, after all. "But Sir Giles couldn't cover this up so easily. Maybe because of Magdalena. Maybe because of Evert Larson, and his own personal connection to the Larson family."

"But if Magdalena contacted the Larsons about what really happened in Spain, why haven't they spoken out?" the Duke wondered. "They wouldn't be conflicted like Sir Giles. It's their son. They'd want the truth known."

Kendra hesitated. "Maybe speaking out wasn't enough."

They were silent for a moment, the only noise the fire devouring the log in the hearth.

The Duke sighed. "If what you say is true—"

"I'm just theorizing."

"—then which Larson? I cannot bring myself to believe Mrs. Larson is the murderer. So is it her son or her husband?"

Kendra wasn't taking Astrid off the table, but decided not to argue the point. "As I said, none of them have a good alibi. They all have motive. Unfortunately, they're close. We can't play them off one another. The innocent will lie to protect the guilty."

She moved to the table and set down her empty cup. *Too much caffeine now*, she thought. Her head was beginning to pound. "We need to find Magdalena. She's the key."

"Let us hope Mr. Kelly will find her," the Duke said.

"There's something else we need to consider," Alec said slowly, and there was something in his tone that made her turn to face him.

"What?"

"If one of the Larsons is behind the murders of Sir Giles and Cross because of some idea for revenge on what happened to Evert, they're not done. Captain Mobray could be his next victim."

"It's possible." Kendra paused, and then shrugged. "Unless Captain Mobray is the killer."

39

The Duke and Alec left for a ride in Hyde Park before darkness fell, while Kendra updated the slate board and murder book. She rubbed her throbbing temples as she paced the room, trying to look at all the information she'd gathered from different angles.

She needed more. *Muldoon*.

Kendra crossed the room to the Duke's desk. She sat down and found a sheet of foolscap, then reached for the elegant quill in the silver inkstand. She scrutinized the nib to make sure it was still sharp. For the murder book, she preferred a pencil, which was easier, if still a little awkward and ungainly for fingers that craved the sleek keyboards and touchscreens of her era. But she'd begun to use the more fashionable quill pen to correspond with Rebecca while she'd been at the Duke's northern estate, Monksgrey. Her first two letters had been messy affairs, marked with thick gobs of ink across the page where she'd allowed the nib to rest to long. Who knew writing a letter could be so damned hard?

Thoughtfully, Kendra stroked the long feather that she was now holding. It had come from a goose's left wing, she knew. The Duke had informed her that the slight curve in the left wing was desirable by right-handed letter writers, while left-handed writers preferred feathers from the goose's right wing. Given most people were right-handed, Kendra imagined there were a lot of lopsided birds running around.

She leaned forward to unscrew the inkwell, dipped in the nib, and scratched a quick note to Muldoon. Carefully setting aside the quill-pen, she reached for the pounce box, sprinkling the sand inside across the page to dry the ink quicker. The Duke used hot wax and his own signet ring to seal letters after folding them several times—there was no such thing as an envelope—but the inkstand had a wafer box. Opening it, she selected one of the waxy wafers, and pressed it down to seal the folded foolscap.

Satisfied, Kendra stood, and went to the bell-pull. When a maid answered, she handed her the letter. "I need this delivered to Phineas Muldoon. I don't have his home address, but he works at the *Morning Chronicle*. Will this get to him?"

The maid's brow puckered. "Oi don't know why not, miss. Oi'll give it ter Mr. Harding, and 'e can 'ave maybe one of the stable lads deliver it."

"I need it delivered immediately."

"Aye, miss. Oi'll see ter it."

It took forty-five minutes for Kendra to receive a response. Not as good as sending a text, but not as bad as it could have been. It certainly made Kendra hopeful that the mysterious Magdalena might actually be found.

She opened the crisp paper. The reporter had written on her original foolscap, below her own writing. *Meet me in the Grosvenor Square park. M.*

Glancing at the time—quarter to five—Kendra jumped up and hurried to her bedchamber to retrieve her cloak. Because the reporter hadn't suggested a time, she suspected he'd delivered the letter himself, and was now waiting for her across the street. Why he'd chosen there instead of the mansion, she didn't know.

She was out the front door before it occurred to her to bring Molly with her as her chaperone. Then she was a little annoyed with herself that such a thing had occurred to her at all. Whether she liked it or not, the ridiculous, backward rules for women in this era were beginning to seep into her consciousness. *I need to adapt, but I don't want to lose myself.*

A shiver that had nothing to do with the chilly outdoor temperature raced down her arms. Once you started giving up pieces of yourself here and there in order to adapt to society's rules, how long before you had nothing left?

She pushed the thought away, mainly because she had no answers. The *clomp-clomp-clomp* of horses' hooves caught her attention. She looked down the street to see Lady Rebecca expertly maneuvering her mare down the cobblestone street. A young groom trailed behind her.

"Good afternoon, Miss Donovan," Rebecca greeted her with a bright smile, pulling up her reins. "Where are you going?"

"Across the street. Sutcliffe and the Duke are riding in Hyde Park. Care to walk with me?"

"I would be delighted. Today is one of the best days we've had this winter," she said, flicking aside her riding habit's long, heavy skirt. The groom hurried around to help her dismount. "Take Sophia around to the Duke's stables," she instructed, handing the groom the reins. She turned to Kendra. "I wanted to come earlier, but my parents insisted on paying a call to my mother's sister in Richmond."

Kendra studied Rebecca's dark blue riding habit. The bodice and sleeves were exquisitely tailored to conform to Rebecca's body, but the skirt was full, with a long, asymmetrical train that only made sense if one was sitting sidesaddle on a horse, but probably wasn't so great when walking.

"Can you walk in that thing?"

"I can manage," Rebecca laughed, and gathered the train, tossing it over her arm like a bridal dress. "So, what have you been doing today?"

Kendra realized that Rebecca hadn't been told about Cross. "Lord Cross was murdered last night," she said.

"Good heavens." Rebecca stumbled to a stop in the street. There wasn't any traffic to mow them down, but Kendra took Rebecca's arm and tugged her toward the pavement on the other side. The cornflower blue eyes narrowed on Kendra. "How? What happened?"

"Strangled, like Sir Giles. Tongue cut out. The killer used his knife to mark the body with a cross—or a *t*. In truth, this one looked more like a *t*. But the unsub was in a hurry, so that might account for the slight variation. Cross was with a girl in an alley, and she fled, screaming her head off. I assume the killer realized he could be caught any second by the people in the Bell & Swan."

Rebecca shook her head. "'Tis either very bold or very foolish for the fiend to kill Lord Cross right in front of the soiled dove with so little time for discovery."

"Yeah, that's what worries me. I don't think he's foolish. In fact, I think he's very clever. He wasn't deterred by a potential witness . . ."

Ella's words came back to Kendra now: *'Is face wasn't right, red and all scaly-like. 'Is eyes were black as pitch . . . evil.*

"What?" Rebecca demanded. "You have that look on your face. There's something else you're not telling me."

Kendra hesitated, feeling like there *was* something else, a shadow in the back of her mind that was trying to take shape and solidify. "No," she finally said. "Not really. The woman was drunk off her ass. And I know that I'm not supposed to say ass."

Rebecca's lips twitched and her eyes danced with merriment. "It certainly would be frowned upon in Polite Society. However, I'm not exactly the arbiter of Polite Society." She waved her free hand in such a way as to dismiss the topic. "You're saying that the woman's intoxication prevented her from seeing anything?"

"Oh, she saw something. She said the devil killed Cross."

"The devil?"

"Yeah, you know, the guy from Hell. Red, reptilian face. Black eyes. The only thing she didn't mention was his horns."

Rebecca said nothing for a moment. Then she glanced sideways at Kendra. "You went to the Bell & Swan last night?"

"Mr. Kelly sent word, and the Duke and I met him there. Unless new information comes out, we can eliminate Holbrooke."

"I daresay that—" She paused, and frowned suddenly. "What is *he* doing here?"

"Who? Oh." Kendra's gaze traveled to the tall man standing with his hands thrust into his shabby greatcoat. A battered tricorn hat was squashed over his reddish curls, his cerulean blue eyes narrowed as he watched them approach.

"You!" Rebecca's long skirt didn't hinder her as she strode forward, her quick gait aggressive enough to have Muldoon falling back a step. "Spying again, are we, Mr. Muldoon?"

His lips curled in a delighted smile. "Not at all, Princess. I—"

"*Stop* calling me that!" she said through clenched teeth, her eyes flashing with dangerous heat. "You ill-bred buffoon!"

"I asked him to meet me," Kendra put in, a little taken aback by Rebecca's vehemence.

Muldoon shot them a cocky grin and swept off his hat in a melodramatic gesture as he bowed. "At your service, Miss Donovan. And delighted to see you again, Pr—" He coughed, and corrected himself, meeting her glare. "Ah, Lady Rebecca."

"Can we get down to business?" Kendra pressed. "This isn't a social call."

He swung his gaze back to Kendra, his good humor vanishing. "No, I didn't think it was. It's about Lord Cross's murder, isn't it?"

"Indirectly. Did you manage to get the official report yet on what happened in Spain?"

Muldoon cocked his head as he regarded her. "I may have."

"Do you care to share?" she asked sarcastically. "Or do you expect me to read your mind?"

He huffed out a surprised laugh. "Since you asked so nicely. Lord Cross and Captain Mobray were part of the Fifty-Second Regiment of Foot—"

"You already told me that."

"Yes, well, I'm telling you again. This is my story, Miss Donovan, in my words. Do you wish to hear it?"

Kendra rolled her eyes. "Sensitive. Go on."

"As I was saying, they were part of the Fifty-Second Regiment of Foot. The company that the captain commanded split off in the mountains and was captured."

"Wait a minute. Captain Mobray was the leader of the regiment that was captured?"

"Not regiment—company. A company is smaller. But yes, Captain Mobray was the unit's leader. They were involved in a particularly nasty battle in the Spanish mountains near the Maya Pass. According to the report, the French launched a surprise attack, split the company, and slaughtered most of the poor sods. The remaining dozen were taken to the French camp as prisoners of war—including Cross and Mobray."

Muldoon's mouth tightened, his eyes turning to blue stones. The expression allowed Kendra to glimpse something beyond the man's charming façade. The reporter had plenty of cheeky wit, but he wasn't *all* cheeky wit, she decided. He cared about what he was writing.

"The conditions were inhuman," he continued. "The soldiers were there two months. According to the report, half of those men died in the camp within the first week."

"Dear heaven." Rebecca's hand went to her throat. "How?"

Muldoon shrugged. "The French officers who ran the camp were products of their country's revolution."

Kendra frowned. "What does that mean?"

Muldoon looked at her. "The French Revolution wasn't like your American war, Miss Donovan. Your countrymen fought to overthrow an outside nation that was controlling them, much like Ireland wants to do. But France overthrew their own people. Just as they toppled their monarchy and aristocracy, they shattered the hierarchy in the army. It became the citizen army. They didn't view those who fought against them as soldiers to be defeated; they viewed the opposition as an evil that needed to be destroyed." He made a disgusted sound in his throat, and shook his head. "Bloodlust was rampant, which was evident by how often la guillotine was used."

Rebecca gave the journalist a sour smile. "I'm surprised you object to the French revolution, considering your own Whig sentiments, Mr. Muldoon."

"I find the end goals of both the American and the French revolutions admirable, your ladyship. However, only a fool thinks self-government is easy to achieve, or that mob rule is best."

"Okay, okay." Kendra waved her hand to get the reporter's attention. "What does this have to do with what happened in the French prisoner of war camp?"

"Before the citizen army took over in France, there were rules on how to treat prisoners of war. But the French revolution changed that. The new army viewed all prisoners of war as evil, and therefore their treatment became vicious. Prisoners were shot or tortured for sport. Napoleon may be a mad little tyrant, but he returned the military to the prerevolutionary code, insisting that prisoners of war must be treated with dignity and respect."

Kendra thought that over. "The French army that captured Mobray and his men operated more like a citizen army than Napoleon's army?"

Muldoon spread his ink-stained hands. "According to the government reports."

"Which were written by Captain Mobray and Lord Cross."

"Yes." He lifted an inquiring eyebrow at her. "Do you have cause to doubt their veracity?"

She was getting tired of that question. She ignored it. "What else did the report say?"

"Ah, there the details become sparse. Larson was captured. The next day, he attempted to escape, and in the process there was a fire, which set fire to the armory at the camp."

"Hence the explosion," Kendra put in.

Muldoon nodded. "Captain Mobray and Lord Cross were in a tent that was being guarded by French soldiers. When the explosion happened, the guards ran to help, and in the confusion, Captain Mobray and Lord Cross managed to escape."

"What about the other British prisoners with them?"

"According to the report, there were only three left. They were held in another tent, and when they tried to flee, they were shot down by the French."

"But not Mobray and Cross." Kendra said nothing for a moment, then became aware that the reporter was studying her. "How did Evert Larson end up in the camp?"

"The French had set up camp near Ximenia, a small village in the mountains. Larson was there to conduct surveillance of the camp, which, as I mentioned, had a sizable armory."

She frowned. "That was in the report from Mobray?"

Muldoon looked impressed. "You are very good, Miss Donovan. No, that was not in the report. That came from Sir Giles's report on the situation. He was the one who'd sent Larson there. The last report Larson sent back with the courier was how he'd infiltrated the camp pretending to be one of the villagers bringing in food. On that mission, he'd discovered English prisoners of war being held at the camp. He was dead shortly thereafter."

"Did he mention that he planned to rescue the English prisoners?"

"No. But given what happened, he must have tried to do that, and been discovered."

"Did he make contact with Mobray or Cross?"

"No. At least, that was not in either report."

"Who recognized Larson?"

"There wasn't anything in the report, but I assume it was Lord Cross. The two had been in Eton together."

"Why was Evert held separately? And Mobray and Cross from the other British soldiers."

"I don't know about Mobray and Cross, but Larson was a spy." He hesitated. "The French most likely wanted to find out what he knew and what he'd shared before they caught him."

"Torture?" But Kendra knew.

Muldoon nodded reluctantly. "Most likely."

Kendra said, "If this is coming from the report by Mobray and Cross, how do they know Evert Larson died in the explosion?"

"How do they know?" Muldoon lifted his eyebrows. "I suppose they saw him go into the tent that exploded."

"While they were running for their lives?"

"The explosion happened first. That's how they escaped. In the chaos," he reminded her, and met her gaze. "What are you thinking, Miss Donovan?"

"I thought Mobray and Cross were being held in a tent under guard, and they escaped when their guards left because of the explosion. As you said, in the chaos. But how did they know Evert caused or perished in the explosion? By their own account, they had no contact with him. They were being held in a tent. I don't remember tents having windows. So how did they know what was happening outside the tent?"

Muldoon's lips parted in surprise. "I'm not certain," he said slowly. "You make a good point. But why would Cross and Mobray lie about such a thing?"

She ignored the question. "Do you know what happened after Mobray and Cross escaped? Did they put in their report where they went?"

"They made it to an ally encampment."

"How long did it take them to get there? What were their physical conditions?"

There was a shrewd gleam in his blue eyes. "That wasn't in their report, but I'll do a little investigating. There must be more. Or I'll find someone who was at the ally base when they arrived."

Kendra smiled. "That sounds like a plan. Let me know what you find out." She turned and began walking toward the gated entrance to the park. Rebecca hurried to catch up.

"Wait! You can't leave it like that, Miss Donovan." Muldoon's long strides ate up the distance, and he fell into step beside them. "Tell me what's going on. What do Captain Mobray's and Lord Cross's imprisonment and escape in Spain have to do with the murders? What are you thinking, Miss Donovan?"

"Get me that report from the ally camp or an eyewitness account, and we'll talk," she said as they exited the park.

"Why don't you tell me now?" He grabbed her arm, stopping her. "Do you think Evert Larson might be alive?"

She gave Muldoon's hand on her arm a pointed glance. He let her go with a sheepish look. "This isn't about Evert Larson," she finally said. "It's about what happened in Spain. Something's not adding up."

Muldoon pushed up his tricorn hat as he regarded her with a strange intensity. "Who are *you*, Miss Donovan?"

Kendra pulled back from him. The last thing she needed was this reporter to turn his inquisitive eyes in her direction. "This isn't about me, either, Mr. Muldoon," she snapped. "Save your questions until you get your hands on that report."

He grinned at her. "Can't help it if I find you an enigma, Miss Donovan. I'm just a poor scribbler with a curious mind."

Rebecca sniffed. "You are beginning to repeat yourself, Mr. Muldoon. You have used that excuse before."

Muldoon laughed.

Kendra spotted a familiar figure walking toward them.

"Good afternoon, Miss Donovan, milady," Sam Kelly greeted them as he came up beside them. He eyed the journalist warily. "Muldoon. What are you doin' here?"

"I asked to see him," Kendra told him. "Mr. Muldoon has promised to look into a few things."

Muldoon cocked an eyebrow at the Bow Street Runner. "And what are you doing here, Mr. Kelly, on this fine Sunday afternoon?"

Sam scowled. "Nothing I'm going ter share with you."

"You wound me, sir!"

Rebecca rolled her eyes at Muldoon. "I am surprised you never tried to make your living on the stage, sir. You have a flare for melodrama."

"Thank you, Princess."

When Rebecca's eyes narrowed, Kendra grabbed her elbow, and shifted her toward the street. "We'll see you inside, Mr. Kelly," she said, then looked back to the reporter. "Send me word when you have anything more to report, Mr. Muldoon."

"She's a spirited creature, isn't she?" Muldoon said, his gaze on the two ladies as they crossed the street and walked up the path to the Duke's mansion.

Sam swung around to face the reporter. "She may be an American, but she's above your touch, Muldoon. Besides, Lord Sutcliffe might have something ter say about it."

"Ah, is that the way of it?" He looked thoughtful.

"Have you discovered anything new?" Sam demanded.

"I read the official reports and have told Miss Donovan everything I know. She actually made a few good points about the reports themselves. Obviously, Captain Mobray provided the information for the French prison camp he was held at. But whether he was entirely honest in his account . . . . that is the question."

"You don't think he was honest in his account?"

"Not after speaking with Miss Donovan. And now Lord Cross was murdered. It's a bit suspicious, don't you think?"

Sam studied the reporter. Muldoon played the fool sometimes, but Sam was well aware that behind his often insolent frivolity was an impressive intelligence. He grunted. "Everything seems suspicious ter me. When you read the reports, did it mention a woman named Magdalena?"

Muldoon's eyebrows rose. "Not that I recollect. Who is Magdalena?"

"Somebody I'm hoping to find. Keep an eye out."

"You realize I work for the *Morning Chronicle*, don't you?" Muldoon groused, and took two steps down the pavement before pausing to look again at Sam. The light was back in the blue eyes, which should have warned him.

"You know, when I said that *she* was a spirited creature, I wasn't talking about Miss Donovan."

Sam's eyes widened. "She's above your touch, too!" he called out, but the younger man had already pivoted around, whistling a jaunty tune as he walked down the street.

40

F ive minutes later, Kendra, Rebecca, and Sam were settling themselves in the study when a footman came in to add more kindling and logs to the fireplace. Straightening, he looked over at Kendra. "Would you like me to light the candles, miss?"

"Oh." For the first time, she realized that the shadows in the room were growing longer. "Yes, thank you."

Rebecca crossed to the side table stocked with decanters. Pulling out a stopper, she glanced at Sam, lifting her eyebrows. "Mr. Kelly? Would you like a whiskey?" She didn't wait for his affirmative, splashing a generous three fingers into a crystal glass and bringing it to him.

He grinned. "Thank you, m'lady."

"Miss Donovan, a sherry?"

"Thanks."

Sam took a sip of his whiskey, watching the footman as he finished lighting the candles. Once the servant left the room, he turned to look at Kendra. "Me men found four women named Magdalena."

She nearly dropped the wineglass Rebecca was handing her. *"What?"*

"Me men found—"

"I heard you," she said impatiently, taking the wineglass from Rebecca and setting it down on the nearby table so she didn't spill it. She looked at Sam. "Go on."

"Not much ter tell. One woman was eighty, if she was a day. Two were still in leading strings. And one was a nun. I quizzed the old woman and the nun. They'd never heard of Sir Giles. The old woman had been in England for nearly twenty years. The nun nigh on five years."

"Are you sure?" Kendra said. "Maybe they were lying."

He lifted his eyebrows. "The *nun?*"

"It's been known to happen."

"Perhaps. But I believed her. Both of them." He lifted his whiskey glass and regarded her over the rim. "Don't be discouraged, lass. 'Tis early days yet. I've got me men spreading out into other neighborhoods."

"It seems an impossible task," Rebecca admitted, sitting down on the sofa near the fire with her glass of sherry. "You can't even be certain she's Spanish."

Kendra chewed on her lower lip. "She could be French. The prisoner of war camp was in the Maya Pass, which borders France."

"A camp follower, mayhap." Rebecca's brows pulled together as she sipped her wine. "Can we even be certain Magdalena is connected to what happened to Evert Larson in Spain?" she wondered, lowering her glass. "Mr. Holbrooke is a rake. Perhaps this letter was about him, and Sir Giles was forced to deal with another of his son's peccadillos."

"I don't think so," Kendra replied. "When I mentioned the name to Captain Mobray and the Larsons, they reacted. It wasn't much, but it was something. She's connected. I'm certain of it."

Sam said, "I went back ter the Holbrooke stables, asked the coachman if he'd taken his master ter anywhere peculiar in the last month."

Kendra remembered thinking Sam was a good cop. She was right. "Good thinking, Mr. Kelly. What did he say?"

"Nothin' much," he sighed, and took a swallow of whiskey. "The coachman said it wasn't strange ter bring Sir Giles all over London Town, even unsavory places. Nothin' seemed unusual ter him about their travels."

"Unsavory places?" Kendra asked. "Sir Giles had a habit of going into rough neighborhoods?"

"Aye. Gin and opium dens, rookeries of the worst sort. Like Rats' Castle, the flash house on the docks."

"*Rats'* Castle?" Kendra wondered if she'd misheard.

Sam grinned at her. "Aye, lass. I suppose he dealt with a lot of ruffians, being a spymaster. He couldn't meet up with them in the nicer sections of the city without attracting some attention. Sir Giles would have ter go ter them if he wanted information."

Kendra frowned, then picked up the glass of sherry and sipped. "Do you think the coachman can give us a list of places that Sir Giles went to this last month?"

"You're thinking of goin' ter each one. Aye, I'll see what I can do, lass."

"At least it's a plan." Absently, she tapped her finger against her wine-glass, and her gaze drifted to the slate board. She thought about the name that was no longer there. "You know," she said slowly, "there's another person who might know what Sir Giles had been up to. Fitzpatrick."

Sam's eyebrows popped up. "Fitzpatrick?" But even as he said the name, he was nodding, golden eyes brightening. "You might be right."

Rebecca frowned, looking at them. "What do you think Mr. Fitzpatrick will say that Sir Giles's coachman could not?"

"Sir Giles's coachman can only tell us where Sir Giles asked to be driven. But if he wanted privacy, he might have taken a hackney or rode a horse. If Fitzpatrick was spying on him, who knows what he saw?"

"I daresay he would have wanted privacy to see this Magdalena," Rebecca murmured.

"Yeah. Mr. Kelly, what are you doing tomorrow?"

"You want ter go to the Liber, lass?"

"I think it's time for me to meet this Irish spy."

A little while later, Sam and Rebecca left and the Duke and Alec returned from their ride. Kendra briefed them on what both Muldoon and the Bow Street Runner had said, finishing up with her decision to make a call on Fitzpatrick.

"Do you really think Mr. Fitzpatrick will be able to help?" the Duke asked, fiddling with his pipe behind his desk.

Alec said, "Perhaps the question ought to be whether he would *want* to help. I'm not certain he would admit to watching Sir Giles."

He was sprawled in a chair next to the fireplace, his hands balancing a crystal glass filled with brandy on his flat stomach. The flickering firelight played across his chiseled features, teasing out hidden lights in his dark hair. He'd been staring at his brandy glass, but he suddenly lifted his eyes, catching Kendra's gaze on him.

"You won't be speaking to Mr. Fitzpatrick alone," he said.

She'd had other thoughts going through her head while she stared at him. But his words and the imperative tone jerked her back to reality. She scowled. "That sounds oddly like a command."

"It's a statement of fact," he returned coolly.

"Are you making that statement because of the ridiculous rules placed on women here or because you don't think I can handle myself with Fitzpatrick?"

He hesitated briefly. "Both."

"How would you handle this in your time, my dear?" Aldridge asked, undoubtedly hoping to prevent the argument he saw brewing—and because he was genuinely interested.

"Well, I certainly wouldn't need a chaperone to interview a subject," she snapped, then rubbed her temples. She'd almost forgotten about the dull ache behind her eyes. "Sorry. Touchy subject." She took a breath and then let it out slowly. "I wouldn't be going into a dangerous situation alone," she answered honestly. "But this isn't a dangerous situation. For Christ's sake, it's a coffee shop. There will be other customers around."

Alec frowned, but said nothing.

"I'll be going with Mr. Kelly," she added. "I won't be alone."

The Duke's intelligent eyes seemed more gray than blue as he looked at her. "And you don't want us to go with you." It wasn't a question.

"I don't want to crowd Fitzpatrick. He's not under suspicion, but he might feel itchy if he had four pairs of eyes trained on him."

The Duke smiled slightly. "Itchy?"

"Paranoid," she said, turning when someone knocked at the door. Her stomach skittered a little when Lady Atwood swept into the room. The firelight danced across the deep maroon evening dress she wore. She'd tucked her hair into a silver turban embellished with two curling feathers that fluttered with each step she took. Kendra hadn't spoken to the countess since the incident with the tongue.

"Good evening," Lady Atwood greeted everyone, sounding surprisingly upbeat for someone who'd declared the family ruined only yesterday. "Dinner will be in twenty minutes," she announced, and frowned when Alec rose to his feet in a lithe movement. "Normally, I do not approve of wearing riding habits at the dinner table, Sutcliffe. But we shall dine en famille, so I shall overlook the gaucheness."

Alec gave a mocking bow. "I am forever your servant, ma'am."

"Insolent boy." But she said it with affection, her lips curving.

The Duke regarded his sister. "You appear to be in remarkably fine spirits this evening. Earlier you were still cast down because of—"

"Do not remind me of . . . of the incident," she warned her brother, her mouth pulling tight. "I swear I shall have nightmares for months. But you are correct, Bertie. My mood has improved. Do you see these?"

For the first time, Kendra noticed that the other woman clutched what appeared to be a thick stack of ivory- and cream-colored cards in her hand.

"All is not lost!" the countess declared with a triumphant smile.

"What do you have there?" her brother asked curiously.

"Invitations, Bertie! They have been arriving all day. Invitations to upcoming balls, soirees, salons, and musical recitals. And, oh, my, look here!" She extracted a small card to wave around, her expression more animated than Kendra had ever seen.

The Duke came around his desk, snatching the card from his sister to scan it. "I can hardly read it with you waving it about."

"It's an invitation to Almack's!"

The name rang a bell, Kendra thought, but not from her own timeline. She'd heard the name mentioned in conversations in the past six months. "That's a social club, right?"

"It is *the* social club, Miss Donovan," Lady Atwood corrected haughtily. "It is the most exclusive assembly room in London, with the most sought-after vouchers. The Prince Regent himself has been known to attend."

Kendra said, "Congratulations. I hope you have a wonderful time."

"Your name is on the invitation as well, Miss Donovan," the Duke pointed out mildly.

The temperature in the room hadn't changed, but Kendra could have sworn it was becoming hotter. "But I don't have to go, do I?" she asked a bit desperately, and then was annoyed at herself for asking. She was a grown woman, damn it. She didn't need permission to *not* go out for the evening.

"Of course, you must go." Lady Atwood snapped, and turned to her brother. "Bertie, tell the creature that she must go."

"Well, I—"

Kendra's hand tightened on her wineglass. "Will the Larsons be there?" Maybe she could use it like the Smyth-Hope ball—

"Don't be stupid." Lady Atwood glared at her. "They're commoners."

Kendra pinched the bridge of her nose in frustration. *So am I*, she wanted to say, but being the ward of the Duke of Aldridge made all the difference.

"Apparently, you are still the toast of the Ton, Miss Donovan," said Alec, not sounding particularly happy over the news. "Receiving a severed tongue as a gift isn't quite the social stigma one might think."

"Curiosity has its own celebrity," she muttered, and saw that Lady Atwood was eyeing her critically. "What?"

"I think I ought to contact my modiste. You'll need new gowns."

"Why do I need new gowns? I haven't worn some of the gowns from the last time we went to your dressmaker."

Lady Atwood ignored her. "And this will require lessons in etiquette. Almack's has the strictest code of propriety in all of England."

"And the worst lemonade, blandest buttered bread, and cattiest ladies in all of the kingdom," Alec mocked.

Kendra raised an eyebrow at him. "Why does anyone go if it's so bad?"

A smile ghosted around his lips. "Because there is nothing more enthralling than to be accepted into a place that turns down everybody else."

Kendra laughed.

"At least we are not the social pariahs that I had feared," Lady Atwood said sharply, and plucked the invitation back from her brother. She shook the card at Alec. "This is a wonderful thing. My dear friend Lady St. James will be green with envy. She was banned from the club for two years now after Lady Jersey flew up into the boughs over some perceived slight."

"I don't have time for this." Again Kendra looked at the Duke to back her up.

"Do not fret, my dear," he said. "The invitation for Almack's is over two weeks away."

"Almack's is not the only invitation," Lady Atwood reminded them, smiling as she lifted the stack of cards in her hand like trophies. Which Kendra supposed they were.

"Have no fear," the countess said, moving toward the door. "I shall take it upon myself to sort through them and decide which ones we shall attend."

Kendra inhaled sharply, then let it out slowly.

Alec sauntered to the sideboard and poured a glass of sherry. He brought it over, smiling slightly as he met her gaze. "Don't look so worried, sweet. When they find out what's behind your newfound popularity, the ladies of the Beau Monde will be sending themselves severed body parts, and you shall soon fall out of favor."

41

Kendra didn't want to think about her newfound popularity with the Ton, or the reasons behind it. She sure as hell didn't want to think about being introduced to the Prince Regent, or wasting valuable time at the dressmaker's being fitted for new gowns. She pushed thoughts of princes and parties to the side, and focused on murder.

After Alec left for the evening and Lady Atwood persuaded her brother into a game of two-handed whist in the drawing room, Kendra quietly slipped back into the study. Using a nearby taper, she lit more candles around the shadowy room. Darkness pressed against the windows, the panes rattling slightly as the wind picked up.

Kendra returned the taper to its holder, picked up the piece of slate, and circled to the slate board. She closed her eyes and let her thoughts drift over what she knew, to isolate each piece of information. Sir Giles may have been murdered four days ago, but that hadn't been the beginning. The beginning was where Sir Giles's ghosts came from a prisoner of war camp in Spain, two years earlier.

Not ghosts. *Ghost, singular,* she decided. She opened her eyes, her gaze immediately falling on one name. *Evert Larson.*

What had happened over there? As usual, she started to pace, jiggling the slate in one hand. Everything they knew came from official reports written by Captain Mobray and Cross. She was sure they'd been debriefed, as well, probably by Sir Giles himself since Evert had died there. At the time, their story was accepted.

Had that changed a month ago with the arrival of Magdalena?

Kendra's mind swung to the Larsons. They'd obviously accepted Mobray and Cross's version of what had happened in Spain as well. They'd suffered the loss of Eric, and by all accounts, they'd picked up the pieces of their lives and moved on—until a month ago when Bertel's behavior had changed, and he'd stopped going to the apothecary shop. It made sense that Magdalena had contacted them as well, told them another version of what had happened to Evert in Spain, and ripped open the wound over Evert's death all over again.

Kendra wandered to the window. The fog had once again rolled in, obscuring the park across the street.

Whoever tries to hide his sins will not succeed, but the one who confesses his sins and leaves them behind will find mercy. What sin had Sir Giles thought to hide? Or confess? And if it was a confession that he had in mind, was that why the killer had cut out his tongue?

She let out a sigh of frustration, pushing away from the window to resume her pacing.

Mobray had a lot to lose. He was the one with political aspirations, working his way up government ranks. He was a military hero of a sort. Maybe not like Horatio Nelson or the Duke of Wellington, but he survived being a POW under the French. That was powerful stuff. Especially if you had an eye on Parliament. She couldn't imagine him *not* trading on it to make his climb a bit easier.

She hadn't paid too much attention to the political climate of the day, except to note that it was depressingly similar to the 21st century. If information had come to light to change his story . . . Mobray wouldn't be the first person seeking a higher position in government who'd killed to keep their secrets from coming out.

Silence Sir Giles, who'd begun asking questions, who was considering confessing his sins and finding mercy. Silence Lord Cross, who knew the truth and was getting cold feet. Cutting out the tongue could have been a sly joke on Mobray's part. The symbols? That struck her as theatrical. Theatrics to cause misdirection? It was possible.

Or maybe it was another joke to which she had yet to learn the punch line.

And if the killer wasn't Mobray . . . She sighed, thinking again of the Larsons. If they had found out that the official story of what happened in Spain wasn't true—if, for instance, Evert had been betrayed by one of his own countrymen—maybe one of the Larsons had snapped and taken revenge.

But which one?

Kendra remembered how Bertel had been standing in front of the stone statue he'd erected for the son he'd lost on the Continent. His grief had been almost palpable, but was there something more? Something—

"I suspected that I'd find you here."

Kendra hadn't heard the door open, but now she turned as the Duke walked into the room. She smiled. "Did you win your game?"

"I did. However, I had the advantage, with Caro distracted by dreams of Almack's and dancing until midnight."

"Don't remind me."

He eyed her with concern. "You look tired, my dear. I find your single-minded pursuit of justice admirable, but I fear you take too much responsibility on yourself. You are not to be blamed for Lord Cross's murder."

She wasn't given to a lot of self-analysis—when you grew up being studied by two scientists, you sort of shied away from analyzing yourself—but she had to acknowledge that the Duke wasn't altogether wrong. "I don't blame myself, exactly," she said slowly. "Though I keep thinking that I've missed something, and that's why Lord Cross is dead."

"You're not omniscient, my dear."

She laughed, but it wasn't a happy sound. "I realize that only too well."

The Duke kept his gaze on her as he lowered himself into his chair behind the desk. "You demand too much of yourself. Did you take the world on your shoulders when you worked for your Federal Bureau of Investigation?"

"Probably." She shrugged. "It's what I do. Who I am." She paused. "It's the only thing I'm really good at. Especially here."

"I think you do not give yourself the credit you should."

She shook her head. "You're giving me too much credit. I'm trying to fit in here, to not look so . . . odd. But you know I don't belong."

He frowned, and looked like he was going to say something, but she lifted her hand. "Do you know what I first thought when Mr. Kelly sent word asking for our help?" she asked.

"No."

"I thought, thank God. Now I can do something where I feel normal—as normal as I can feel in this century." Her chest was tight; she drew in a deep breath to ease the pressure.

"My dear . . ."

"Don't feel sorry for me. I'm just trying to explain why I may seem a little intense sometimes."

The Duke regarded her with somber eyes for a long moment. Then he leaned forward, opened a drawer on his desk, and brought out what looked to be a pendant attached to a long, delicate gold chain. "I had meant to give you this earlier," he said, and pushed himself to his feet. He came around the desk, offering it to her.

Only then did she realize it was the arrowhead that he'd been given the other morning. "Oh."

He smiled slightly at her confusion. "I sent it to a jeweler to drill a hole into the stone for the chain. Of course, he thought I was mad."

"It's . . ." *Beautiful?* It wasn't polished or pretty. She didn't know what to say.

The Duke chuckled. "I know this is not a traditional frippery, my dear. But it comes from your America. Not *your* America, but—"

"I know what you mean." She stared down at the ancient weapon, and felt her heart give a hard tug. "Arrowheads are still being found in my America." She put it on. The chain was long enough for the arrowhead to hit below her breast bone. Lifting her eyes to the Duke, she realized she had to blink back tears. "Thank you. It's beautiful."

The Duke's mouth curved in a gentle smile. "It occurs to me that mankind has been picking up rocks for one reason or another since the beginning of time. They've been used as punishment to stone sinners, walls to keep in livestock and keep out intruders and the elements. They've been cobbled together to pave streets or, like this one"—he tapped the arrowhead lightly—"fashioned as a weapon or as a tool for hunting.

"The stone is the same," he added softly. "It is what we do with it that matters. And whatever it eventually becomes has nothing to do with where it comes from—or when."

Kendra was silent for a long moment. "I think I understand what you're saying," she said. "But I'm not sure it's that simple." She lifted the stone, felt the cool surface of it beneath her fingertips. "This arrowhead may be here now, but it doesn't really belong. I won't be using it to slay my enemies or hunt for food. It's still in the wrong place and time."

"My dear, you are not looking at it correctly. It is now a pendant. It has changed, but its new purpose, I think, fits perfectly in this time and place." He waited a moment, then smiled. "Maybe it's something to think about. Now, I shall bid you good night, my dear."

She waited until he was at the door before she spoke. "Your Grace?"

He paused, lifting his eyebrows in inquiry.

"Thank you." She wanted to say more, to tell him that she was grateful to have him with her in this crazy new life, but her throat burned.

He waited a moment, then nodded. "Good night," he said again. Then he was gone, leaving her standing there, clutching the pendant and wondering how she could find her own purpose here without losing herself.

Ten minutes later, Kendra let herself into her darkened bedchamber, and nearly screamed when two arms came around her. But she recognized the hard, masculine body and faint scent even before she was spun around and pushed up against the closed door. Alec's mouth came down on hers in a kiss long enough, passionate enough, for her toes to curl in her slippers.

"Jesus, Alec," she managed to pant when he finally lifted his head. "Are you trying to give me a heart attack? What are you doing here? Are you crazy?"

"Too many questions."

She caught the burning in his green eyes before he lowered his head again and kissed her. She gave herself up to the sensations that slammed into her, sliding her hands around his neck, her trembling fingers tunneling through his thick hair as she kissed him back. God, she had missed this, missed him.

"I *am* mad—for you," he whispered when he released her again.

She found herself grinning suddenly, foolishly, the somber mood she'd been in vanishing in an instant. "I must be mad for you, too, because I'm not kicking you out. In fact . . ." She loosened the knot on his cravat, unwinding the delicate fabric. "Stay."

"Good. Because that was my plan. I love you." His hands glided over her. Paused. "What's this?" He frowned, fingering the arrowhead pendant.

"An idea that I need to think about . . . later," she whispered, tugging at the ends of the loose cravat as she stepped backward toward the bed. "Much later."

42

Of course, Alec was gone by the time she woke up. Kendra lay watching the early morning light play over the bed's canopy until Molly poked her head into the room, and then popped in fully when she saw that Kendra was awake.

"Good mornin', miss," she greeted, and began picking up the gown, shift, stays, and stockings that had been discarded in a crumpled heap on the floor the night before. "Do ye wish fer a bath?" she asked with a sideways look at Kendra as she folded the clothes into a neat stack, placing them on a nearby tufted chair. If the maid thought anything about the clothes or Kendra's nakedness, she didn't let it show on her face.

"God, I would *love* a bath." But that was a complicated procedure, involving maids and footmen heating water in the kitchens and transporting it in buckets to the copper bathtub that was in the dressing room. "I don't know if I should."

"Why shouldn't ye?" Molly didn't wait for an answer, crossing the room to yank the bell-pull.

Forty minutes later—twenty of them spent luxuriating in the hot waters of the copper tub—Kendra pulled on a fresh shift, yanking the stays over the soft lawn material and tying it. Six months ago, the undergarment had baffled her, but she'd gotten the hang of it. *Maybe I am transforming.* She wasn't sure how that made her feel.

Her gaze fell on the arrowhead pendant. She scooped it up, lowering the thin chain around her neck.

"W'ot's that?" Molly asked.

"An arrowhead. His Grace had it made into a pendant for me."

The fifteen-year-old's brow crinkled. "Why?"

Kendra laughed. "I had the same reaction." She stepped into the green-and-white striped dress Molly held out for her, tugging the material up and thrusting her arms into the long sleeves. "It's a very thoughtful gift, actually," she insisted, presenting her back to Molly so she could be buttoned up.

"If ye say so, miss. Oi was thinkin' of the gold silk for this evenin'," said Molly, handing Kendra a fresh pair of white stockings and two garter ribbons.

"The gold silk?" She sat on the bed, wiggling into the stockings and tying the garters.

"Aye. The ball gown, miss."

Hell. "Is there a ball tonight?"

"Miss Beckett said there was."

Miss Beckett was Lady Atwood's personal maid. Kendra tried not to groan as she sat down in front of the vanity for Molly to brush her hair. "Well, she'd know."

"So, then, the gold silk?" Molly asked again.

"What? Oh, yeah. Let's go with that." She didn't want to think about it. It was one thing to adapt; that didn't mean she had to like it.

The sky was a gunmetal gray, the heavy clouds threatening to spit either rain or snow, the cold wind blustery enough to send Kendra's skirts ballooning outward as soon as she and Sam stepped down from the carriage in front of the Liber. She briefly wondered if the weather would have Lady Atwood changing her plan to attend the ball later that evening. Unless a raging blizzard incapacitated the city, the Beau Monde tended to stick with their social calendars.

Sam hurried to open the door for her. Kendra's gaze traveled around the coffee shop. Despite the fireplace, which had a nice fire blazing in its blackened hearth, and the lit oil lamps lining the walls, it wasn't too different from a modern-day Starbucks or Coffee Bean & Tea Leaf with its booths and tables and the pleasant scent of brewing coffee in the air. Instead of sipping a salted caramel double mocha skinny latte and typing away on their laptops or texting on their phones, the dozen or so men here were drinking plain coffee—maybe doctored with cream and sugar—from earthenware mugs, and either reading newspapers or talking to each other.

Besides the serving maid, who was running a rag along the counter, there were no women inside the Liber. Unlike London's gentleman's clubs, women weren't banned from coffee shops per se. Maybe it was just too early for women in society's upper tier to be out and about. Because she was the only woman, Kendra was conscious of heads turning, conversations stopping, and eyes following her and Sam as they found a table.

The serving maid began to approach, but a dark-haired man stood up, tapping her lightly on her arm to gain her attention. He gave a jerk of his head, which sent the girl scurrying back behind the long counter. Her gaze was on Kendra, too, as she picked up her abandoned rag and resumed polishing.

"Well, now this is an unexpected surprise," said the man, the lilt of Ireland in his voice. He sauntered over to their table, his teeth flashing white in a tanned, rugged countenance. "Are you here to accuse me of another murder? Lord Cross's, perchance?"

Sam's eyebrows lowered. "Once again, I have ter say, you are remarkably well informed, Mr. Fitzpatrick."

The Irishman shrugged. "Well, now, why wouldn't I be? Plenty of people come in here to talk about the events of the day. Havin' a lord murdered while tryin' ter cup a doxy is sure to set tongues wagging."

Kendra spoke up. "Mr. Fitzpatrick, we haven't been properly introduced. I'm Kendra Donovan." She indicated the chair. "Please, won't you join us?"

Fitzpatrick eyed her with both surprise and curiosity. "You're an American by the sound of it, Miss Donovan."

"I am."

"The lady in the *Morning Chronicle* helping Bow Street with the investigation." He grinned at her. "I read."

Sam glowered at him. "Keep a civil tongue in your head."

"I wasn't being uncivil. If you're here about Lord Cross, I can tell you that I didn't kill the viscount. Unfortunately, I have no better an alibi than the night Sir Giles was murdered."

Kendra said, "You're not a suspect. We're hoping you can provide us with information."

Fitzpatrick stared at her for a long moment before turning to look at the girl behind the counter. "Pru, bring us coffee, there's a good lass," he shouted, and grasped the back of a chair. He spun it around so he could straddle it. Folding his arms over the chair's back, he eyed Kendra. "What sorta information are you seeking, Miss Donovan?"

"We're interested in Sir Giles's movements before he was killed."

The Irishman didn't so much as bat an eyelash. "And how would I know such a thing?"

Sam gave Fitzpatrick a hard look. "Because you were probably keepin' your peepers on him, just like he was keepin' his peepers on you."

Fitzpatrick slid his gaze to the Bow Street Runner. "Why would I be spyin' on the man? I'm a simple proprietor of a coffeehouse."

Sam snorted.

"Mr. Fitzpatrick, we are not the government," Kendra said. "My only interest is in finding the man who is now responsible for two murders. I think you can help us."

The Irishman scratched his chin. "See, now, everyone knows that Bow Street works hand in fist with the Home Office."

"I'm not workin' for the Home Office," Sam said.

"Your reports don't make their way there?" Whatever Fitzpatrick saw on Sam's face had him laughing softly. "Ah, I thought so."

Kendra leaned forward, catching the Irishman's gaze. "Hypothetically, let's say a gentleman was spying on a businessman, and that businessman decided it might be worth his while to in turn keep tabs on the gentleman. Let's say—hypothetically—that the first gentleman's routine was observed. Maybe that routine was pretty normal. The gentleman goes to his office. He goes to his club. He goes home."

Fitzpatrick's lips curled, his gray eyes glinting with amusement. He seemed to enjoy the game they were playing. "What are you asking—hypothetically?"

"I'm wondering if maybe there was a break in the routine. If the gentleman went somewhere that seemed out of place. Or met with someone who seemed odd for the gentleman to meet. Maybe a woman."

Fitzpatrick stared at her for a long moment, only breaking off eye contact when Pru arrived, carrying a tray with coffee mugs, a sugar bowl, and a pitcher of cream.

"Will ye be needin' anythin' else?" she asked without a smile. Her gaze scanned the table, lingered on Kendra. It wasn't hostility so much as distrust that Kendra saw in the other woman's eyes.

Fitzpatrick waved off the maid in a dismissive gesture, and leaned forward to pluck the mug off the table, wrapping both hands around the cup. He was looking at Kendra, seeming to debate about what to say.

"We're looking at about a month ago," Kendra added.

"Why should I tell you anything—hypothetically? What's in it for me?"

"Probably nothing," she admitted, instinctively knowing that Fitzpatrick wasn't the kind of man she'd be able to bribe. "Don't you think it's important to see a murderer brought to justice?"

She saw the gray eyes glint with bitterness. "For an English spymaster and an English lord? Justice might have already been done, depending where you're standing."

"Then we're at a stalemate," she said, keeping her eyes locked on his. "Because I want justice no matter what. I want the truth, no matter what."

"The truth is not an easy thing to have known."

"No," she agreed, knowing he was thinking of his sister. "But that doesn't mean we stop trying. We don't give up."

He took a long sip of his coffee. "Hypothetically," he said, lowering his cup, "let's say this clever merchant knew about the gentleman's comings and goings. Made it his business to know. Maybe there was one time the gentleman went down to the docks and boarded a ship. That wasn't the thing that was queer, though. That came after he left the ship."

Kendra leaned forward. "What happened after he left the ship?"

"He cast up his accounts into the River Thames."

Kendra frowned. "Do you know who the gentleman met on the ship?" she asked.

The Irishman rolled his shoulders in another shrug. "As I wasn't there, I can't say. But if, hypothetically"—he seemed to have warmed up to that word—"someone else was following the gentleman, he wasn't in a position to see who he met with on the ship."

"Okay," Kendra said, nodding. "Did that someone happen to see the name of the ship?"

"Aye. 'Tis a Spanish galleon. The *Magdalena.*"

43

"ood heavens. Not a woman, then. A ship," Rebecca said.

She'd arrived at the Duke's mansion to find Kendra, Sam, the Duke, and Alec in the study. A gust of wind rattled the windowpanes along with a light patter of sleet against the glass. Even though it was not quite noon, the overcast skies made it seem much later. Wall sconces had been lit to combat the gloom. Earlier, a footman had brought in more wood, stoking the fire in the hearth into a roaring blaze, while a maid had brought in a tray with tea, coffee, hot chocolate, and porcelain dishes of fruit, cheese, and hot buttered rum cakes.

Kendra debated about having another cup of coffee. She already felt like she was on a caffeine high, unable to sit still, which was why she was pacing. Yet she believed her hyperactivity had less to do with the caffeine and more to do with the situation. The puzzle she'd viewed before had changed, the pieces rearranging, forming a new picture. After a moment of indecision, she headed to the table and poured herself another cup.

"Here's what we know. A month ago, the *Magdalena* docked here in London and someone from that ship sent Sir Giles a note," Kendra said, returning to her position in front of the slate board. "Obviously the ship was a rendezvous point."

"Pray tell, why would he burn the letter if it was only requesting a meeting?" Rebecca asked.

"If it had anything to do with his business in government, Sir Giles would have done so as a precautionary measure," Alec said. "When I worked for him, it was standard procedure to burn all communications."

Fire—the 19th-century version of a shredder, Kendra thought. "First, we don't know what was in the letter," she said. "But whatever it was brought Sir Giles to the ship. I think we can also safely say that this wasn't business, it was personal. After he left the ship, he threw up," she reminded them. "Whatever happened inside, whoever he met was disturbing enough for him to be physically ill after the meeting."

"The Sir Giles I knew was not fainthearted," said Alec.

Kendra nodded. "So whatever happened inside that ship seriously shook him up. And he continued to be seriously shook up until the day he died. There's something else—" She broke off when the door opened, and Lady Atwood came into the room.

"Forgive me for interrupting," she said, her gaze sweeping across them before focusing on her brother. "I only wish to remind you that we shall be attending the Duchess of Bedford's ball this evening."

The Duke nodded. "I haven't forgotten, Caro. I have an appointment with my man of affairs this afternoon, but never fear, I shall be back in time to accompany you."

"Very good." Lady Atwood glanced at Rebecca. "Will you be attending with your parents, my dear?"

"Mama mentioned Mrs. Livingston's soiree this evening. However, I shall ask them to leave me off here, if you would allow me to attend with you?"

Lady Atwood relaxed enough to smile. "You know you are always welcome." The smile vanished when her gaze drifted over the slate board, touching on Kendra before returning to her brother. "I shall leave you to . . . do whatever it is you do in here."

There was a moment of silence as Lady Atwood withdrew from the room, then the Duke looked at Kendra. "You were saying, my dear?"

"What?" Lady Atwood had a way of throwing her off. "Oh, yeah. I don't think it's a coincidence that the *Magdalena* is a Spanish galleon. Another connection to Spain." She circled the name on the slate board. "And Evert Larson."

"This seems to confirm your theory that new information came to light about what happened to the man in Spain," said the Duke.

"Yes. Information that upset Sir Giles enough to become ill," she said. "We have to find the captain of the *Magdalena*. Either he's the one who brought the information to England, or he knows who Sir Giles met with on his ship." She smiled. "We're getting closer."

"Aye." Sam swallowed the slice of buttered rum cake he'd been chewing, and pushed himself to his feet. "I don't know if the *Magdalena* is in port, but I'm going ter go ter the docks ter find out. If it's not there, maybe I can find out when it's scheduled ter return, and anything I can about the captain."

Kendra nodded. "If the ship isn't in port, how long would it take to get the information we need?" she asked, but she knew it could be weeks, perhaps even months.

"Depends on the voyage, and when it's scheduled ter return, lass," Sam told her. "I'll see what I can find out."

Alec stood up. "I'll go with you, Mr. Kelly. Two of us ought to cover more ground than only one."

"Three," Kendra said.

"No." Alec held up his hand as he met her eyes. "And before you say it, yes, I am well aware that you can take care of yourself. But the docks are the most dangerous area in London. You shall only be a distraction if I am worried about your safety. I'll be occupied enough worrying about my own safety."

"His lordship has the right of it, lass," Sam put in. "Makes the hairs on the back of me neck go up, it does, whenever I have ter go there. Full of the worst sort of cutthroats and rogues."

Kendra's jaw tightened. "Sounds like you both might need someone along to watch *your* backs."

"I know you're vexed." Alec walked over to her, his gaze on hers. "For the sake of my sanity, Miss Donovan, will you please stay here while Mr. Kelly and I make inquiries? If the *Magdalena* is in port, we shall send word to you immediately."

"And if it's not in port? What are you going to do?"

Sam said, "We'll try the taverns around the docks. The *Magdalena's* captain and its crew had ter have come ashore. If this is a regular route for them, they have regular spots."

Kendra shifted her gaze to the Bow Street Runner. "And if it's not a regular route?"

Sam lifted his shoulder in a half shrug. "They were here a month ago. Hopefully somebody remembers them."

It was only legwork that they'd be doing, but she didn't like being left behind. Still, she knew she was wasting time arguing. She let out a sigh. "Fine. If the ship is in port, you'll send word, and wait for me?"

"Yes." Alec was too smart to smile, but he ran a hand down her arm that felt both caressing and consoling. "Thank you."

"You'd better watch your back," she muttered, and threw a glance at Sam. "Both of you. You're not any more indestructible than I am, you know."

"We will." Alec looked like he wanted to kiss her, but instead turned away. Kendra frowned as she watched them leave, and tried not to worry.

44

The River Thames was why London had always been an important trading post. Sam couldn't remember a time when the wharves hadn't been crammed with ships from all over the world, waiting to unload their cargo. Tempers were known to flare between crew and dockworkers as patience snapped. Arguments often ended with a blade stuck into a bloke's gut. Adding to the tension, thievery was rampant among the ships anchored in the river.

Sam had been a young man when Parliament had finally had enough of the crime and hired Magistrate Patrick Colquhoun to form the River Police to stop the looting. That had been eighteen years ago. A few years later, the nobs had refashioned the docks themselves, taking roughly thirty acres in Wapping to build the Western and Eastern docks, connected by the Tobacco Dock, a massive brick building that stored imported tobacco. Walls had gone up around the new ports, as well as enormous storage warehouses and auxiliary businesses to service the sailors and workers. To Sam, the new design only meant that more ships were allowed to come into port. The River Police may have reduced some of the thievery by catching many of the scoundrels, but the docks were still the busiest—and most treacherous—place in the city.

Which was why he was now carrying a blunderbuss, tucked into his belt, at the ready, a pistol in one pocket, an extra knife in the other pocket, and his four-inch Sheffield blade in his boot. Alec, he knew, carried at least two pistols on his person. The thought that Miss Donovan had wanted to come along with them still sent a chill down his spine.

Despite the foul weather, including icy swirls of fog rolling off the Thames, the waterfront was crowded with workers of every nationality and race. They carried hemp bags across their shoulders and rolled barrels down ship planks to stack up on the wharf. The air crackled with foreign languages mixed with broken English. Sam's hand moved to rest on his blunderbuss when he heard the snap and snarl in some of the voices. He didn't need to speak their tongue to know trouble was brewing. Mingled with the voices were the cries of seagulls, the slap of water against the wharf, and the creak and groan of the countless sail masts as ships bobbed to and fro on the wind-chopped waters of the Thames.

"We'll cover more ground if we separate," Alec said in a low voice.

Sam nodded, but glanced at the marquis. Alec was wearing a greatcoat, but the quality of his clothes was noticeable. "Will you be all right?"

"I can take care of myself," he said, then gave a surprised laugh. "Good God, I sound exactly like Ke—Miss Donovan. You know, it *is* a bit annoying."

Sam grinned. "Owe her an apology, do you?"

"I wouldn't go that far. Why don't you take that side of the docks, and I will take the other. We'll work our way to the center."

They separated, and Sam moved through the crowds, asking the same question over and over again. "Do you know the *Magdalena*? It's a Spanish galleon."

Most of those he stopped shook their heads and hurried on. About a dozen responded with foreign chatter. Sam didn't know if they were telling him where the ship was or if they were insulting him. A few made hand gestures.

Sam had quizzed at least three dozen men when the scent of roasting chestnuts rose above the brackish and fishy smell of the Thames, luring him toward a stall where a man was currently shaking a wire basket over an open flame, tossing the chestnuts inside. Seven men were in the queue. Sam joined, his gaze on the vendor, who somehow managed to take the offered coins and slip them inside a pocket in his waistcoat even as he dumped hot chestnuts into scraps of paper he curled into cones.

"Have you heard of a Spanish galleon named the *Magdalena*?" he asked the two Chinese men ahead of him.

"*Bù! Bù!*" they said, shaking their heads, and shuffling forward.

"How about you?" Sam asked a wiry sailor in front of the Chinese men.

"The *Magdalena*?" Beneath his knit cap, the man looked like he could be a hundred, his swarthy skin crisscrossed with lines. "Aye, Oi've heard of it. Don't think it's in port at the moment. W'ot's yer interest?"

"I need ter speak with the captain," Sam said, shuffling forward two more paces. "Do you know him? Or the crew?"

"The Spanish deal mostly in textiles," the vendor spoke up, glancing at Sam as he dealt with the wiry sailor, and then the Chinese men. "Couldn't help overhearing. If ye're looking for a Spanish ship, ye might try yer luck where the textiles are being traded, down a bit on the Eastern docks."

"Thank you." Sam took the chestnuts and handed the peddler a coin.

Sam turned and began walking. He recognized the figure materializing out of the fog. "Any luck, milord?" he asked, offering Alec the cone filled with chestnuts.

"No." Alec dug into the paper for a couple of chestnuts, and bit into the soft meat. "You?"

"Maybe. We should go ter the area where they trade Spanish textiles. The Eastern dock."

It still took another twenty minutes before they found a Spaniard unloading long fabric bolts wrapped in rough hemp. Sam managed to stop him from walking away by planting himself before the dockworker, but his accent was so thick that Alec finally stepped forward and took over the questioning in Spanish. Sam finished the chestnuts, crumpled the paper, and stuck it in his pocket.

"*Gracias*," Alec said, and produced a coin for the man. He turned to Sam. "He said he knows the *Magdalena*. The captain's name is Suarez. He's not in port at the moment, but when he is, he and his crew have been known to frequent a brothel on Croft Street called the Zamora."

"Never heard of it."

"I was told it's run by an abbess who goes by the name Araceli. Captain Suarez appears to be quite close with the woman."

"Do you think she'd know anything?"

"I don't know. If not her, maybe one of her harlots. Men who have been out to sea not only want a willing body, they want someone to talk to as well."

Kendra tossed aside the foolscap she'd been studying and stood with more impatience than grace. It didn't help that her mind had once again returned to Alec and Sam. She wasn't worried—exactly. She *was* irritated that she had agreed to stay behind instead of canvasing the docks with them.

She began to pace the room, pausing to kick the nearby chair, a gesture more suited to a petulant child. She was glad no one was around to witness her flash of temper. Fifteen minutes ago, the Duke had left for his appointment with his man of affairs, and Rebecca had returned home to persuade her parents to let her join them later for the Duchess of Bedford's ball.

Kendra willed herself to think about the investigation rather than being relegated to a supporting role because she was a woman. As if having a Y chromosome was any protection against a bullet or a knife.

She was peering down at the loose pages of foolscap from the murder book when Harding came to the door.

"Forgive me for disturbing you, but there is that young . . . *person* here to see you again. He is saying that you offered him some type of employment." He looked at her in a way that made it clear he was hoping that she'd correct him. "Shall I give him some bread and cheese and send him on his way?"

"No. I did—well, His Grace agreed . . . You know what, never mind. Just send him up here." She recalled Snake's thin face. "Actually, you can send up some bread and cheese as well. And a glass of milk."

Harding's eyes flickered. "You do remember that you have the Bedford ball to attend."

"I didn't hit my head in the last four hours, so yeah, I remember."

He didn't seem to know what to say to that, so he bowed. "Very well, miss."

Kendra found her lips twitching as she watched the butler depart. She could almost feel sorry for him. She was an anomaly in his and Mrs. Danbury's carefully constructed world, and they were still trying to figure out how to deal with her. Just as she was still trying to figure out how to deal with them.

She moved back to the slate board, allowing her gaze to drift over the names, the symbol, the manner of deaths. It was coming together. She could *feel* it. She just needed a couple more puzzle pieces. Hopefully, Alec and Sam would be able to provide them.

Kendra didn't know how long she was lost in thought, cycling through theories, before the door opened again. She turned to watch Snake lope into the room with Harding frowning after him.

"Thank you, Harding," she said. It was a dismissal. The butler responded with a brief, stiff bow, and then melted away. She looked at Snake's slight figure in his raggedy coat and moth-eaten scarf. His hair stuck out at weird angles from beneath the soft cap he wore. His cheeks were red from the cold. "I take it you're here because you made your decision," she said carefully.

He looked down at his boots. "Aye. Bear said Oi'd better not spit inter fortune's face."

Kendra smiled. "Bear's quite a philosopher."

Snake glanced up at her, frowning. "A filo-what?"

"Philosopher. A thinker. The Duke is out right now, but he's agreeable to finding a place for you in his household. Or maybe the stables. Would you like that?"

"Oi don't know much about 'orses."

Kendra wasn't surprised. The kid was a Londoner, and a *poor* Londoner, at that, which meant he probably had about as much experience with horses as she did. "You can learn, if you want. Or there are other duties."

Snake nodded silently.

A maid pushed open the door, carrying a tray with the promised bread, butter, and cheese. And a glass of milk. She set it on the table, careful to keep it away from the pieces of foolscap strewn across the surface.

"Will that be all, miss?"

"Yes, thank you." She gestured to the tray. "Would you like to have something to eat, Snake?"

The boy moved his bony shoulders. "Oi could use a bite."

"Well, then." She walked over to the table and pulled out a chair. "Why don't you sit down?"

"Why're ye doin' this, eh? Wantin' me ter come an' work fer a nob?" he asked suddenly. His eyes were suspicious as he came over and hopped up on the chair. He kept his gaze on hers as he reached out with a grubby hand to snatch the bread.

Because I feel sorry for you. Because I want to help. And I hope to God that I'm not changing the future with my actions. She said aloud, "Maybe I think you can do better." Beneath her dress, she felt the weight of the arrowhead pendant. "It might take a little work on your part, and, of course, a desire to change."

"Ter change into w'ot?" he asked with his mouth full.

"What works best for you."

Snake regarded her for a long moment, then turned his attention to the food. As she watched, he demolished the cheese and rest of the bread so quickly that she worried he might choke on it.

"W'ot do yer got that fer?" he asked between bites.

"What?"

"*That!*" He pointed a grubby finger at the foolscap on the table.

Kendra looked down, and saw it was the symbol she'd drawn. "Oh. It's a cross. I think."

"Ain't no cross."

Kendra arched a brow at the boy. "How do you know?"

"'Cause Bear 'as that on 'is arm. An' Bear ain't one fer the church."

Kendra froze. "Bear has a tattoo like this one?" She snatched up the paper with the symbol. "*Exactly* like this?"

"Aye."

Holy shit. Maybe they wouldn't have to wait for the captain of the *Magdalena* after all. "Stay here, Snake. Right here. Drink your milk. I'm going to get my coat." *And reticule and gun.* "I'll be back."

"Then w'ot?"

"Then we go see Bear."

45

Kendra didn't want to waste valuable time finding Molly to change into servants' clothing, but she hoped by using her hooded cloak she would achieve some sort of anonymity. She doubted that she'd be so lucky as to leave the mansion without being seen, but she tried, hustling Snake down the servant's stairs and hauling him toward the back entrance.

"Where are you going, Miss Donovan?"

Kendra glanced back at Mrs. Danbury, who'd stepped out of the kitchens to frown at her.

"Gotta check something out. I'll be back," she said, and didn't stop.

"This is quite outra—"

Kendra shut the door on the rest of the housekeeper's words. She let go of Snake's thin wrist and hurried down the back alley that faced the mews. The cold was an unwelcome slap in the face, but she ignored it, as well as the dirty puddles that soaked the hem of her dress and cloak and froze her feet in the thin-soled shoes. She kept up the half-jogging pace until they were on the street, and she spotted the hackney about fifty yards away.

"Hey," she managed, huffing a little as she skidded to a stop. She looked up at the driver on his perch. "I need you to take us to Cheapside."

She watched the man's eyes widen in the shadow of his tricorn hat. "Watcha want ter go there for?" he asked, his voice muffled slightly by the thick wool scarf that he'd wound around his neck, nearly up to his bulbous nose. She thought of what a good disguise it was for the murderer.

"Just get us there," she said, and fished out a few extra coins from the reticule. This time it was pure greed that widened the man's eyes.

"Aye, m'lady. Get in." He waited until they'd climbed into the cabin before he shouted down at them. "Where'd ye want ter go in Cheapside?"

"The Iron Maiden," Snake yelled back.

"Christ," the hackney driver muttered. "Does the lady know that's one of the worst flash 'ouses in London Town?"

"This lady can speak for herself," Kendra shouted. "Now move your ass!"

The smoke inside the Iron Maiden's tavern was almost as thick as the fog outside. Rough-looking men with scarred, hard faces were gathered around tables. Despite the gray haze in the room, Kendra had no trouble identifying Bear. He was more than double the size of any of the other tavern's customers. Her hand dipped into her reticule, closing over the comfortable weight of the pistol as she and Snake wove through the crowd. The money and baubles scattered on the tables—without dice or cards—seemed to signal that she was witnessing highwaymen or housebreakers counting their stolen property.

Sweat dampened her palms and her heart pounded. Her pistol had only two lead balls. If things got ugly . . .

She decided not to think about what would happen if things got ugly. She wasn't counting on her pistol to get her out of the Iron Maiden alive, but Bear's protection. Which was ironic, given how many times she'd threatened to blow the man's balls off.

An eerie silence descended as she made her way to where Bear was sitting.

He stared at her in disbelief. "God's teeth, ye are a madwoman." He flicked his massive hand in a gesture of dismissal, instantly obeyed as the men at the table with him scraped back their chairs and scattered. He frowned at Snake. "Have ye come ter return the boy?"

The fact that he had sent Snake to her in the first place made her believe that the criminal had a spark of humanity inside him. Her gaze traveled across the coins spilling from pouches on the table before raising to meet his flat brown eyes. "No. I'd like to see your arm."

"Me *arm?*" he echoed. "Ye *are* touched in the attic, wench."

"It's important."

"Yer daft."

Kendra said nothing, mainly because she thought he was probably right.

Bear thrust himself to his feet, his eyes never leaving her. He shrugged out of the jacket he wore, tossed it on the chair. As she watched, he unbuttoned the cuffs of his workman's smock, and pushed up both sleeves. "What are ye lookin' for?" he asked, sounding intrigued despite himself.

Kendra remembered his sleeve of tattoos from the time he'd threatened her and Alec, but she hadn't paid any attention to them. Now her gaze swept one arm and its many images. Nothing. She shifted her gaze to the other arm, and saw the symbol.

"There." She pointed to the image that had been painted on Sir Giles and carved on Lord Cross's torso. "It's not a cross?"

He snorted. "Nay, it's not a bleeding cross. It's a Naudhiz rune," he said finally, and shrugged his massive shoulders. "'Tis about survival. Willpower." His lips curled in a hard smile. "Fate."

Kendra drew in a harsh breath. "That's Scandinavian, isn't it?"

"Aye. Me folks go back to the Viking invaders."

That didn't surprise Kendra, but she barely registered the boast. She was busy reviewing everything she knew—namely, the Larsons and their Scandinavian heritage.

She thought she knew which Larson would have used the symbol.

She started to turn, then became aware of her silent audience. She glanced back at Bear. "Am I going to have a problem getting out of here?"

A glint of amusement brightened Bear's flat eyes. "Maybe ye shoulda thought about that before ye came, eh?" But he shifted his gaze to the room at large. "Let the mad gentry mort pass," he yelled. "Toby, ye go with her ter make sure she gets inter a hackney."

A man in rough garb with a face only a mother could love hoisted himself to his feet. "Aye. C'mon, then."

Kendra grabbed Snake's arm, and they followed the man out the door. Outside, Kendra was shocked to see how quickly night had fallen, with lamplighters going about the business of lighting the oil lamps hanging from street posts. A damp mist surged around their ankles, and Kendra thought she felt several icy raindrops hit her hood by the time they found a hackney.

Kendra stopped Snake from jumping into the cabin. "I need you to take another hackney, Snake. Go back to Grosvenor Square." She leaned down and pressed a coin into his palm. "Tell the Duke that the symbol is a rune. Okay?"

Snake's face scrunched up. "W'ot's 'okay' mean?"

That made her grin. "It means all right." She straightened and dug out another coin, thrusting it at Toby. "Find him another hackney."

He flashed rotting teeth in a grin. "Aye."

Kendra gave the hackney driver an address, and then climbed into the cab.

"W'ot are ye gonna do?" Snake asked before she could slam the door shut.

"Hopefully save another man from being murdered." She yanked the door closed and reached up to pound on the ceiling. "Go!"

46

A young, pretty maid opened the door of the Zamora. After a quick inspection from smoky brown eyes generously lined with kohl, the girl stepped back to allow Alec and Sam entry. Alec surveyed the small, wood-paneled foyer. Only three wall sconces were lit, leaving most of the space draped in dusky shadows. The air was laden with a spicy, exotic scent. The wide staircase at the end of the foyer climbed to a balustrade that overlooked the foyer. He heard faint noises, a soft cry, low masculine laughter, a higher-pitched feminine giggle.

"Welcome to the Zamora," the maid said in quiet and oddly cultured tones. "If you will follow me."

"A moment." Alec stopped the maid. "We're here to speak to your mistress, Araceli."

The girl hesitated, then said, "Please, follow me . . ."

She brought them to a drawing room that was as shadowed as the foyer. Logs crackled in a delicately carved fireplace. The velvet burgundy curtains were trimmed in gold, and closed to shut out the blustery night.

The exotic scent was stronger here. Alec suspected that someone had added incense to the fire, allowing the spicy aroma to saturate the room. Half a dozen women in varying states of dress were lounging on velvet tufted chairs and settees. A girl, lovely enough to be a Cyprian, her dark hair left loose and flowing, was playing Mozart on the pianoforte. One man was in the corner with a young lady. Based on the cut of his clothes, Alec thought he was a merchant, not gentry or nobility. He looked to be in his fifties, with sagging skin and a paunch. The girl who rose with languid grace from the Egyptian settee, clasping his hand to guide him from the room, was no more than twenty.

The remaining girls sent them coquettish looks, but had apparently been trained to keep silent when customers arrived to inspect the wares. Obviously Araceli was trying to create a more sophisticated brothel than Drury Lane, where whores called out for a gentleman's attention from doorways.

The maid glided over to a side table and poured them each a glass of mulled wine. "Who shall I tell Miss Araceli wishes to see her?" she asked.

"Alec Morgan"—Alec hesitated, then decided to leave out his title—"and this is Mr. Kelly." Not that anybody in the Ton would blink about Alec visiting a brothel, if they heard. It was expected of men of the Ton, just as were affairs with actresses and ballet dancers. But he thought it best not to identify the Bow Street Runner. If the Abbess proved reluctant to speak, they could always inform her then. With a coin or two. Bribery was always welcome.

The maid quietly departed. It took less than five minutes for the door to open again, and a tall, strikingly beautiful woman swept into the room. She wore a black silk empire dress that had no adornments other than an ebony sash tied snuggly beneath her breasts. The color was slightly shocking, given its association with widow's weeds, which was most likely why she'd chosen it, Alec thought cynically. Or maybe she realized the stark simplicity—and low décolletage—only served to enhance her beauty. Her raven hair was pulled high and covered by a black lace mantilla, framing her oval face. She was not the gold-and-white Cyprian so fashionable these days, but rather a clever contradiction. Instead of downplaying her obvious Spanish heritage, with her long black eyes and warm skin tones, she played them up, with black kohl and red painted lips. The effect was stunning.

"Mr. Morgan? Mr. Kelly?" Her voice was throaty and, consciously or not, seductive, with the faintest hint of a Spanish accent. She glided over to an alcove with two empty settees and sank down onto the plump cushions. Her gaze never left them as she held out her hand, waiting for the maid to pour red wine into a crystal glass. "You have no interest in *amor*?" She smiled slightly, her bold lips curving.

The maid brought over the wineglass, pressed it into her hand, and then quietly left. Araceli took a dainty sip of the burgundy. "*Mis chicas* are well versed in the arts of pleasure. They would leave you well satisfied."

Alec smiled. "I have no doubt, but we are here only for information. I can pay. Your time, I know, is valuable."

A glint entered her eyes as she regarded him. "*Si*, it is. I am happy you recognize this." She indicated the settee opposite her. "Please, sit down, be comfortable." She took another slow sip of wine, watching as they sat. She waited until Alec retrieved several gold coins, stacking them on the side table. She didn't pick them up, but her gaze flicked to the coins, then back to Alec. "What do you wish to know?"

The notes of the pianoforte provided pleasant background. Having become aware that Alec and Sam weren't customers, a few of the girls began to talk softly amongst themselves.

Sam said, "Captain Suarez. We've been told that he visits you when he's in port."

"*Si*, the captain and I have a long friendship." The dark eyes went cold. "And I do not betray my friends. Not even for gold."

"Admirable. And we would not ask it of you, señora," Alec said mildly, lifting his glass to sample the mulled wine. Not as inferior as he'd expected. He lowered the glass. "A month ago, while the *Magdalena* was docked here, a man of some consequences went onboard. Sir Giles. Perhaps you've heard of him? Or read about him?"

The red lips parted in surprise. "*Si*. I have read about the terrible murder. But I know nothing about him visiting Captain Suarez."

Sam scratched the side of his nose as he regarded her. "Captain Suarez said nothing to you about Sir Giles meeting someone on his ship? Another passenger, perhaps?"

"*Nada*. No." She hesitated, her dark eyes studying them. "A month ago, you say?"

"Yes." Alec's eyes narrowed. "You remember something?"

"The captain did have a passenger. He brought him here." The delicate throat worked as she swallowed, and she looked away. "The man was . . . I don't know how to say . . ."

"Violent?" guessed Alec.

The dark eyes flashed in surprise. "No . . . nada, nothing such as that. It was more of . . . an aesthetic."

Alec frowned. "An aesthetic."

She gave a husky laugh. "*Mis chicas* know that our patrons are often not the most handsome, young, or virile of men. But we must keep up the pretense, *si*? With some men, the pretense is more difficult than others." She paused to take a swallow of wine. "With that man, Captain Suarez's passenger, it was very difficult. One of his hands, it was little more than a stump. And his face . . . *Dios*."

A chill raced down Alec's spine. "What about his face?"

"One of his ears was gone, and he was scarred. So horribly scarred." She moistened her red lips. "He looked like a demon."

Sam drew in a swift breath, and threw Alec a look.

"I know he was not," Araceli continued. "Obviously he had been in a terrible fire. But *Madre de Dios*, looking at him was like looking into a *pesadilla*—a nightmare."

"Evert Larson," Alec said. "Evert Larson is alive."

"I do not know his name," said the Abbess.

Sam leaned forward. "What happened to the man? Do you know where he is?"

She shook her head. "He stayed the night with Giselle. But when she woke the next morning, he was gone."

47

Impatience snapped like a live wire inside Kendra's chest, and she had to bite her lip to restrain herself from yelling at the driver to go bloody faster.

Breathe in. Breathe out.

The meditation technique didn't stop her racing thoughts. The image of the swastikas on Larson & Son rose up in her mind. The family, she thought, had always been into symbols. The compulsion to put a mark on the victims symbolizing survival, willpower, and fate made sense, she supposed, if Evert Larson didn't die in Spain as everyone had thought.

But why hadn't he returned two years ago? Why had he allowed his family to mourn? She'd briefly considered the possibility, but she hadn't believed Evert would have allowed them to suffer. Was that her own bias? She'd never had a loving family, so she had no point of reference.

She frowned as she considered what she knew of Evert. Something had happened over there to flip the golden boy into a killer, to be so cruel as to let his family think he was dead.

Did his family know he was alive now? She remembered their reaction when she'd mentioned Magdalena, and thought yes. Did that mean they also knew Evert was responsible for murdering Sir Giles and Lord Cross?

In her mind, Kendra shuffled through their actions and reactions. *They know*, she thought. *They're protecting him.* Maybe they felt he was justified in what he was doing. Maybe they thought they could talk him out of killing anyone else. But if he'd come back for revenge, Evert wouldn't be satisfied until he'd killed Captain Mobray, the last person who had any connection to Spain.

The hackney seemed to shiver and shake as it barreled around a corner, then slowed to a crawl. Kendra leaned forward to look out the window. They'd reached Piccadilly. Despite the foul weather, traffic ensnarled the street. *It might be faster getting out and running . . .* Kendra could only imagine what Lady Atwood would say to that.

She rubbed a hand over her face and tried to calm her racing heart. Her foot tapped an impatient rhythm. It seemed to take hours, but probably was no more than ten minutes before the hackney sped up again, eventually turning down Sackville Street. Kendra barely waited for the carriage to jerk to a halt before she thrust open the door and jumped down. The fog-shrouded street wasn't as busy as Piccadilly but it wasn't deserted either. Through the gray mist, Kendra saw several carriages and a hackney parked against the curb. One carriage had just begun to pull out, horses clomping down the street. She ran toward Captain Mobray's building. Two riders on horseback gave her astonished looks as she passed, and pelted up the steps of the Georgian mansion.

She was reaching for the doorknob when the door jerked inward suddenly, and a man loomed on the threshold. She didn't know whether she or Mobray was more startled to come face-to-face.

"Captain Mobray."

"Miss Donovan." He recovered quickly, glancing beyond her to skim the street. "What are you doing here?" Then his eyes widened. "You didn't come *alone*?"

Kendra nearly laughed at his suddenly wary expression. "Relax. I'm not trying to compromise you." This was the flip side of the marriage coin, she knew. Being alone with a woman of quality (which she was, given her relationship with the Duke) left a man as vulnerable to being forced into a marriage as the woman. Refusing to marry a woman that he'd compromised was one of the few things that could destroy a gentleman's reputation.

She said, "I need to talk to you."

His eyes flickered. "I fear that I cannot accommodate you, Miss Donovan. I am meeting someone, and am already behind schedule." He brushed past her, moving down the steps. He looked up and down the street and began to walk toward the nearest hackney. "Perhaps I shall call upon you tomorrow," he threw at her over his shoulder.

She followed him. "This is important. Make time."

Mobray shot her a cold glance as he yanked opened the hackney's door. "You are an impertinent creature. Does His Grace realize you are running about London without a chaperone?" He hoisted himself up into the cab and called to the driver, "Drury Lane!"

"This is a matter of life and death."

"I don't need female hysterics—Good God, what are you doing?" He gaped at her when she grasped the handrail and catapulted herself in behind him.

"I'm coming with you. It will give us an opportunity to talk." She raised an eyebrow at him. "It's probably ill-bred to toss me out of the carriage."

He glared at her for a moment, then lifted a gloved hand, giving the ceiling a rap as a signal to go. After a moment, the hackney started to move.

"This is highly irregular, Miss Donovan." In a gesture that bespoke extreme irritation, he yanked off his gloves, and reached into his inner pocket and retrieved his porcelain snuffbox. Flicking it open, he took a pinch of snuff, sniffing it into each nostril. "What, pray tell, is this melodrama about? Life and death." He snapped the snuffbox closed. "You have been reading too many of Ann Radcliffe's novels, I suspect."

Kendra kept her gaze on his when she said, "Evert Larson."

Something flashed in his eyes. "Why do you persist in this matter? What happened to the man in Spain was tragic, but it was two years ago."

"Evert Larson is alive."

He stilled. "You *are* mad," he finally bit out, his voice harsh.

"Evert is alive. And he killed Sir Giles and Lord Cross."

"I don't believe you."

"Didn't Sir Giles tell you? He met with Evert when he returned on the *Magdalena*."

"This is ridiculous. As I said, you are obviously a hysterical female prone to fantasies," he snapped, trying to sound dismissive, but Kendra heard the crackle of fear.

She pressed, "You must have realized something had changed when Sir Giles began questioning you and Cross about what had happened in Spain." It was an educated guess, based on Cross having sought out Sir Giles.

"I was captured and tortured. That's what happened in Spain." His voice rose, and he made an effort to lower it. "'Tis not a time that I care to discuss."

"Afraid that you might say something incriminating?"

"Hardly."

A muscle pulsed along his jaw as he tore his gaze away from hers. She waited, hoping the silence was working on his nerves. But he continued to stare out the window into the night, ignoring her. Maybe the silent treatment wasn't working because it wasn't exactly silent. Kendra could hear the clatter of carriage wheels and horse hooves, the buzz of voices beyond the quietness inside the cab. After about ten minutes, she released a sigh.

"What happened in Spain, Captain Mobray?"

He said nothing.

"Evert is alive," she repeated. "He murdered Sir Giles and Lord Cross." She waited. Silence. "You are his next target."

That brought his eyes back around. His face hardened. "You are wrong," he said, but she thought his lips quivered slightly. "I saw the explosion and fire myself. No one could have survived that."

"According to the reports, you were being held in a tent. How did you see the explosion and fire yourself? How did you know Evert had been caught in it?"

He shifted his attention back to the window. She thought he was going to ignore her again, but he finally spoke. "If Evert Larson is alive, why did he wait two years before returning?"

"An interesting question, but I find it strange that you don't ask the obvious one."

"What obvious question?" he demanded, turning back again.

"*Why me?*" Kendra watched him closely, saw his mouth tighten. "People who feel wronged always ask that question. But maybe you didn't ask because you know exactly why Evert would target you. What happened in Spain?"

"*Nothing, damn you,*" he hissed.

He seemed relieved when the hackney drew to a stop. He suddenly leaned forward, close enough for Kendra to see the coldness in his gray eyes, like chips of dirty ice. "You would do well to stop with these inquiries, Miss Donovan." He thrust open the door and stepped down. "They are dangerous."

"That sounds like a warning," Kendra said, and slid over to follow him. "It's only a matter of time before the truth comes out. I'm not the only one making inquiries."

"I am giving you sound advice—What the devil?"

Kendra saw the horror on Mobray's face an instant before she heard the scrape of a shoe behind her, and too late she realized her mistake. Her muscles tightened, and she began to spin with some thought of kicking out, but in the next instant, her world exploded with pain, her vision going red before splintering into darkness.

48

Alec and Sam's greatcoats flapped open as they ran up the steps to the Duke's mansion, and, without ceremony, catapulted themselves through the door. They came to an abrupt stop when they came upon the Duke and Harding facing Snake. At their sudden entrance, the Duke spun around, and there was something in the man's eyes that sent a terrible fear spearing through Alec. Instinctively, his gaze swept the entrance hall for Kendra.

"Where's Kendra?" he demanded sharply.

The Duke straightened. "I don't think there is any cause for alarm," he said, but his expression was uneasy. "Snake and Kendra went to see Bear—"

"*Bear!*" Ice clutched at Alec's stomach. The woman was going to drive him mad. He grasped Snake's thin arm and fought the urge to shake him. "Why the devil did she do that? Where is she?"

"*Oy!* Let go!" Snake tried to squirm away, but Alec kept a firm grasp on him.

"Alec, let the child go!" Aldridge ordered.

Alec yanked the boy to the door. "Take me to her. And if the bastard has touched a hair on her head, I swear to God—"

The Duke shouted, "Alec, stop it!"

"She ain't with Bear now, gov'ner!" Snake cried, struggling. "As soon as she laid 'er peepers on his tattoo, she told me ter come 'ere and tell ye gentry morts w'ots 'appened."

Alec stopped, but didn't let go of Snake. "What in God's name are you talking about?"

Sam frowned. "The lass wanted ter look at Bear's tattoo? What for?"

"Let the boy go," the Duke said again, catching Alec's gaze. "Kendra learned something important. The symbol—it's not a crucifix. It's a rune."

"Nod His—that's its name," said Snake.

The Duke eyed the boy. "Yes, well, I don't think that's the correct name. But Snake here says it means survival, willpower, and fate. I think—"

"Evert Larson is alive," snapped Alec, and waved his hand at his uncle's shocked expression. "I know."

"How—?"

"Never mind that now." He looked at Snake. "If she's not with Bear, where did she go?"

"Calm down, my boy," said the Duke. "Snake said that she went to save a man from being murdered. Obviously she was referring to Captain Mobray." Alec began striding for the door, but the Duke called, "Wait! She may be on her way back home right now."

"Then it won't matter, will it?" Alec hoped to God that it wouldn't matter. He'd rather be chasing after Kendra like a fool than sitting on his arse, waiting for her to come home like a bloody half-wit.

"I'm coming with you!" Sam called out, and sprinted to catch up with the marquis.

"Take the carriage!" the Duke shouted after them.

"Gor!" exclaimed Snake, ogling the Duke. "Is it always so excitin' in yer 'ousehold, Yer Grace?"

Aldridge's eyes dropped to the boy while Harding rushed forward to close the door. "Only in the last six months, Snake."

A light snow had begun falling by the time Alec and Sam jumped out of the carriage in front of Mobray's residence. In the distance, Alec could hear the sounds of traffic, but Sackville Street was fairly quiet, save two dandies drunkenly meandering down the pavement, their arms slung over the other's shoulder.

A sickening fear burned a hole in Alec's gut as he rushed up the outer steps. He whipped open the door and raced up the stairs to Mobray's rooms on the third floor. Behind him, Sam huffed up the two flights.

"Christ." Sam bent over after coming to the third-story landing. He placed a hand on each knee as he tried to suck in deep gulps of air.

Alec was already at Mobray's door, pounding his fist against the panel. "Captain Mobray! Open up! Mobray!"

Sam finally managed to regain his breath. "He ain't home, milord. No reason ter not open the door. He ain't done nothin' wrong."

A door across the hall opened, and a thin young man glared out at them. He was in his shirtsleeves, clutching the ends of his loose cravat. "What the blazes is going on out here? I am attempting to create the Mathematician, you know," he informed them with a haughty accent, glancing down at the cravat around his neck. "It may look simple, but it is devilishly tricky. And it certainly doesn't help when you are making such a god-awful commotion!"

"Do you know where Captain Mobray is?" Alec demanded.

"I don't know. I believe he mentioned receiving an invitation to attend the theater. Or perhaps it was—"

"Did you see a young lady around here? Dark hair, dark eyes, beautiful." Alec brought up his hand, let it hover in the air. "About this high?"

The other man's lip curled. "No, but she wouldn't be a lady if she came here to see Captain Mobray, would she—*oof*!" The air was pushed out of his lungs when Alec sprung across the hallway and shoved him up against his doorframe.

"I'd think very carefully before you say anything derogatory about the lady," Alec said with silken heat, his arm across the other man's throat. "How long ago did Captain Mobray leave?"

"I don't know," the man squeaked. "Forty minutes ago? An hour? I-I only heard his door slam when he left. The walls in this building are as thin as paper. I'm certain he hailed a hackney and went to the theater as he planned. Perhaps you ought to look there."

"Which theater?" But then Alec's knees went weak as his words registered. *"A hackney . . ."* He let go of the man, who clutched at his throat and slumped against the wall.

Alec's gaze met Sam's, and he saw a matching horror. He spun back to face the dandy. "Did you see the hackney?"

"No. I told you, I only heard the door shut when he left!"

"How do you know Captain Mobray had plans for the theater?"

The man gaped at him. "I encountered him earlier in the afternoon. I inquired whether he would be attending the Duchess of Bedfordshire's ball tonight, but he said that he'd been invited to the theater. That is all I know!"

Alec looked at Sam. "Do you believe it?"

"I'm telling the truth!" the man swore.

Alec shot him a scathing look. "Not you, you bloody fool!" To Sam, he said, "Do you think it was a trap?"

"I don't know. It could have been," Sam said. "But we don't know whether Miss Donovan is with the captain. She may have come here, but that doesn't mean she encountered him. She may be back at Grosvenor Square as we speak."

Alec knew that was true, and he might be overreacting. Except he still had the gut-clenching sensation that something was seriously wrong, and Kendra was in danger.

He sucked in a shaky breath and lifted his hat to run agitated fingers through his hair. *Think.* "All right," he finally said. "We'll go back to Grosvenor Square. If Kendra is there, she'll want to accompany us to the Larsons."

"And if she ain't there?" Sam asked.

"If she isn't there, the Larsons will most likely be able to lead us to their son."

"And if they don't know where he is?" Sam persisted, but then his mouth compressed, as though he regretted asking the question.

"They'll know," Alec snapped out, ignoring the ball of ice in his gut that was telling him that he was wrong.

For the second time that evening, Alec burst into the Duke's house, startling the footman who was flirting with a maid in a shadowy corner. Alec demanded, "Is she here?"

"Sir?" The footman, flushing red, straightened, while the maid melted away.

"Kendra—Miss Donovan," Alec said sharply. "Has she returned?"

"I-I'm not certain—"

Hell. Alec pushed past him, sprinting up the stairs. He knew—God, he *knew*—even before he thrust open the door to the study that Kendra wouldn't be inside. His gaze locked on his uncle, who was rising from his desk chair.

"Alec?"

"Kendra has not returned?" he demanded.

The Duke frowned. "No. Did you speak to Captain Mobray?"

"He wasn't at home. His neighbor said that he'd been invited to the theater. He left in a hackney." He saw alarm flare in his uncle's eyes, and turned back around.

"Where are you going?" demanded the Duke.

He paused, glancing back at his uncle. "The Larsons. They should know the whereabouts of their son!"

The Duke came around the desk. "I'm coming with you."

Alec hesitated. "If Kendra has been delayed for some reason—"

"Harding will send word. Where is Mr. Kelly?"

"He's waiting for me in the carriage."

"Good." Aldridge grabbed Alec's arm. "Kendra does know how to take care of herself, Alec."

"I pray to God you're right."

49

Awareness came to Kendra with the hot, stabbing pain behind her left ear, and a vague sense of discomfort everywhere else. She heard a groan. It took her a minute to realize that she'd issued the broken sound. She struggled to open her eyes, the fluttering movement like a spike being driven into her eyeballs, followed by a wave of dizziness. She instantly reacted by squeezing her eyes shut, groaning again as nausea rolled through her. *Shit, shit, shit.*

Sweat popped up on her brow as she fought the queasiness twisting her stomach. Christ, did she have a concussion? At least she hadn't been gagged. If she threw up, she wouldn't now choke on her own vomit.

After a moment, the pain and dizziness receded slightly. Most of her physical pain was coming from her head, where she'd been coldcocked. She became aware that she was on the floor, slumped against a wall. The cold and damp penetrated her layers of clothing. Her wrists were bound with rope—hemp, she was sure. It pinched her wrists, causing her fingertips to go numb. Though that could have been the chill in the room.

She became conscious of the smell of dust and decay. Not the human kind, thank God, but the kind brought on by neglect, like rotting wood and mildew. There were other odors, as well: linseed oil, and something chemical. And . . . was that blood?

Breathe in. Breathe out.

She wasn't the only one breathing. She became conscious of the ragged sound beside her, then the clink of metal against glass farther away.

Ignoring her throbbing head, Kendra forced her eyes open. The room was long and narrow, seething with deep shadows kept at bay by several candelabras and a half dozen oil lamps. The candelabras were set on a rough bench against the wall on the other side of the room. The flames from the candles glinted off an array of glass beakers, test tubes, and flasks. The oil lamps were scattered across the grimy floor, illuminating the pallet in the corner topped with a pillow and thick quilts.

Kendra's gaze locked on a tall, broad-shouldered figure standing in front of the workbench. His back was to her, his concentration on mixing some sort of concoction in a glass beaker, the source of metal clinking against glass. He still wore the greatcoat he'd worn as a hackney driver, but he'd removed the tricorn hat and scarf. As she watched, he turned slightly, and she caught his profile, the murky light in the room limning red, twisted flesh.

He was a demon. A demon straight from Hell. She remembered Ella's horror.

"He's mad."

Carefully, Kendra turned her throbbing head to look at the man who'd issued that rough whisper. Captain Mobray was sitting beside her, back against the wall, his legs out. Instead of rope, his wrists were manacled together, his fists clenched on his lap. His face was ashen and sweaty with fear. As she met his gaze, she saw that his pupils were dilated with horror.

Kendra straightened, curling and uncurling her fingers to bring some feeling back into them. Thankfully, he'd tied her hands in front of her. Not that she couldn't have gotten out of having them tied behind her back, but it would have required more of an effort. Effort that would draw his attention.

Slowly she brought her bound hands to her chest. Beneath her cloak and dress, the arrowhead pendant lay heavy against her breastbone.

"*We must do something,*" Captain Mobray hissed beside her.

"Where's my reticule?" she whispered.

Mobray stared at her. "Your reticule? Who fucking cares about your reticule?"

She had a brief flash of the pouch on the hackney seat. Damn. She'd gotten down so fast to keep pushing Mobray, she'd left it behind. *Stupid.*

"Are you listening to me?" Mobray hissed.

"No." She focused on sliding her bound hands up to her throat, her fingers tangling with the delicate chain, tugging.

"He's going to kill us," the captain persisted, his breath hitching a little. The man's arrogance had crumbled. She shot him another glance, saw him lick his lips. His eyes darted to Evert Larson, still occupied at the workbench. "He's going to kill us just like Sir Giles and Cross."

"And why is that?" she finally hissed back. "What did you do to him in Spain?"

"'Tis a story I want to hear as well," Evert Larson said with eerie calm, slowly turning around. "It is the only reason you still live, Captain Mobray."

Kendra's throat tightened as she turned to the macabre visage. And realized she'd made her second mistake that evening.

"Is your master at home?" demanded the Duke as soon as the Larsons' butler opened the door. "We must see him immediately."

The servant blinked, clearly startled to find such an august personage as the Duke of Aldridge knocking on the door. His gaze traveled to Alec and Sam with much the same bemusement. If the situation hadn't been so serious, Sam would have been amused by the other man's expression, given how many times he'd encountered butlers who'd looked down their noses at him when he'd knocked on the doors of his betters.

"Now, if you please," snapped Aldridge.

The servant jerked to attention. "Please, come inside." He stepped back, allowing them to enter. "I shall inform my master that you wish to see him—"

"Take us to him, or I'll find him myself," Alec said, the look in his green eyes lethal.

Astrid emerged from the shadows of the hall, the skirts of her blue silk evening gown whispering over the floor. "What is the meaning of this?"

Aldridge said, "We are here about your son, Evert."

Sam couldn't identify the emotion that rippled across the beautiful face. "Evert?"

"We know that he survived his ordeal in Spain," Alec said harshly. "He returned to England on the *Magdalena* a month ago—"

"*Ordeal?*" She cut him off, practically spitting out the word. Her eyes were like a blue flame as she gave them a contemptuous look. "Is that what you call it when a brave young man serves his country, and is betrayed by his own countrymen?"

"Where is he?" Alec demanded. "Where is your son?"

She glared at him, her jaw becoming rigid. "Evert is dead. He died in Spain."

"Bloody hell," Alec swore. "Where is your husband?"

She laughed, but it was sharp crack filled with bitterness. "Do you think he will tell you anything different?"

The Duke said, "Your son returned from Spain. We know this is true. We also know he murdered Sir Giles and Lord Cross. Now he has taken Captain Mobray. But we think that my ward, Miss Donovan, was with Captain Mobray, and she may have been taken too. We need to know where your son may have taken her. Please, Mrs. Larson, I beg of you . . . you must tell me where your son is!"

"My son would never hurt Miss Donovan," she whispered, balling her one hand into a fist and pressing it against her stomach. Sam saw the flicker of fear in her artic blue eyes.

"Where is your husband?" Alec demanded again.

Astrid squared her shoulders, her look scathing. "He is not home. I've told you everything. You must leave now."

A muscle jumped in Alec's jaw, and he took a threatening step forward, but the Duke laid a hand on his arm to stop him. He looked at Astrid. "Mrs. Larson, we must find Evert. This . . . vendetta of his must be stopped before anyone else is harmed."

She shifted her gaze to meet his. "I'm telling you the truth. Evert is dead," she said coldly. "You may search this house if you don't believe me."

The butler shuffled forward. "If I would be so bold, my mistress is speaking the truth, sir. The master and Mr. Larson are not in residence. They left earlier for the apothecary shop."

Sam said, "This is an official Bow Street investigation. If you're lying ter us—"

"He's not lying," Astrid interrupted, glaring at Sam. "Nor am I." Her lips twisted in a mockery of a smile. "Evert is in Valhalla. Where he can no longer be harmed."

The man was wearing a leather mask stained red and carved with hideous furrows and gashes.

"You were not supposed to be here, Miss Donovan."

Kendra caught the glitter of eyes in the shadowy holes of the mask as he regarded her. "Funny," she said, "because I don't remember hitting myself over the head and bringing myself here."

"But you got into the hackney with *him*, didn't you? I think the gods must have ordained that you were meant to bear witness to his confession." The mask turned to look at Captain Mobray. "'Tis time for you to speak. To tell us of your betrayal."

Captain Mobray swallowed hard enough for his Adam's apple to make a clicking sound. "You're a lunatic."

The man stared at him for a long moment, then he pivoted abruptly, retreating to the workbench. Kendra saw the glint of the blade in the candlelight as he picked up the knife, and knew that Mobray had seen it as well when a strange mewling sound came from his throat.

"If you do not speak, there's no reason for me not to cut out your tongue now, is there?" the killer murmured as he walked toward them. "And I shall not wait for your death to do so."

"For God's sake, it was *war*!" Mobray cried desperately. "They were starving us. Torturing us!"

"Lies. All lies! Tell us of your betrayal!" The man slowly pushed up his mask. "Tell us *now*."

50

The apothecary shop's windows were dark when they pulled up to the curb. Alec jumped from the carriage, driven by a sense of urgency that had him wanting to break down the shop's door. Instead, he banged his fist loudly upon it.

Sam pressed his face against the windowpanes to peer inside. "I see a bit of light behind the counter. The laboratory is in the back of the shop, I think. There must be a rear entrance."

Alec was already running for the alley between the apothecary shop and the haberdashery next door. Rats scurried out of sight at the sound of their pounding feet. Alec spotted the back door and rushed to it. He rattled the doorknob, and was shocked when it swung inward. He thrust open the door fully, his gaze on the man hurrying toward them.

"What's this about?" Bertel Larson demanded, stopping to stare in shock at his unexpected visitors. "My God . . . Your Grace. What is happening?"

Alec pushed past him to the other door, his gaze sweeping laboratory workbenches filled with sacks of herbs, measuring equipment, beakers, and dishes. Empty. He spun around. "Where's your son?" he snapped, and clenched his hands into fists to stop himself from laying hands on the apothecary. "Where is Evert?"

Sam's golden eyes narrowed as he shot a cursory glance around the laboratory. "Where's David? Ain't he supposed ter be working with you tonight?"

Bertel was shaking his head. "What is the meaning of this?"

"My ward is missing," said the Duke, stepping forward. "We know she went to speak to Captain Mobray. We think your son has Captain Mobray and Miss Donovan. You must tell us where he would have taken them!"

Bertel pressed shaking hands against his temples. "I cannot believe this!"

"Damn you! Now is not the time to express your incredulity," Alec snapped. "Tell us where you son has gone!"

"I don't know." Bertel dropped his hands and looked at them helplessly. "I swear to you that I would tell you if I knew! I have no wish for this. He—he is not in his right mind. You must see that? You must see that his mind was shattered by what happened . . ."

Ice cold terror arrowed through him, and Alec looked at his uncle and Sam. "My God, where has Evert taken her?"

Bertel raked trembling fingers through his hair, his horror building to match Alec's. "No, no, Evert is dead . . ."

"David." Kendra breathed the name as she stared at the strikingly handsome face.

The blue eyes sparkled with tears of fury and vengeance. The finely sculpted lips peeled back in a snarl. "He killed my brother!"

Kendra's head swam. And it wasn't from the concussion. It felt like the earth had tilted on its axis, and she had to scramble to make sense of the new world order. "I thought Evert had survived . . . that he had returned to England a month ago. On the *Magdalena*."

Tears spilled over and ran unheeded down David's cheeks as he flicked her a glance. "Living isn't surviving, Miss Donovan."

She looked at him. "Is Evert alive?"

"No. But he didn't die in Spain, either," he whispered brokenly. For a long moment, he stood there, breathing harshly, staring at nothing in particular. "We couldn't believe it when we received a note from the *Magdalena*," he finally said. "We didn't believe it, thought it must be somebody's idea of a cruel jest, someone who wanted to hurt us." He swallowed hard. "But I went to the ship that night."

"And found Evert," Kendra said softly.

"I found a monster . . . because of *him*." Without warning, David lurched forward and kicked Mobray in the kidneys. The other man cried out in pain, falling to the side and curling up like a shrimp as David landed two more vicious kicks.

"Stop it!" Kendra screamed. "Stop it! Goddamn it, *stop it*!"

David shifted back, the sound of his ragged breathing and Mobray's groans filling the room. "Evert had been in an explosion in Spain. That much of what he said was true. His face—it was gone. His fingers . . ." A sob rose in his throat, and his hand clenched the knife, knuckles whitening. "The pain that he endured was inhuman. Do you know how he survived? The French thought he was dead, his flesh burnt and rotting! They threw him in a cart with the other dead, hauled away by the villagers . . ."

Jesus. Kendra said nothing, horrified.

David continued, "A peasant saw that Evert was alive—barely. He brought him home, tended to him. God knows why. It would have been kinder to kill him then. But he lived."

David fell silent again, his handsome face twisting.

"But he came home," Kendra said after a moment.

"He had no intention of returning home. It had taken more than a year to mend, and when he was fit, he chose to stay in the village. Do you know what he did?" Kendra caught the wild glitter in David's blue eyes as he let out a sudden laugh. "He became an *apothecary*! Tending to peasants' mosquito bites and complaints!"

"He *survived*," Kendra said.

David shot her a scathing look. "Survived. He *died*!"

She didn't ask why Evert hadn't returned home. She knew why. Evert Larson had been his family's golden boy. In the 21st century, he would have been the star quarterback, the brilliant politician, the Wall Street whiz, the model or movie star. Everything she'd learned about him told her that he was the kind of guy who would've excelled in whatever his chosen profession. Talent, brains, and good looks were a powerful combination.

But what happened to someone's psyche when you took away one part of that trifecta?

The first thing she'd noticed about David was how strikingly handsome he was. People hadn't spoken of Evert's gorgeous face when they'd remembered him, but based on the oil painting hanging in the Larsons' home, he and David had been nearly identical. Like most blessed with beauty, Evert had probably taken his looks for granted. All youth did. Until time wrought changes on a person's face and skin.

But there was a big difference between time's slow encroachment on beauty, and having it ravaged by fire.

"What made Evert finally return?" she asked.

David's lips twisted. "Because of *him*." He glared at Mobray, who seemed to curl into a tighter position, awaiting the next kick. "With the war over, people began to travel again. Peddlers, tradesmen. A merchant from England passed through Evert's village, and left a London newspaper behind. There was an article in it that mentioned the good captain." He sneered. "It speculated about his political aspirations. Evert knew he had to return, to tell the truth."

"He sent Sir Giles a note as well as you."

"Sir Giles—a man that he thought he could *trust*," David spat, his eyes glittering with fury. "Sir Giles was more concerned with how Captain Mobray and Lord Cross's treasonous actions might put England in a bad light! The bastard asked Evert to keep quiet while he investigated. *Investigated*. He was trying to figure out how to stop the truth from being known!"

"I don't think so. I think he just needed time to figure it out."

"Bullocks! He lied! And Evert knew he was lying!"

"Why didn't you bring him home with you after you found him on the ship?"

He glared at her. "You think I didn't *try*? I *begged* him to come home with me. But he refused. He . . . he was ashamed." David had to blink back tears. "He came here," he said, his voice hoarse, "and lived like a bloody animal. Because of *him*."

Kendra's gaze traveled to the pallet and blankets.

"I tried to make Evert understand that it didn't matter," David said, his breathing heavy. "I tried—and then it was too late."

Kendra swallowed against the bile that had risen in her throat. Her lips felt stiff as she asked, "What happened?"

"He took a knife—*this* knife"—David's breath caught on a sob as he lifted the blade he held—"and slit his wrists. I found him here. Christ, the blood . . . there was so much blood. That was scarcely three weeks ago. He'd been in England for three days."

Kendra's gaze slid from the pallet and blankets to the grimy floor, now recognizing a large stain near the pallet as blood. Her stomach knotted. "I'm sorry, David. It's not your fault."

His face twisted on a spasm of pain. "Do you think that I believe it's *my* fault?" he shot back. "It's *his* fault!" He surged forward, and kicked Mobray again, eliciting a moan.

"Tell her!" he screamed. "Tell her how you betrayed your own men! You and Cross! Cross recognized Evert when he came to the camp with the villagers. He told you, didn't he, you bastard? And you realized you could trade that information for food, comfort, and freedom!"

Mobray slowly pushed himself upright, angling his body in such a way to protect himself from any more blows. "We didn't want to harm anyone," he muttered. "It was *war*, for Christ's sakes!"

"You turned on your own men!" David shouted. "You made a deal with the French—my brother for your sodding freedom! Evert saw you when he escaped. He went to try to destroy the armory, and saw you pick up a rifle and shoot and bayonet your own men!"

"*Lies!*" Mobray hissed, but Kendra saw the truth in his eyes.

"Did they realize that you and Cross had been plotting with the French?" David's bitter gaze was locked on Mobray. "You killed them all because you didn't want witnesses to your perfidy!"

"No!" Mobray suddenly threw out his shackled arms. In that moment, Kendra realized that the captain had been playing possum when he'd lay curled on the ground. With his body as cover, he'd been clawing the broken stone floor, and now threw a handful of grit into David's eyes. As David fell back a step, his hands automatically lifting, Mobray shoved himself to his feet, and charged.

51

Lifting her frothy organza skirts with one hand while pulling down the hood of her velvet cloak with the other to protect the elaborate coif that her maid had spent the last two hours arranging, Rebecca dashed up the path to Number 29. With her head bent and her hood obstructing her vision, she didn't see the man at the door until she ran into him. She gasped, and would have fallen off the steps if hands hadn't grabbed her, yanking her forward into a hard embrace. The scent of wet wool enveloped her as her face was smashed against the man's chest.

"Ho, there, Princess."

Muldoon. Irritated, Rebecca pulled back, shoving her hood back so she could glare up at him. "What are you doing lurking outside the Duke's house?" she demanded.

"Well, now, here I was thinking that I was behaving in a civilized fashion by knocking at His Grace's door," the reporter said, grinning. "How was I to know that one of my betters would be rushing at me like one of the Furies."

Her jaw tightened. "You persist in giving me mythological identities, Mr. Muldoon. First a guard dog to Hell, and now one of the goddesses seeking vengeance."

"'Tis the writer in me." His gaze roamed over her face. "You are looking particularly lovely this evening, Princess. Where are you off to, then?"

For just a moment, Rebecca's breath caught, and her wits seemed to scramble. She'd never been called lovely before, not by someone outside the family. But then she reminded herself of the glibness of this particular journalist's tongue. Stiffening, certain she'd heard mockery in his voice, she scowled at him. "What are you doing here?"

"Miss Donovan asked me to look into something, and I thought to leave this note for her, requesting a meeting tomorrow." He pulled out the damp missive when the door opened, and Harding stood regarding them.

"My lady." Harding opened the door wider to allow them to enter, although he frowned at Muldoon. "Sir?"

Rebecca undid the frog closures at her throat and handed the butler her cloak. "Mr. Muldoon is with me," she said, and saw the flash of surprise in the reporter's eyes. "Trust me, Miss Donovan will not want to wait until tomorrow to find out whatever you've discovered," she told the reporter, and began walking toward the stairs.

Harding cleared his throat, drawing her attention. "Miss Donovan is not at home, my lady. His Grace is quite concerned."

She now saw the worry behind the butler's habitually somber expression, and her chest tightened. "What has happened? Where is she? Never mind." She lifted the skirts of her evening gown and ran toward the staircase. "I trust the Duke is in the study?" she called out the question as she hurried up the steps.

Harding said, "Yes."

"What's going on?" Muldoon asked, easily keeping pace behind her.

Rebecca ignored the reporter as she jogged down the hallway. The door to the study was open, so she barreled through, coming to a skidding stop as her gaze scanned the occupants in the room. The Duke and Sam were standing at a table, their attention fixed on the map spread across the surface. Alec's gaze was on the slate board. All their heads snapped around when she and Muldoon burst into the room.

"What is happening?" she demanded, the three words burning her throat. "Where is Kendra?"

"What's he doing here?" Sam asked, his golden eyes narrowing on Muldoon.

"He has information for Kendra." She waved that aside with a jerky gesture, her eyes focusing on the Duke. "Where is Kendra?" she asked again, her breath hitching a little.

The Duke shook his head, his blue eyes dark with concern. "I don't know. Kendra learned something and went to warn Captain Mobray that he may be in danger. Now they have both disappeared."

"Dear heaven." Rebecca fought to draw air into her lungs. "How long has she been missing?"

"A few hours," said the Duke.

Rebecca stared at him, her thoughts whirling with all the terrible things that could happen to a person in a few hours. "Who took her?"

Alec looked at Muldoon. "What information have you discovered? Could it help us find Kendra?"

The reporter took off his hat, raking his fingers through his bright hair, and shook his head. "I don't see how. She asked me to look into the official reports regarding Captain Mobray and Lord Cross's time in Spain."

Alec said, "You already gave her those."

"This was the official reports from the English camp that Captain Mobray and Lord Cross fled to after escaping. It was curious. Both gentlemen were in remarkably good condition for the ordeal that they claimed to have endured. I located an officer who'd been at the English camp, and he confessed that there had been rumors among the men at the time that questioned the captain and Cross's account. They thought Mobray had embellished his ordeal."

"Goddamn it. This doesn't help at all," Alec muttered and began to pace.

"Who do you think took her?" Rebecca asked again.

The Duke said, "David Larson."

"*David Larson?*" Muldoon repeated.

Alec circled back to the map. "Where the bloody hell did he take them?"

"The same place that he must have taken Sir Giles," Sam said, his expression grim.

"David Larson?" Muldoon asked again.

Sam scowled at him. "You sound like a bloody parrot, Muldoon. Aye, David Larson—the brother of Evert."

"But why—"

"Oh, dear heaven." Rebecca's legs turned to liquid. Suddenly, Muldoon's arms were around her, and he half dragged, half carried her to the sofa.

"Someone get smelling salts!" Muldoon yelled. "She's fainting."

She clutched at his arms, staring at him. "*Parrot*. The old crone. My God." She shoved the reporter aside as she got to her feet. "I think I know where he took her!"

The Duke gazed at her. "What are you talking about?"

"There was an old crone when we visited Trevelyan Square," she said, her breath catching in her excitement. "She came out of one of the buildings and she said, 'Go away,' over and over. I told Kendra that she was harmless, and the madwoman began to repeat that as well. The woman repeated only what she heard. Trevelyan Square is abandoned. So who told her to go away?"

Sam glanced at the Duke and Alec. "It makes sense. The proximity might be the reason that he chose ter put Sir Giles's body in the church."

Alec was already moving toward the door.

Rebecca said, "I'm coming with you."

"My dear—" the Duke began.

She cut him off. "There are quite a few tenements in the square. Do you really want to search all of them when I can point to the one that the crone came out of?"

"Becca's right," Alec shot back. "Come on!"

52

Mobray rammed his head straight into David's solar plexus, sending both men flying to the floor and the knife spinning away from David's hand. Kendra considered going after the knife, but the men were between her and the weapon. The air filled with grunts and groans, and the unmistakable sound of fists connecting viciously with flesh and bone.

Her own breath whistling through her teeth, Kendra focused on maneuvering the arrowhead between her fingers in order to use it to saw through the hemp rope. It was an awkward angle, and time had worn the stone's edge down to the sharpness of a butter knife. She leaned forward, putting effort into the back-and-forth motion.

Something thudded, and glass shattered. She shot a quick glance toward the men. They'd gotten to their feet, locked in what looked like a wrestling embrace, crashing into the workbench with enough force to send several beakers flying, liquid splashing across the floor. A strong chemical stench rose up. Mobray and David ignored the debris. Glass crunched under their feet as they fought, their faces twisted in rage. No one had to tell her that this would be a fight to the death.

Shit, shit, shit. Kendra continued to saw desperately at the rope. One of the three woven strands broke free. Despite the cold, sweat rolled down her brow, stinging her eye. She shifted the arrowhead slightly and continued to rub.

She tried to block out the heavy breathing, the cries of agony and anger, but gave a startled jolt when a howl rose up. *"Die, you bastard!"*

David had fallen to the ground now, with Mobray straddling him, using the chain of the shackles as a frontal garrote against David's throat. His arms trembled as he pressed down, his bruised and bloodied face a mask of fury.

Fingers cramping, Kendra nearly doubled over in her efforts to saw through the rope. There was another scream and she looked again at the men. David's hand swept the ground, finding a glass shard from one of the destroyed beakers. The flame of a nearby candle struck sparks off the glass as David plunged it down in a violent arc, slashing Mobray's cheek open. Blood spurted in a macabre fountain. Mobray reared backward, clasping his face, a momentum that allowed David to dislodge the man. Mobray fell, his body twisting to the side, the shackled hands stretching.

"No!" Kendra screamed, because she'd seen what Mobray had. Their battle had brought them around to where the knife lay forgotten on the floor.

Kendra held the arrowhead necklace by its chain and hoisted herself to her feet just as Mobray seized the knife and thrust it into David's stomach. As she watched, David fell backward, sprawling across the floor, blinking rapidly. His chest continued to rise and fall in quick, jerky movements.

Mobray managed to lurch to his feet, breathing heavily. He bent over and spat out a stream of blood. Then he looked over at Kendra, and their gazes locked. Ice pricked at the back of her neck. Kendra knew that he wouldn't let her leave alive. *I've heard too much.*

Slowly, the captain turned and grasped the hilt of the knife. David let out a harsh cry when Mobray yanked it out with a sickening sucking noise. Kendra put all her strength into pulling the rope apart, straining against the hemp. Her legs were already mobile, but she needed her hands free for defensive maneuvers.

Mobray's head turned, his eyes tracking her movement like a cobra.

"You can't keep Spain a secret anymore, Captain." Kendra yanked against the rope, and thought it gave a little.

He smiled. Kendra noticed that his teeth were smeared with blood.

"Everybody who knows about Spain is dead," he said, and took a step toward her. "Or soon will be."

"Other people know. Evert told them. You don't think he told the captain of the *Magdalena* his story when they were sailing to England?"

That gave the captain pause. But after a moment, he shook his head, his lip curling back into a contemptuous leer. "A *Spaniard*. Do you really think anyone would believe a *foreigner* over me?"

Kendra pulled harder, and relief flooded her as the last strand gave way. She shook her hands free and moved backward, keeping her eyes on Mobray's instead of the knife that he held. She saw the exact moment he decided to attack, and dodged as he leapt forward, swinging the knife in a wild arc. She whirled around, aiming a strong kick at Mobray's kneecap. She missed, but hit his thigh instead, the impact sending him staggering to the side. Although he didn't lose his grip on the knife, he was disoriented enough for Kendra to rush forward and slam her fist into his nose. Pain stung her knuckles, but satisfaction surged through her when she heard bone crunch, and Mobray screamed. She darted backward.

"*Bitch!*" He shook his head like a wet dog, sending droplets of blood everywhere.

Nose swelling, face twisting in rage, Mobray charged. Ironically, the shackles keeping his wrists together made counter defensive maneuvers difficult—Kendra couldn't grab his wrist and twist his hand behind his back to subdue him.

Heart pounding, she raced toward the pallet, whipping one of the blankets off the bed. She whirled and snapped it at Mobray. *Never bring a blanket to a knife fight*. Still, it made him hesitate. And that was all she needed to spin the blanket into a bulky rope and toss it around Mobray's hands and the knife like a lasso. Before Mobray could react, she rammed her shoulder into Mobray's chest with enough force to send pain reverberating all the way down her arm.

Mobray staggered backward, but recovered quickly. With his hands disabled, he managed a sharp kick to the shin. She yelped and stumbled backward. Jerking her gaze away from Mobray, who was already disentangling himself from the blanket, Kendra scanned the room for another weapon. Her breathing, already ragged, hitched when she saw David move behind Mobray. In an unsteady movement, he rolled to his knees, and used the workbench to pull himself up.

Hearing the movement, Mobray glanced behind him. He hesitated, as though deciding who was a more dangerous opponent. Apparently, Kendra wasn't it, because Mobray whirled around, lifting the knife as he began to advance on the wounded man. Kendra was stunned when David smiled suddenly. For one strange moment, everything seemed to freeze. Then David grabbed the candelabra off the workbench, and launched it at Mobray. It fell a good twelve inches from Mobray's feet. Mobray looked like he was going to laugh. But everything changed in the next second. David hadn't missed, Kendra realized. The flames hit the chemicals on the floor, and in a dazzling swoosh, the puddle ignited, racing across the surface to where Mobray was standing. In a matter of seconds, Mobray's leather boots and pantaloons had caught fire.

He screamed, a high-pitched, animalistic howl that sent a shiver down Kendra's arms, and dropped the knife. His shackles rattled as he tried to beat down the flames that were devouring his pantaloons, but the fire was like a living thing, and leapt to his greatcoat. Shrieking, Mobray ran around in panic as the inferno engulfed him. Spinning, flailing . . . then, as suddenly as he'd been consumed, he collapsed.

Kendra reeled back. The fire jumped to the workbench and walls. Great billows of black smoke competed against the hot orange and red flames. Glass shattered; wood beams creaked dangerously. Kendra grabbed her cloak, pressing the material against her nose. Through the haze and fumes, Kendra saw David fall to his knees. She started in his direction, her instinct to rescue him from the flames, but she knew it was too late. Even as she watched, the fire attacked him like a greedy beast, roaring over him. Within seconds, he was consumed.

Kendra stumbled back, choking despite the material across her nose. For the first time, she realized that the fire was all around her, climbing the walls, speeding across the ceiling. Heart pounding, Kendra ran for the door. A sharp crack pierced the roar of the fire. She glanced up just as the ceiling caved in.

53

"My God! Fire!" the Duke gasped as soon as the carriage came to a stop on the narrow lane leading to Trevelyan Square. Already crowds had gathered, men, women, and children racing to bring buckets sloshing with water.

"Form a line! Form a line!" The cry rang out in the square, pulsing with the kind of panic every Londoner understood. The city had gone up in flames too many times for anyone to take the matter of fire lightly.

Alec shoved the door open, jumping down. *"Kendra!"*

He started to run, but the Duke caught his arm, dragging him back. "Alec, no!"

Their gazes locked on the building that was burning the most aggressively, smoke as black as the night pumping out of windows and into the night sky. Long orange-yellow-red tongues chased after it.

"Sweet Jesus," Muldoon muttered as he climbed down from the carriage, automatically turning to assist Rebecca.

"Oh, dear heaven . . ." Rebecca's voice trembled, caught on a sob, and Alec turned to see tears in her eyes.

His gut twisted sharply, despair ripping through him. Then he yanked his arm from his uncle's restraining grasp and bolted toward the inferno.

"Alec!" the Duke shouted after him.

Vaguely, Alec heard other shouts, strangers thinking he was a madman running toward his death. They might have been right, but he couldn't stop himself, couldn't imagine living if Kendra died inside that burning building. Fear of that possibility thrummed through his bloodstream and lent wings to his feet. Ahead of him, the door was open; he kept running. Within seconds, he crossed the threshold into the mouth of Hell.

Kendra gasped and choked as acrid smoke slithered into her lungs and stung her eyes. Most people didn't die from being burned to death in fires, she knew; they died of smoke inhalation. Even with her cloak held tightly to her nose as a safeguard, her head was beginning to swim, her vision to blur. The heat was oppressive, pressing against her, sending greasy rolls of sweat running down her face. She could feel her hands burn, and with a jolt realized that she'd caught on fire. She swatted the flames out and kept moving.

Behind her, sharp cracks, shrieks, and groans filled the air as walls began to collapse in the devouring flames. *I'm in a house of horrors*, she thought. She realized she'd made it to the stairs. Her knees were wobbling, but she began to descend, jerking back when a burning beam crashed down right in front of her.

Fuck. There was no way . . .

She had to go through. She had to.

Gathering her courage, she ducked under and knew the instant her cloak had caught on fire. She abandoned the garment and kept on down the steps. She tried to hold her breath. A wave of dizziness assailed her. She missed a step, and plummeted down one flight of stairs, the pain dazzling. On the landing, she sucked in air, which was filled with oily black smoke. Coughing violently, she tried to push herself off the ground, conscious of the roar of the fire all around her.

"*Kendra.*"

She raised her head, and wondered if she was hallucinating. But then Alec was reaching down to haul her up, too solid for a hallucination.

"I can walk," she gasped, but buckled over in a fit of coughing.

"Christ," he swore, swinging her up into his arms, and raced down the last flight of stairs as burning embers flew like a horde of irate fireflies around them. She clutched at his shoulders as they burst out of the building. Sleet was falling lightly. Grateful, she lifted her face to the sky as Alec carried her away from the flames. People handed buckets of water down a long assembly line to toss on the blaze, and several burly men pumped water from an old-fashioned (to her, anyway) wagon. Kendra stared in disbelief at the hose, which was squirting out a miserable stream of water. No wonder London had burnt down so many times.

"Is that Rebecca . . . and Muldoon?" Her voice was an unrecognizable croak.

In the line was Rebecca, looking bedraggled and bizarre in her evening dress, as she handed off the wooden bucket to Muldoon. Rebecca spotted her, and waved enthusiastically, and then turned to give Muldoon an impulsive hug. Even from the distance, Kendra saw the reporter's start of surprise. Almost instantly the two broke apart and hurriedly went back to working the water line.

"I believe it is." Alec set Kendra carefully down on her feet, like she was made of glass. He brought his hands up to cup her face, laughing softly. "You are a mess, Miss Donovan."

She gazed into his soot-streaked face and had to grin. "So are you, my lord." She leaned into him, her arms going around his waist. If Rebecca could hug Muldoon . . . "Maybe we make a pretty good match after all."

54

Three hours later, after a long bath and a lot of soap to scrub away the smut and the sharp stench of smoke, Kendra sat in the Duke's study, gingerly sipping a strong tea doctored with honey and lemon to ease the dryness of her throat and occasional coughing fit. It would take a few days for her lungs to recover from smoke inhalation. Her blistered hands, currently slathered with an ointment made of lavender oil and honey and bandaged with strips of linen, might take a little longer. On the plus side, her headache from being coldcocked was pretty much gone.

A gust rattled the windowpane, drawing her attention. White snowflakes swirled against the darkness. Earlier, at Trevelyan Square, sleet had turned to snow, which had sent up a rousing cheer among the volunteers fighting the inferno. Everyone knew that without Mother Nature's helping hand, the blaze could have been much more serious. As it was, the fire had leapt to two other tenements before it had been finally extinguished by the snowfall.

Kendra had been caught up in the jubilation of the crowd, but that joy had quickly ebbed, replaced by a somber reflection. The bodies of Captain Mobray and David Larson would remain buried in ash and rubble until morning, when Sam could return with men to dig out the corpses. Both would end up on Dr. Munroe's autopsy table. Kendra had told Sam that she'd seen Mobray burn to death, but whether David had succumbed to his knife wounds or perished from smoke and flame, would eventually be revealed by Dr. Munroe.

It probably didn't matter. It certainly wouldn't ease Bertel and Astrid's suffering. Sam had the unenviable task of informing them that their son was dead.

Muldoon had a thousand questions for her. She'd managed to deflect most of them until Alec had cut the interview short. The reporter had then hurried off to the *Morning Chronicle* to put together a story for the morning edition, but Kendra had dealt with enough journalists in her own time to know that she hadn't seen the last of the reporter. That was good. Kendra was hoping Muldoon would bring Mobray's perfidy to light. She was a little more ambivalent about having David's madness dissected for the public. Or Evert's fate.

Still, she pushed aside those troubling thoughts as they'd piled into the Duke's carriage to drop an exhausted Rebecca at her residence before continuing on to Grosvenor Square, where they'd shocked the staff with their grubby appearance.

"No one knows about the lad—Evert—except for us," said Sam as he entered the study. He'd returned five minutes earlier—perfect timing, since she, Alec, and the Duke had only just settled in the study. Sam had also bathed and changed into fresh clothes, but he still appeared rumpled and weary, his eyes hollow following his visit with the Larsons. Even the glass of whiskey that Alec thrust into his hand couldn't erase the sadness in his golden eyes.

Sam continued, "He was a war hero. I'm not sure we ought ter change that."

"Nothing should be able to change that," Kendra muttered hoarsely. But, of course, she knew that wasn't true. In this era, suicide wasn't just a tragedy. If it became known that Evert Larson had taken his own life, his reputation would be besmirched, his soul damned for eternity.

"I think Mr. and Mrs. Larson have suffered enough," said the Duke, his own gaze bleak. "To know that their child was in such despair and there was nothing they could do . . ."

"Mr. Larson told me they begged Evert ter come home, but he couldn't bear the idea of their pity." Sam took a swallow of his whiskey, his gaze on the fire crackling in the hearth. He shook his head. "He also told me why Evert chose Trevelyan Square to hide himself like a hermit. Apparently, Mr. Larson and Sir Giles own much of the property there. It was something they invested in together. They abandoned it after they had their falling out, and it quickly fell into disrepair."

"Snake said anyone left in the area had fled because they'd seen a demon," Kendra said softly. "Evert lived for two years in that small Spanish village with people accepting him. But the moment he returned to England, people regarded him in horror. I can't imagine what that did to his mental state."

They fell silent for a long moment. Evert might not have wanted pity, but it was difficult not to feel sorry for him.

The Duke broke the silence. "I wonder if the Larsons will remain in London. There is nothing here for them now."

"They won't go," Kendra stated. "They won't leave their son's grave."

Sam sighed heavily. "After Munroe's finished with his examination, they'll be able ter take their son's remains and have a proper funeral."

"I wasn't talking about David." She looked at the Bow Street Runner. "You don't think they'd dump Evert's body somewhere where they couldn't visit him, do you?"

He frowned. "I never thought about it, but I reckon you're right. They must have buried him somewhere."

"They buried him in their garden, and put up the stone rune as a monument," Kendra said, remembering when she'd first seen Bertel standing outside in the cold. He'd been visiting his son's grave; she just hadn't realized it at the time. "Bertel said they hadn't been able to give him a decent burial, not that they hadn't buried him."

She let that sink in. "In their own way, they were just as bad as Sir Giles," she said. Her throat tightened. This time it wasn't because of the smoke, but anger.

Sam regarded her. "How so, lass?"

"Sir Giles kept silent over what had happened in Spain because he thought Cross and Mobray's actions would embarrass England. But the Larsons kept quiet about their son's suicide for the same reason. They didn't want scandal."

The Duke shook his head. "It's not the same thing, my dear. It wasn't pride that kept the Larsons silent. It was love of their son."

"But what of their other son? David idolized his brother. If Bertel and Astrid had told the truth about what had happened to Evert in Spain instead of hiding it, maybe they could have gotten justice. Maybe David wouldn't have felt driven to avenge his brother's death."

Alec frowned. "What David Larson did wasn't justice."

"I'm not saying that exactly." But it was a trigger, she thought.

The Duke let out a heavy sigh. "I daresay we'll never know."

The window rattled again. Sam glanced at it and drained his whiskey before pushing himself to his feet. "I must take my leave." He paused, and looked at Kendra. "Forgive me, lass. I didn't realize that I'd be puttin' you in danger when I sent word. I nearly got you killed."

"I'm not going to let you blame yourself, Mr. Kelly." Kendra set aside her teacup and rose. "I was so focused on Captain Mobray that I didn't even realize that David had set the same trap for him as he had for Sir Giles. That's on me."

Sam didn't look like he was buying it.

She added, "Besides, David wasn't going to kill me, any more than the hackney driver or Ella."

"They didn't see him," argued Alec. "You did. You could have identified him."

She shook her head. "David didn't want another victim. He wanted a witness."

"A witness?" the Duke echoed.

"For Captain Mobray's confession." In the last three hours, she'd thought this through. "Once Mobray confessed, David intended to kill him. But I think he was going to let me go. He needed someone alive to tell the truth."

"But he could have . . ." Sam began, then seemed to understand. "Ah. I suppose nobody would pay him any mind if he accused the captain. He was a murderer. And the way he'd gone about it, a madman too. Why'd he do it that way, lass? Putting that symbol on the dead men?"

"Survival. Willpower. Fate," she murmured. "It's what the Naudhiz rune stood for. I suppose it was David's way to honor his brother. They both shared a love of Scandinavian folklore."

Sam looked at her. "And the tongue?"

"Another kind of symbolism, I'd say. Sir Giles for either luring Evert into danger or failing to speak up. Cross knew Evert from Eton. He must have recognized him in the camp and told Mobray, and Mobray told the French soldiers."

Alec's mouth tightened. "They traded Evert's life for their freedom."

"Not only Evert's life. Mobray killed what was left of his own men in the camp. He and Cross were already separated from the rest of the POWs, collaborating with the enemy. I don't know if the other soldiers knew, but Mobray couldn't take a chance. Just like he wouldn't have let me live." She remembered the way he looked at her after he'd stabbed David. "David wasn't the one I had to fear—Captain Mobray was."

"Where do you think David would have tried ter escape ter, if his plan would've succeeded, and he'd killed the captain and let you go?" Sam wondered, circling back to the earlier point.

She shook her head. "I don't think he had any intention of leaving there alive," she said. "Captain Mobray was the last of it. Once he got his confession . . ." She shrugged. "But that's just a hunch. I can't prove it."

Sam nodded, and moved toward the door again. He paused there, looking back at her. "Muldoon will be coming around, lass, lookin' for his story."

"I can handle Muldoon."

"Aye, lass." A smile ghosted around the Bow Street Runner's mouth. "Aye, that you can."

"A moment, Mr. Kelly. I'll walk with you," the Duke said suddenly, and followed Sam out of the room.

Kendra smiled, turning to look at Alec. "I think His Grace is giving us a moment of privacy."

"My uncle is a brilliant man." Alec set down his glass of brandy and walked over to her. "I died a thousand deaths when we arrived at Trevelyan Square and I saw the fire," he admitted, his green eyes bright as he searched her face. "I love you."

So simple, she thought. *And yet so complicated.*

"I love you too." She wrapped her bandaged hands around his waist and smiled when his arms automatically came around her. "Thank you for saving me. I don't think I would have made it out without your help."

"We made it out together."

Kendra's lips curved. "As I said, my lord. We're a good match."

ACKNOWLEDGMENTS

Writing is a solitary endeavor—sitting behind your computer for long stretches of time, both researching and writing. But the *business* of writing, thankfully, is not, and I am surrounded by an amazing group of people. As always, I am grateful to my agent, Jill Grosjean, for being with me on this journey, and a big shout-out to the wonderful team at Pegasus, including my editor, Katie McGuire, and publisher, Claiborne Hancock. Also, I want to thank Derek Thornton of Faceout Studio for creating another awesome cover with *Betrayal in Time*.

I continue to be blessed to have people in my life who not only support me, but understand when I cancel plans at the last minute so I can tackle a particularly difficult chapter. Bonnie McCarthy, Karre Jacobs, and Lori McAllister—you were with me from the beginning of this endeavor and will always hold a special place in my heart. I am also grateful to fellow writers Olga Grimalt, who helped me with the Spanish in this book, and Leslie Smith, who manages to find time in her busy schedule to organize much-needed writer's retreats (a.k.a. happy hours). I am once again touched by the support of the nation's librarians and LibraryReads, which put *Caught in Time* on their Must-Read list for July.

One of the joys of writing a mystery that is set in the past is always finding out something new about history. Some research makes it into the book (such as the nod to the real-life Duchess of Bedford, who was a well-known hostess in the Beau Monde, and is said to be the originator of the English custom of afternoon tea), and some ends up on the cutting room floor, as it were. And still other research inspires characters. The Duke's chef, Monsieur Anton, is based loosely on the first celebrity chef, Antonin Carême, who whipped up dishes for the likes of the Prince Regent and Napoleon. *Cooking For Kings* by Ian Kelly introduced me to Antonin Carême—and his distrust of English footmen, who he believed were trying to sabotage him.

White's is the oldest gentleman's club in England, *very* exclusive, and its members were known to make outrageous wagers. According to an article in the UK's Daily Mail, in the early nineteenth century, Lord Alvanley bet a friend £3,000 (roughly $300,000 in today's currency) which raindrop would reach the bottom pane of White's famous Bow window. It is unknown whether he won or lost the bet.

London has always been a hotbed of political intrigue, and the government—like all governments—employed spies. In fact, intelligence and counter-intelligence was quite common. I found Sue Wilkes' book, *Regency Spies: Secret Histories of Britain's Rebels & Revolutionaries* to be an insightful read.

Finally, *The Morning Chronicle* was a real newspaper that was founded in 1769, with a partiality toward the Whig party. It was shut down and resurrected many times throughout its history, but I found it especially interesting to discover that Charles Dickens started as a reporter for the newspaper in 1834, and used it as a platform to publish his short stories under the name "Boz." I like to think that Dickens would have been friends with Finn Muldoon.

The *In Time* books are works of fiction but I make every effort to be as factual as possible when it comes to history. Any errors are mine, and mine alone.